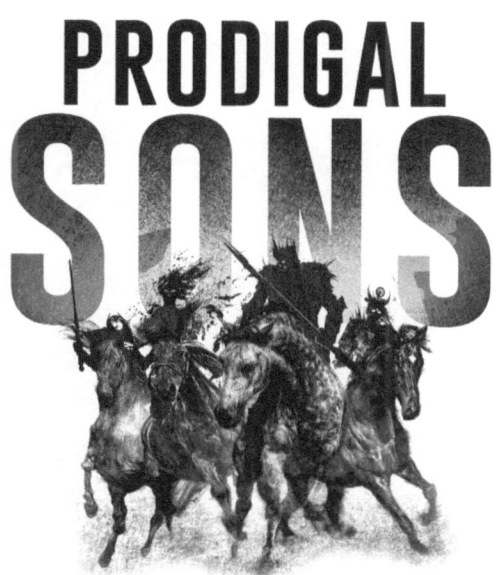

PRODIGAL SONS

CHRIS GROOTE

To Jamie, you make me want to be a better man.

"And I looked, and behold a pale horse: and his name that sat on him was Death, and Hell followed with him. And power was given unto them over the fourth part of the Earth, to kill with sword, and with hunger, and with death, and with the beasts of the earth."

- REVELATION 6:8

FEBRUARY, 1989

MATTIE O'TOOLE LOOKED OUT over her class at River's Ford High School. Most of the classes she taught, and had taught, since 1961, had been typing and experiential work-study courses, but she was actually one of two teachers on staff with some real-world experience with law and accounting. Granted, she had never practiced either, but she did teach a basic accounting course to seniors.

Second period every spring, though, she always seemed to be teaching "Introduction to Business Law" to uninterested seniors looking for an easy elective to get them to graduation. This year was the first time in three years that any underclassmen were on the roster. Merrick Gose and Jon Crockett were both young men who lived in the same subdivision she did, and though Mattie knew the names, she didn't personally know the students. With an experienced teacher's intuition, of course, she had quickly figured out the two boys were inseparable, probably on account of both being the only boys either of their families had. Mattie had quickly separated the two for talking in class, but the two boys had the highest grades in the class, and not by a small margin.

The fact they asked intelligent questions, turned in their homework on time, and at least seemed to be interested was a nice feature she rarely expected from students these days, and while she was fairly sure her husband had played golf with one of the boys' fathers, she got the sense their families had some degree of substance – at least for Graniteton County – and what she really liked was the fact anyone at all was paying attention in class.

Nonetheless, this Tuesday, Mattie had begun the new section of study for the class, Personal Law, and as she explained to the group of disinterested young people how felonies and misdemeanors worked – and why minors generally weren't prosecuted as adults, even for capital crimes – she wasn't surprised to see four of the twenty-eight students in her class asleep, a dozen or more distracted, and only two actually paying attention.

Jon Crockett had his hand up.

"Yes, Jon?"

"Umm, so, Missus O'Toole, so you're sayin' that if a minor … ummm … robbed somebody, they wouldn't be in the same kind of trouble that a grown up would?"

"Well, within reason, yes, that's correct. Jon, the law is really complicated, but if the District Attorney didn't think he could win the trial with a minor being judged as an adult, he may not even choose to prosecute it.

"Honestly, a lot of it depends on where you are, and, unfortunately, who you are. Down here, in the deep south, courts tend to only want to try felony cases – remember, those are crimes punishable by over a year in jail – when the perpetrators are over the age of 18 when the crime was committed. Maybe if you were in New York, they'd see it differently.

"In fact, I can only remember a handful of cases in the last decade or so when anyone in the Atlanta area was tried as an adult when they were under 18 – and those cases were extremely violent."

Across the room, Merrick Gose's hand shot up. "Miss O'Toole?"

"Yes Merrick?"

"So, if a good guy killed a bad guy, like, umm, I don't know, a drug dealer or something, even if it was in cold blood, you're saying the District ... uhhh ..."

"Attorney..."

"Yes ma'am! Attorney! The District Attorney might not even choose to bring the case? That's actually legal? Shouldn't the judge be, well, the judge of that?"

"Well, like I said Merrick, it all depends on what the exact circumstances of the case were. Please don't go kill a drug dealer and tell the sheriff I told you it would be okay."

The few students who were paying attention laughed, as did the two boys who had actually asked the questions.

The rest of the class had passed with few other interjections, and, when the bell rang, Mattie had to smile. At least Merrick and Jon had been taking notes. They might just be football players and freshmen, but at least they were trying. Crockett would almost certainly go on to graduate with honors and Gose was adamant he was joining the Marines after he graduated, but given what she had to deal with among all the other students, it was refreshing to see somebody was paying attention, even if the two boys couldn't drive a car yet.

She swore, the students were worse every year; the skirts got shorter, the sexuality got more overt, and the disrespect became more and more obvious. Just look at the music! Rap, heavy metal, even country was getting harder to understand. More than a decade before Columbine, Mattie O'Toole was one of the few educators who was surprised there wasn't more real violence in schools. She would be happy to retire in a few more years and get out of teaching; because the next generation was really screwed if these kids, comprising the wealthiest part of Graniteton County, represented the best and brightest.

As she walked down the empty rows of student's desks towards her own at the back of the room, she stooped to pick up a scrap of paper, carefully folded up and obviously a note. In the clean block print she recognized as Jon Crockett's was the cryptic phrase, "You know what I'm thinking." No question mark, simply a period. The desk she found it beside was, of course, Merrick Gose's.

DUNDEE BAY, GRAND BAHAMA
AUGUST 24, 1992

ROOSEVELT BIDINGS HAD LIVED on Grand Bahama his entire life, and despite the violence and squalor that existed in the slums on every island in the Bahamas, he had never seen desolation like this.

Hurricane Andrew had systematically destroyed vast swaths of the island he loved and that his ancestors had lived and worked on for three hundred years. Now, despite having recently been made a detective on the Freeport Police Force, he was essentially relegated, in the aftermath of the most destructive hurricane in two generations to hit the Bahamas, to a traffic cop.

Services all over the islands had broken down. Hundreds were feared dead, thousands were missing, and even when power was restored – whenever that might be – he feared the actual death toll from Hurricane Andrew would still be incredible ... and likely never accurate. As he stood watch over what little traffic there was at the intersection of Santa Maria and Pinta Avenues, he knew he was really there as a show of force. He represented The Government. The Government was working to bring back order and electricity. The Government wasn't taking the day off.

Of course, he and the other officers on this stretch of road were really there to limit looting in the merchant areas where the white tourists and expatriates shopped and along the coastline of Dundee Bay where they lived.

"A lot of money theah, Roosevelt, and we ha' to have a pre-sance for the folks who have chosen to join us…" his sergeant had told him in his island lilt that morning. Of course, he had only a radio and a sidearm, all the police vehicles were reserved, in the aftermath, to ensuring services were restored promptly.

What a joke! It would be weeks before the Bahamians had the tools and supplies from mainland Florida to begin, much less finish, any work. His small block home, far inland from the breezes that cooled the rich white families on the coast, would become a sauna. He could plan on long hours and perhaps sleeping in the locker room at the precinct. At least they would likely have a generator running electricity and air conditioning within a few days.

Suddenly, a voice was screaming from Biding's radio. "Roos'velt! Roos'velt! There's been a massacre!"

Bidings didn't immediately recognize the voice, but he knew it was a young officer, Smithfield, who had just joined the police force two months ago and today, had been sent to check on the luxury homes on the only road in and out of Dundee Bay. Perhaps twenty homes, all monstrous, lay hidden past the small security gate and one lane concrete bridge that connected the thin sliver of land to the main island. The security company, headquartered in Florida, had pulled its people out on the last boat two nights ago, leaving only a skeleton crew of locals to man the post and finally, calling them off hours before the storm surge began to hit. They had simply told the residents remaining they were on their own.

It hadn't mattered. Most of the wealthy owners had boarded up their homes and headed away, their servants steering yachts north to Jacksonville, Florida, or south to Biscayne Bay to escape the storm while they had simply boarded private planes to other homes in New York, or London, or Moscow.

Having money in Grand Bahama meant not having to take care of your property, others would clean up the mess and, in a month, or two, or six, they would return and regale their visitors with how bad the storm had been, but how their faithful staff had helped them to beat Mother Nature and they had emerged victorious.

All this went through Bidings' mind in a flash, and by the time the young officer had screamed for him a third time, he was running at full speed down Pinta Avenue, looking for Smithfield.

Smithfield gasped out a "follow me" when he saw Bidings and the two men had run down to Dundee Point Road, past the crumpled guard house, wrecked trees, windtorn hedges, and mountains of debris until they had come to the sixth home on the street. Number 15.

Smithfield, breathing heavily, leaned with his hands on his knees and gestured towards the house. "In theah. A lot o' killin', Roos'velt. A lot o' killin'..."

• • •

Roosevelt Bidings followed Smithfield up the driveway, past a wrecked gate that only hours before had likely been thousands of dollars in wrought iron and masonry work. One thing about Dundee Bay, the people that lived here had plenty of money. Granted, most of it was dirty money, from drugs, or criminal organizations, or, in at least one notable instance, the American pornographic film industry, but officials in the Bahamas were far more worried about taxes and good publicity - and tourism dollars - than what was legally, morally, or ethically right.

The rumor was that this particular house, built in the 1970s, had been originally commissioned by a Russian oligarch who was branching out into capitalism years before his countrymen would do so.

It wasn't surprising he never lived to see the house completed.

The first resident of the home actually was Russian, but a high-ranking member of the Politburo who was gifted the mansion for his sage advice on what would become the Soviet invasion of Afghanistan.

All these things Roosevelt Bidings knew because it was implied to every member of the police force they should look the other way in matters concerning Dundee Bay. As long as the wealthy kept to themselves and buried their own bodies – or at least cleaned up their own messes - there was little worry from reprisal by the authorities if they were just killing each other.

Islanders who were somehow wronged by these wealthy owners could expect little in the way of recourse, unless they too had some substance.

Dundee Bay was a private playground - Grand Bahama's own Island of Dr. Moreau.

Kill a hooker? No problem. Kill your gardener while you were in a drunken rage? You'd likely never even be questioned by the police.

• • •

Now, as Roosevelt and the young officer eased cautiously up to the main house, all Bidings could think of was the home looked like every other one he'd seen in the last day - waterlogged and abused, but nothing suggested the young man's story of a massacre.

The other man gestured to the path that led around to the back, and they carefully eased around the house.

When the home had been built, the architect had obviously envisioned a grand vista for the owners and occupants, allowing easy access to the small private beach and the long dock that stood ruined out into the channel.

Every part of the walls on the back of the house that faced the ocean was glass. Double doors, floor to ceiling windows, and vast open spaces on the patio that flowed seamlessly into and out of the house proper were torn away by the storm surge. The door frames were intact, but nearly every pane of glass on the first floor was gone.

"Roosevelt! I ha' come around heah, exactly like we are walking now. No one had answered the door, but the Sergeant had said to ensure the homes were empty and the people were safe. I called at the front door, then ah came around heah. No one has answered my calls, so I stepped up the stairs to that first landing. Come with me..."

Bidings followed the other man as he picked a path through the debris littering the floor. Surprisingly, it appeared that the house's slight difference in elevation - maybe only three feet from the surrounding land-scaping, had actually saved the structure of the house. Water had come inside, and much of the glass that made up the western wall of the home had blown in, but the house was surprisingly intact. Pots and pans hung normally from the racks in the kitchen undisturbed, although Bidings could see where at least two were on the ground.

Someone seeing the back of the house from a distance might not even notice the glass missing, but they could easily see how grand the home was – it offered the occupants a commanding view of the western ocean and the channel hugging the southern part of the island.

On the marble staircase leading down from what Roosevelt assumed were the bedrooms was blood. A lot of it.

The storm surge had washed it away from the lower steps, but Bidings could see smears and smudges where others – the perpetrators? - had walked through the pools of it sometime earlier - and he could make out the young man's steps in the sticky mess that was now the landing and the upper flight of the staircase.

The two men proceeded carefully up the steps.

At the top of the stairs, Bidings tried to understand what the hell had happened. From what little experience he had in crime scenes, he thought he could make out at least seven distinct blood trails, all coming out of various rooms and leading to the staircase.

What the hell had happened?

Roosevelt's hands were shaking when he reached for his radio to call his Sergeant.

Seven hours later, Roosevelt Bidings was finally released from his watch. It had taken nearly three hours to get his Sergeant to the site and another two to get a team - well, a medical assistant and an investigator - to the house.

In the end, there was little more to do than takes pictures of the bloodstains and trails. Precious little evidence remained of what had happened to what they assumed were bodies once they reached the first floor. Each blood trail was photographed and then a sample of it was taken from the point of origin upstairs, identified and tagged, and placed as evidence. At the same time, what made this evidence collection even more frustrating was that all the personal items - luggage, clothing, and even toiletries - had been removed from the guest rooms. Only the items that could be associated with the master bedroom were still present, and none of those were personalized. The team had found two monogrammed pieces, bearing the letters JRA, in the master suite, but little else. No pictures, no wallets, and an empty safe with the door ajar, hanging open in the master bedroom closet.

On the first floor, they did find several fired cartridge casings - a couple of 32 ACP handgun shells, three empty 12 gauge hulls, and bullet holes in the eastern wall, and the men all agreed this must mean the intruders - whoever they were - had come in from the back door. But how could they have gotten through the gate? The guardhouse at the entrance to the Dundee Bay enclave? It had been occupied nearly until the hurricane had hit.

The men marveled at the idea a team of assassins could have planned such an attack in the face of a Category 5 storm.

The medical examiner was convinced it was another occupant of Dundee Bay, "Dese are all bad men, I tink dey have simply killed off some kind of competition. Perhaps a drug dealer was trying to expand? You know, like you see in the movie shows?"

The sergeant nodded. It was a plausible theory in a sea of questions.

The investigator shook his head, "No, no, no. Dese are bad men, yes, but this was an inside job. Look – no one shot back. Dat tells me that friends killed dese men. They were ambushed by de very men dey trusted. I'd say at least six men must have done this."

The sergeant laughed, "Six men? To kill at least seven? To empty a house of the personal belongings of all dese peoples? No, I think perhaps even more, but then, we don't even know who was killed. Perhaps the men who did the killing were the ones who had been staying here - which would explain why dat is all missing."

In the back of his mind, something nibbled at Roosevelt Bidings.

Upstairs, they found other shells - thirteen 45 ACP empties scattered through the guest rooms and near where blood trails inevitably started, but little else. Although the shells had not been soaked by the saltwater of the storm surge, there were no identifiable fingerprints on the cases. Just as importantly, the men noted there was no evidence of exit wounds, which was strange, given the heavy-hitting ballistics of the 45 ACP. There was a single blood trail that led out of the master bedroom. The sergeant, a man who had been to several training seminars in the United States sighed. "Two shots to each person maybe? In the U.S., dey call this a "double tap" – lots of security forces and the military train dis. You want to make sure your man is dead.

"I've never seen a Bahamian man do this…"

As Bidings went outside to smoke a cigarette, his eye caught something in the corner of the doorjamb. It seemed odd, as he later realized, but all the men processing the crime scene had kept the door closed throughout the day even with the entirety of the back of the house open to the outside as a result of so much broken glass.

There, in the dark oak of the heavy edge of the door, where the frame met the actual door, was a bullet hole.

A bullet hole that could only have been made if the door was open. Even as he called for the other men to join him, Bidings realized that whoever had done all this killing had either been shot coming into the home or while leaving it. They must have come to the house, not been there beforehand.

Around that hole was the tiniest spatter of what appeared to be blood.

Here, finally, was something to suggest that at least one of the poor dead bastards had fired back and hit somebody. Despite the exhaustion he felt, he and the other men thoroughly documented their find. Pictures, as good a sample of the blood as possible sealed into an evidence baggie, and they carefully dug out the bullet.

Even after hitting the heavy frame of the door, it was obvious the bullet was much smaller. Maybe a .32 caliber – but whether from a revolver or a semi-automatic, no one could say. Bahamian policework, as practiced in the early 1990s, did not have the technology to determine these things, and in the midst of the aftermath of Hurricane Andrew, there were other things to consider.

Besides, with no bodies or identification, there was nothing to prosecute yet. All the men agreed this was something they had never seen or even heard of.

It appeared the attackers had encountered some kind of resistance, but who? What? Why? The evidence pointed to a massacre, but it left as much unknown to the investigators as it told. As the day ended, it appeared the only things they knew and could prove in a court of law was that someone had fired unregistered weapons in a home and at least seven – now eight – people had been injured, some lethally. It seemed likely, based on what they had seen so far from bullet holes and shell casings, that the men must have come through the back door.

At least one had been shot. If they were of average build, the shot would have taken them in the upper chest or the flesh of the shoulder or perhaps bicep, but it could have been a lethal shot.

But how the hell did the attackers get past the security?

Bidings finally told the sergeant his idea – the one that had been rubbing his mind all afternoon - the attackers had come in by boat.

"Roosevelt, you been out in the sun too long, boy! Ain't no man goin' to try to take a boat out in that weather! Hurricane blowin' an' you tink a bunch of killers gonna row in here to do this killin'? Not even de white men are dat crazy! Besides, a boat big enough to hold all dese men would be so very hard to handle in dat channel. Remember, de sea draws back on dese flats before the storm hits. It'd be a gamble to run it, even in a boat dat drew only 18 inches of water. Nobody needs killin' dat bad!"

The others had laughed, even Roosevelt had smiled, but he still thought it was possible. In fact, the more he thought about it, the more sense it made.

"But sir, may I say someting? If we tink a man was shot right here, which must be the case, then doesn't it make sense he was either going out of this door or had just come in it? If that's the case, then it means these attackers had to have broken in here, doesn't it?"

A cry from outside from the medical assistant brought the team quickly to the corner of the house.

The man was excitedly pointing to a pulverized piece of brick on the side of the house that would have been invisible if the shrubs that had stood in front of it had not been wrenched away by the winds.

The sergeant nodded, "Dat's a bullet strike, Roos'velt." Someting fast and heavy - a rifle, maybe thirty caliber. Bullet'd be all blown to hell and God knows where, but maybe we can figure it out."

While the rest of the team remained noncommittal, Bidings realized there was only one place such a shot could have come from.

The dock. He pointed out an impact like they were looking at could have been to kill a guard on the corner, watching the property.

Begrudgingly, the old sergeant acknowledged that Bidings' theory of a team coming ashore via boat was plausible, but with no one to question and no clear idea of who had been there, much less what happened to them, their work could only document what they had found.

At the same time, did the owner have a boat? Where was it? The house and the clues left far more questions than answers to the men trying to investigate. In the aftermath of Hurricane Andrew, little of the dock except for broken pilings remained, and they were silent to what they had witnessed.

In the end, no one was ever caught or prosecuted for what had to have been the deaths of at least seven people. The owner of the home was found to be a Panamanian corporation and, when inquiries were made - months later - the company merely responded they had no employees or agents missing, nor anyone on their corporate team with initials matching those that had been found on the set of cufflinks and the eyeglass case, so it must have been local criminals killing each other in a robbery gone wrong. Roosevelt, intrigued by the case, followed it, and watched as the home was rebuilt by local contractors nearly two years later, but little, if anything, ever came of it.

The Bahamians had an island to rebuild. If no one was missing or missed, then there must not have been a crime.

Dundee Bay kept its secrets and Roosevelt Bidings kept a copy of the report in his own files for the rest of his career, looking into it at odd times or as new technology or data became available. He never expected an answer, but he always hoped to at least understand.

Nearly a quarter century would pass before the answers came, and when they did, Roosevelt Bidings didn't like them.

1

THE AUTOMATIC DOORS closed with an audible whoosh and Presley Franklin slipped out of the Atlanta Police Department's annex near Mitchell Street and the United States Federal Building. The heat was on, but he felt invigorated. He was still holding on to a pension and all his retirement benefits, despite the investigation from Internal Affairs, and with little luck, if he made it six more months, he would be able to retire with the honor due a thirty-year cop.

Not that it had been easy. Back when he'd started as a beat cop covering the area around Georgia Tech, Techwood homes, and over to Spring Street, there weren't many worse places to be. He'd busted addicts, he'd cleaned up after rowdy college students imbibing too much but with daddies in the legislature, and he'd done a good job of upholding the law.

He knew the exact day he'd crossed the line steering him to corruption - November 14, 1987, right before he began his fourth year with the department. His wife had been laid off at AT&T, his sons were both in elementary school, and Christmas was around the corner.

He'd busted up a verbal argument between two drunken black guys in front of a strip club on Spring Street and in the altercation, one had dropped a wad of cash out of his pocket.

It turned out to be $4250. Two months' pay – before taxes - for Franklin. By then, Franklin had the two men handcuffed on the side-walk and the bouncers had gone back into the club. Then the bastard had gone off running his mouth, both at the man he had been fighting and at Franklin, and something had snapped in Presley.

"I make more in one day than your ass makes in a month, pig. Let me go and let me finish off this bastard and yo' cracker ass can go fuck with someone else."

He'd pistol-whipped the man with his backup gun and left him rolled in the bushes on the side of the club and given the other man $500 to walk away. The other man, a light skinned kid, had disappeared so quickly Franklin was unsure he'd ever been there, but the blood on the butt of the little Smith and Wesson and the wad of cash in his pocket told him it *was* real. His conscience, if it had been there at all, felt nothing.

From there it had been the usual slow downward spiral of corrup-tion commiserate with his position. He'd actually become a detective two months later and elevated his game considerably due to the fact he could meet even more criminals. He'd quickly mastered the art of extorting dealers, protection money from traffickers, and by the time Franklin had been on the force twenty years, he was making four times his police salary (now as a detective bucking for captain) in tribute from gangsters on the street.

The little fish he'd shook down in the late eighties had grown into big fish and now, Franklin and the bad boys had simply agreed to a monthly payment for Franklin to look the other way or to derail investigations if they looked likely to start.

He'd also developed a sort of sixth sense for figuring out what cops would look the other way and which ones were going to be hard asses.

He could sniff out the newest Academy graduate or a new transfer from another department or agency and know whether they were dirty or not.

It was a handy skill to have.

The irony, of course, was the catalyst for all this – his family - had dissolved within months of that first episode. Presley divorced his wife a year later and hadn't seen or spoken to his sons in fifteen years.

On the other hand, he had grown into quite the source for "his" criminals. If they wanted to get a rival out of the way, they sent word to Franklin through his network of confidential informants and he leaked this information to the right department.

Internal Affairs had been trying to shut down this criminal behavior since his eighteenth year on the force. The downside was, one of two things always happened - a tragic accident for the accuser or - *three times now* - a loss of the evidence or a problem in the chain of custody for the evidence. Presley Franklin had become a thorn in the side of Internal Affairs and the worst part was no one knew how he had escaped prosecution so many times.

Except, of course, for Presley Franklin. He had an eye for the talented criminals in the town and when he busted them, he would try to get them to play ball. He left it open for them to say yes, but never in such a way he could have been busted if the crook had been wearing a wire. His talent extended only to the blacks – he knew they could be bought and more importantly, he understood their mindset – they'd never trust an honest cop – society and life had taught them cops were only going to take advantage of them or railroad them into prison on trumped up charges.

Franklin had been smart, though, he never took too much, just enough. Years before, he'd heard a quote that summed him up perfectly, "Pigs get fat, hogs get slaughtered."

He was brilliant when it came to breaking the law. He had taken a fake ID years ago and used his own contacts in the force to create - unbeknownst to them - all the documents he needed to open up fictitious bank accounts and money market accounts and, through his own good luck, the banks he had started them in had all been bought out by others. Today, he had nearly two million dollars in untraceable assets, all made possible through smart investment of ill-gotten gains and United States' banking laws.

As he approached his thirtieth year as a cop, though, it was just vanity; Franklin wanted to retire as a cop - not a *disgraced* cop, but with all the honor and credit due a lifetime of law enforcement.

In some ways, this was to thumb his nose at the system that had tried so hard to shut him down. Realistically, though, it would be nice to have the pension, too. He needed to be able to show some kind of income on his taxes after retirement. Besides, with the cost of health care, that benefit alone was worth ten thousand or so bucks a year. He planned to live a long time into his retirement, so he had to make these advantages last awhile. Next year, he'd be 54.

2

AS HE WALKED TO HIS CAR, his cell phone began to ring. He flipped it open and spoke gruffly, "Franklin."

The jovial voice on the other end was Franklin's boss, Captain Jonathan Scott. Scott, like many oldtimers on the force, knew what Franklin was and despised him for it, but he also believed in due process. If IAD hadn't gotten enough on Presley to fire him or send him to jail, then he was still technically innocent, even if everyone knew he was crooked. In a lot of ways, Scott hoped the bastard would double cross the wrong crook and just get killed.

Nevertheless, Scott's voice sounded happy to speak to Franklin and he soon told him why.

"Presley, the mayor just called the Chief and the Chief just called me, you're on administrative leave until further notice. Paid. Don't bother coming back to the office."

"For what? I'm innocent, IAD didn't find anything - again, I might add - so I'm on my way back right now."

"No, Presley, you're not. Look, jackass, you and I both know you're a crook, but the department is trying to not get caught and put on the spot.

It's easier for us to pay you to stay away than it is to risk a scandal, especially with all the shit that has gone down in the last few years in Atlanta. I'm telling you to stay the fuck away. For your own good. You might trip and hurt yourself on the staircase here.

"Look, Franklin, you've got plenty of time to play that line somewhere else. You're not coming back in for awhile, so take a few weeks, go to the beach, go to the tittie bars, go jerk off, do whatever you want, but don't come to work.

"Your paycheck is still coming."

"Captain, with all due respect, fuck off, I'm innocent."

"Don't piss down my back and tell me it's raining, Franklin. We'll call you when you can come back on the reservation. Don't wait up late on that call." And with that, the line went dead.

Franklin *hated* someone else getting the last word. Hated it with a passion. But he had to smile. Paid vacation? If he played it right, he might end up retiring on administrative leave and never deal with another IAD investigation. When he retired, of course, he wasn't planning on sticking around Atlanta. He'd always wanted to have a place on the beach and every year, he'd travel to some little out of the way place to check it out with the idea of coming back and living there.

Most of those places sucked, of course. Once you got past the tourist whitewash and got yourself dirty with the locals, you saw the shitty little people with the same problems that plagued everywhere.

This year, though, he'd decided to check out the Bahamas, and even though he'd been there years ago, he hadn't looked at the place with the critical eyes of an investor with money and free time.

That night, Franklin booked two flights, one from Hartsfield-Jackson to Fort Lauderdale and one from Lauderdale to Grand Bahama. He also found a small family-run hotel on the beach for virtually nothing and booked two weeks there, to start.

3

PRESLEY FRANKLIN SAT on a lounge chair on the beach in front of the Royal Villas and soaked up the sun. Fall was right around the corner, so the American tourists and their screaming little bastard children had gone home and he'd actually enjoyed himself the last week.

He'd gotten no voicemails or emails from Croft, so he figured he still had a job and IAD had continued to chase bumblebees in their investigations, so he'd decided another week here might be great.

The food was good, the proprietor was nonchalant, and the beer was ice cold.

The thought of a cold beer drove Franklin from the beach up to the tiki hut that served as a snack bar for the Royal Villas at the complex's pool.

As usual, the bar was deserted, and as the bartender, a huge black man named, of all things, Collete, handed Franklin a cold bottle of Coors Light, another black man stepped up to the bar and in the rapid-fire patois of what appeared to be all black Bahamians, began to speak to Collete.

Franklin could make out some of the words, things like "good, sir, yes," but struggled to follow the conversation. Nonetheless, a lifetime of being a cop, especially a dirty one, had taught him to always listen.

Collete and the other man seemed to reach a flat spot in the conversation and the man pulled out a business card and handed it to Collete. Presley could plainly see a gold star on it.

The other man was a cop.

Franklin stood up and faced the man, then extended his hand. "Always nice to meet a brother officer on the job. Detective Presley Franklin, Atlanta Police Department."

The other man's face broke out into a big smile, "Roosevelt Bidings, Inspector, Bahamian State Police. I certainly hope you're not at work, Detective."

"Absolutely not! I told your teams at the Customs House I was here on vacation, checked in with my embassy and my boss, and let my hair down. The only things I'm investigating are the effects of these cold beers Collete keeps giving me in the afternoons and how many conchs I can eat each day."

Bidings laughed and gave Franklin a somewhat harder once-over that only a cop could have noticed, then said, "It's a pleasure to meet you, Detective. I've always loved meeting other law enforcement professionals from other countries. Perhaps if you have time on your vacation, we could meet for lunch to share stories of your big city and my little country."

"You know where to find me, Inspector. Feel free to come lift a bottle with me and we'll exchange war stories."

With that, Bidings smiled and tossed a half-hearted salute to Franklin and made his way back to the lobby of the hotel.

Presley Franklin smiled. It *was* nice to meet cops from other places. Maybe they'd get the chance to shoot the shit, have a few drinks, and share some stories. Bidings was about Franklin's age, so he was sure he'd seen some shit in that time, especially in the damn Bahamas.

Besides, his sixth sense told him Bidings was dirty, too.

• • •

Two days later, the cabana boy at the Royal Villas had knocked on Franklin's door to inform him he had a guest. Waiting in the lobby was Roosevelt Bidings. The men shook hands and Bidings apologized for not calling beforehand but asked if Franklin would like to meet that night for dinner at a small diner down the street. Bidings left after they agreed the man would pick up Franklin at 6:30.

At 6:35, Bidings' well-maintained but older Ford Contour pulled up in front of the hotel and Franklin got in. Three hours later, the two men, hopelessly drunk, had begun to reminisce about their own pet cases – ones that had left them pondering the truth of the case for years or simply grown cold and haunted them.

Bidings shared his own favorite – a drug dealer who had kidnapped another dealer's girlfriend and held her for ransom. After the ransom had been paid, the girl and the kidnapper had run off to Miami together.

At least that was the story the police had been able to put together. Years later, two bodies had been discovered in a shallow grave on a tiny island far to the south and later identified as the man and the woman. No one had ever been arrested, the dealer who had paid the ransom was devastated, and there was never anything to suggest the man had been anything but honest in his reporting to the police – he'd even volunteered information about his drug dealing outfit, but nothing had ever come of it.

On Franklin's side, his talents working both sides of the law rarely meant he couldn't crack a case, but plenty of times, he'd been unable to prosecute it.

He began telling Bidings about the Four Horsemen.

In the late eighties and early nineties, law enforcement's theory held that a group of shadowy men had supposedly begun moving large amounts of heroin into the Atlanta area. Crack cocaine had begun to devastate the inner city, but heroin was showing up in overdoses in the Atlanta hospitals. No dealers claimed it, and the young black men that were making thousands of dollars a day selling crack cocaine to other blacks in the inner city had little use for a drug that cost too much and didn't provide the near-instant addiction of crack – and required them to move into the traditionally white neighborhoods to find the users they'd need.

Powdered coke and heroin were the white man's drugs. Better to sell rocks on the corner of your own ghetto where it would be harder to be busted.

At the same time, the APD as well as other agencies in northern Georgia had begun to investigate the deaths of multiple drug dealers in the area. At first, of course, it was all unrelated. A drive by shooting of a street corner in Dekalb county bore little resemblance to a home invasion in Douglasville, but the results were the same.

Bad men dead in bloody ways.

Early investigations centered around, of course, Columbian cartels trying to capture market share or rival gangbangers looking to increase their own market share, but the handful of witnesses always claimed white men were present.

At the time, of course, white bad guys spelled Mafia and organized crime *did* have a history of heroin trafficking. A small timer named Jimmy Allitini had been rumored to be the logistics man in Atlanta for organized crime up north, but in Atlanta? Despite its reputation as a transportation hub, La Cosa Nostra only wanted to move products *through* Atlanta, not into it.

In the end, though, even Allitini had just disappeared and the usual theory was he'd gotten out of the game and moved to some non-extradition treaty country. His old man had died in prison, the result of a decades-long RICO indictment, but no one ever knew where Jimmy Jr. went. Dead in an unmarked grave or living life in the sunshine, it didn't matter. He'd only been operating for a couple of years when he'd gotten out.

For Presley and the rest of the departments looking into these killings, it was both frustrating and liberating. No cop liked the idea of protecting bad guys and if they were killing themselves, who really cared?

In every case, once they began to link those cases together, the perpetrators had executed bad men while ensuring no civilians had been injured. Or no witnesses.

Over a nearly four-year period, at least 46 drug dealers, traffickers, or related bad guys had been killed and the last one the joint task force had identified was killed on August 4th, 1992.

That one had been as nasty as any of the men investigating crime had ever seen. A recently released suspected dealer and a presumed associate of Allitini had been found in an abandoned building near a golf course in south Dekalb county. The Medical Examiner had been able to confirm the man, Jamontay Morgan, had been tortured, his body burned in multiple places with a torch, he'd had a chain wrapped around his body and been suspended – hung really – so he could get no respite from the wounds that had been inflicted. Only his destroyed feet could touch the ground, unable to take the pressure off the toes and the cauterized wounds. In the end, six of the man's fingers and all of his toes had been severed from his body and the wounds seared with a torch. Finally, he'd been shot in the head with a big, soft lead bullet that had bounced around inside Morgan's head and was so misshapen when the coroner dug it out in autopsy he could only guess as to what caliber it had been – either 44 or 45. Burn marks on Morgan's body had also suggested he'd been electrocuted multiple times.

The bullet had become the telltale sign they were dealing with the Four Horsemen. Not every case had those, sometimes traditional jacketed slugs were used - especially when these guys used rifles, but if a large caliber handgun was used, it was almost certainly a solid, soft lead slug, presumably from a 45 ACP and obviously hand cast and handloaded. No manufacturer, in those days, loaded factory bullets with such a soft lead alloy.

Even the seasoned ME, an old man named Moorman, had said he'd never seen anything like what had happened to Morgan in forty years on the job.

"Goddammit, Franklin, this looks like something from *The Godfather*, not *Gone With The Wind*. I mean, these damned niggers'll kill each other and not think of it at all. This, though? This takes a whole different level of medieval for one man to do to another."

Off the record, Moorman told the investigators he didn't think a killing like this was black on black violence, but from Mafia-backed or from the cartels in South America. "You guys watch, this is the sort of shit that will become commonplace. They don't care about pain in others and life doesn't mean a thing to these bastards. At the same time, not a lot of the brothers handload their own ammunition, so maybe it's a white thing. Damned if I know why."

The worst part of all the deaths is that not a single agency had turned up a single significant lead in the investigations. The few witnesses had been able to describe white men, and any variety of cars had been associated with the crimes, but after four years, about the best anyone had was that at least four men had been whacking drug dealers in new and creative ways, stealing the drugs and the money, and simply going away.

"In the end, Bidings, the task force the governor created to look into this ran out of things to do. Along the way someone – maybe Joe Barber over in Bunko – had nicknamed these guys the Four Horsemen, because they damned sure brought death and judgement to whoever the hell they were after. We never found a single instance where these guys had injured an innocent and we never even were clear on how many of the bastards there were. The best witness we ever had – a valet in Buckhead – even said the two guys he'd interfaced with were young, polite, well dressed, and tipped well.

"I never forgot the case, but nothing, absolutely *nothing*, ever came up afterwards. It was like they had accomplished their mission and they got called back into Hell. After Morgan, they disappeared."

Bidings was shocked. In the Bahamas, death could be nasty, but it was usually simple – a knife, maybe a hammer. Firearms were involved from time to time, no doubt, but for the most part, Bahamians killed other Bahamians in boring but passionate ways.

"Presley, what do *you* think happened?"

"No idea. If I had to guess, I'd say they got killed by the same people they were bankrolled by. I don't know, maybe? I've stayed up a lot of nights trying to figure it out. I mean, there wasn't enough organized crime in Atlanta in those days to orchestrate the wholesale killings of a bunch of unrelated gangsters."

"Were they actually unrelated though?"

"Good question, I don't know. In about 1989, a couple of newer gangs had moved into the metro area, but for the most part, it was the usual Crips and Bloods and all their derivatives. One group, an offshoot of the Folks, tried to make a run, but the Crips and Bloods killed them out. The Latin Kings were always there, but they dealt strictly with the Mexicans and the immigrants. Honestly, they did more for the Spanish immigrant community than most Americans did. I had a CI who was a gang member of the Kings who was fencing stolen property at night and teaching illegals to read in the day.

"All in all, the heroin was the part that never fit. Everything we'd heard about it was just that – hearsay. There was never anything to suggest these guys were moving it, although we *had* been making more busts with heroin involved at that time. I guess we had to make some assumptions – why would anyone else be killing these poor bastards if not for the drug market? Yeah, we assumed it, but if you took that assumption out, it became even harder to try to begin to figure it out. Whoever they were, they made a helluva dent in the market in Atlanta. Even now, some of the guys you bust talk about it. It's become a kind of curse on the streets for the old guys – 'rat me out and the Four Horsemen will find you.'"

In his drunken state, Bidings laughed at the story Franklin had told. "You know, I know what happened to your bad boys – they took all that money and just came down to live in the islands."

Still, though, something about what Franklin had told him about the Four Horsemen had stuck in his mind. There was something about that date. It was almost there for Bidings, but alcohol in his system slowed his ability to think clearly.

After another two hours of drinking and telling stories – they'd both moved on from cold cases to women, then ex-wives, and finally professional sports – the bartender called the two men a cab and the old policemen, moving carefully, maneuvered into the waiting car and the driver took Franklin back to the Royal Villas and steered him into his room, then took Bidings back to his home, much closer to the beach than it had been years ago.

• • •

Nearly a week later, it hit Bidings. August 4, 1992. Three weeks before Hurricane Andrew hit the Bahamas. Three weeks before the killings at Dundee Bay. How could he forget? Bidings knew, of course – he'd been drunk. He pulled out his phone and called the Royal Villas, looking for Franklin. The man was out – he'd said he wanted to explore the island a bit this week, so Bidings left word at the front desk to have Franklin call him.

He had one more story to tell about a cold case.

• • •

Four hours later, Bidings, still in uniform, knocked on Franklin's door with a six pack of beer in a brown paper bag under his arm. Franklin had called him back soon after Bidings had left the message and Bidings said he had something to share with Franklin.

In his hand was the case report on 15 Dundee Point Road.

Franklin ushered Bidings into the room. The view was nice and the sliding glass doors were open to the sea and the breeze blew the curtain slightly. Franklin had the air conditioner on and the room was cool and the overall effect was pleasant.

"Presley, please forgive me. The other night, when we spoke of cold cases, I neglected to speak of this one. I don't usually drink to excess, so this one slipped my mind. Today, I realized that it is a lot like your Four Horseman ... I'd like to share it with you."

Presley Franklin smiled, sometimes it was nice to be able to play the role of a real cop, not being seen as a crook, or having to cover for people you had on the take.

"Well, let's have a look. Tell me about it."

Bidings began retelling the tale of what he and Smithfield had found in the home all those year ago.

Nearly thirty minutes later, Franklin was impressed.

He bit his lip and asked Bidings about the boat.

"Presley, I think it must have sunk in the hurricane. The seas were terrible and with the storm pushing water off the flats and once you get into the deep water past Bain Town, it drops to thousands of feet fast. You might be in sight of land and still past 1000 fathoms. To me, it was no surprise the boat was gone."

"Roosevelt, I meant the boat these men took to the house, not the boat at the dock."

For a moment, Roosevelt Bidings looked confused. Then, his eyes flashed with insight. "A second boat! Presley, we never thought of that! 'Where was the fucking boat' was the wrong question. 'Where were the fucking *boats*?' There were two of them!

"Where the hell did they go?" said Bidings, as he looked out the window to the channel beyond.

Presley followed his gaze and added, "It would make sense to think the boat that was moored there was either moved before the storm or was lost in the storm. But where would a team of men, faced with a storm the size of the state of Texas, try to outrun that weather?"

"Presley, it only makes sense these men and their boat were lost in the storm. So much damage, so much wind, it would be virtually impossible to get to safety in any kind of craft and even if they did, the entire island was virtually awash. Nowhere was safe. If they beached it anywhere on the island, the result is the same – the boat would have been damaged or lost and the men would have been stranded here. If they tried to run to another island though..." He let the sentence trail off. Both men knew what would become of a small craft in 25 foot seas and 150 mph winds.

"So now, this is even more confusing. Now, instead of one boat, we need to try to figure out if ... *if* ... there could have been two boats. And where those could have gone. After the storm, there would have been flotsam and jetsam and debris for miles out to sea, so any debris from the boats sinking wouldn't be noticed. Does it even matter how many boats were at the crime scene?"

Presley Franklin smiled, for being stuck in the third world, these Bahamian cops had done good work. It was definitely interesting, and then he saw it in the report.

The blood trails. No exit wounds. 45 ACP cases. A head or a body shot, with that heavy of a cartridge, should have gone through whatever it had hit. Especially considering how most 45 ammo was hardball – or non-expanding - bullets. It was hard to overlook the similarity to what they had found in Atlanta at crime scenes for at least two years previous to the attack in Dundee Bay.

Bidings and the team *had* found blood that day, even if they hadn't found any expended bullets that had been used to kill the people in the house. Seven trails of it, and a tiny sample from an eighth person. Admittedly, only a tiny amount, but it did pique Franklin's interest.

DNA could potentially be pulled from those eight samples.

In the last thirty years, an awful lot had been discovered and the databases and policework had shifted to use more and more scientific evidence stored neatly in bank after bank of computer networks.

"Roosevelt, is it possible that I could get one of the U.S. agencies – I'm thinking the FBI – to analyze those samples?"

"I don't see why not, Presley. I mean, we've still got them and it's not like the Bahamians can do anything with them. We're still in the stone age when it comes to how we do things here. I can submit the paperwork this week, but the red tape might take some time. I cannot think of anyone who would have a problem."

Presley Franklin smiled. If he could work this out in his favor, he would be able to crack a case - an *international* case - long ago deemed lost.

It might even salvage his reputation and he could ride off into the sunset as a hero. At the least, it would make IAD eat crow, and no matter what they found in the ensuing years, they couldn't deny a collar like this.

He was starting to like the Bahamas.

4

IN THE END, it had taken a lot of favors called in from Presley Franklin to get the blood samples from the Dundee Bay incident to be shipped by courier to the FBI field office in Miami. He wasn't prepared for the storm he inadvertently created.

Very few people wanted to be involved with Franklin, but he finally managed it nearly four weeks after he had left the Bahamas and returned home to Atlanta. The good news is that he did have some seniority and, outside of Atlanta, many of the people he would interface with would simply acknowledge him as a senior law enforcement officer. Despite the tenuous link between the Four Horseman and the events of Dundee Bay, he was one of the only men still involved in law enforcement that had been on the joint task force back in 1992, so he could rubber stamp a few things to make the process easier.

Now, though, he had to wait.

Miami wasn't going to move him to the front of any lines for a cold case … make that a *foreign* cold case that had no evidence tying it to a real crime.

Agencies still knew it was a vanity play, including Presley, so he simply had to wait.

September came and went and what had started out to be a promising season for Atlanta sports – and really all of Georgia – had devolved as it always did. The Braves petered out in the playoffs, the Falcons were 3-5, and even the Georgia Bulldogs – long the only hope for parity in Georgia sports, were struggling to break .500 this season.

Franklin had honestly forgotten about the FBI reports when he received an email from them in mid-October. They had completed their analysis and would be sending their reports via encrypted email to his APD address, as well as his captain's. As to what that report contained, the email was silent.

Twenty minutes later, Jonathan Scott called Presley Franklin and the tremor in his voice suggested it wasn't with good news.

"Franklin, I don't know what you've done, but you *have* to quit trying to fuck up this precinct. You're in so much shit over this right now, I don't even know where to start. How soon can you be here?"

"What are you talking about? I'm 100% on the level!"

"Presley, you've really fucked up now. Get down here."

Eighteen minutes later, Presley Franklin sat in Scott's office and read the report. As to the blood evidence in the upstairs bedrooms, little was found. There were two possible familial ties to known criminals in the INTERPOL database, one of which was also in the FBI's, but the matches only suggested family, not necessarily parents. Uncles, cousins, the people you only saw once a year at a cookout. The real problem was the bloodstain from the door frame.

It was a positive match to one Merrick Gose, Gunnery Sergeant, USMC, (deceased), Navy Cross recipient.

"Now how did you manage to fuck this up, Presley?" asked Scott, "I mean, I know you're trying to keep the heat off of you, but to try to say that a kid – and he *was* a kid at that time – barely 18 – to say a kid, who went on to win the fuckin' Navy Cross and die for his country – was a shooter in a … *fuck!* A non-crime? In another country? I can't even follow that logic!"

"Captain, I don't know, I really don't." He sat down heavily on the chair opposite Scott and told him what he knew from Bidings' report. He also explained the tenuous relationship the events in Dundee Bay may have had on the Four Horsemen case.

"Oh fuck me with a stick! Presley, you go trying to dig up the dirt on a hero and IAD will be the last problem you'll have. The fuckin' Marines'll probably kill you with their bare hands when they find out. Just because this kid's a local boy, can you see how the press will play this or are you too fuckin' stupid – or worried about your own skin?

"Jesus, Franklin. Have you seen the story this kid put up? He graduates from River's Ford out in Graniteton, he buries his parents after they're killed in a car wreck, raises his kid sister and gets her sorted out into college, then he joins the Marines and does God knows what for them and then dies a hero? Let me tell you, in this day in age, you don't have enough friends to pull this off and the press will have a field day. Man, they'll be lookin' up your ass with a microscope and in case you don't understand that, it means they'll find all the shit that IAD didn't yet. They'll nail your ass to the barn door in a trial of public opinion. One, I might add, that the APD has been losing for the last few years thanks to crooked cops."

Swift peered over his readers at Franklin.

"Look, I don't know what this means, but I'm giving you some advice as a guy that doesn't like you but doesn't want our department run through the grinder: Leave this alone. Let the dead stay dead."

Franklin had a faraway look on his face, but he snapped right back. "I get it, I really do. I can't let it go, but can you at least let me keep looking? I get it – I never thought this thing would turn this way, I was honestly trying to do a solid for Bidings in the Bahamas. I never thought this would – or could – lead back to this. It's the only lead we've ever had on the Four Horsemen – ever. If it's shit, then it's shit."

"You are so *full* of shit! If you didn't think this was about the god-damned Four Horsemen, then you'd never have pushed it through. For once in your shitty life, quit lying when you know you're caught!"

Franklin looked despondent. "Honest to God, Captain. I'll swear on it. I may be a lot of other things, but on this one, I'm on the level. There's no angle here – at least there wasn't. I sent off the samples and simply used the old case to lubricate the process. I never in a million years thought it would come back here." He decided it might be better to stay mum on his idea the shooter was using the same kind of soft lead bullets in both instances.

Scott looked unimpressed, "Look, Gose is dead and the evidence is shot. No court would allow it and any attorney would have it laughed out of a court if it somehow was allowed to be admitted. Chains of custody broken, storage conditions, you name it. It would never play, even if the poor bastard was alive. You want to check it out? Go ahead. But check it like you're following up on old stuff, not trying to ruin a dead hero's reputation."

With that, Scott abruptly went back to the mountain of paperwork covering the left side of his desk and Franklin assumed he was dismissed.

5

THE BLACK LINCOLN TOWN CAR backed slowly out of the garage at a house in Pickett, Georgia. Situated on the northern side of Lake Lanier, it was a quiet and distant suburb of Atlanta, but its location allowed easy access to anywhere in the metro area. Jon Crockett put the car into drive and pulled out onto Lakeview Drive.

Crockett stood slightly over six feet tall and his weight hovered around two hundred pounds. Now over forty years of age, his body still was in excellent physical shape – not the mass of muscle he'd been as a football player, but it was clear to anyone who saw him he still worked out. He wore his hair short, not quite a crew cut, and was going grey at the temples.

Crockett hit the Bluetooth headset and began calling other real estate investors, pitching a house he had just put a contract on. It was a far cry from the way his father had done real estate – even the few times the man had handled single-family projects for people - but two different methods had made both men wealthy and now it allowed Jon Crockett time to not be stuck in the office. It was as simple as it could be – buy a beat-up house, put a contract on it, add a few percent, and "flip" it to someone else.

He hardly ever even did anything to the homes he bought and sold. Have his people pressure wash them, make sure the carpets were reasonably clean, and sometimes, if he was optimistic about the neighborhood, he might have them paint the interior. For the most part, he just had a team of contractors come in and make sure the house was empty and clean. Maybe a dozen houses a year, if they were in up and coming markets around Atlanta, would be completely remodeled and sold in more traditional ways – listed with agents, pretty pictures for the MLS, and sold to new buyers with traditional mortgages.

For a lot of reasons, Crockett had built a minor, albeit wealthy, empire where all the people who worked for him knew very little about the overall company that paid them. Over the years, he'd learned the power of keeping people – nearly all of them – at an arm's length.

Honestly, his real love was the freedom this gave him. If he wanted to take the month off, he could. He loved the outdoors – fishing, hunting, hiking, you name it. He'd settled on real estate because it allowed him to do exactly as much as he wanted to.

It had paid off handsomely. Now, at 45 years old, he not only owned the house in Pickett free and clear, he had parlayed the inheritance his parents had left him into a 1,458 acre property near Hoback Junction, Wyoming owned by an LLC he had created as a tax shelter. Ultimately, Crockett knew he would leave for the west, but for at least a few more years, he wanted to play the real estate markets in Atlanta.

Jon Crockett loved to talk about how much real estate gave him freedom and free time, but the reality was he still routinely worked fifty and sixty hours a week at it. Wheeling and dealing, the way his old man had taught him, was in his blood. Besides, you couldn't hunt or fish every day.

Now, as he headed south on highway 400, he was on the phone with his virtual assistant, Terry, running through loose ends on homes they had offers on, paperwork and comps for other houses, and the state of three closings Crockett had scheduled in the next two weeks.

"Jon, everything is ready for the Alcott deal, all we'll need to do is have a copy of the Proof of Funds to be able to move that forward. Mr. Gerber's office called to confirm you're meeting him today at 12:00 for lunch regarding your two properties on Old Norcross, and Joel Habersham called to remind you money goes hard on the Fleming contract in one more week."

Crockett smiled, "Yes Terry, I've got all of those under control. I think we're full steam ahead on everything. Is there anything else in your notes?"

"No sir. If that's all, I'll be going for the day."

"You do that. It's nearly ten there, so have a nice evening."

"Thank you, Jon, good day."

And with that, Terry, from her cubicle in the Philippines, signed off. She had worked for Crockett for more than five years and he had never met her in person. He'd seen her, on Skype calls and video conferences, but never physically met the woman. Crockett had constructed his business to allow him to use VAs from all over the world to handle the mundane tasks of tracking down ownership of potential properties, title issues, even running comparables for the homes he was looking at. Many of the attorneys and lenders he worked with had similar relationships with Crockett. They knew him only through the phone or video conference. He was intensely private.

Using VAs had been among the smartest thing he'd ever done. No offices, no overhead, and they could do all the legwork and research he needed, for a fraction of the price of his time.

Not that he paid poorly. While others looked to offshore labor as a way to save money, Crockett looked to save time. On average, he paid his people, regardless of where in the world they were located, twice the wages they might expect for similar work elsewhere, but he knew exactly what that got him – loyalty and a place at the top of their list.

He'd loved that about money: when you spread it around in places where it wasn't common and treated your people well, you made harder for them to leave you, or betray you, or not show up when and where you needed them. He tried to explain that to others, even his ex-wife, and they rarely got it, even if it was as simple as tipping well at a restaurant.

Crockett smiled at the memory of the first time he'd taken his ex-wife to Mexico. They'd checked with the concierge at the hotel for a nice restaurant; the man had shared his recommendations with the Crocketts' driver, who took the couple to a quaint restaurant situated on a cliff overlooking the Bahia Banderas. While waiting to be seated, he'd watched the wait staff. A few minutes of observing them told him exactly who he wanted to serve them, an older man who was moving fast and obviously working multiple tables. They'd requested to sit in the man's section – his name had been Guillermo - and the service, as Crockett had known it would be, was excellent.

He tipped the man $50 on a bill that had only been $64 and his wife had freaked out. "Jesus, Jon, he just waited on us, he didn't do anything special."

"Just watch, Jen. We'll ask what his schedule is this week and you'll see."

Three nights later, the couple had come back – the food had been excellent, after all – and despite the wait, Guillermo saw the couple and immediately began finding a place for them. Two minutes later, they sat at a table and Guillermo was already bringing their drinks from the bar.

That night, Guillermo had brought the head chef, the bartender, the proprietor, and even his cousin, now only a busboy, out to meet *"his old friends, Senor Juan y Yenn…"*

The Crockett's bill had been $47 but included far more than they had enjoyed on their previous visit. He gladly left the man another $50. This sort of thing had continued for nearly two years as the Crockett's visited Puerto Vallarta at least three or four times each year. They didn't eat there every night, but they were instantly remembered by the staff.

It reminded Crockett of Hemingway's tales of France in the 1920s and his own father's of growing up in Chicago, buying real estate for men who wanted to remain anonymous or didn't want to explain where their money had come from. He remembered riding in the old man's Eldorado through the crummiest parts of Atlanta, on their way to pay contractors.

"Johnny, there's two kinds of people in this world: those that can be bought and those that do the buying."

The man had looked over at his son and addressed him with his steel-blue eyes, "Don't be one who can be bought."

As Jon Crockett smiled at the memory of his father, his phone buzzed again. He knew the number and he knew he need not identify himself to the caller.

"Yes?"

"Merrick Gose's name kicked out on an FBI search 27 hours ago. Since Mr. Gose is deceased, I elected not to inform you until I was able to monitor for any further activity."

"And has there been?"

"No sir. It seemed to be a random search, there were several samples submitted from Atlanta police to the FBI, but all appear to be dead ends; his was the only one with a clear marker."

"Thank you Dimitry, as always, keep me informed of any searches."

With that, the two men hung up simultaneously.

6

THE VOICE ON THE OTHER END of the phone was emphatic. "Roos'velt, you've got to do sumtin', even if it is wrong. Dis is why we pay you."

Bidings, for all of his faults, understood why he was asked by criminals on the island to help solve problems for them – he had taken the bribes and the kickbacks for nearly twenty years to do just that. It was one thing to look the other way about traffic citations, or a drunk driving charge, but another completely to manufacture or hide evidence with violent crimes.

After so many years of working both sides of the law, he was slowly coming to realize he'd become a slave. The calls would never end – the money wouldn't, either – but in the end, he understood there were only two ways out of this: he'd be killed or exposed as a criminal.

In the Bahamas, both amounted to the same thing. If he wasn't killed outright, he'd die in Fox Hill, shived by some young man trying to make a name for himself in the country's primary prison.

Bidings was snapped out of this fugue by another call. It was Presley Franklin.

"Roosevelt, I don't have too much time, but listen carefully. The FBI finally came through and it looks like we have an identification on one of the shooters and some suggestions as to who else was in the room at the time. I've checked them all out, but the only solid lead is on an American kid who's dead now."

A broad smile crossed Bidings' face. "That is excellent, Presley. Now what shall we do?"

"Well. That's kind of the problem. I've got some troubles up here that are keeping me busy, but I wanted to know, where would a guy – an American – go if they were shot? Would there be any kind of record of the treatment?"

Roosevelt thought hard. The problem, of course, was the hurricane bearing down on the island at the time of the shooting. Normally, someone who had a gunshot wound would only be treated once a police report was taken.

"Presley, these men – would they have even stayed on the island? I mean, 'dere is a huge storm coming in on them. Where would they go? I believe they came in from the sea, but it would be suicide for them to have attempted to cross in that storm, no matter how fast a boat they had. They would be fools to stay AND fools to leave.

"If they stayed, they would have been referred to the primary hospital on the island and treated with the police present. Then a report would have been made and that would have been filed.

"That storm, though, knocked out communication for days, except by short wave radios. If they stayed, it's likely they'd be stuck for days, as the police wouldn't release them. I don't think he could have been sewed up here."

Franklin lost it, "Goddammit, Roosevelt, you're not the only dirty cop on that island! Somebody could've been bribed. Do you think these guys swam back to Miami with their boy bleeding out? How long is a ride like that?"

"Presley, in a go-fast boat, the kind we see traffickers using, those men could make it back in less than two hours, depending on the conditions. They were on the dry side of the hurricane as it came across the Bahamas, so they would have had a following sea and wind.

"For a man with the necessary skills, it would not be hard, but the timing has to be perfect. Like we said some time ago, the ocean could help them to escape or simply be their grave. We've never been able to be sure of when the attack took place. We know when we found it, but it could have been as much as thirty-six hours before that. There's no way to tell. There's *never* been a way to tell."

Franklin realized this was a dead end. The entire Bahamas was a dead end. Gruffly, he told Bidings goodbye and hung up the phone.

● ● ●

At his kitchen table in Atlanta, Franklin turned over facts and timelines again and again in his mind. He'd pulled up the data on the hurricane from the National Weather Service and knew when it hit Grand Bahama and when it hit south Florida, but he was no sailor. He could paddle a rowboat, but he stayed away from the water. Knots, nautical miles, and high and low tides were a mystery to him. He fell back into thinking like a cop, but he understood he had to make assumptions.

In the end, all Franklin could do was to ask the state of Florida Criminal Research Center (CRC) to look into all the gunshot wounds that had been reported in Miami-Dade County in the four-day period from August 22 to August 25, 1992.

The CRC had been funded to make it easier for prosecutors to build cases against criminals operating in multiple areas and was supposed to lead the way for other states to model their system on Florida's. Unfortunately, 9/11 happened and Homeland Security had been formed and made the CRC virtually obsolete before anyone outside of Florida and her neighboring states ever found out.

Presley Franklin dutifully filled out the online form for the CRC – months, days, years, and then listed his credentials and badge number, as well as his agency. Franklin hated computers, but he knew this search would go through data far faster than a human randomly pulling open files, so he crossed his fingers and hit "submit."

Almost immediately, the computer came back with news – "No Positive Matches Found."

"Fuck," he said to the empty house.

He looked at the map and decided to include all of southeastern Florida, so he widened the search parameters to include St. Lucie, Palm Beach, and Broward this time and set about re-entering all his information, then hit submit.

He got an error message.

On the screen, the database had popped open a new window, "Date field not inputted properly."

Muttering under his breath, Franklin re-entered the dates and didn't catch the mistake he made – he searched for August 22-25, 1992- 1995.

Almost immediately, he realized his error as well as the fact he'd forgotten to narrow the search down to only Caucasians, so instead of the half-dozen or so names he'd expected, he had 25.

He was able to easily move through most of them – the Pablos, Demetrius', and even a stray Molly – and he came to three possibilities: Troy Carter, Stan Ellison, and Jon Crockett.

Pulling up a copy of the actual police report showed that Carter had caught a 25 auto round in the leg and walked in and out of the hospital under his own power.

Ellison was involved in a botched drug deal and caught a 9 mm in the abdomen and died on the table.

Jon Crockett, aged 22, had been shot in a liquor store holdup in Delray Beach. A 32 Smith Long round had caught him in the upper shoulder, just inside of the rotator cuff. The bullet, a simple round-nosed slug, had gone right through the man and a good Samaritan had not only killed the perp, he'd helped treat Crockett on the scene until the cops and paramedics had shown up.

The problem was the dates didn't match up.

Crockett had been shot on August 24th, 1995. Three years *after* Hurricane Andrew.

Fuck.

With little else to do, he decided to backtrack and carefully look into the Marine, Merrick Gose and if those inquiries didn't go anywhere, he could always see what the deal with this guy, Jon Crockett, was. At least it would kill some time. Besides, what else did he have to do?

7

FOUR MINUTES AFTER Presley Franklin's search spat out Jon Crockett's name, Jon Crockett's phone rang.

"Yes?"

"Sir, your name was just kicked out in another search, this time originating from an Atlanta police officer named Presley Franklin."

"And what was it?"

"The police report filed on your behalf in Delray Beach, when you were shot in 1995."

"Is this related to our call earlier this week?"

"I'm unsure, but quite possibly."

"Thank you Dimitry. Please prepare me a file on Franklin and send it to the old address."

"As you wish."

Again, the men hung up the phone at the same time.

This news presented either a bad coincidence or a potential problem. Crockett, twelve years ago, after his divorce, had been seen dating a local former debutante and the social pages of the local papers had begun digging into his past. Mistrustful of most people and their intentions and wishing to keep the few interpersonal relationships he had private and discrete, he had hired several legitimate companies that helped business professionals protect their own privacy as well as to protect their online reputations. Relatively quickly, Jon Crockett became much harder to research. Online databases bearing his information were buried, his companies – or at least the formal documents of incorporation – were remanded to include only the names of the registered agents, and those inevitably were in states besides Georgia. It wasn't that he couldn't be found, it was just that he was a lot harder to find.

One of the men who owned one of those companies had recommended a specialist to Crockett – the man known only as Dimitry. Crockett had never seen him, only spoken to him on the phone, but he had come to understand Dimitry was in a position to monitor thousands of online databases and systems for names. In certain circumstances, like newspaper articles, social media posts, and blogs, Dimitry could make things disappear or have them edited to misdirect the reader elsewhere, while in others, such as Federal and State law enforcement systems, he could only parlay that inquiries had been made and what those inquiries had said.

Part hacker, part librarian, he was very good and Crockett had put him on retainer to only search for four names: Jon Crockett, Merrick Gose, Peter Claiborne, and Brandon Jones.

As a rule, the two men spoke several times a year – local newspapers carrying hometown interest stuff, Memorial Day and Veteran's Day filler, and, once in awhile, a photo op from Jon Crockett or Peter Claiborne, the only two men on the list still alive.

• • •

It was past seven that night when Jon Crockett was finally able to get home. He went upstairs to his office, started up his computer and logged in to the first email address he'd ever had – an old AOL.com listing that was only monitored once a month or on an as-needed basis.

Today, though, Jon Crockett opened it, saw the email from an address that Dimitry used, and then printed the zipped file the man had sent on Presley Franklin. He'd hit "print" before realizing the damn thing was 67 pages, so he had to rummage around the office to find the printer paper and then, of course, stop in the middle of printing to change out an ink cartridge.

Who the hell *was* this guy?

He retrieved a Diet Pepsi from the refrigerator, made himself comfortable on the overstuffed loveseat on the other side of the office, and began reading. One of the man's two cats, Bella, jumped neatly up into his lap despite her age and began purring loudly as the man read the dossier Dimitry had prepared from multiple sources inside and outside conventional search parameters.

Franklin was quite a piece of work. He'd been on the force nearly 30 years and been hounded by Internal Affairs for most of the last twelve. He'd come from next to nothing, grown up in Coweta County, the son of a farmhand, and joined the force at age 25, after an unsuccessful stint in the restaurant business.

Crockett shook his head that the powers that be on the Atlanta police force in the 1980s had thought a failed burger flipper could make a good cop. Not unused to dealing with blue collar men, Jon Crockett felt he knew the exact type of man Presley Franklin was – angry at everything. Nothing life could give him would ever be considered enough. Crockett noted that Franklin's marriage had ended in divorce after only a few years and the man was estranged from his children.

Every few years, it seemed, there were accusations made against Franklin – starting back in 1987. Harassing witnesses, sloppy paperwork accounting for no less than six censures from the District Attorney, at least another nine cases that had ended in mistrials based on chain-of-custody troubles originating with Franklin. It had certainly cost him advancement and nearly cost him his job – multiple times.

If he wasn't a crook, he was at least inept.

Crockett shook his head. If there was something to Franklin's inquiry – make that *inquiries* – Jon Crockett didn't believe in coincidence – then Franklin was either too incompetent to ever piece together the truth or he was too dirty to reveal how good he really was.

Secretly, Jon Crockett hoped Franklin was the former and not the later. *But what did the man know … and how had he known it?* In a sea of unsolved crimes in Georgia, how did this bastard find the only loose end that could unravel the whole thing?

Besides, it wasn't even a real loose end.

Franklin knew something, but *how* did he know it? He looked back through the last pages of the report and there it was: Franklin was under a seemingly never-ending administrative leave as of now and his file included his plans to leave the country. His passport had been flagged into and out of the Bahamas two months ago. Working on assumptions – which he hated to do – Crockett realized the man must have gotten his evidence there.

But how?

Jon Crockett looked down at the now sleeping cat in his lap and scratched her under her chin. Her quiet snoring became a loud purring and he said to her, "I guess we'll figure it out, Bella."

8

WHEN HE WAS IMPRESSED, Presley Franklin was known to let out a low whistle.

He did so now. He'd sent an inquiry to the Veteran's Administration asking for the best way to access the file on a deceased Marine, Lance Corporal Merrick Gose, and they had politely emailed back how he could do so and what credentials he would need. Since Gose was a hero, such inquiries were routine, so Franklin had little problem getting the man's file. Despite having won the Navy Cross, Franklin was surprised to find out how little of any substance was really in the files of a Marine.

A lot of stuff he didn't understand.

Absently, Franklin logged into his laptop with his police credentials, then logged into the heavily redacted file that had been delivered to his email account. The file was over one hundred pages in length and contained virtually every document the government had specifically on Gose. Franklin scanned the pages, but it didn't offer much he wasn't already aware of.

Gose had joined the Marines on the Delayed Entry program in 1992, after he had buried his parents and gotten his younger sister enrolled in the University of Georgia. He'd actually graduated from River's Ford High School with honors and a year later gone to Parris Island for Basic Training. From there, he'd been sent to Camp Geiger for Basic Infantry training, then on to another four weeks of Advanced Infantry training. He'd been an Expert Marksman and had been stationed with Headquarters and Service Company in a STA Platoon at Camp Lejeune.

Franklin kept scanning the rest of the documents, but the truth of it was, he couldn't figure much of it out. There were documents pertaining to the man's time at Parris Island, then on to combat training in North Carolina. A single sheet of paper acknowledged Gose had married and three documented his divorce from Tina Hilliard less than a year later. Another page, dated from the fall of 1995, indicated that, in the case of his death, his estate was to distribute any funds paid from his Servicemember's Group Life Insurance policy to the Shady Dale S. C., some kind of a trust fund in Wyoming.

Franklin took a moment to Google the name, but aside from an out-of-date, one-page website, he found little else. The Wyoming Secretary of State website was even less useful, only stating the Shady Dale S. C. existed and giving the name of the Registered Agent, an attorney in Cheyenne. He could assume was it must have been something Gose was passionate about nearly two decades ago.

Continuing to try to sort out the file, he noted Gose had been to 29 Palms, he'd been on multiple deployments into the Mediterranean, he'd volunteered for and been accepted into the Marine's Scout/Sniper training school at Lejeune and graduated at the top of his class. Finally, towards the end of the file, Franklin found the letter of recommendation for Gose to receive the Congressional Medal of Honor for his actions in, of all places, Sierra Leone in 1997.

It was signed by none other than the United States Senator from Georgia, Steven Berryhill, Gunnery Sergeant, USMC (ret).

Unfortunately, the actual details of the letter were virtually illegible due to the action of the censors. Whatever Gose had done, he'd done it in a place where the government didn't want anyone to know about it.

Franklin decided to see if he could schedule a call with Senator Berryhill to discuss what had occurred in Sierra Leone in 1997 that made Merrick Gose so damned important.

• • •

Knowing that setting up a meeting with a sitting senator could take some time, Franklin decided to look elsewhere. Picking up the phone, he called the local police department in Gose's hometown, Graniteton, thirty-five minutes east of Atlanta.

After being bounced around on hold for several minutes and with four different people, Franklin finally got Officer Peyton Flanagan on the phone. After the usual exchanging of law enforcement pleasantries, Presley started in.

"So, officer, what I'm trying to do is to get a little local flavor on some of the men and women that have served our country in the Atlanta area. Anyone around here knows about Merrick Gose, so I'm wondering if you could share anything about him with me?"

Flanagan was quiet for a moment, then, carefully and formally, he asked, "And what would this be pertaining to, Detective?"

Obviously, Franklin had struck a nerve, so he tried to quickly backtrack and build on a good lie, "Well, I'm coming up on retirement and was thinking about writing a book about the men and women in north Georgia that have given their lives for law and order and their country. You can't not talk about Gose when you do something like that, can you?"

Flanagan seemed to consider what Franklin had just said and then responded, "He was the finest young man I ever met, Detective. I was about four years younger than him but knew the family. He lost his parents his senior year in high school and Merrick stayed in school and managed to make sure that his sister did so, too. She was a year or so younger than he was and when she graduated high school, he made sure she was enrolled in college and all set to go. Once she'd been gotten sorted out at school, he went ahead and enlisted in the Corps.

"I think that was all he had ever wanted. To be a soldier, to fight. He wasn't a bad man or a troublemaker, but he was ... I don't know ... driven? Maybe that's the word ... driven to do the right thing and to see it done. He hated the way people took advantage of other people. He had a real moral compass, and he saw the Marines as being the answer to that.

"I guess you already know about his service record. He was a bad ass. He could shoot pretty good as a kid – he and his friends used to hunt and target shoot out in Newton County somewheres, but that boy loved to push the envelope with guns. I remember he and some of his buddies talking about blowing up a gun with handloads just to see how strong the action on it was – and they were still kids – teenagers for sure – but kids. What kid reloads ammunition and knows enough to figure out what's safe? I never heard of anyone doing that, much less intentionally, but that's the kind of stuff they were into. I guess that's better than what some kids'll do with free time."

"I guess so," said Presley, still trying to sort out the hero worship from the rest of the story. "Tell, me, Officer, what was he like in high school? I know you were younger than he was, but do you remember anything? His friends? Did he work somewhere?"

"Sorry, Detective, I really don't remember that much, given the difference in our ages. I mean, he was on the football team, so I'm sure he had plenty of friends there, and I think he worked cutting greens at one of the golf courses around here – seems like one of them do a Merrick

Gose Memorial Day event. I guess you could look it up. You'd probably need to just come out here and visit folks to figure out how to word it best."

"Well, officer, I appreciate it. As I get closer, I'm sure I'll end up in Graniteton, so I'll look you up then. Thanks, and stay safe out there."

"You too, Detective."

As he hung up, Flanagan looked at the phone. He remembered a lot more than he'd told, but he didn't see any need to disparage a hero.

9

JON CROCKETT PUT DOWN THE FILE *and felt the melancholy. Over the decades, he'd managed to file a lot of it away. The losses, the pain, the ... detachment? It had been tough to define what he felt. He'd tried counseling, he'd done the therapist thing at the behest of his ex-wife.*

Nothing. Nada. Zip.

Sometimes, at the end of it all, the nights were just tough. Sleep wouldn't come or, if it did, some of the same old dreams did.

That was really the problem – the dreams. For the most part, the flashbacks and the nightmares had died down in the last decade, but every once in awhile, the little parts he had blocked out and walled up in his memory broke loose.

Tonight was one of those.

Crockett, even though he knew he was dreaming, was powerless to stop it. Once begun, nothing stopped the onslaught. This show would run until it ended...

There he was, sitting in Mrs. Lindsey's seventh grade English class, when the New Girl walked in, dirty blonde hair and green eyes.

Her name had been Leigh.

In the funny way of adolescents, Jon Crockett felt her in his heart. The new girl was Something. What? He wasn't sure. He only knew, that day, as sure as the sun had come up, that she was special – or would be special – to him.

From there, like a roller coaster gaining speed, The Dream began to speed up. Images and memories flashed in his mind like the cards of a blackjack dealer...

Leigh, looking beautiful on their first "date," even if the boy's mom had to drive them to the movies and they were on the strictest of time schedules. What could you expect, though? He'd been in whatever passed for love as a kid from the moment he'd laid eyes on her as the "new girl" in class, just transferred in from Griffin Middle School.

In the end, they'd found friendship, then commonality, then some version of love as ninth grade kids. The downside?

Her parents forbid her to date, and whatever the young couple could have had beyond friendship, it required a vehicle, and that required an adult – or at least somebody old enough to drive. The irony was that the one boy that Leigh could trust to treat her with respect was the one boy her parents had decided to keep her from.

"Our daughter is too young to date, young man." That had been the line her father had told a very nervous young Crockett who had, of all things, ridden his bike to her house to ask the man before he'd even asked the girl.

In the ensuing months, she'd moved past Crockett and on to others, keeping as much of her life a secret from her parents as possible. She dated upperclassmen who could drive, attended parties where the kids drank and smoked with older siblings, college students, and sex, drugs, and rock-and-roll was the norm. Still, Jon Crockett's ignorance, along with some primitive (or basic) idea of love, had kept him loyal to her.

Another scene played out across Crockett's mind, this time Leigh calling from a payphone where she'd been unceremoniously let out of the car by her "boyfriend" because he was too high to do anything and didn't want to worry about her. Crockett, sixteen now, had snuck out of his house, pushed the old truck out of the driveway and down the street before starting it, and then gone to find her on a street in southeast Atlanta. He'd gotten her back to her home and she'd assured him she would change.

Awkwardly, Crockett asked her to go out the next weekend and she had said yes.

That Friday, Leigh's parents had been out of town, leaving her to babysit her younger brother and she had quickly earned the kid's silence by renting him a movie and promising she wouldn't tell if he wouldn't, and Jon had picked her up at seven. They'd gone to eat in Graniteton, of course, but they had held hands walking into the restaurant.

Later that night, he had taken her home and the two had sat out on the porch swing for two hours, his arm around her. Crockett was filled with the quiet gratitude of a man-child for whom a dream had come true.

Silently, she had leaned over and kissed him.

As he left her house, nearly floating to his truck and still a slave to the curfew his parents insisted upon, he bravely tried to kiss her again on the cheek. Leigh turned suddenly and caught his lips on hers, and he melted into their softness.

His heart sang, in love, not with anyone, but with the young woman his soul knew was The One.

The Dream, ever the Trickster, then began to twist and turn, as it always did, into the dark places.

A phone call, late at night less than two weeks later, this time from a nurse who knew the boy's family, stating that Leigh had been dropped off at the emergency room by persons unknown, overdosed on heroin that had been spiked with something. She wasn't expected to make it but had been asking for the boy. Could he possibly come in? His father had acquiesced and driven Jon Crockett to the hospital. The boy, scared, nervous, and trying to hold himself together, still noticed his father had pushed the car – this year, a new Seville – far faster than the speed limit to get them to Graniteton Memorial.

The end of something, be it a day or a life, need not be dramatic, but nevertheless, it is an end. The girl, the only one Jon Crockett had ever kissed, the only one he would ever truly love within the innocence of his youth, had slipped into unconsciousness and never woke up, never knew Crockett was there. The machines keeping her alive with their monotonous beeping slowed, then became an incessant alarm. The boy and his father were rudely ushered out along with her family, and Jon Crockett watched in horror as one of the nurses rapidly pulled the curtains across the window and a steady stream of nurses, staff, and doctors raced around the floor, attempting to save the girl's life.

After that, the scenes and the faces of The Dream change. Leigh, always Leigh, her memory driving Crockett further and further into the madness and the bloodlust for revenge against somebody.

Anybody.

Everybody.

Crockett the Sleeping Man watched as Crockett the Boy stood over the girl's grave on what would have been her seventeenth birthday. The early spring rain pasted his hair to his head, and he laid a dozen white roses on the marker and walked back to the truck. The rain running down his face had hidden the tears.

Now we see the young man with three other young men, all in the flower of youth, facial hair only barely beginning to sprout from their cheeks and yet, they have become hunters of men. They have curfews, they have football practice, they have girlfriends and homework and parents and families to come home and eat dinner with. All four of them are on the honor roll.

The man-boy who ushered them down this path seems far older than the date on his driver's license suggests, and with the peculiar passion of all young men, the four pursue the dealers, the peddlers, the predators whom they see preying upon on the well-to-do middle-class children whose parents gave them too much allowance and not enough supervision. More importantly, they have sworn to kill the men that run it all, ignorant of the fact that others will simply move into whatever power vacuum they create. The solutions of youth are often not long-lived.

And despite their cleverness in violence, they are still blissfully ignorant of the world. They understand how the bullet kills a man but shift nervously from side to side when trying to ask a girl out to dinner and a movie.

Newspaper clippings flash in the man's mind, of nameless men killed for dealing drugs or being in some way connected to the dealers that had brought drugs into the area. The boys – young men now – hunt slowly. One dealer may take weeks to find, to track, and to finally kill, but each one brings them closer to reconciling the deaths of the boy's love and, now, of other classmates. Three killed in a car wreck while smoking laced marijuana. Two more killed in 'accidental" drive by shootings while visiting their cousin on the other side of town. One suicide from a bad trip on psychedelics. The dark side of the experimentation so many people their age do.

Now, snapshots of briefcases of money, of guns – not the hunting rifles or shotguns they had begun this journey with, but now semi- and fully automatic weapons and pistols stolen from the men they kill, of bags of white powder and dark green buds being cut open and thrown from a bridge on the south end of the county, sinking into the dark depths of the Southern River.

Finally, after what feels like hours, the sleeping man knows it's almost over. He sees the man hanging from the chain, he feels the weight of the old Colt 1911 as he puts it to the man's head, and he feels the recoil as the big 255 grain slug breeches the cranial vault. One road trip left.

One last snake to kill.

The oldest of the four is seven months past his eighteenth birthday.

As he always did, Jon Crockett woke bathed in sweat. This one had been bad. Wide awake now, he got out of the bed and walked silently down the hall of his home, past the liquor cabinet, to the kitchen, where he drew a tall glass of water from the sink. Still maneuvering in the dark, he walked out onto the back porch, his eyes making out the lake beyond in the shimmer of the stars and the faint sliver of moon.

It was a long time before he went back to sleep.

10

PRESLEY FRANKLIN WAS MODERATELY surprised to find his appointment with Senator Steven Berryhill accepted in a matter of days instead of weeks. He decided he'd dress for the occasion, less to look like a cop and more to look like a respectable businessman, so he rummaged around, pulled out one of his better suits, and drove to meet the Senator at his office in Vinings the next Wednesday.

Virtually nothing had happened and, while his investigation wasn't really at a standstill, he didn't know where else to go until he understood Merrick Gose.

He found the senator's office to be in a rather generic looking office park that contained the bare minimum of security. Since he was technically on leave, he elected to leave the little Glock in the glove compartment and proceeded into the atrium, where he noted two agents obviously tasked with guarding the senator.

Franklin announced himself to the secretary, who showed him to the coffee machine and explained the senator would be with him in a few minutes. Nine minutes later – exactly at the time of Franklin's appointment, the secretary called to Franklin and opened the door to the senator's office, after requesting Franklin's cellphone.

Steven Berryhill was 100 percent Marine. He'd graduated from UGA and gotten his law degree and still volunteered for the Marines as an enlisted man, not an officer. Once in, he'd fallen in love with the Corps and gone on to serve his "twenty" and come back to Georgia, where he had successfully run for and been elected Senator over a decade ago. Although Berryhill had retired as an NCO, specifically a Gunnery Sergeant, he had received multiple awards, meritorious citations from bravery, and had parlayed his experience into the U.S. Senate and a seat on the Senate Armed Forces Committee.

Steven Berryhill was 100% Marine and 100% Hawk and pulled no punches, in politics or life.

The two men sized each other up even as they exchanged pleasantries.

"Detective, please come in and sit down. Can I get you another cup of coffee?"

"No thank you, Senator. I really must tell you how much I appreciate you taking the time to speak with me."

"Well, that's not a problem Detective Franklin."

"Please, Senator, call me Presley."

Berryhill's face seemed to darken visibly, and he shook his head, "Honestly, Detective, I'll need to be frank with you. Your reputation is shit. I make it a point to understand every person that is seen coming into and out of this office and I'm not at all sure I wish to be seen as friends or even a nodding acquaintance of yours. I'm intimately aware of the current investigations into your actions at the APD and I'll further advise you that this entire meeting is being taped, in case you try to throw me under the bus or imply things that aren't true.

"Do I make myself clear?"

"Yes sir. You do. I understand your concern and I'm not here under the guise of anything that the Atlanta IAD might or might not be investigating. I'd just like some information."

Berryhill's eyebrows raised up, "On what?"

"A man you served with in the Marines. Merrick Gose. You recommended him for the Medal of Honor."

Berryhill leaned back in his chair at the mention of Gose's name and his eyes flashed to a picture on the opposite wall. "That's Gose there. Second from the left, holding the M107. Go look for yourself."

Franklin stood up and moved over to the picture. It had obviously been shot somewhere in the world on some mission, as the three black men not in standard Marine Corps BDUs had on fatigues from somewhere. Gose was dark skinned and bareheaded, sleeves on his fatigues rolled up, holding a huge rifle that looked to weigh forty pounds and had a tremendous telescopic sight on it. The five white men in the picture were all smiling, including Gose, and each casually held some weapon, most of which were M16s or the shorter M4 carbine.

All of the men in the picture, white and black, exuded the smooth professionalism of warriors who were trained to solve one problem – defend the interests of the United States and her allies.

"Gose was the baddest son of a bitch I ever served with. He had a coolness about him. He simply never got rattled. The man to his right in the picture is his spotter, Danny Finn. Great kid, from somewhere in the middle of Arkansas."

Franklin recognized the name from the file. Finn had been the second witness for Berryhill's nomination of Gose for the CMH.

Franklin studied the picture, the man identified as Gose was deeply tanned. "Was the Lance Corporal Spanish?"

Berryhill laughed, "No, I think he was German or Scottish or something, but he had a deep streak of Cherokee from his father's side. I swear, the man could get a tan holding a flashlight."

"So was this taken in Sierra Leone, Senator?"

"No, that picture was the year before – 1996 – Operation Assured Response in Liberia. We'd jumped over there as part of the 22nd MEU right at the damned beginning of our deployment. I think that time we'd come in on the USS Ponce. Essentially, the whole mission was a show of force and peacekeeping gig, but Uncle Sam had added a couple extra snipers to our billet. The idea was that we'd have extra cover for civilian evacuations and not need to have close air support hovering around making the natives restless."

"Did it work?"

"Of course. Actually worked better than you might think. There was a fair amount of skirmishing, but not real battles like CNN wanted to report on. The breakdown of the Liberian press and more exciting things to report back home allowed us to do what we needed to and not get any press. You might remember that at that time, we had so much good PR on Desert Storm and Panama that DoD didn't want to lose anything. Of course, the fact that it was black folks fighting and not the white ones in Bosnia was probably just as good of a reason for the major networks to not cover it, too."

"What did Gose do there?"

"Same thing he did wherever he went – deal out death from 2,000 yards. He wasn't the best Marine sniper ever and his confirmed kills barely scratch the surface of what some guys have done in Vietnam or even now in Afghanistan or Iraq, but he was damned good. I think he had a dozen or so by this time. Some guys get caught up in it, but to him, it was just doing what needed to be done. I never saw him overthink his job or the mission, which happens from time to time with anyone. To Gose, it was simple – if you were the enemy, he killed you or he tried."

"Mostly, though, he killed you."

"Bad ass Marine, huh, Senator?"

"We're all bad asses, son. But Gose? He was what Marines want to grow up and become."

"Senator, that's why I'm here, I'd like to know more about the circumstances of Merrick Gose's death. Unfortunately, the information I've got access to was heavily redacted, even your letter recommending him for the Medal of Honor. Would it be too much for you to elaborate on it?"

"And why do you want to know about Lance Corporal Gose, Detective?"

"Well, sir, I've been chasing cold case files and, odd as it might sound, a sample of blood from a scene in the Bahamas in 1992 came back as positive to Merrick Gose. It doesn't make sense that it could be there, but it was."

Berryhill was unfazed, "And you trust the Bahamian government, their chain of custody, their evidence collection techniques, and a score of years of sketchy storage to produce a quality sample?"

"Honestly, no sir, I don't. But I'm a cop, good or bad, and I've got nothing else to do, so I'm trying to understand why that young man could have been there. More importantly, I'm trying to understand the young man the DNA says was there. It doesn't make any sense, Hell, everyone that was there seems to be dead, and yet here's this sample of Gose's DNA in a bloodstain in a place it shouldn't – or can't – be."

Berryhill's gaze suddenly went far away. Franklin could see he was thinking hard about what he'd just been asked, and after a long minute, he sighed, reached under the desk where Franklin heard a slight "click" and flatly stated, "Detective, I'm turning off the recorder. I'll explain this one time and only once, and if you repeat any of this, then IAD will be the least of your worries."

Berryhill hit the buzzer on his desk phone and simply stated, "Patrice, please come into the office."

Franklin expected the young secretary and instead, a door opened up immediately behind the bookshelf to his right. A very large black man in an impeccably tailored navy-blue suit walked in and asked Franklin to stand up and hold his arms out from his sides.

As Franklin stood there, the man produced a small electronic scanner, roughly the size of a pack of cigarettes, and ran it over Franklin's body.

"He's clear, Senator, no listening or recording devices." With that, Patrice, or who Franklin assumed was Patrice, disappeared back through the bookshelf door.

"Detective, what I'm about to tell you is still classified, for any variety of reasons. If you utter one word of this to anyone, understand, you will not be tried for treason, you will simply go away. No press, no jail time, no questions asked. Do you understand?"

Presley Franklin didn't often get nervous, but he felt the first cold trickle of sweat on his forehead. What the Hell was going on?

"Now, Detective, I'm going to give you the Cliffs Notes of that day. The "what" and "why" are not important to your question, and I think you now understand not to go wagging your tongue on this. Merrick Gose died a hero's death, but the politics of the situation in which he died made it virtually impossible for him to receive the commendations he deserved.

"Our stated mission in Sierra Leone in 1997 was simple: to evacuate any refugees and American nationals who desired to leave the country after the coup. Obviously, there were other components at work here, which is why you're not getting the background I think you'd like to have.

"The operation was called Noble Obelisk, and in order to effectively handle the stated mission, the 22nd MEU – again – was called on to assist. Normally, we would have rotated out of an active deployment, but the nonsense in Bosnia as well as some other unrest had us bounce out of Camp Lejeune and back to active in the Mediterranean. We had intel already in the area and by the time Marines were on the ground in late May, MEU command was situated in the U. S. Embassy in Freetown. As Marines are wont to do, the enlisted forces soon took to calling it Mamba Station.

"Now here's the deal: Freetown sits on a peninsula and the challenge was trying to keep those roads open for anyone who wanted to evac. We decided, after about 4 days, that we'd put the word out by the jungle drums and our sources in the area that anyone who wanted a lift out could meet our people in a convoy roughly fifteen miles from Freetown, at the borders of the Northern Province and what they called the Western Area and we'd get them out.

"To do that, though, takes logistics and infrastructure – two things that are notably lacking in the third world. We decided that the risk was worth it to line the primary extraction point with scout/sniper teams spaced out by 1500 yards. They'd provide intel and cover fire for any friendlies as well as recon for any air support we might end up needing if it turned nasty.

"Does all this make sense to you, Detective?"

"Yes sir."

"Good. Maybe you're not as dumb as you look. So, we've got scout/snipers in place recon'ing the area for nearly three days, documenting everything – cattle grazing, people moving, even wild animals, making sure that there's nothing exciting going down or being planned. The sniper teams had all drawn straws to see who set up where, and Gose and Finn drew the long straw – first choice. Gose took the far edge. He and Finn were on point for the whole operation – 43 hours in the bush, six-mile hump in, and they set up outside of a burg called Katu Town. From the spot Gose had chosen, they had an unfettered view of our pick up zone roughly 1000 yards out."

"Was the 1000 yards by design?" asked Franklin.

"No, it just worked out that way. It wasn't optimal, because that's at the operational limit of the usual weapons Scout/Sniper teams used – the M40A ... basically an accurized Remington 700 in 308 Winchester. Gose could hit with the M40 at that range, but it really was the hairy edge for anyone, even with Merrick's skills. Danny only had confidence in the gun to about 800 yards.

"Which is why they had the big gun out there, the Barrett M107. Shoots the .50 caliber Browning Machine Gun Cartridge and is accurate on vehicles and light armor past 3,000 yards and bad guys out to 2,500."

Franklin leaned forward, "So what happened, Senator?"

"Simple, our convoy rolled in and was evac'ing refugees and after about 12 minutes, Gose and Finn observed hostiles rolling towards us. The usual stuff, cobbled-together old trucks with homemade sheet plating, a bunch of locals armed with small arms and at least a few RPGs. Finn issued a warning by radio, over on the *Trenton*, the LPH we'd deployed from, they started warming up the Cobras despite the cloud cover, and my team at the pick up started scrambling to get everyone onto the carriers we'd brought.

"Gose engaged the third vehicle in the convoy at 2,100 yards and disabled it at a natural choke point on the road, which blocked the vehicles behind it. We later found he'd killed the driver with a shot *to the head*. Next, he took out the two lead vehicles – blew the engine block in the first one and caught the second one in the transmission. Understand, he was using the Raufoss Mk 211 ammo in that Barrett, so the effect was, shall we say, dramatic."

"What makes it so special?"

"It's an anti-matériel projectile. High-explosive incendiary and armor-piercing ammo designed specifically to break hard stuff. Once the bullet hits, it triggers a small explosive charge in the nose of the bullet. If it hits you, it likely wouldn't go off *inside* of you, but it tends to blow through soft targets and explode immediately after exiting. The first guy Gose shot? The round actually blew out of him and killed three men in the back of the truck.

"The second and third vehicles didn't fair much better. In three shots, Gose had killed six men and disabled three vehicles.

"By this time – maybe twenty or thirty seconds, he'd re-engaged the initial convoy, and began taking out soft and hardened targets within it. By now, I had our team on the ground rolling and as we retreated back down the road, unfortunately, our lead Humvee got hit by what we would now call an IED. We lost two men there, the top gunner and the driver and the deuce and a half behind it pushed the wreckage out of the way.

"In the meantime, Gose had engaged a total of eight vehicles with ten shots. At that range, he'd still managed to kill 17 men. The gunners on our Humvees had opened up a time of two, but we didn't have a clear line of sight, so they were told to stand down until they could engage freely.

"In Lance Corporal Finn's AA report, he stated Gose had reloaded the Barrett and begun to engage single targets – men – on the ground. He killed one as the man was readying an RPG, even though that weapon was far out of range. At that point, though, Gose and Finn began to take fire from their right flank as roughly four dozen irregulars began shooting towards them from a treeline less than 200 yards from their position. It was just plain bad luck. No one had any idea they were in the area – they'd heard the sounds of Gose's .50, obviously seen something, and just started spraying fire where they thought the shots were coming from.

Berryhill's expression was a long way off, "That was the shitty part of the whole deal – no one knew who these guys were and it was a complete fluke that fucked the whole operation.

"Finn was hit twice, once in the leg, breaking his femur, once in the upper chest. Gose got Finn down low and began applying first aid and unfortunately, their comms were screwed. We could hear them but they couldn't hear us. Gose shucked part of his ghillie suit and got Finn into it to provide some kind of concealment, then took the M4 that Finn had and began engaging these targets. He killed another six men there, then he left his position to draw fire. From what we were able to deduce, he left Finn's position armed with the M4, three twenty round clips, and his sidearm – a 1911 and three magazines. He engaged this irregular force for the next 300 yards – over a total of perhaps ten minutes and led them away from Finn and the road my team was on.

"My team began trying to flank the troops that were flanking Gose while Finn got evac'ed. We could hear the rattle of AKs and Gose's M4, then it went silent and there was only the heavy 'boom' of his .45 … with fewer AKs. Finally, nothing for several minutes, and two RPG rounds hit back to back."

Berryhill smiled a sad smile. "That was the end of Merrick Gose."

Franklin shook his head and had to acknowledge that this type of bravery and courage was not something he could ever find in himself.

Berryhill snapped back and continued, "I ordered the convoy to move out and leave us two Humvees. I kept a team of six of the original 36 Marines that had rolled out and we moved into the creek bottom that Gose had bounced into. What we found was bodies everywhere. Merrick had engaged these guys at every turn and killed 19, and based on the blood trails we found, at least another twelve were hit. He'd killed a half dozen more with his pistol, which we found – broken due to taking a hit on the slide by an AK-74 round. At least four more men had been killed by Gose with either his knife or his bare hands.

"Somebody finally got around him and hit him with the RPG. Then hit him again. All our team – or the investigation team the next day – could ever find of Merrick Gose was his left ring and pinkie finger, his dog tags, and a patch of skin from his leg."

"Jesus," said Presley Franklin, slowly.

"Yes, maybe now you can see why this man was so special?"

"Is it possible he could have survived the fight? Maybe?"

Berryhill's disposition changed nearly instantly. "You *bastard*! Do you think *anyone* gets hit like that and walks away? If you're being serious, then no. Gose is dead. We had people in the bush for weeks – spooks from the Company, missionaries on our payroll, and a whole native speaking team of informants. No white man walked into a mission in the ensuing weeks. No white man made it back to Mamba Station. The best we could do for Merrick Gose was to make sure his sacrifice was recognized.

"It was the single bravest thing I've ever seen any man do in my life. The worst part was, it was for damn near nothing. Finn caught a round in Afghanistan eight years later and came home under the flag he swore an oath to."

Franklin tried to empathize, "Well, Senator, he protected those civilians…"

"You never served, did you Detective?"

"No sir."

"Then you could never realize that what Gose did – all the killing, all the maneuvering, all the training? It wasn't for those blacks in the bush, it was for his *team*. His platoon. His Corps. His country. The faces of civilians always look the same, but the men you serve with? They're who you're there for.

"When I got in that night and completed the after-action reports, I wrote my recommendation for Merrick Gose to receive the Medal of Honor. While Finn recovered, I met him on a hospital ship and had him sign the paperwork too. You have to have two witnesses to an event for it to be considered."

"And why didn't Gose receive the Medal of Honor?"

"Oh hell, politics, you numb bastard! The military wants good press, and snipers are usually *not* good press. Snipers killing ragtag civilian irregulars is *terrible* press and if you kill the dumb bastards on a "peacekeeping" mission, it's really a bad deal. Gose deserved the CMH, but I guess the Navy Cross was as good as I could expect."

"Senator, may I ask you a question?"

"Perhaps."

"What makes this mission such a classified operation? I mean, what you've shared with me seems like it could have taken place anywhere."

"Detective, you don't need to worry about it, but suffice to say, it was far more important than simply evac'ing civilians. There were two very specific people we got out that day, and it doesn't make any difference who they were. They were important to the United States' interests.

"Now, Franklin, if that's all, I believe you know the way out. I hope this clears up any questions you have and, more importantly, I hope you understand the importance of tact in this situation and how any "slip of the tongue" will be dealt with."

"Yes sir, Senator. Thank you." Franklin extended his hand and Berryhill made no move to shake it.

"Goodbye, Detective."

...

Presley Franklin made it out of the Senator's office and back to his car in a daze. He wasn't sure what he could do with the information that Berryhill had shared, but it certainly hadn't hurt to fill in the blanks, even if they didn't move the case forward.

So now what? The lead he had, the tiny little insignificant lead he had, was gone in an RPG blast in a place he couldn't find on a map.

Damn.

Even worse? Merrick Gose was a hero – that meant people would likely only remember the positive things he'd done as a kid. Oh, they might remember some stupid stunt he'd pulled while drinking beer at a party in high school, but they'd never throw him under the bus as a criminal.

Downtrodden, Franklin put the car in gear and drove home.

11

PRESLEY FRANKLIN SAT in his dining room that night with the files laid out in something approaching order. He understood what had happened in Dundee Bay, he knew that Merrick Gose had been there, and he knew that, somehow, it was possible that Merrick Gose had been involved in the killings in Atlanta years ago – the young man *could* have been one of the Four Horsemen, and that led him back to that cold case.

No, that wasn't quite right.

There was no reason to think Gose was part of the Four Horsemen, was there? There wasn't anything to link the events of Dundee Bay with anything in Atlanta, other than the drunken ramblings of two dirty cops sitting in a bar in the Bahamas three months ago.

Now, he tried to understand what the police had actually known about the Four Horsemen.

He flipped absently through the file he'd copied from the master case file in the bowels of the APD.

The downside of cold case files assembled, in some cases, years after the initial crimes had been committed was that someone had to make a call on what that initial crime was. In the case of the Four Horsemen, it was widely believed the first killings had started taking place in late 1989 and concluded by August of 1992.

But *why* had they stopped?

Franklin tried to be objective. Why do you stop committing crimes?

You get killed?

You get caught?

You move?

You get ... done?

Was the motivation for all the killings in the Four Horsemen case about revenge? The police had usually floated the theory that some criminal enterprise had decided to take over the street level dealings in parts of Atlanta, but no one had ever really put forward a workable theory on who that could have been.

In the power vacuum that was left, the sergeants of the street gangs had almost exclusively stayed small instead of getting bigger. In fact, it was nearly 1997 before anyone had risen to prominence in the Atlanta underworld to create any type of cohesive organization, and that had only lasted a few years before falling apart.

Franklin rubbed his eyes. He was getting nowhere. He began putting the files back in their respective folders and when he got to his own notes, he remembered the real estate guy.

Crocker? Crockett! Jon Crockett. He'd been shot in a liquor store robbery in 1995 in Florida. Who the hell was he?

Absently, Franklin typed Crockett's name into his computer and promptly found ... nothing.

No social media, no LinkedIn, no website, no company.

Who was this guy?

Digging deeper, Franklin was able to pull the man's records from the DMV – he lived in Pickett, on Lake Lanier and his first driver's license on record showed he lived in Graniteton, Georgia as a kid.

Jon Crockett was six months younger than Gose. They'd grown up in the same town. They'd both attended River's Ford High School.

Suddenly, Franklin wasn't as tired and he set out looking for more information about the reclusive real estate investor. He dug up the police report from when Crockett had been shot and found the good Samaritan was named Peter Claiborne, also a resident of Georgia and on vacation at the same time as Crockett.

Claiborne had also grown up in Graniteton.

He, too, had attended River's Ford High School and graduated in 1992.

With Merrick Gose. With Jon Crockett.

Something didn't add up.

The math was wrong. In 1995, Gose was enlisted in the Marines doing God knows what. Claiborne, it appeared, was in college at UGA, and Crockett was in school in Tennessee. Who the fuck gets shot in a liquor store 500 miles from home?

Franklin, far from being frustrated, pushed his laptop into databases he'd never tried to get into and found very little. He looked at his watch, it was after midnight. Finally, he decided there wasn't anything else to be done this evening and he decided the next day he could ride out to Graniteton and poke around for himself.

12

HUNDREDS OF MILES from where Presley Franklin was making painfully slow deductions on a cold case, Roosevelt Bidings was cleaning up a mess made by the son of a Russian mafioso who paid Bidings to do things like this from time to time.

A woman – little more than a girl – sixteen years old, had been murdered and sexually assaulted four miles from Freeport. Roosevelt was busy burying the corpse well off the dirt road where she'd been dumped and hoping no one had seen him in the early morning darkness that draped the edges of Freeport. He was also blindly hoping he'd managed to grab all the evidence left at the scene to suggest Sergei Karamunin had, in fact, been involved.

Sergei was the 21-year-old son of Andrei Karamunin – an expatriate arms dealer who dabbled in arming whoever paid top dollar. His company, Chernaya Voda Vlozheniya, meant God-knows-what in Russian, but operated in the Bahamas on account of its Panamanian corporate registration.

Unfortunately, it was a little too open-and-shut to discredit in the usual ways.

The dumb fuck had left his wallet at the scene of the crime and even the substandard investigatory tactics of the Bahamian State Police would gather enough evidence and build a case against the kid that would land him in jail for life.

Times like these were when Roosevelt Bidings hated ever having been on the take from the bad guys. He'd made well over fifty thousand dollars over the years from Andrei, and, of course, Andrei had already reminded him of that by phone early this morning.

At fourteen minutes past four, to be exact.

"Roosevelt, I'm sorry to wake you, but my son Sergei needs some attention."

Bidings, drug out of a dreamless sleep, had only been able to mumble into his phone a garbled, "mm'kay."

"It would seem he had a little too much fun with a young woman this evening and has potentially injured her. He is in my home now and I'll need you to assist me," there was a pregnant pause, "as you have so many times in the past. Yes?

"I know the police will be happy to send him to jail over this … indiscretion … shall we say … but I am personally handling his discipline as a parent. I merely need you to ensure the police will not find anything to indicate young Sergei was involved."

Roosevelt, awake now, dutifully took down the location of "indiscretion" and began putting on old clothes to hopefully avoid easy identification while he heeded the calls of one of his masters.

In his mind, the voice of his father, long since deceased, laughed and said, "Roos'velt, son, you da one who put dese chains on you'self. You's made dem link ba link and foot ba foot. Boy, you choosed to become da slave, so who da dumber one in dis deal?"

It wasn't the first body he'd had to hide from … well, from himself.

He looked at his watch – 5:39 a.m. Today was a payday for Bidings. He had to meet one of several different men in the market at 6:30 that morning, where they would exchange pleasantries and, seemingly accidentally, matching backpacks.

The difference, of course, was the one Bidings arrived with was empty – unless he was "losing" a file from the police – and the one he left with contained $5,000 in U.S. dollars.

Small bills, as he had stipulated when he began taking the bribes years ago. From time to time, the men who paid him would pull a prank. Once, they had paid him in Euros at the correct exchange rate. Another time, he had gone to pick up the backpack and found it contained hundreds of dollars in coins as well as folding money.

Three hours later, as he sat at his kitchen table filling out deposit slips to four different banks in three different fake identities, Roosevelt Bidings idly thought about Presley Franklin and wondered where his cold case had gone. He made a mental note to call the man later on and check in.

13

FLUSH WITH LOADS OF circumstantial evidence, Presley Franklin got into his car the next morning and took the 40-minute ride to Graniteton, Georgia. Here was a town gone to rot. In some places, you could still make out the lazy, rural background of the city, but everywhere, the impending sprawl of Atlanta loomed. Three hundred thousand-dollar homes stood in stark relief to their surroundings – the neighborhoods they were being built in had been cattle pastures only a few years before. Along the interstate, commercial buildings advertised everything from motorcycles to new cars to bedroom sets and, immediately beside those businesses sat single-wide trailers with trashy whites sitting on their porches and beaten and broken cars decaying on what passed for lawns.

In the old part of the city, centered around the railroad, it wasn't any better. Here were the suburban blacks, with battered cars sitting on big rims, with booming stereo systems that seemed to ignore the oil leaking from tired engines. Nail salons, "African Hair Studios" and pawn shops lined these streets and, with a sigh of relief, Franklin made it to the southern part of the county, where at least some of the sprawl had been halted.

Here was River's Ford High School, built in 1976, home to 1,500 students and the alma mater of Claiborne, Gose, and Crockett. Franklin didn't know what he expected to find at the school, he was simply driving to get the flavor of the town, although he knew precious little of 1992 was to be found there. Absently, he pulled up into the visitor's parking and walked into the school. He announced himself at the front office and flashed his badge. The lady behind the desk, Loretta Smith, smiled and asked what the purpose of his visit was. Franklin mumbled something about doing some research for a book about suburban teens he was writing when he retired.

She brightened up considerably and offered to give him a quick tour of the common areas of the school. All around them, students flowed, oblivious to the adults in their midst. Presley was no fan of kids, but he was always amazed at how easily teenagers could maneuver around – and not even acknowledge – grown-ups.

With little better to do, Franklin agreed. Loretta began by sharing that she had been a student at the school years before, graduating in 1989. She'd gone on to get her teaching certificate and then come back to Graniteton after her parents had become ill in the early part of 2001. She'd taught until 2006 and then moved into the administration for the school, preferring the hours and schedule to the small pay cut she'd had to take.

Finally, after wandering around for twenty minutes and having seen everything he'd secretly not wanted to see, Loretta stopped in front of a black marble statue in the Common's Area.

"I don't know if you know anything about the history of this school, Detective Franklin, but it had a real run of bad luck in the early 1990s. In total, twenty-six students, from three graduation classes, were killed or died of drug related causes or accidents."

"Damn. That's terrible!"

"It was, I remember reading about it while I was away at college. As administrators, we always have to expect that one or two kids will having something terrible happen to them, but this was like a scourge. Four died in drive by shootings – unheard of back then around here, nearly a dozen were killed in car wrecks or random problems from bad drugs, and several more were just doing stupid crap that high schoolers all do, but usually survive. So you have this here."

Franklin looked at the statue. It was a riderless horse, nearly eight feet tall, with saddle, scabbard, and all the tack still in place. At its base, there were the names of the dead students inscribed and below that, a phrase Presley Franklin had never seen and could not easily pronounce. "*Nemo Me Impune Lacessit.*"

"Who did this, Loretta?"

"Well, that's the weird thing – no one knows. It was delivered in the middle of the school year in the late fall of 1994 and even the delivery men and the company that created it didn't know who commissioned it. Honestly, the school left it in place as they figured it was something that one of the victim's families had sanctioned. It's strange, though, because the company that created it said they were paid over one hundred thousand for it and I know that kind of money doesn't grow on trees for our students' families. Some could have afforded it, but danged few."

"So what's with the horse? The school's mascot or something?"

"That's *another* weird thing, Detective, our mascot is the Patriots. Nothing to do with horses or cowboys, or cavaliers, or anything like it. *Nemo Me Impune Lacessit* is the motto of Scotland, and Graniteton has little, if any, Scottish heritage."

Franklin, a strange look on his face, looked at the woman, then back to the statue. "What's it mean?"

"No one will touch me with impunity."

Franklin shook his head. It damned sure *sounded* like something a vigilante might say.

"Loretta, can I ask you a weird question?"

"You can try, but remember, I work with kids."

73

"Does the phrase, "The Four Horsemen" mean anything to you?"

"You mean, like the old professional wrestlers?"

Franklin laughed, he'd forgotten about them. "No, not those guys, just the term."

"Actually, that's funny, in the library, there's a picture of four men on horseback drawn by one of our students years ago. Would you like to see it?"

Presley perked up visibly. "Yes. Yes, I would."

In the back corner of the library, in a separate room obviously reserved for some special reason, Loretta showed Presley Franklin the print, framed on the wall. It was done in pencil, or charcoal, or something and the best term to describe it was "haunting."

It showed four men, wraiths, really, all on horseback, stopped and facing the viewer. The men were a depiction of the Four Horsemen of the Apocalypse. Long removed from church, Presley struggled to remember who was who in terms of the biblical horsemen of Revelation, but he could see one of the men held scales, another held a broken sword aloft, a third wielded a huge scythe, and the last one, on the far right of the page, could be seen to be little more than a skeleton wearing clothing long ago moth eaten and riddled with holes. Unlike some depictions of the Four Horsemen in Renaissance art, the creatures depicted in this image were all huge, muscular beings – or at least had been.

The image was haunting and it created a sense of incredible foreboding in Franklin – like opening up a grave you knew contained something supernatural that would destroy you.

The overall effect of the picture was intense and, while none of the wraiths in the image was moving, the artist had imbued a sense of *something* about to happen in the work. You knew, just knew, this was the end for whomever observed these men. Franklin felt the hair on the back of his neck stand up simply looking at the damned thing.

Whoever had drawn this was not only an artist, they were intensely motivated by the subject at hand. Franklin could feel the passion of the artist from across the years. This was far from a high school kid's art project, it was the product of someone who *felt* the subject matter.

"Who did this piece? It's amazing."

Loretta smiled, "Unfortunately, that young man might have been as cursed as the rest of his class. That was done by Brandon Jones, he graduated in 1992 and was killed in 1995. Some sort of training accident in the Army – he'd enlisted right out of high school. I knew his family and he was a wonderful guy. He'd played football here as a student."

Franklin leaned in closer to the picture and could just make out "B. Jones" in the lower corner. Here was another piece – circumstantial again – but a piece – that tied the Four Horsemen killings back to Gose and company. Was Jones the fourth? Or did he simply know what was going on? Had he been killed because he knew?

More questions bubbled up into his mind but he silenced them and turned back to Loretta.

"I'm wondering if you have a picture of this young man? Maybe the yearbook from the class of 1992?"

Loretta smiled, "Well of course! We're in the library, silly. We've got all of them, all the way back to 1978, the first graduating class. Let's go talk to Miss Sally, she's the head librarian here."

Sally Colleton was 100% librarian. Stern-faced, horn-rimmed glasses, and obviously far more comfortable with books than people, she nearly made eye contact with Franklin twice in the four minutes they interacted but was noticeably warmer to Loretta while they talked. She directed them back into what she called the "archives" – really a small room used for all school yearbooks, playlists, papers published by the teachers on staff, and a myriad of other assorted paperwork that was somehow deemed appropriate to hold on to.

Two minutes of searching produced the 1992 yearbook, titled "Gettin' Done" with an odd graphic on the cover with a stylized Patriot. Flipping absently through it, he looked at the senior class.

Here was Gose, flattop haircut, smiling broadly for the camera.

Next, Franklin found Jones, hair longer, the faint outline of a mustache on his upper lip, undoubtedly grown for months to get it to this point.

Flipping back one page, he found Claiborne and Crockett, both looking like generic teenagers, with no hint of malice or concern on their faces.

As seniors, all of the young men had been wearing tuxedos for their class photos, so Franklin couldn't gauge how they might have dressed. He flipped to the back of the book and found an index. He noted that the four men were pictured multiple times in the book, and they each had played football all four years of high school. Finally, on page 35, he found a casual picture of the four boys together.

All wear wearing jeans and t-shirts, all looked to be at least six feet tall and had obviously spent years training in the gym and on the athletic fields. In the photograph, they were smiling and showed not a single bit of stress while they leaned casually, laughing at some private joke, in a hallway wall between classes.

The caption simply read, "Four old friends, Merrick Gose, Peter Claiborne, Brandon Jones, and Jon Crockett pause for a laugh between classes."

It wasn't a smoking gun – far from it, really - but Franklin did realize the importance of the picture – these kids knew each other well.

...And there were four of them.

He replaced the yearbook, and thanked Lorretta. He apologized for keeping her so long from her regular duties and she laughed, "Detective, do you know what I'd have been doing if you hadn't shown up?"

"No ma'am."

"Well, it would have been a lot more mundane than this. Thank you for coming by today."

She shook hands with Franklin and walked him to the front door.

"I appreciate the education and the history lesson, Mrs. Smith. If I get back to Graniteton, I'll look you up, maybe buy you a coffee."

Smith laughed and waved at the cop, then turned back into the school.

14

WITH TWO NEW NAMES, Peter Claiborne and Brandon Jones, Presley Franklin had new places to look. He dove into Brandon Jones first and found out that Loretta Smith wasn't very accurate in her storytelling. Jones *had* enlisted in the Army, but not until 1993, same as Gose. In his case, though, it was different.

He'd gone to Furman to play football on a partial scholarship and come home a year later. His grades had suffered, but since he'd graduated with honors at River's Edge, the U. S. Army was more than happy to have him enlist.

Unlike Merrick Gose, though, the file Franklin reviewed from the VA was fairly boring and only a few pieces were redacted – Basic training in Fort Benning, Georgia, then several MOS's in the States, and finally, he was sent to Jump School, again at Fort Benning, in 1996 and died in a training accident early that year.

Open and shut and no heroism.

He'd been buried in his family's plot in Wrens, Georgia, two hours east of Atlanta.

Franklin found it an odd comparison to the heroic death of Merrick Gose, but figured, in the end, most soldiers don't die heroes and most also don't die in wars, or even battle, so it wasn't unexpected.

Maybe the whole graduating class was just damned from the beginning.

Franklin moved on to Peter Claiborne.

Here was a kid that *wasn't* damned.

From several law enforcement databases, Presley was able to determine that Claiborne had grown up in Graniteton, his parents had been divorced, and his father had been in an executive position with the long-defunct Eastern Airlines and then had moved to Delta.

After graduation, Claiborne had gone on to UGA and then law school, and as the years went by, he'd become one of the top intellectual property attorneys in the United States. He and his family had moved to just outside of Nashville, Tennessee in 1998 after he married and lived there ever since.

Aside from taxes and the occasional newspaper article, there was little else to go on – no arrests, ever, and not even a speeding ticket.

The guy was as straight as he could be.

On social media, Franklin found Claiborne's wife's accounts – apparently Claiborne had no social media presence. Her profiles and feeds were filled with pictures of the family – their three kids and what looked like a spacious home surrounded by rolling hills and fields and other pictures of the family in a home on some body of water, with the caption, "The view from Bird Key."

Another dead end. Shit.

On a whim, he decided to call in a favor from the computer nerds in the APD Cybercrimes division – with a total staff of three nerds buried in the bowels of the APD – and see if they could find anything linking Claiborne to the reclusive Crockett.

Picking up the phone, he called the main switchboard at the department and was quickly transferred.

A nasally voice picked up the phone, "Uh, Cyber, this is Joey."

"Hey Joey, it's Detective Presley Franklin, I've got a question for you."

Perking up, Joey Krakowski sounded more alive, "Yes sir!"

"Is it possible – and legal, of course – to see if two individuals are friends on, like, social media, or if they exchange emails regularly?"

"Oh, yeah, Detective, there's no problem with that. Patriot Act covers it for us and NSA has that data for us to use. In fact, you can probably do it yourself..."

"Joey, I'll bet you can do it faster than you can explain it to an old man like me – could I simply give you some names and you check it out for me? Of course, this is hush-hush, so we need to be quiet about this – it's a big case, so I can't tell you too much."

"You got it! I'll get right on it." And promptly hung up.

Presley stared at the phone, then redialed it. As he did, his phone beeped with another call coming in.

It was Joey. He clicked over.

"Umm, yeah, Detective, sorry, I forgot to ask the names. Sorry, it's been kind of slow down here."

Franklin rolled his eyes. He wondered if the Cybercrimes Division had to qualify with firearms? If they did, he figured the good news was they'd shoot themselves before they could do too much damage. He gave Joey the names, thanked him, reiterated the need for tact and quiet on this, and hung up.

From there, Franklin opened up the box containing the entire Four Horsemen file and began trying to look at it with fresh eyes. Pulling a small table up beside him, he took out the Dundee Bay file and tried to compare.

After four hours, Franklin realized he was no further towards reconciling any real evidence with circumstantial evidence, then the phone rang.

It was Joey.

"Umm, Detective, I'm sorry it took so long, and I've gotta tell you, there really isn't much. A couple of times a year, it looks like Crockett has called the Claiborne home – maybe to wish him a happy birthday – that's in mid-February, by the way – and then there's a call at Christmas time. Other than that, they aren't even really on social media. It's kind of weird, they both went to school together and … I guess … just grew apart."

"So there's nothing?"

"No sir."

"Shit. Thanks Joey."

"No problem, call anytime. We don't get a lot of people actually talking to us, you know."

"I can't imagine why, Joey. I'll ring you up if I need anything."

Presley hung up the phone, looked at it for a moment, then looked at the mountain of paperwork before him. There was nothing in it. No smoking gun. No motive. Nothing.

In frustration, he got up and walked quickly out of the room.

15

THIRTY-EIGHT MILES AWAY, while Presley Franklin sat mulling over missing motives and circumstantial evidence, Jon Crockett sat in the evening light on his back porch looking over Lake Lanier. Dimitry had already notified Crockett of Franklin's searches, and while Crockett knew there was little to find, he silently worried about the things that *could* be found.

In his mind was all the evidence Presley Franklin ever needed, but he'd put it far, far away. Tonight, though, as it sometimes did, it all came gushing back to the forefront of his memory, prompted by some odd outside stimulus or event.

Sometimes just one or two random memories peeked out, like some sort of rodent from a burrow. Other times, the whole damn thing came back with the violence of pack of wolves seeking blood.

Now, long after the bodies had been buried, someone had come along to kick over the gravestones. It had seemed like a simple thing then, almost childish in its simplicity – kill the drug dealers that were killing his friends. It had taken no convincing to get Merrick to help, or Brandon, and even Peter had come along with no remorse or second thoughts.

Their success had been due to naiveté, though. What dealer was worried about white high school kids? They were buyers, right? The plan had been simple, gleaned from too many old western movies - "clean up the town" and ensure no one else came in, but just like so many dreams that young men aspire to, there is always another bastard to sell drugs, just like there is always another bastard to buy them.

Outlawing sex, drugs, and alcohol seemed to be about the dumbest thing anyone could every think they could actually do, especially if all they did was sentence you to jail for a few years.

Right or wrong, the four teenagers – not the Four Horsemen yet – that would have to wait another 16 months before that nickname was given - had decided that criminals, especially those dealing drugs, had to die.

They'd been smart, that was for sure, they knew the kids who were buying and using – they were the upper middle class kids the boys didn't hang out with at school; the ones with new cars, big weekly allowances, and parents who had assumed the television made an effective babysitter. The problem, of course, is their friends were using, too. And dying. It didn't take much effort to figure out who was the seller, then who they bought from, and figure out who the bigger fish were.

Teenagers couldn't keep secrets worth a damn.

Barely old enough to drive, Merrick and Jon had killed the first dealer as he leaned into the window of Merrick's mother's car to see "what ya'll needs, tonight?" and Jon had shoved the little 38 Special – his dad's - into the man's chest and pulled the trigger three times. They'd sped off in the Camry and had pulled over on the side of the road two miles later to vomit. At the same time, they realized the side of the car was soaked in the man's blood. They wiped what they could off of it with a towel from the trunk and searched for nearly 20 minutes to find a car wash.

Both boys noticed that the dealer's death was not reported in the news the next day, and when it finally was two days later, it was only one paragraph on the police blotter for Dekalb County.

Nothing ever came from it. No arrests, no outcry, nothing to suggest that anyone was looking for the murderer of a drug dealer.

They'd tracked and found the next five over the course of two more months and by then, Peter and Brandon had begun helping the two to sort out and find the suppliers of the drugs that laced the streets of Graniteton. Peter, ever the organizer, had suggested they take the cash and the guns the dealers inevitably had on them or in their cars. No one else was going to use it and, with the stories in the paper about crooked cops selling and dealing, too, at least the four of them could guarantee the shit was off the streets. Quickly, the boys learned that cash – especially the wads of cash they found – was a problem.

There was simply too damn much of it. No bank teller was going to allow a kid to deposit $17,549 in small bills. In the end, they came to realize that everyone – or at least *nearly* everyone – was dirty in one way or another. If you had cash, you didn't necessarily need to be 18 to open a bank account. Parental signatures could be bypassed as long as you passed some of the money around; people looked the other way. Once in a blue moon, someone might get morally incensed, but for the most part, bribes and graft and letting others "dip their beak" opened doors none of them could have ever believed.

In less than a year, they had over $200,000 in two separate accounts in different banks, smoothed over by bribing assistant branch managers.

The worst part? Everything about it had been easy. Three of the boys worked in jobs with plenty of outdoor labor and blue-collar employees who were more than willing to smoke dope or do a quick hit of meth or a snort of coke, all the while sharing information on who sold what. From there, it was simple: meet a dealer, befriend them, and start asking questions. Several times, they had actually been invited to go pick up "shipments." The beauty had been their age. They were kids. Nobody would even prosecute them.

Why worry?

In the end, it was still remarkable they hadn't been caught or killed. The secret, they determined, was making sure that all their parents thought they were somewhere they actually weren't. Merrick's family cabin on their hunting lease in Shady Dale, or down at Brandon's family cabin on the lake. Peter's grandparents home in Sarasota, where the four were invited to spend two weeks every summer, playing at the beach. Or simply going out to celebrate a victory after the football game. Juggling curfews and liberal timeframes allowed them to kill a drug dealer on the same night they beat their cross town rival and merely edit out the hour or so a murder had taken. Two times, they had killed men on their way home from a date.

In the days before cell phones and social media, it was easy to be somewhere you weren't supposed to be.

In time, though, they began to understand they could never kill enough small dealers to ever impact the river of drugs flowing into east Atlanta. Peter, ever the visionary, floated the idea of killing suppliers and smugglers in the fall of 1991.

"Look, if they don't have the shit to sell, what are they going to sell? Let's whack those bastards and be done with it."

Brandon had leaned forward by this time, the four had been sitting in the Waffle House on the interstate in Graniteton after fishing one evening, "Yeah, but how do we do that? Those guys aren't around here. What, are we going to drive to Columbia? Bitch, please. We can't fly to some banana republic and start blasting people. That shit won't work."

Peter, rising to the idea he had just suggested, smiled. "We just need to ask. Somebody knows where the shit comes from."

Jon Crockett began to smile. "Why don't we do a report on it for school?

The looks his friends shot at him said, "*You've lost your fucking mind*," but he continued.

"...You know, for school? All of us know the Sheriff and half of the deputies from the football games and stuff, so we just go to the Sheriff's department and ask for an interview? Tell them we're doing a group project for Social Studies or something?"

Merrick Gose was warming up to the idea. "And we could ask the cop that comes to talk about the DARE Program in school, too. Remember last year when Coach made us do that silly-assed photo for the paper with the cops? The Graniteton police gotta know the same shit the Sheriff's do, right?"

Four young men nodded in assent. The game was changing.

Less than a month later, the four had gone on no less than three separate "field trips" to the Police Department and the Sheriff's Office and had, through feigned ignorance, gotten information about who many law enforcement officials in northern Georgia felt was behind the current issue of the drugs flowing into Atlanta – the black sheep son of a small-time mafioso from St. Louis named Jimmy Allitini.

It was at that same time that the Deputy first mentioned the Four Horsemen.

"The wrestlers?"

"No, you dummy, the drug dealers. It's some crazy bastards from Columbia or something, killing off the local scumbags. Some GBI task-force is on it, but I swear, I think they're smoking what they should be busting. There's no radical group of Mexicans whacking guys. But to hear Atlanta tell it, the Four Horsemen are cutting a swath through the local scumbags."

Crockett leaned in closer to the Deputy, he had to admit, it had a nice ring to it, the Four Horsemen. "So how long have they been doing it?"

"Oh, hell, I don't know, kid. Couple of years? No one's really sure, but they got some guys on film and they got some witnesses. Nobody knows. This Allitini guy, though, he's a real piece of work."

Allitini Sr. had won the rights to move drugs through Atlanta on account of his strong ties to certain trucking companies and unions and his son, a royal fuckup if there ever had been, had been put in charge of making sure the right load got put on the right truck. Despite not being overly smart in terms of school – he'd quit high school as soon as he could, Allitini Jr. had excelled at the logistics of shipping and then, seeing the chance to get rich, had begun making side deals with other suppliers to move – and stay – in Atlanta. At only 30 years of age, Allitini had been ostracized by his family and replaced by the criminal syndicates that controlled distribution, but that made no difference to Allitini, he'd created his own distribution chain into metro Atlanta and made a small fortune every month. He wasn't "made" like the men who ran the big outfits in places like Vegas, or Philly, or New York or Chicago, but nobody was going to mess with him as long as he kept to himself in Atlanta.

He'd only been operating solo for two years, but his distribution network was the biggest one in the southern United States besides the Cubans and Columbians in south Florida.

The challenge? Allitini didn't even live in Atlanta. He'd show once a week, verify things were going well, and then fly back out. Some of the officers said he lived in Florida, some believed he'd gone home up North, and still another, seemingly smarter, believed the man lived somewhere in the Bahamas.

The boys all agreed Allitini seemed to be the key, but no one knew where the hell the man was – or where he could be bounced.

Jon Crockett smiled at the memory of those four innocents, plotting murder and mayhem amongst the drug dealers in Atlanta. Babes in the woods who had nearly pulled off the impossible. Nearly.

At least they'd gotten a helluva nickname for what they'd done.

16

Summer, 1992

THE MAN, BARELY A MAN at all, sat looking through the scope of the Winchester Model 70. Two months ago, it had been legally purchased from a classified ad in the Graniteton Citizen. After purchase, it had been stripped down by Merrick Gose and Jon Crockett, the stock bedded in a stiff two part epoxy to guarantee alignment and proper spacing between the action, the receiver pillar bedded with aluminum bushings through the stock for the action screws, the scope rings lapped for concentricity, the trigger pull hand smoothed with Arkansas stones, and the locking lugs trued with polishing compound. They had pieced together most of this process from books they checked out of the library and the marksmanship and firearms safety Merrick's father had taught them as kids.

Still chambered in 30-06, it had started life as a deer rifle, but now, despite the sporter weight barrel Winchester had screwed on to it years before in their factory, the gun would place five shots into a dime at 100 yards. The Leupold 10X scope was bright and clear and even in low light, such as one might find on a private airport runway late at night, targets were far clearer than either of the young men could believe.

Gose and Crockett had spent long hours poring over ballistics tables, both internal and external, and finally decided upon the Sierra MatchKing, a 168 grain bullet, loaded with 50 grains of IMR 4064 powder. Handloading these bullets in the old single stage RCBS press Gose's father had given him for Christmas three years ago, they could push the bullet nearly to 2850 feet per second, giving the rifle a maximum point-blank range – where no adjustment of the hold on the target was needed to impact within a six inch circle - of nearly three hundred yards.

The old rifle, more accurate than ever, adhered to the strange physical phenomenon of truly repeatable accuracy – it shot sub MOA groups.

MOA, or Minute-of-Angle, was the odd paradox of accurate rifles and shooters to shoot into an ever-growing concentric ring. One MOA was nearly the equivalent of an inch at one hundred yards, two inches at two hundred, and so on. Coupled with the speed of the handload they had developed and its point blank range, a target the size of a human head only needed the crosshairs centered on it to achieve a hit from nearly three football fields away.

In other words, farther than they needed for the shot they intended to take.

They had "run the ladder" on the handloads, weighing and testing ten shots at each possible charge weight of powder until they had found the sweet spot where bullets seemed to magically fall into the same hole, no matter the range. 50 grains of 4064 was a warm load, but it was a damned accurate one.

Peter had used a modified version of their "Social Studies report" strategy, along with the information they had gleaned from dealers they hadn't killed, to determine that Allitini flew into Charlie Brown airport on Friday afternoon and flew out on Saturday night or Sunday morning.

He'd shared it with the other members of the Four Horsemen at another dinner, sitting in the McDonalds on West Avenue in Graniteton two weeks prior.

"So here's the deal, I talked to my pops last week and told him I had a report due on air traffic controllers – you know, the guys Reagan fired years ago. Dad called one of his guys at Hartsfield International and they said I could come in and see how the tower works for approaching flights."

Brandon laughed at the idea, "Well, brilliant, to bad 'Montay says that's the wrong fuckin' airport."

Crockett was smiling. He understood. "No, Brandon, I get it. Peter's gonna play dumb, look around Hartsfield a day or two, then ask his old man if he can let him go check out Charlie Brown, where your boy says Allitini comes in at." Claiborne was nodding his head and smiling.

Brandon's face lit up. "Ohh. You sneaky bastard. So you think you can get into Charlie Brown to see when this douche shows up?"

Peter shook his head. "I don't know. I know dad's got plenty of pull at Hartsfield, so he should at Charlie Brown. The problem is we don't know what kind of plane this guy even flies. Is it a Cessna? Is it a Lear?" He turned back to Brandon, "What's your boy say?"

"Jamontay says it's some kind of jet. That's all he knows."

Peter was not impressed. "Well, that's good news. Show that spook some flashcards or something. We need to know what we're looking for. When do you see him next?"

"I guess we'll both be working at the golf course this weekend."

"Hit his pager and figure it out. The sooner the better."

The young man turned to Crockett, "What's the story on the rifle you girls have been playing with? Gose got your barrel nice and clean?" The boys – and they really were boys – still laughed at a good penis joke.

Gose, silent until then, reached into his back pocket and pulled out the metal lid of a snuff can, only slightly more than two inches across. The center was shot out of it. He tossed it haphazardly on the table and said simply, "I did that with an old Coleman lantern set up twenty feet from it two nights ago at the deer property. That's seven shots."

Claiborne looked at the lid, about the size of the top of a can of soda. "How far?"

"Two hundred fifty yards at ten o'clock at night."

Jones and Claiborne said, "Jesus!" in unison.

Crockett laughed and said, "I guess my barrel's clean, faggots."

The plan had been simple, Peter would be at Hartsfield's tower this weekend, then ask his dad if he would pull some strings to put him at Charlie Brown the next weekend. In the meantime, Brandon would press Jamontay Morgan, a coworker who was a full time dealer but smart enough to have something resembling a job. The four young men had bought drugs from Morgan occasionally just to add to the story they floated as casual users, and, due to his quiet ascension up the ladder of the Allitini organization, he occasionally had been called on to drive Allitini from Charlie Brown Airport to one of several hotels in the Atlanta area. Hopefully, Brandon could get the man to admit what the plane looked like, and Gose and Crockett would try to figure out where they could take a shot from that would kill the Allitini and allow them to get away.

It was a good plan, but a slow one.

"It's at least three weeks to pull this off," said Brandon Jones to no one at the table in particular.

At that moment, Merrick Gose's pager went off. "Lemme out, that's little sis." He scooted out of the booth after Crockett and went to the back of the restaurant to the payphone.

The other three continued to talk, and as teenagers are prone to do, girls, graduation, and college soon began to phase out the planned killing of a drug runner. The sting of Leigh's death was still too painful, but Crockett could at least acknowledge there were a lot of nice looking bottoms attached to girls at their school.

Crockett was the first to notice Gose walking back from the pay-phones, tears streaming down his face. He was making no attempt to hide it and his entire body looked smaller.

"What the fuck? What's wrong?"

Gose tried to talk, tried to verbalize the call he'd just gotten, tried to say something, but the words wouldn't come. His face was crushed with pain and grief and the three men could see he was making a huge effort to regain control.

Taking a deep breath, he held it, lost it, and then, through sheer force of will, he managed to simply say, "My ... parents..." and then lost control again and collapsed, sobbing, on the table.

17

Summer 1992

THEY'D GOTTEN GOSE HOME that night, calling each of their families to relay the message they were staying at the Gose home and that both of Merrick's parents had been killed in a car wreck. Merrick's sister, Julie, younger than him by less than a year, had locked herself in her room. The boys had called Merrick's surviving grandmother, but the police had already been there.

The three young men had given Merrick four strong fingers of bourbon from his father's liquor cabinet to calm him down and gotten him to at least lay down in his own bed.

Quietly, the three sat downstairs.

Jon Crockett was the first to speak.

"Did anyone catch what happened? I mean, really, what happened?"

The other two, understanding his meaning, both shook their heads. "Deputy Morse simply said it was a crash, they went off the embankment on Salem Road. Car flipped and they were killed as a result."

"I don't think it was a message for us."

"We need to find out…"

"We need to figure it out before Gose does. With his temper, if it was a message, we'll pay hell trying to keep him careful like we have been."

Finally, several hours later, the young men fell sleep on couches and chairs in the main parlor of the home where so much warmth had always been shown to them by the Gose family. Each of them mourned quietly and feigned sleep.

The next morning, Jon Crockett pulled Peter Claiborne aside and instructed him to stick to the plan. They each still had work to do.

Two days later, Crockett had driven Gose out to where the car had been towed after the wreck. As they pulled up to the wrecking yard, he looked at Gose. "Are you okay with this?"

"What the fuck do you think? Mom and Dad are dead and we're about to go have to clean their belongings out of the car they were killed in."

"I'll file that under 'okay.' I can do this, man, you can stay here."

"You won't think I'm a puss?"

"Shit no."

"You gonna tell the guys?"

"Not now, maybe in ten years or so. Man, I don't fuckin' know. Sit here and drink your coffee. I'll be back in a few."

With that, Jon Crockett had grabbed the police paperwork, opened the door to his old hot-rodded truck, and walked into the office of the tow company.

Five minutes later, he was staring at the car where his best friend's parents had died. He was surprised there had been so little blood. Merrick's parents had been wearing their seatbelts, but the Sheriff's Deputy they had spoken to that morning to get the accident report had indicated the way the wreck had actually occurred, it likely wouldn't have been survivable no matter what.

"Just a fluke, men. I'm sorry you lost your folks, Merrick, truly I am. No finer people in the county than your family. Your dad had a kind word for everyone, no matter who, and your mother was an angel, no doubt. How's your grandma takin' it?

Gose had the smallest of smiles on his face, "We're all just doing what we have to do. The funeral is in three days, so I guess that's when the real hard part starts. I don't think Julie has figured it out yet. It's been shitty, no matter what, sir."

The Deputy nodded. "Well, here's the report, I already called the tow company that are holdin' it until the insurance adjusters come to handle it, so this will let you get any remaining personal property out of the vehicle. I'm real sorry, son. I need you to sign here for their personal effects from the hospital and the car."

When Merrick did, the Deputy reached down behind the counter and produced a large brown paper bag with the Gose's effects. Merrick didn't look inside.

"Thanks."

And with that, the two young men had left.

Now, looking at the wreckage of the Pontiac Bonneville in the bright morning light, Crockett could see how devastating the wreck had really been. Not a single piece of sheet metal on the body was untouched. Fenders, quarter panels, trunk, hood, and grill – all were broken and bent. The accident report indicated the car had slipped off the road and into a small depression running parallel to the roadbed and when Rick Gose had tried to correct it, had caused the car to pull against the rear passenger tire, ripping it from the axle and causing it to slew wildly in the road. The end result had ultimately been the car running back into the culvert on the side of the road, impacting at the front passenger-side grill, and flipping end over end at least four times.

What didn't make sense was *why* it had happened. As Crockett stared at the wreck, the bright sunlight at his back illuminated a small smudge on the left quarter panel of the car. It stood out in stark contrast to the rest of the crumpled sheetmetal, and it was only by pure accident the area around it had not been damaged. Despite the wrecked body panels and mud-splattered exterior, it looked for all the word like the smudge was part of a slightly larger dent.

Like the car had been hit on the side like the stock car racers did in a bump and run, spinning out the car they hit.

Crockett buried the thought and continued looking into the car, gathering the few personal items that Merrick's parents kept in the vehicle. A cassette tape, a tube of lipstick, and loose change were scattered on the floorboards. A pack of Lucky Strikes, which Mr. Gose smoked exactly three cigarettes out of each day.

Nothing of any real consequence.

Still, the small dent on the side bothered him. He knew the road where Merrick's parents had died and he knew Mr. Gose drove it nearly every day going to and from work. It bothered him, thinking how the man likely knew everything there was to know about that stretch of road: how fast he could go, how to handle the turns, and how his car, three years old, would react in any driving condition.

Crockett looked at the tires – all were still inflated, even the one that had broken loose and was simply placed behind the car. No blowout to force them into the ditch.

What the hell was going on?

Just then, he heard the crunch of gravel behind him and knew it was Merrick.

"I thought I told you to stay in the truck."

"Fuck off, it wasn't your parents."

"Yeah, but they were damned close. Your old man taught me a helluva lot more about the outdoors than mine could have. If I had to depend on Dad to teach me to shoot a deer, I'd still be trying to get the gun loaded."

"Yeah, you're right."

Crockett didn't want Gose to see the odd dent in the car, and he tried to wrap up their visit. "There just isn't much here, Merrick. All their personal effects were at the police station."

"You knew I'd want to see it."

"I did. Will it change anything?"

"Like as not." The young man grew silent. He'd always been quiet and introspective and this was no exception. He reached out his arm to touch the car and placed his hand tenderly on it. Taking a deep breath, he held it, then exhaled. "What do you think about the dent on the side?"

'Damn!' thought Crockett. *'This sumbitch doesn't miss anything...'*

"I don't know. It does look like someone hit it, like Rusty Wallace did a few years ago in one of the races – spinning that guy out. Maybe it happened in the wreck, or in a parking lot."

"Jon don't bullshit me. You know Dad, he would've lost his shit if that dent was on his car. He'd talk about a scuff on the tires, you think he'd have missed this?" he said, gesturing to the dent. "You know he would have seen it and you know he'd have told anyone who would listen.

"Come on, Crockett, I want to see where my parents died."

18

Summer, 1992

FIFTEEN MINUTES LATER, the bright red 1963 Chevy pickup with a mountain of a motor built from stolen drug money rumbled to a stop on the side of Salem Road. Gose and Crockett got out and began looking at what was left of the accident scene. Both young men had learned – from the elder Gose – to read the land and the sign that was left upon it – tracks and trails in the woods, and to infer what had occurred based on what was left, or *not* left, behind by something's passing - and while they looked at the scene silently, they both saw the same things. There was little difference in understanding how humans or their machines moved through a space; it was usually far easier to see than what nature gave you.

Here was the first skid mark, slewing six feet back into the road with a parallel gouge indicating where the now-broken axle had drug. Then, another skid mark, this time showing where the driver had regained some tiny bit of control with a car that was quickly becoming uncontrollable. Into the culvert, they could see the main impact point of the Bonneville, then a series of impact points for nearly eighty feet in the red clay and fescue grass that lined the road along this stretch.

Merrick and Jon, without saying a word, both walked slowly to the edge of the culvert and began climbing down into it. It was really no more than two feet deep in some places and nearly seven feet across. In most spots, running off the road wouldn't have resulted in anything dramatic happening. In reality, this was the only spot where something bad could've happened to a motorist.

Something sparkled from the blackberry bushes forty feet from the culvert and nearly eighty feet from where the wreck had begun.

It was a hubcap from a Nissan. Clean and shiny, like it had only recently been lost.

Gose nudged it with his foot and simply said, "Jon."

Crockett, five feet away, looked at it and nodded. Gose bent and picked it up. Looking at it, he asked the hubcap, "Who are you? Where'd you come from?"

They looked at the scene for perhaps ten more minutes, but no more insight came to them. Absently, Gose placed the hubcap into the bed of the truck, the big motor roared to life, and the two men drove back to the Gose home.

Five days later, two days after the funeral, the four men met at the Gose home. Family from across the area had come for the ceremony; aunts and cousins, uncles and great-uncles, all had made casseroles, pies, hams, and chickens, as well as any other manner of foodstuff, following that peculiar Southern tradition of feeding everyone in the wake of death, and now that the Gose's had been buried, they had left for their homes – but at least once a day, the phone rang with a cousin or aunt checking on the two children. Merrick was 18 now, so their main concern was Julie, but death, especially accidental death, ensured the extended family was keeping in touch.

The unintentional family, that is to say, the four young men now gathered on the back porch, had much different things on their minds.

"Montay says he doesn't know. To him, all planes look the same. I pretty sure, from his description, it's got to be a jet, but that's as good as I can get him to do." Brandon quietly reported.

Peter Claiborne was next, flipping through a ringbound notebook for his "project", "Okay, the two nights I was at Charlie Brown there were only two real jets that came in. Once was from New York, but the tower guys said they'd never seen it before. The other one, though, they said it flew in every weekend from Freeport in the Bahamas. The air traffic dudes said the plane was owned by some company in Panama or something and the guy was an American. If it's our guy, he came in with a briefcase and nothing else, the customs guys looked him over, patted him down, opened the case, and then he got into a dark four door, right at the end of Aviation Circle Road, west of the tower."

"Okay, so now what?" asked Jones.

"The guy's traveling light. Simple as that. He probably still has a place up here and catches a lift from one of his soldiers."

The other three had agreed to continue to develop the plan with or without Gose, and Crockett would be the trigger man if need be. He wasn't as good as Gose, but he was still a helluva lot better than most. Gose could deliver one inch shot groups at 250 yards, Crockett could deliver two inches.

The difference on a human being was negligible. There were no degrees of dead.

For his own research into killing Allitini, Jon Crockett had decided to go fishing. The Chattahoochee River flowed beside Charlie Brown Airport and so Crockett had simply driven there after school afternoon and began wandering around with a rod and small tackle box. In his pocket, though, he'd carried an old rangefinder. Nothing special, it had been designed in the 1960s and, by pairing the two floating images between the twin eye-pieces, you merely read the range on a dial set on the top. For the unknowing, it looked like a camera. He'd bought it as a novelty in a pawn shop in

Graniteton and was amazed at how accurate the thing was. Just because something was old didn't mean it was bad.

He began to tell what he'd found. "For one thing, the damn whole place above the river bank is briars and vines. Lotsa thick shit in those bottoms, but when you come out of that, you've got Sandy Creek Road. It's just a dirt road the county maintains. From there, you've got about four hundred yards, we'll have to cut through the fence beside the second runway, then we could set up for the shot. It's gonna be right at 300 yards, though. There's a chance we could take the shot from the other side, off of Airport Road, but there is some security on that side. Guy in a truck swings by every fifteen minutes or so, and you know the bastard'll show up right as you squeeze one off."

Peter looked at the rest of them and said, "What if we take him out?"

Brandon looked shocked, "Whack the guard? Why? He's innocent."

"No, no, we set up something to distract him, I don't know, one of us, broken down on the side of the road a little further on."

Crockett shook his head, "No, that won't work. Too many of us there. If it all goes tits up, then we have to explain why three or even four guys from a town fifty miles away are all at the same place at the same time. No cop would believe that. If the shot goes wrong from the runway side, Merrick and I can bail back to the river and head downstream to I-285 and get out there.

"Peter, it'd be good if you can arrange another field trip to the tower again, just to page one of us when the guy's landing. It seems odd they'd think anything about a kid on a fieldtrip, even if somebody gets killed. We could ditch the rifle in the river and no one would be the wiser."

"There's something else to consider, guys," continued Crockett.

Gose, silent until now, simply said, "What?"

"We're all legally adults now. We're not talking about killing some gangster wannabee, we're talking about the premeditated murder of a businessman on a state-owned facility."

"Fuck that, he's a criminal."

"You guys know it doesn't matter to me, but that's what they'll say he is. Shutting this guy down might send a real message to the bastards who are moving shit into the town. At least, I hope so. If we really *can* get this guy and get away, we have to think about how we get away from what we've done."

Crockett looked at the other three, boys who were men now, the brothers he'd never had due to his mother's inability to have any more kids. He'd been a surprise, too.

Now, he realized, the longer they stayed together, the better the chances were they could be found out or killed. "What I'm sayin' is this: when this is all over and done, we gotta plan to get the hell out of Graniteton and Atlanta. Maybe never come back. After this summer, we gotta cut ties."

Gose laughed. "Shit, you think I want to stay here? I gotta get Julie's mind unfucked and then, once she's out of school and in college, I'm enlisting. You know that. Semper Fi, bitches." He smiled and flashed the "peace" sign with his hand.

Brandon smiled, "I got enough shitty memories of Graniteton to last a lifetime. No way I'll stay here, and the way Dad talks about his commute into Atlanta every day, there's got to be better places to live than here. Furman is offering me some kind of scholarship, and if that doesn't work out, Dad and I talked about me joining the Army, maybe learn a trade."

Peter, more introspectively, looked at Crockett, then the other two, "All I want to do is get to college, get my degree, and then, yeah, you're right. Getting out of here is high on my list. Too much city for me, any-how, and dad only has a few years before he retires, so I know he'll be gone, too."

The three looked at Crockett. Merrick smiled. "You got the short straw. What are you gonna do?"

"I been thinking, maybe I'll get my degree in something easy, like political science, you know, just to have a degree, then go work in something like real estate, the way my old man does."

"Yeah, but your old man invests money for the *real* gangsters, not these punks like Allitini."

"No, most of Dad's guys are old money now. Their fathers were the crooks. Now, he really only works for families that are legit.

"But I think maybe I *do* need to stay. At least to see what happens."

The next Friday was Memorial Day, and Brandon, working with his would-be informant Jamontay at the golf course, had paged Jon Crockett to tell him 'Montay planned to be at the airport at nine. Allitini was coming.

19

Summer, 1992

MERRICK AND JON HAD PACKED up Gose's Toyota four-wheel drive truck with several fishing rods, a battered old tackle box, and, of course, the Model 70, twenty rounds of the handloaded ammunition, and a few small tools to make maneuvering into the airport runway section easier. They both packed pistols, battered looking old Colt 1911s on the outside, while the insides were like new – Wilson Combat barrels, Ed Brown ambidextrous safeties, hand lapped National Match barrel bushings and hand fitted hoods, all topped by combat sights: again, loaded with their own handloads and the big 255 grain soft lead bullets they had learned to cast from the wrong mold, but that left little, if any trace of rifling on the slug due to the deformation from the hit, no matter where it hit someone.

When their friends had been figuring out how to get high or drunk, Gose and Crockett had been learning how to gunsmith.

The question mark was the weather. Rain was scheduled to move into the area that evening, beginning at or around 7 p.m.

By five p.m., Gose and Crockett were on the treeline, some six hundred yards from the tower and nearly seven hundred from the pickup zone Peter had identified on an Aero Atlas. Each of them wore full camouflage and had added small amounts of the vegetation that surrounded them. The good news was clouds have moved in and, even though they would be moving in the gloaming half-light of the late evening, they wouldn't have to deal with the harsh angles of the sunlight throwing shadows less than an hour before.

In essence, they needed to move two hundred fifty yards to the fence, cut through it, and then nearly another two hundred to a small depression where they would be invisible to planes and, they hoped, the lackadaisical security that Crockett had noted patrolled this perimeter of the airport.

They couldn't control the sound of the shot, but they could hope that with only one, no one could vector in on where the sound originated from.

At 8:58, Jon Crockett's pager went off, with a simple numbered code they had worked out years ago. The message was simple, "Incoming." Perhaps five miles to the east, landing lights had clicked on, and Crockett leaned closer to Gose and simply said, "That's him."

Three hundred yards from where they sat camouflaged, a sedan had pulled up, and Crockett turned a pair of Steiner binoculars to face it. He watched as a black man he recognized got out and the spit dried up in Jon Crockett's mouth.

Jamontay Morgan was driving a new Nissan Maxima. It was missing the front passenger side hubcap.

"Fuck me…"

Gose, watching the plane intently, didn't move, but whispered, "What's up?"

"Morgan is here."

"Yeah, no shit? A black man that's on time? Better call the Atlanta Journal to report it. Come on, man, focus."

"Merrick, the car he's in is a Nissan that's missing the front right hubcap."

The effect was both sudden and dramatic. Gose pivoted the rifle perhaps ten degrees from where he'd estimated the shot would need to be taken and looked for himself. In the harsh lights of the terminal, he could barely make out the tiny bit of body damage and see the black steel wheel that, only weeks before, would had been covered by the hubcap that might very well be residing in Jon Crockett's truck bed toolbox.

Gose took two deep breaths and suddenly stopped and Crockett knew him too well and for too long to not know what he was doing. Gose's finger had taken out nearly a pound of weight from the rifle's two-pound trigger. In a harsh whisper, Jon spat out, "Merrick! No! Take the shot we came to take. We can end it all in ten more minutes! Kill Allitini, throw the bolt, and kill Morgan. I don't give a shit. *But don't fuck it up right now.*"

In the tower, Peter Claiborne was watching the Lear 28 come in when one of the men in the tower suddenly turned to him and said, "Hey kid, your old man is with Delta, isn't he?"

"Yes sir. He works in the offices downtown, not at Hartsfield, but yes sir, he does."

"Well, walk with me and check this out, you can add this to your report."

"Um, Mr…" Peter squinted at the man's nametag, "Randolph, I don't think I'm allowed to go anywhere too exciting."

"Come on, kid, I want you to meet some of the guys that do the real work around here. U. S. Customs guys."

Peter suddenly felt more nervous than ever. He was about to be on the tarmac, with Customs, and he knew the shot was going to come soon. He didn't mind the blood, but it could make questions get asked. He'd figured if he was in the tower when Allitini got whacked, he'd be fine.

But in *front* of the motherfucker?

He also knew Morgan might see him and *that* would shit the bed, too.

Jack Randolph walked Peter down to the two men that were on duty at Customs that night, introduced him, and the three adults all began chatting. It was obvious they all shot the breeze regularly, and the talk went to golf, to the Braves, and by the time Peter could hear the Lear jet taxiing into Gate A, he was about to piss himself he was so nervous. Fortunately, he could see Morgan, still another 75 yards away and obviously in no hurry to get too close to the agents.

Gose and Crockett had kept their theory about Gose's parents being run off the road to themselves, so Peter merely noted humorously the drug dealer had some body damage and wondered why, with all money Morgan made on the side, he had not repaired the car.

Three hundred yards away, Gose and Crockett suddenly saw Peter appear with the agents on the ground and Merrick flipped the safety on the rifle.

"We can't do it with him there, he'll be fucked. We gotta kill the son of a bitch, and I need to have a little talk with Morgan, but we can't do it now, the police'll be all over Peter and his story doesn't hold any water."

As the plane taxied down the runway, Crockett and Gose were already nearly to the fenceline and on their way out.

Peter, now in the line of fire, tried to follow the conversations the men were all having. Now, as the plane pulled up and the stairs were flipped down to allow passengers to deplane, all he wanted to do was disappear. No such luck.

Only one man had gotten off the plane, Peter could only assume it was Allitini, and now he walked over, casually, to the Customs agents, sat his briefcase down, and began emptying his pockets.

Only one of the agents even stood up. "Nice flight Mr. Allen?"

"Of course," Allitini responded, "How's your family, Joe?" Allitini looked at Peter Claiborne, "And who is this, new trainee boys? Son, you're a little young for Customs work, don't you think?"

Peter, his wits back about him, smiled, "No sir, this was a school project about Air Traffic Controllers and Mr. Randolph just sort of pulled me down here to meet these Customs agents."

Allitini laughed and said, "Well, you ought to think about coming to work in Freeport. *Those* guys are a bunch of assholes. You gotta prove who you are everytime you walk in, no matter how many times they see you. A nice white kid like you'd probably end up running the whole damn place in no time." All four men laughed and Peter smiled.

Peter, whose grandparents had money to tour the world freely, didn't miss a beat, "Freeport? I went there with my grandparents two years ago, they were visiting some friends that lived in Windsor Park. Are you near there?"

Allitini laughed, "Kid, I'm a member there at the Reef Club. Yeah, I live a few miles away, in Dundee Bay."

"I'm sorry, I've never heard of that spot." Peter looked at the jet the man had just stepped from, "I guess it's a couple levels up from Windsor."

Allitini nodded, "A few, kid," and laughed.

The Customs agents, grown complacent with the routine of Allitini's weekly visits, waved him through after a glance at his personal items.

20

TWO HOURS LATER, the Four Horsemen sat in a diner in Gwinnett County, twenty-odd miles east of the airport and nearly the same north of Graniteton. Merrick Gose was furious but kept his voice low. His anger was directed at Brandon Jones.

"Goddammit, you could've shared what Morgan was driving."

Brandon, ignorant of the connection that Gose and Crockett had made, was confused and puzzled. "What the fuck are you talking about?"

"I'm talking about the fact we think he killed my folks, you son of a bitch!"

Crockett leaned into the table and hushed the two men, "Dammit, you two bastards need to quiet the fuck down or I'll pistol whip the both of you!"

By now, what Gose had just conveyed had sunk in to the others. Trying to keep calm, Gose shared the story about what he and

113

Crockett had found at the accident scene. With everyone caught up, Gose asked Brandon if he remembered when Jamontay had gotten in the accident.

"Shit, I don't know, I don't keep up with body damage from coworkers. He just bought the car this spring, and I guess…" he let the sentence trail off.

The other men leaned further in.

"I guess it did happen… *fuck*. It did happen sometime that week. He was out that Saturday, called off work, but that Sunday, the Sunday after … you know … the wreck; I'd gotten there right before I was scheduled, seven o'clock, and he was just pulling in. I saw the dents and the scuffed paint and said something and he said he'd hit a guardrail drunk earlier that week.

"Man, I didn't think anything of it. Fuck…" Brandon Jones hung his head, then laid it on the table. Crockett kicked his foot, "Dammit, get your head out of your ass. Now, though, we've got to think. How the hell did he know? Who could have tipped him?"

None of them had any idea. Each man retreated into his own thoughts and replayed scenes from the previous two and a half years. Nothing jumped out at them. Amidst all the death they had doled out, there was nothing to suggest any of the men they had killed had any direct ties to Jamontay Morgan.

Fifteen minutes later, Crockett and Gose stood by the Toyota in the parking lot. Gose was drinking a Dr. Pepper from a cooler in the bed and Crockett was sticking a pinch of snuff under his lip.

"What are we going to do, Jon? You've been the brains of this operation since we started it. Peter and Brandon have always played a part, but they didn't get their hands dirty as we did. If that black son of a bitch killed my folks, you know what I'm going to do."

"Yeah, and I'll help you. But you gotta promise me one thing, 'Rick. Just one."

"What's that?"

"When you do what you do, we do it smart. We get what we need to get. I lost someone I loved, you lost your parents – hell, they were like parents to all of us and have been for years. Brandon don't have anything at home, Peter's mom's gone God knows where and his dad is married to Delta. My folks're great, but they're trying to save everything they lost when Big Tony went to jail. Your Mom and Dad, though?

"They were *all* of our parents, too. They *choose* us, they *had* you and Julie. This isn't just about revenge and you know it," Crockett looked up at the clouds in the sky, still ripe with the promise of rain, "this is about doing what's right."

"Fuck you, Jon. It's not your fight."

"Fuck me? No, fuck *you*." The young man's voice rose slightly, and with a noticeable quiver. "You think a day goes by I don't think about Leigh? You think I don't wonder what might have been? I see her in my dreams at night. I wake up thinking about her. I jump out of the fuckin' bed to call her and about halfway to the goddamn phone I remember she's dead. Sittin' in motherfuckin' Holly Grove, rotting... And you know what? I can't think about who could replace the feeling she gave me. That goofy little smile of hers. The silly shit she would say to me that just made me giggle like a sissy with a bagful of dicks. All gone to hell now..."

Crockett looked around, suddenly aware his voice had gotten louder. He blinked back tears, then he continued, "We do this right and we'll get bloody. Then we're out. We take the money, we split the accounts up, and we all fuckin' bail out. Leave Atlanta, leave it all. Start over somewhere the fuck else as college students from Bumfuck, Georgia."

Gose looked at Crockett. He smiled that crazy-assed smile of his and simply said, "You know this is liable to get bad, don't you?

"Yeah I do, brother, but this is family. Always has been."

With that, Gose started the Toyota, dropped the stick into first gear, and the big tires began rolling back to Graniteton.

The next week, the four boys graduated from River's Ford High School.

21

Summer, 1992

JAMONTAY MORGAN DIDN'T SHOW UP for work the next day, or the week after. Scanning through the police blotter, no word of the man's whereabouts could be found. Peter had gone to his grandparent's home on Bird Key in Sarasota, Florida for the rest of the month, even though they were actually on a two month tour of the Western Rockies.

Brandon Jones, angry and feeling he had somehow let down Merrick by not being more forthcoming about Morgan's car and feeling he had somehow let something slip that might have gotten Merrick's parents killed, got to the golf course well before the rest of the grounds crew one Tuesday morning and deftly broke in to what had to be the most lax set of locks any office could offer.

Rifling through the employee files, he found, then photocopied, Jamontay's application and ID they had on file for the man. Putting everything back into place, he locked the file cabinet, then the office, and went and met the other two men for breakfast.

Sliding the paperwork over the table, he simply said, "This is the bastard's address, and here's a copy of his driver's license. I hope the motherfucker lives at one of these two addresses."

As it turned out, Morgan didn't live at either home, but, acting like dumb high school kids, they had asked the old woman at the second house if she knew where their "friend" had moved to.

The old woman had laughed, "Ya'll here to buy drugs from dat little shit?"

Jon, who introduced himself as Brandon Jones, laughed, "No ma'am. If I needed that, I would've just stayed in Graniteton. I know I could get it and not have to come all the way into Dekalb to get it. I really need to see him, the week before he quit work, I loaned him fifty bucks 'cause he said he needed it. I'm just trying to get it back, but we did work together for over a year, so I really was worried about the man."

"Well, sonny, you ain' gwonna ta find him here, because the law done got him. He done got arrested one night an' went to fightin' wit' da law. Dey got him down in the Dekalb County jail and ain't nobody want to go his bail. His hearing ain't for another four o' five weeks, so I'm sorry, child, but you and your money gwon'na have to wait in line for it."

"Dang, I hate that," said Merrick, "you think he'll come back here when he gets out?"

"He gonna haf to! He ain't got nowhere's else to go! That girl he messin' around wit' ain't got no time for a sorry-assed nigga like him. I'se tell him when he gets here you been around, but don't hold yo' breathe. 'Montay ain't one to hurry an' repay no debts, but if you here when he is, and he's got the money, I know he's good for it."

With that, the woman waved at the two men and slammed the door she'd been standing in.

Jon looked at Merrick and the two men smiled. The bastard was in jail.

That afternoon, as the real Brandon Jones was walking out to his car, a newer Camaro IROC with plenty of motor in it, too, Gose and Crockett were sitting on the tailgate of Crockett's '63 Chevy with a small cooler between them. As Jones walked up to them, they tossed him a Dr. Pepper.

"Your boy is in jail and doesn't have anyone to bail him out."

Not missing a beat, Brandon began to laugh. "So, by extension, his car is in the impound lot, correct?"

"Sounds about right."

"So, what we need is to see if the hubcaps match and if the damage matches what we should expect from hitting Mr. Gose's car?"

Merrick winced at the thought, but he nodded his head as he swallowed another drink of the soda. Summer was in full bloom and the temperature hovered near ninety-five degrees. "That's what we thought, too."

"How the fuck do we do that?"

22

Summer, 1992

TWO DAYS LATER, Jon Crockett pulled up to the Dekalb County impound yard and knocked on the door of the office. A young black uniformed officer was sitting in the air conditioning and opened the door. Crockett held out a bottle of Coke and in his best country accent, stated flatly, "I've got a dumb question, sir, but I figured I'd buy you a Coke and smile, like the commercial says."

The officer, used to dumb questions but not white kids buying him a Coke, was trying to figure out what the kid wanted. "What's that, son?"

"Well, a few weeks ago, my sister was riding with a guy and the dummy got arrested. The guy, I mean. Anyhow, the police called my dad, my dad came down to the precinct, and he picked her up. The officers that took her in said she could pick up her personal property at the desk on the way out, or something. The problem, though, is she left her class ring in this guy's car and," Crockett looked around, like he was telling a secret, "I think she's too embarrassed to tell Dad and ask for his help.

"Anyhow, she didn't know what to do and I don't either, but I got off work today and figured I was almost here anyway, so I'd stop and ask. No harm in that, is there?"

"No, son, there isn't. But I can't let you into an impounded car. And I really can't let you take any property in that car."

"Yes sir. I figured that, too. To tell the truth, I'm not even sure if it's here. Is there any way I could just go look around?"

The cop laughed, "Boy, where are you from? I know it's not around here."

"We live in Graniteton."

"Figures. Look, in order to take any property out of the impound yard, whether it's personal or an entire vehicle, you have to have a mountain of paperwork or proof of ownership. It doesn't sound like you have either."

Jon Crockett, still playing the dumb kid card, decided to keep playing, "Sir, can I be frank?"

The cop's face had a confused look on it, but he nodded.

"The guy my sister's dating is ... well ... black, and daddy's not ... I don't know how to say it ... real open to that kind of thing. Francine – that's my sister – she's a big girl and she likes black guys, she always has. If there was any way you could let me just take a quick look, I ... I'd really appreciate it."

Then Crockett played his ace, "Look, I've got Montay's – that's the guy's name – Montay Morgan – I've got his danged hubcap in my truck, it fell off when he was leaving the house a few weeks ago! Daddy hadn't graded the gravel in five months, so it was rough as a cob!"

Before the cop could say anything, Crockett had run back to the truck, opened up the toolbox in the bed, and grabbed the hubcap he and Merrick had found at the accident scene. He ran back up to the officer, sweat from the heat of the day beginning to bead on his forehead.

Still playing the dumb hick from the boondocks, he proudly held it aloft. "This is Montay's hubcap! If you walk out there with me, I'll even snap it back on! Please officer, I don't want Francine to get in any more trouble with daddy, and you and I both know it's gonna be crappy when … if … he finds out. I'm sorry I tried to bribe you with the Coke, but it was all I could think of. You won't arrest me, will you?"

The officer, tired of the rube he was entertaining and the humidity that was taking the starch out of his uniform as he watched, finally shrugged his shoulders. "Look kid, you got five minutes. I don't have the keys to it, but if it's open, you can have a look around. Put the damned hubcap on, get your sister's ring, and please, get the hell out of here before you give me a stroke thinking about your family tree.

The guard walked into the office, looked on a clipboard, and walked back out to Crockett, "Morgan's Nissan is in Row 6, space K. Can you remember that?"

"Yes sir!" He snapped a salute at the perturbed cop and looked around for a few seconds. Finally, the cop pointed out the signs that labeled the impound lot and steered the crazy white boy towards where the car was parked.

Crockett thanked the man and began walking down the row with the hubcap clutched tightly in his arms, still playing dumb. When he was out of sight of the guard shack, his gait changed completely and he slipped the Slim Jim out of the small of his back and made his way to the Maxima, which he could now see in the distance.

Walking up to the car, he could see the hubcap was an exact match. As he walked around the passenger side, he could make out the slightest amount of damage to the front fender – a stark contrast to the Gose's Bonneville. He leaned in close and could see a faint smudge of paint.

It was a dead match for the red of Rick Gose's car.

Fuck.

Working quickly, Crockett snapped the hubcap back on and slipped the Slim Jim into the passenger door windowsill. Four seconds later, in one fluid motion, Crockett sat in the sauna of the Nissan, smelling the dead odor of cigarettes and weed and he quickly and effortlessly snapped open a large Ziploc bag, grabbed the contents of the glove compartment and the center console, and slipped them into the bag. He ran his fingers under the seats, checked over the sunvisors, and peered into the pockets on the side of the doors.

The car was clean, but, with minutes to spare, he popped the trunk and took a quick look.

Empty.

He closed it, locked the doors, removed a handkerchief from his other pocket and wiped down all the places he had touched, including the hubcap. He replaced the Slim Jim in the small of his back and, with some effort, got the contents of the Ziploc bags to lay flat there as well. As he walked past the office, he waved the exaggerated wave he knew the cop expected and then, he got into his truck and drove away.

Total time? Twelve minutes.

Total cost? Fifty cents for the coke.

It was the cheapest bribe he'd ever made.

23

Summer, 1992

CROCKETT'S PARENTS WERE OUT OF TOWN for two weeks, ostensibly for fun, but Jon Crockett knew enough of his father's dealings to know they were in Chicago and his dad was meeting with one of several powerfully connected men who had made hundreds of millions in organized crime and now, invested those monies into legitimate businesses.

Everything Roger Crockett did was on the level, but both he and his son wisely knew where to quit asking questions.

With the home to himself, Crockett paged Gose and Jones; when they each called him back, he asked them to meet him when they all got off work. All of them worked at golf courses or in construction, except Peter, and from his call with him the other night, he would be staying in Florida the rest of the summer until college started – his grandfather had gotten him a job at the Yacht Club in Sarasota, and even though his grandparents had decided to go to Tahoe until Labor Day, they were happy that someone was using the house.

Finally, at seven thirty that night, Jones, Gose, and Crockett sat down at the big dining room table to pore over what Crockett had gotten from the Nissan that day.

Aside from the assurance that Morgan's car had run Merrick's parents off the road, there wasn't much. In fact, much of it was simply trash. Finally, after passing scraps of paper back and forth for thirty minutes, Jones spoke up, "What the fuck is this?"

He held up the back of a check stub with faint penciled wording on the back.

There were, in good light, two addresses.

One was Merrick Gose's, the other, Peter Claiborne's.

"Someone figured it out," Gose said quietly.

"Who?"

Jon Crockett grabbed the check stub and flipped it over. "This dumb bastard, I think."

The name on the check stub was Demetrius Vines. Killed by Crockett in a parking lot outside of the Silver String strip club in Buckhead, Georgia.

"I killed him eight months ago. He was walking out with two briefcases, one with coke and one with cash. He used to deal on the northside. When I asked him about it that night, he pulled some shitty little piece and shot at me twice. Missed me and I popped him in the lid. I think the haul on that one was a little over $80,000 in cash and five or six pounds of coke. How'd we find him?"

Jones looked confused, "Montay had said something about him, hadn't he? That was before we'd figured out Allitini was the shot caller. Demetrius was a big fish and we thought we could end it there."

The three men sat in the dining room, mulling over what they knew and what they didn't. Finally, Gose spoke. "I think this spook's been playing us a long time. I think Montay either guessed what we were doing or picked up on it, and in the end, I wonder if he didn't just feed us the intel he wanted to move himself up the ladder." He looked around the table. Almost as an afterthought, he added, "Or Allitini did…"

"Does that sound right?"

Jon Crockett was trying to think. He looked hard at Brandon Jones. "You ever been shitty drunk around Montay? Even a little buzz? Could you have said something, let something slip?"

"Man, I don't …"

Gose slammed his hands down on the table, "Think goddammit! Think! This nigger doesn't appear to be trying to kill you, but he damn sure got my folks! I noticed your fuckin' address isn't on here!"

Brandon Jones looked like he was about to cry. Stammering, he stuttered out, "I swear, I swear, no way. Look, I don't know, but I can't remember ever saying anything to the guy. If I did, then shoot me now. I swear I haven't said shit."

Gose, despite his short temper, looked into his friend's eyes. He knew Brandon was telling the truth. He put out his hand, "I believe you, I really do. Shake on it and mean it."

The two men shook hands and went back to planning what to do about Jamontay Morgan.

24

Summer, 1992

THE PROBLEM WASN'T HOW to get to Morgan, all they really had to do was to hire a bondsman to bail him out and kill the bastard. The problem was that plan would leave a paper trail. June turned to July, and July began to get old and the problem had still not resolved itself.

Jones, Gose, and Crockett all went down to Peter Claiborne's grandparents' house for the July Fourth holiday and acted their age for the first time in months. Peter had gotten his boating license three years before and his grandparents let them take out the forty-two foot sportfisherman, the Honey Chile, that Grandpa Claiborne owned.

Peter had been driving it for several years, under the watchful eye of his grandfather and even the old man, a seasoned boatman, had to acknowledge Peter was as fine a boat captain at his young age than many men two or even three times older. The four men loaded the boat up with food and drink, pumped the tanks full of six hundred gallons of diesel, and ran the Wellcraft all the way to the Keys to fish that weekend. They'd hit calm water and easy winds and Peter had set the big diesels up to run at 25 knots. Less than nine hours later, they were in sight of Key West.

Coming back had been an adventure. Big winds were pushing swells up on the Gulf, rain squalls lashed the windshield, and, even though the boat worked through it all with ease, it was tough going. Jon and Merrick, comfortable steering the big boat – and silently approved by Grandpa Claiborne from summers past - had each done their fair share in the deep waters, but in the end, it was Peter that brought the big boat back in safely to Sarasota Bay.

The next day, the four men had eaten lunch on the veranda of the home, tried unsuccessfully to plot their next moves with regards to Morgan and Allitini, and finally, after breakfast, left Peter to the mansion his grandparents had built on Bird Key and gotten back into the IROC and pointed it towards Graniteton.

On August third, Jamontay Morgan was released from jail. He and Merrick Gose disappeared that night.

• • •

Brandon Jones had paged Crockett three times in two minutes, their own sort of "SOS" call, on the morning of August 4th. Crockett, working construction, had asked his boss if he could borrow the phone in the trailer that served as an office and called Brandon back four minutes later.

"What's up?"

"Gose's gone. Julie called me last night asking if he was at my house. I didn't see him yesterday, did you?"

"Yeah, he was checking on Morgan, it was his turn to call the jail." The men had rotated calling the Dekalb jail at different times twice a day to see what Morgan's status had been so as not to raise too much suspicion from whoever answered the phone or to create a pattern of calls. It was unlikely that the jail had lines tapped, but the men took no chances. Even

Peter was in on it, calling from Florida every other day, then updating Crockett or Gose via a coded page.

"You call the jail today?"

"No, it's Gose's turn, both calls today. But I don't know where the fuck he is."

Crockett, thinking quickly, told Jones he'd call him right back. He dialed the number of the jail from memory, having been doing so for the last three weeks.

Whoever answered the phone always seemed to use the exact same words, no matter who it was, "Dekalb jail."

"Hey, I'm wondering if you could see if my homeboy Montay Morgan is still there?"

"Hold please."

Two minutes later, the same soulless voice picked back up. "No sir, he's been released on bail last night."

"Was it a bondsman that got him out?"

"It doesn't say, only that a cash deposit was made in Mr. Morgan's name, $15,000. His court date is set for September 14th."

Crockett thanked the man and hung up. *Damn!*

He immediately called Brandon back. "Look, you gotta stick around work and see if he comes in for a check or something. I'll try to get out early and figure out where the hell Gose is. Right now, let's figure Gose has Morgan and hope he doesn't do something stupid before we find him."

Hanging up the phone, he dialed one more number – Merrick Gose's pager – and used their simple code to ask "Where are you?"

He hoped he'd get something back from Gose.

Crockett put the phone back down on the cradle, thanked his boss who was standing outside the trailer talking to a foreman, and went back to smoothing the concrete his team was pouring that day. He wracked his brain trying to think where Gose could be.

It wouldn't be anything that could be traced to them.

It wouldn't be anywhere public.

Crockett winced at the next thought:

It wouldn't be somewhere anyone could hear the man scream.

Three hours later, his pager went off. It was Gose.

The coded message simply said, "Pole Bridge Creek," one of he and Gose's favorite spots to fish. Feigning a stomachache, he asked the foreman if he could leave early. The heat was oppressive, after all, and they had been knocking off early several times a week when the temperature hit the century mark.

The man, whom Crockett knew only as "Buddy," grinned under his hard hat, patted Crockett on the back, and said, "I got you, kid. See you in the morning."

Crockett steered the souped up truck onto the interstate and again, wracked his brain trying to figure out where Gose had gone. He'd undoubtedly left the Nissan in impound, but Gose's cryptic message bothered him.

Jon Crockett knew in his soul Gose had taken Morgan. The men had grown up together and regarded one another as brothers. The other boys were family, too, but Merrick was the brother Jon Crockett never had.

Where would he have taken Morgan? Pole Bridge Creek was a trickle of a stream, and the boys had fished miles and miles of it, before it inevitably turned west and ran into the Southern River.

As he neared the county line, it hit him. There were the remnants of an old gravel operation not far from the golf course where Jones and Morgan worked. Most of the buildings had fallen down, but at least two were still standing. Plenty of times, the men had gone there to fish, but in all those times, they had never seen another person.

It was possible to get a four-wheel drive there, but cars - and even some trucks – might have trouble. "*Fuck it, I don't have a choice. I can always call Triple-A.*" Crockett pushed the transmission shifter down into third and headed for the off ramp.

25

THIRTEEN MINUTES LATER, Crockett carefully picked his way down the road. He'd had the old truck lowered slightly to give it better on-road handling, but now, as the rocks grew larger and the ruts deeper, he gritted his teeth and merely hoped to get through. He knew if Gose was there, he'd hear the engine long before he saw the truck, but he wasn't looking to surprise him, he was hoping to stop him. He grimaced as the frame hit another rock and hoped the traction would hold.

Finally, he came out of the big rocks by the old river bottom and the road smoothed considerably.

Ahead, he could see Gose's Toyota pulled to the side of the building with the hood up. Surprisingly, he also saw Gose, standing outside. As Crockett got closer, he could see the man looked badly shaken, like he had seen something he didn't want – or need – to see.

Crockett pulled the truck up and parked besides Merrick's Toyota. Merrick gave him a knowing glance and a tired smile. "I wondered when you'd pop by."

"Well, 'Rick, we were a little worried about you. Everything okay?"

"Oh, it's alright." He let out a long sigh, "Been a busy day. How about you?"

"I managed to get off work a little early and I figured, from your message, you might be down here. I'm guessing you've got Morgan in there?"

"Yeah I do, Jon. And it ain't pretty. I'm not proud of what I done ... can we ... just leave it at that?"

"Fuck, what *did* you do, Merrick?"

Merrick Gose's face was an absolute portrait of mental anguish. The man, barely old enough to be called one legally, but one who had seen violence, inflicted it, and been touched by it, broke down. Tears streamed down his face, his breath came in heavy gasps, and all he could do was to lean against the big tires of the truck and sob.

"Jon ... I ... I ..." his body shuddered, and Crockett could see how much anguish Merrick was going through. Finally, Crockett could see Gose pull himself together mentally, focus, and he looked at Jon Crockett with bloodshot eyes and simply said, "I snatched Morgan. Brought him here. He admitted to killing my parents. He's admitted to doing a lot.

"Everything was going pretty well and then, he started talking about Mom and Dad, how he'd sat there on the side of the road, listening to them die. He said forty minutes, but I know there's too much traffic for that.

"But the motherfucker said it. Then laughed."

Crockett could see Gose was fighting to stay above the point of breakdown. He knew his friend was embarrassed by showing emotion – all of them were – but Merrick more so than any. All of them had cried on each other's shoulder over the years, but to openly display emotion as a man was still hard, even if it was with family.

"I'm sorry, Jon..."

Crockett turned to go into the decrepit building beside him and as he opened the door, an anguished groan came from the corner. As his eyes adjusted, he could see the carnage. It was Morgan, or what was *left* of Morgan.

In a weak voice, the man looked through swollen eyes at Crockett. "Jes kill me, man. I told that other boy all I know. I took everything from him and he done me the same way. Just end it here, now, white boy."

The breathing was labored, and now, with his eyes focused to the dark surroundings, Jon Crockett could see what his friend had done. Here was the battery from the truck. Jumper cables. The logging chain that had resided in a Gose truck for generations, with the big log hook on one end. Over there was a set of pruning shears and a propane torch.

He leaned in close to Jamontay Morgan and the smell was as bad as the man's appearance. Fear. Fear was pouring off of Morgan, but so was exhaustion. Here was a man who had lost everything and no longer had any reason to live – except to die.

"Morgan, I'll end it right here, but tell me who put the hit on his parents?" Crockett whispered, nodding his head to indicate Gose outside.

"Allitini. He been running you boys for almos' a year. Ya'll fucked up when you killed D'metrius. Allitini been anglin' on ya'll ever since…" Morgan began coughing and gagging and his breathing got raspier.

Crockett leaned in closer, "Where's Allitini live? Tell me that and it all goes black for you, right now."

Morgan looked at Crockett and simply said, "Anywhere he wants to. He got some big house in Dundee or sumpin' in the Bahamas. That's all…" Morgan's face screwed up as another bolt of pain shot through his body from his wrecked feet and missing fingers. His head lolled to the side.

He had passed out.

Jon Crockett walked outside, passing Gose, still leaned against the big tire of his truck with a distant look. He opened the door to his own truck, pulled the seat forward and popped open the lockbox bolted behind the seat. Out came the 1911. He knew the gun was loaded with the big 255 grain slugs in front of 7.5 grains of Universal powder and he knew what it was going to do.

He walked back inside the shed. Jamontay Morgan was just coming out of the fugue the pain had put him in.

Crockett held the big gun in front of Morgan. "Is that all, Montay? 'Dundee' is the best you can do?"

"Dat's it, white boy. I be seeing ya'll in hell."

"It'll be a while, you bastard."

Crockett put the gun to the man's head and pulled the trigger.

26

SOMETIMES, DRUNK OR DREAMING, ideas come to you. Other times, an offhand comment in the right place actually helps you connect dots you'd never thought about.

For Presley Franklin, the "ah-ha" moment happened in the grocery store checkout line.

He'd been fourth in line behind some ancient woman trying to write a check with glacial speed, then a young black man buying a twelve pack of beer, then a young woman with three kids all scurrying around. The youngest, perhaps two, sat in the shopping cart and was laughing and smiling at her brother and sister, who looked like they could only be separated by two years in age.

In fact, the entire family looked like the woman likely never quit having sex and must've been the most fertile woman Franklin ever met.

As he marveled at the reproductive capacity of poor white trash, he watched the youngest child carefully reach out and slap both siblings on the top of the head. The sister had freaked out at the blow and the brother stayed quiet.

It was a marvel of coordination for a kid that age and, as the middle child – the little girl – cried to her mother that "Sadie hit me!" and the mother remonstrated Sadie for the blows, Franklin smiled and thought, "She doesn't know the other one got hit."

Somehow, that sentence seemed to hit Franklin differently.

"She doesn't know the other one got hit."

What the hell did that mean?

Finally, Franklin got through the line and was walking to his car when it hit *him*.

...The other one got hit.

Gose had been hit in the Bahamas.

Crockett had been hit in Fort Lauderdale *three years later to the day.*

But that wasn't what had happened, was it? Presley Franklin dropped the two bags of groceries he'd been carrying to his car.

They'd doctored the police report. Somehow they'd changed the dates. Both men had been shot in Dundee Bay!

Bribery? Extortion? Nepotism. Something *had* happened.

The police report said Peter Claiborne had brought him in. The treatment for two pass-through gunshot wounds would be the same as for one, so both men could use the prescription.

Couldn't they?

Franklin looked at the two bags he'd dropped. His eggs were broken and battered, his loaf of bread was squashed, and he was sure the tomatoes were pretty well gone, too. He left the bags laying in the parking lot and drove quickly home.

When he got there, he flew up to his little half-assed office on the second floor and tore open the new file he'd been building on the Four Horsemen case.

Sure enough, as he looked at the medical report and the subsequent police report on Crockett, he could just convince himself that the hand-written date – August 24th, 1995 – back when so many police and medical reports were filled out and left handwritten to be photocopied and placed in files – had once said "August 24th, 1992" and someone had added a simple "-" on top of the "2" to change it to a "5."

But when?

Presley tried to think – Hurricane Andrew would have bearing down on Florida – or in it – by then, so police resources would've been stretched. The men could have gotten to the mainland, fabricated the whole thing, killed some would-be attacker and even paid off the liquor store owner.

Right?

He looked up the signature of the officer who had filled out the report, a "Brad Simmons" and typed it into the Law Enforcement Officers Database, hoping to be able to track the man down.

No such luck. Simmons had been killed in the line of duty when his squad car had run off the road in a high speed chase in December 1995.

Shit. Shit. Shit.

Franklin went and got a beer from the refrigerator. Coming back up the stairs, he decided to "clean sheet" the case, just like he knew the DA would do before he would ever bring it to the Grand Jury.

Franklin knew that Crockett, Claiborne, Gose, and Jones had been the Four Horsemen. Of that much, he was sure.

Now what could he prove?

The blank sheet looked back at him.

Franklin couldn't prove a lot. Everything was circumstantial.

27

THE NEXT MORNING, he got up and drove down the headquarters building, but never went near his desk. Instead, he went to the third floor, past his good friends at IAD (he'd briefly considered bringing them coffee, but he just had too much shit to do to poke *that* bear) and knocked on the door of Jamie Noroughs, one of the department's psychologists.

Surprisingly, she was in her office and welcomed Franklin in, "Why, what brings you here, Detective? I heard you were on leave, but I never thought you'd darken my door." She exuded a sort of feline grace that Franklin's sixth sense could never pin down. He honestly was never sure if she was – or could be – crooked or she was so good at hiding her feelings while she dug into yours, so he'd always been guarded in her presence.

"Well, Doc, it's like this. I've got an old case and it's a doozy. It happened years before you were on the force, but I've been playing with it a little since I … you know…"

"Got suspended with pay?"

"You don't pull a lot of punches, do you?"

"Detective," she said, "let me be frank, you're used to police work and I'm a police shrink. There is a degree of doctor-patient privilege here, but let's make sure we're still 100% on the level. Does that make sense? Don't use pretty language with me and I'll not use it with you. Innuendo and nuance is why so many people are fucked up in the world today.

"Nobody wants to give a straight answer."

Franklin smiled, "Okay, then. I'll put it out there. I think I found this guy. He and some other guys – a group of friends from childhood, committed a string of violent crimes years ago, then they simply went away. For a lot of odd reasons, I've been able to find a lot of circumstantial evidence that *might* tie him to those crimes.

"But I haven't found the smoking gun. And I don't think I can. I'm asking you, as a pro, do you think he would *admit* it? Is there some part of the vigilante mindset that might make him want to admit that the men he killed years ago died because he thought he and his friends were doing the right thing?"

Jamie Noroughs thought about it and the look on her face told Franklin she really was searching for an answer. "He might. You might be able to put him in a room, with a good interrogator, and get him to open up about it. You'd have to move fast, though, because the best you'd get from the DA would be a 96 hour hold."

Franklin held up his hand, "We could do 14 days under the Patriot Act."

"So your guy is a terrorist?"

"Well, in a certain light, you could call him one."

"Detective tell me a little more about his background. Where does he come from? What does he do?"

"His name is Jon Crockett, and he's a real estate investor. Honestly, he's very under-the-radar. No social media, lives alone, divorced. No arrests."

"College educated?"

"Yes, from some private school in Tennessee."

"Siblings? Family?"

"His parents are deceased, no siblings. He played sports throughout his time in school and from what I've seen, he's fairly wealthy."

Noroughs was thinking again. She leaned back in her chair and absently clicked the pen in her hand. "How smart is he?"

"Smart? I don't know. I never looked at his transcript or anything. I know he's built a successful business and has a big house out in Pickett, but he might just be a dumb jock who got lucky – you know – here in the south, football players get away with a lot in school. There's politicians in Georgia that are only in office because they played for UGA."

The psychologist laughed at the joke, but Franklin could see she was still thinking. "There's a chance you could break him. If he committed these crimes for what he considered "good" then he might admit them. Who were the victims?"

"Almost all were, to our knowledge, drug dealers or traffickers."

"So he's living some sort of weird Clint Eastwood fantasy? 'Cleaning up the town' to keep out the riff-raff?"

"That's what it looks like, yeah. It's the only motive that makes any sense."

"Was there any publicity about the crimes when they happened?"

Franklin began laughing, "You could say that! The Governor had a task force, the GBI was losing their minds, and the APD was up to their arms in it, and nothing, I mean, *nothing*, ever came from it. These guys were killing folks left and right and they just … disappeared."

Noroughs leaned closer. "Franklin, I don't want to be involved with you directly, because you're poison. But from what you've said, I think your man might want to finally get credit for what he did. Is there anyone who can corroborate this guy's actions? An accomplice who could be turned?"

"One of them is still alive, living out, as far as I can tell, some sort of perfect upper income lifestyle. Plenty of money, beautiful family, success the way a lot of people define it. Maybe he could. The other two, though? They're dead."

"Did your guy kill them, too?"

"One hundred percent *no*. One died a Marine hero, the other died in the Army in a training accident. No reason to suspect anything different."

The shrink looked up at the clock on the wall, "Detective, I'm going to be late for a scheduled meeting, so I really have to ask you to close off our conversation. Can you get me the files on this case? Just email them to me and I'll see if I can't help you out. Can you give me a week or so, though?"

"Yes ma'am. Some of the files are digital, some are still on paper. How much do you need?"

Jamie Noroughs shrugged and sighed, "Just give me the digital stuff for now. I'll assess and get you my thoughts as soon as I can."

"Deal." Franklin stood to leave and reached out his hand. The two shook hands and he walked out of the office and quickly back to his car.

Ten days later, Jon Crockett was arrested and charged with the murder of Chad Spanning.

28

PRESLEY FRANKLIN KNEW it wasn't a solid case, but hoped, based on what Jamie Noroughs' report to him had said, it would be strong enough to get Crockett to talk about what he and the other members of the Four Horsemen had done two decades before.

The psychologist had reviewed the information as well as the personality analyses' Franklin had been able to provide her and believed all four of the men had been classic "Type A" personalities. Hard charging, take-no-prisoner types who all jockeyed for first place in whatever they choose to do. Each of them wanted to be the best in whatever they had done and Noroughs, correctly, felt there was a hint of sibling rivalry involved as well.

In her report, she had written:

"Note the relative behavior of all four men indicates the same obvious patterns – leadership coupled with intelligence. At some point, each self-selected into fields of endeavor where they could excel with no fear of beating their close friends. Even on the football field, each of these young men played different positions – one offensive line, one defensive line, one in the backfield and one as a linebacker. In their private lives, after graduating high school, it

is the exact same pattern – each man left the others to pursue "life" in different ways. Schools in different states or the military in different branches."

"A review of their lives since leaving Graniteton reveals much of the same – one was a Marine, one training to be a paratrooper, one is the premier IP attorney in the country and the last, a respected real estate investor."

"Each of these men was or is driven to succeed and, at the same time, to protect the reputation of the other men, allowing them all to "save face" by NOT allowing only one to be the "most" successful among them all."

"It is indeed a fascinating study…"

Armed with that, he had corralled an assistant DA to review his information, gotten a green light, and actually – shockingly – gotten an arrest warrant issued two days later.

That was when it had started to get weird.

The arrest warrant had been issued at 9:38 a.m. At 10:46 – Presley checked the records on it - Jon Crockett appeared at the APD headquarters building with his attorney, surrendered, and posted bail in less than two hours.

How the fuck did this guy know this?

Anyone who seemed to know – that is to say – Crockett and his attorney, one Joel Habersham – was mum on the point, but the reality was, Crockett had been arrested for Murder One and had actually never set foot into the jail.

No interrogations.

Even worse? Within minutes of Crockett leaving the APD, Franklin's phone rang. It was Captain Jonathan Scott, Franklin's boss.

"You dumb fuck. I told you NOT to go poking shit with sharp sticks. Do you want to know who just called me? The fuckin' Atlanta Journal-Constitution. Guess what they were asking me about? Internal corruption in the ranks of *my* department. Specifically, they were asking about *you.*

"You wanna know what I think? I think you've pissed off the wrong people. I don't know *how* you did that, and I don't really even care *why* you did that, but I told you "leave this alone" and what did you do? You kept picking at this fucking scab. *Oh fuck me...*"

There was an audible crash on the other end of the line and then it went dead.

Two minutes later, Scott called Franklin back, yelling into the phone, "NOW I just got notified that the fuckin' Journal-Constitution just filed a Freedom of Information Act review for your entire IAD file from 1999-present. This wasn't a fuckin' cub reporter, either, it's from the fuckin' editors – *plural* - you dumb bastard!" The phone slammed down.

Franklin had been expecting the hard work would be starting soon, but in actuality – convincing the Grand Jury to indict – wasn't his problem. He'd surrendered his evidence, all of it circumstantial, to the Assistant DA and he, a young man named Shane Tillerson, had been trying to run it through the proper channels. Tillerson had reached out to the FBI to corroborate the blood evidence reports, he'd gotten the gunshot wound from Ft. Lauderdale and sent that on to the FBI labs to study the handwriting and try to determine if it had been doctored, and there was little else for Franklin to do but keep his head down. To his credit, Tillerson tried to get the blood evidence from the Bahamas introduced, but his boss had nixed that idea post haste.

There was even an added bit of good news in all this – Tillerson and the DA, citing the obvious RICO influences of the case, had gotten Jon Crockett's assets frozen. Even if he didn't go to jail, he'd pay hell trying to get the Feds to give him his money back.

Franklin smiled at that. Poetic justice, in the least, would be served. In the meantime, he decided to begin by calling the local newspapers, except the Journal-Constitution, trying to turn the court of public opinion against Crockett, and while he tried to drum up support for the case, only two reporters actually took the time to find out more on the case.

More importantly, Franklin found it odd the only mention of the arrest was on the police blotter in the next morning's paper, and it failed to even list the crime. Who was protecting this guy?

It seemed like a straightforward case they had, too. Chad Spanning, the man Crockett had killed, had been a small-time dealer who had been found dead in his wrecked car on the side of the state highway 212, near the Dekalb county border in September of 1991. He'd been shot in the head with a high-powered rifle and all his personal effects had been taken out of the vehicle and the car had obviously been wiped down.

In the initial report, taken on the scene, the investigator had used the term "sharpshooter" to describe what might have occurred, but the case had lain dormant since then.

The decision to use Spanning had come down to the fact the murder had occurred close enough to Graniteton to likely implicate the Four Horsemen and Franklin's hope to get Crockett to simply step up and admit what he and his cohorts had done.

Finally, on the third day after the arrest, Franklin began to see some tidbits in the news. An exposé in the weekend edition had mentioned Crockett's arrest with few details, while the rest of the article took a decidedly negative stand on how the case had been handled by law enforcement while the case was still active in 1991.

The wheels had begun to fall off when the writer began to pick at the common thread then and now, one Detective Presley Franklin, on a nearly permanent administrative leave from the APD as a result of multiple ongoing investigations by the Internal Affairs Department.

The next article was on the survivors of the gang wars in Atlanta in the late 1980s and early nineties, again, with no mention of Jon Crockett and his arrest stemming from those same events or of the Four Horsemen.

What the fuck was going on?

Here was an incredible story and no one wanted to cover it.

On a whim, Franklin had asked – and been granted – permission to send an officer to interview the reclusive Peter Claiborne at his home in Nashville. He had no desire to do so himself, but the DA's office had dutifully gotten permission from the Tennessee Bureau of Investigation to meet one of their agents and interview Claiborne at his home in Nashville. That had yielded some surprising revelations. Fortunately, Claiborne – and then his wife – had happily agreed to allow the interview to be taped and Franklin had poured over the audio multiple times.

It hadn't gone the way he'd hoped…

29

THE YOUNG COP, Charlie Ott, had happily accepted the orders he'd gotten to go to Nashville to interview some rich white couple about some other dude that was being prosecuted for some ancient unsolved case. He'd dutifully checked out the sensible beige Chevy Malibu from the fleet and drove the six hours to Nashville where he'd met his "mirror" on the Tennessee Bureau of Investigation, a man named Todd Braun.

Braun had explained he'd already made an appointment to meet the Claiborne's at their home on the outskirts of West Nashville at nine the next morning. After a half hour of idle chat, the two men shook hands and Ott drove to the hotel that the APD had booked for him for the night.

The next morning, Ott's phone buzzed while he sat drinking a cup of coffee and eating a stale Danish ion the hotel lobby. Braun was in the parking lot.

In Braun's bland grey government issue Malibu, the two men talked about the case.

"Basically, this guy Claiborne was friends with – or maybe worked with – a guy we just busted on Murder One for a cold case. We can't find a thing to link Claiborne to the crime, but the DA wants us to interview him."

Braun laughed, "Charlie, do you know anything about Peter Claiborne?"

"Other than what's in the file? Nothing."

Braun smiled. "Well, let me try to fill you in. He's about the best attorney in the free world, but not one of those ambulance chaser types. He defends companies and their intellectual property."

Ott let out a "Oh-kay" that immediately showed he didn't understand. Braun jumped in, "Basically, he defends your *ideas*. Let's say you invented a copier, right? The patents on that keep – or at least attempt to keep – some company in China from knocking off your system. Claiborne does that, but with ideas – maybe you gotta catchphrase, like "Coke is it" or 'You deserve a break today.'

"Claiborne keeps others from using that – or, like, some idea you wrote in a book. Get it?"

Ott shook his head, "Isn't that copyright stuff?"

"Yeah, sort of, look, I ain't no expert, but it's not like the police are gonna bust you for it. Gotta get a lawyer like this guy."

After another fifteen or so minutes of idle conversation, Braun pulled the Chevrolet onto a long driveway flanked on both sides by white fences and a dozen or more horses. Off to the west, a massive barn stood and atop the small hill they were driving up, a spacious modern home stood amid an ancient grove of oaks.

The overall effect was stunning.

Braun and Ott parked and got out of the car, looking around and an attractive woman, obviously in her forties but still beautiful, opened the door and walked out on the porch.

"You gentlemen are the police?"

"Well, sort of, yes ma'am. I'm Todd Braun from the TBI and this is Detective Charlie Ott, from the Atlanta Police Department. We're happy to meet you and we're only here to ask a few questions, nothing more."

The woman smiled warmly, extended her hand and shook both men's hands firmly, "Well, thank heavens. I'm Tricia Claiborne, Peter's wife, and I wasn't too worried. Please, come in."

The house they walked into was impeccably designed and decorated and, despite the look of a farmhouse on the outside, the interior exuded a very modern style. Tricia gestured to the two men to sit on the couch and asked if they would like coffee. Somewhere in the back of the house, obviously an office, they could hear a man's voice, not quite clearly, talking on the phone.

"Peter's got a bit of an emergency with a client, but he'll be off in a minute. In the meantime, I'll grab you gentlemen your coffee and be right back. Maybe I can help clear things up, too." She flashed a smile that bordered on flirtatious and moved easily into the kitchen, out of sight.

Ott looked over at Braun and smiled. He leaned over a bit and whispered, "So this is how the other half lives?" Looking around the room, there were literally dozens of pictures, mostly of family – kids, parents and grandparents, but Ott noted there were also at least three pictures of the couple taken with famous entrepreneurs and politicians.

Here was Claiborne with Jeff Bezos, of Amazon, another with *both* President Bush's, and then, the entire family with Shigeru Miyamoto, the man who had largely built Nintendo.

The picture looked like the Claiborne's were in Miyamoto's office in Japan.

Who was this guy?

A few minutes later, Tricia walked in with a tray holding a warmer of coffee, several cups, sugar, and cream. Smiling broadly, she said, "Dive in, boys," and then, unceremoniously, sat down opposite the two men.

"So, what brings you men all the way out here today? Peter said this was something about a guy he went to school with was arrested?"

The two men looked at each other – this wasn't the way most spouses acted.

"Oh, fellas, cut the crap. You know I've been to this movie before. Peter has had more people come here to ask questions of his clients than you can ever imagine. FBI, TBI, Justice, Homeland Security, even Mossad and MI-6. You think this is the first time I've had to serve coffee?"

Ott, unsure of how to react, managed to gather himself. Tricia Claiborne was obviously a lot more than a pretty face. He decided to go all in and just share his information, confident she would be telling her husband anything he'd missed as soon as he and Braun were back in the car. At the same time, he removed a small notebook from the jacket of his sportcoat and began to take notes.

"Well, Mrs. Claiborne, years ago, when your husband was still in high school, he was friends with a man named Jon Crockett. We recently arrested Mr. Crockett on murder charges. Our meeting here today is really not about your husband, but about his relationship with Mr. Crockett.

"We're hoping he can help shed some light on Mr. Crockett and his dealings."

Tricia Claiborne had a faraway look on her face, like she was deep in thought. "Crockett? I think I remember him. If he was Peter's friend from school, I'm sure he was invited to the wedding, but..." she let the sentence trail off.

"Well, I know Jon Crockett," came a deep voice from the kitchen. Peter Claiborne, well dressed but casual in an open collar shirt and wearing slacks and Oxfords, walked in and introduced himself.

"Good morning, gentlemen, and welcome to my home. How can I help you today?"

Claiborne shook hands with the men like he meant it.

"Well, Mr. Claiborne..."

"Peter, please."

"Yes sir. Peter, an old acquaintance of yours from River's Ford High School was recently arrested on Murder One charges. Evidence indicates Mr. Crockett shot and killed a man named Chad Spanning."

Peter shook his head in disgust. "Jon Crockett. There's a name I haven't heard in a long, long time. Yes, Jon and I were pretty close in high school. Played ball together, went on some vacations, and then, a few years later, we'd gone down to Miami while we were in school and he got shot in a liquor store robbery."

Ott nodded his head. "Yes sir. I know that was a tough time for you, I've read the police report. My condolences about that day."

Tricia looked up from her coffee, "Peter? What happened?"

Claiborne looked at his wife, "Tricia, I had to kill a man in self defense that day after he'd shot Jon."

Her reaction was severe and instant.

"You killed a man! Oh my God! You never said that. Jesus! Honey, I'm so sorry – I know that's not who you are."

She leaned over an gave her husband a long hug and he responded by taking her hand. For all her bravado only minutes before, she suddenly seemed to shrink before the two officers.

Claiborne quietly "shhhh'd" his wife as he hugged her, and the pure emotion of the moment was difficult to watch. Finally, after a few minutes, Peter looked up.

"Gentlemen, obviously, I'd like to not talk about that day. That was one of the last times Jon and I were together socially. When he was released from the hospital that next day, we packed up our stuff and simply drove home.

"End of vacation. I did invite him to our wedding, of course, but I can't remember if I even had the chance to speak to him that day. By then most all of us from River's Ford had gone our own ways, gone to college, gotten married, hell, some folks had already had kids and gotten divorced.

"Our childhood friends often got left behind."

For the next thirty minutes, Peter Claiborne described a long ago friendship with a young man tortured by the loss of his first love and already naturally a loner. Crockett was an only child of parents who were also only children, so the extended family was negligible.

In the end, Peter Claiborne offered very little in the way of new material or insight into the enigma that was Jon Crockett.

Tricia spoke up after a moment, "He sounds like he was a good man. Peter. How come you two didn't stay close?"

"No reason, really. He was building his business in Atlanta and I was still in the firm at the time. We just lost touch. I've missed calls from him over the years – my birthday, Christmas, and so on. Jon was always the one who remembered those things. I guess it's the same story for a lot of friends from high school, wouldn't you gentlemen say? "

Ott and Braun both nodded their heads in agreement.

Claiborne looked down at his phone. "Gentlemen, would you excuse me? That's a call I have to take. Maybe ten minutes?"

"Go right ahead, Peter. Thank you."

When he stepped out the room, Tricia leaned forward. "Do either of you guys actually know Jon Crockett?"

Braun and Ott shook their heads. "No ma'am."

"I remember Peter mentioning one time that a lot of kids in his class had been killed in weird accidents and drug stuff. Do you think was related? I mean, this was all so long ago. How do you even try to prosecute something like this?"

"Well, the good news, Mrs. Claiborne, is that we don't have to. We're just here to try to see if your husband knew or remembered anything about Crockett. Obviously, being with him when he was shot in 1995 implies to us they were pretty close friends, but that was still twenty years ago. In all honesty, our visit here was less about evidence and more about context.

"…And the simple fact that your husband may be the only close friend Jon Crockett had in high school that is still alive. Two other men, Merrick Gose and Brandon Jones, died in the service of their country, so even as tenuous as this investigation and questioning today was, it was still valuable to us."

Tricia nodded, "I don't think there was a lot you learned today, I'm sorry."

Just then, Peter walked back into the room. "Sorry men, that was a challenge I needed to take care of. What else can I help you with?"

Ott extended his hand and smiled at the couple, "Mr. Claiborne, we appreciate your time and your wife's hospitality" and Tricia smiled broadly.

Braun shook hands and the two men turned to leave.

"Detectives, high school was hard for a lot of us. Jon was – and I hope still is – a good man. Whatever happened to him since then, I can't speak to, but I don't know the man you say he killed. Could Jon have done it? Personally, I don't think so. Yeah, he hunted and liked to shoot, but killing a deer or shooting a target is a lot different than a human being. I guess I'll follow your case as it develops. Safe travels, gentlemen."

With that, Peter led them to the door.

As the two men drove off, Tricia turned to her husband, "Did he really do it?"

"Jon did a lot of things back then, but he didn't kill Chad Spanning." Peter Claiborne abruptly turned and walked back inside, leaving his wife on the front porch of their home.

She stood there a few more minutes, watching the horses in the lower field. She knew a lot about her husband's past but had wisely never asked too many questions. Her surprise with regards to her husband's killing of the attacker in a south Florida liquor store was merely another act in the decades-long drama she had long ago agreed to play a part of when she married Peter Claiborne. She'd known about it for years, but for this meeting, Peter had explained it might be a lie they needed to tell. Of course, she and her husband also knew Jon Crockett far better than they had let on to Braun and Ott, too.

30

FINALLY, TWO WEEKS LATER, Presley Franklin got what he thought was lucky. Joel Habersham, Crockett's attorney, had called Tillerson and asked if the two men, along with Crockett, could meet at Habersham's office in Vinings.

Then Habersham threw a curveball to Tillerson – could Presley Franklin also attend the meeting?

Two days later, Franklin and Tillerson arrived in Tillerson's government-issue Chevy Malibu sedan, painted the same boring color of grey that all such vehicles seemed to be. Franklin had taken some convincing to come, but finally, Tillerson had gotten his consent.

"Presley, we're just meeting. It's not unheard-of, in high profile cases, to have this kind of give-and-take."

"Shane, I get that, but I don't get why I need to be there. I mean, I've been investigating the Four Horsemen, and I was on the Task Force years ago, but are they playing some angle? Are they going to try to say, since I was under investigation from IAD that I'm tainting the evidence or some shit?"

Tillerson shook his head, "I doubt it. A lot of times, I think it's just window dressing – the guy under investigation may not even *want* a cop there, but his attorney might … it gives some sort of official decorum to the whole thing. Just relax. I'll pick you up at nine, we gotta be there at ten, and Habersham already said he's got another appointment at 11:30, so we'll be outta there by 11:20 at the latest.

At 9:43, Tillerson and Franklin were pulling into the office park where Habersham's practice was located. Franklin was peering intently around the perimeter and asked Tillerson to make a complete circuit through the parking lot.

"Why?"

"Just humor me. I want to be sure we're not walking into something stupid."

Tillerson sighed and drove through the entire parking lot, which, although a weekday, was surprisingly empty. As he pulled back around to the front, by Habersham's office, he looked over, "Are you happy, Detective?"

"As a matter of fact, I am Shane, and check that damned tone with me. I'm alive and I intend to stay that way."

"No offense, Detective, but I'm not sure killing a cop is what Mr. Habersham or his client are planning today. Come on, let's go."

Joel Habersham was everything you expected a southern attorney to be except tall. In heels, the man might have been five feet, eight inches and 155 pounds, but his presence seemed to fill the room. He had made a name for himself as a District Attorney, trying and convicting the first white man ever executed for the murder of a black man in, of all places, Graniteton, and then, tiring of that game in the 1980s, he'd gone into private practice for two decades before finally entering a pseudo-retirement and representing only a very few private clients.

Today, most of his business was real estate and that was where many other lawyers underestimated him. They'd forgotten how good he really was.

This morning, though, as Tillerson and Franklin walked into his suite, a young lady greeted them and asked if they'd like coffee. Franklin shook his head but Tillerson, to the exasperation of Franklin, took a cup with cream and sugar. Four minutes later, she showed them into Joel Habersham's conference room, where Habersham, dressed in an impeccably tailored grey suit, greeted them warmly with his faint southern accent. Despite his diminutive size, he did indeed evoke a room-filling presence.

Jon Crockett, dressed in a sport coat, jeans, and an open collared shirt, stood up and shook the two men's hands as well, and held Franklin's stare for a solid five seconds before Franklin glanced away.

Habersham made sure the men were comfortable and then began "Gentlemen, first of all, I'm legally required to tell you I'm recording this conversation. If at any time, you feel this perfectly legal operation on my part somehow infringes upon your rights, I will be glad to turn it off. If that indeed becomes the case, however, then I shall consider our conversation to be finished. Should you, Mr. Tillerson – may I call you Mr. Tillerson? "Assistant District Attorney Tillerson" is just too damned hard to say every single time – request a copy of this recording, I will provide it.

"With that being said, I need to respectfully ask that both of you gentlemen return your cell phones or any other potential recording devices to your vehicle. I will not authorize any other recording device in this office, and I will not accept the responsibility of your personal belongings being in my care or the care of my staff."

He turned to Shane Tillerson and smiled, "Good fences, Mr. Tillerson, make good neighbors. I'll give you gentlemen a moment to do that and then please come back in so we can get started."

Tillerson and Franklin looked at each other and Tillerson nodded his head. A few moments later, the two men were seated back in the conference room.

Turning to Franklin, Habersham addressed him, "Detective Franklin, if you should require a copy of the recording of this meeting, I will not provide it directly to you, but only through Mr. Tillerson. It *could* potentially constitute a breach of my attorney-client privilege, which Mr. Crockett has consented to already today, by allowing me to call this meeting and subsequently record it.

"Is that clear to you, gentlemen? Is so, please audibly say your name and verbalize your consent."

The two men both did so.

Almost immediately, Habersham's voice dropped right back down to a sort of aw-shucks tone that completely hid his motives, even with leading questions. He quickly summarized the point of the meeting that morning, "Gentlemen, I've asked you to come down here today for a sort of preview of what the DA's office is thinking by charging my client with a murder from nearly a quarter century ago and at the same time, invoking the RICO statutes and freezing my client's assets." Habersham looked at the two men and continued, "Jon Crockett is innocent of these charges and this unlawful seizure of legitimate monies his business uses for its operations is negligent and illegal."

For the next few minutes, Habersham introduced, for the recording, who was present and went through what Franklin could only assume was a blanket restatement of the current meeting. To Franklin, it felt formal, although he knew from Tillerson there really was no set protocol for this type of meeting.

"Mr. Tillerson, can you elaborate on the evidence you'll bring to trial on this matter?"

Tillerson immediately sat up, like a kid called on by a teacher, and quickly stated, "Well, sir, Detective Franklin has been able to draw several powerful inferences about the Spanning case, and it is the opinion of the DA's office that your client, Mr. Crockett, was, in fact, the man who murdered Chad Spanning."

Habersham nodded. "Mr. Tillerson, your use of the word "inferences" is interesting to me. By that, would you say the lion's share of your evidence is circumstantial?"

"Well, Mr. Habersham, in some cases, yes. But our office also feels there is strong evidence that Mr. Crockett, along with three other men – Brandon Jones, Peter Claiborne, and Merrick Gose – operated a vigilante-like group, nicknamed "The Four Horsemen" by the GBI Drug Task Force."

Habersham looked unimpressed, "I see. And when was this?"

"Beginning in the late 1980s and going through at least August of 1992."

Habersham seemed to be stumped. He looked up at the ceiling, then at Tillerson, and then back to Jon Crockett. "So my client, as a *high school student*, not only was a highly recruited by colleges as a football player, but also plotted to kill drug dealers, and *killed* them; all while working a part time job and maintaining an "A" average in classes?

"That's an interesting premise, Mr. Tillerson. I understand your office is still contemplating how, exactly, to bring these charges to the Grand Jury, but might I ask what has led you, the District Attorney, and, presumably, Detective Franklin to make this accusation?"

"Well, sir, we've found strong evidence to tie Mr. Crockett to a shoot out in the Bahamas in 1992, based on evidence from the scene of that incident and a wound your client was treated for Fort Lauderdale."

"I see." Habersham looked, for all the world like he was confused. "Just so I can get this straight in my own mind, your office is seeking to besmirch my client's reputation and put him on trial as a murderer, and at the same time, drag the reputations of three other men based on hearsay and inadmissible … evidence – and I use that term loosely – obtained outside of the United States, with no clear chain of custody, and additional "evidence" gathered from an event that took place in 199 – excuse me…" he said, turning to Crockett, "When were you shot in Florida?

"August 24ᵗʰ, 1995. Peter saved my life that day."

"1995, and from all that, you were going to charge my client with the capitol crime of First Degree Murder?"

"Young man, do you know these other three men?"

Tillerson looked confused, "Umm, no sir."

"Well, Brandon Jones graduated twelfth in his class at River's Ford and went on to serve his country – and die for it – in the United States Army. He was killed while training at Georgia's own Fort Benning, down in Columbus.

"Peter Claiborne is one of the most highly paid and successful intellectual property attorneys in the world. Google has *him* on retainer. By the way, he graduated sixth in his class, right behind Mr. Crockett.

"Finally, there's Merrick Gose, a volunteer for the United States Marine Corps, killed in action and posthumously awarded the Navy Cross. He was the dumb one of these men, he graduated twenty-first. In a class of 296.

"Mr. Tillerson, you understand my client firstly maintains his innocence on these charges, but also, just how, frankly … *silly* this sounds? I mean" he turned and looked at Jon Crockett, "my client is a successful businessman and well respected in the real estate investment world nationwide.

"And you'd call him a murderer?"

Tillerson looked sheepish, turned to Franklin, and in a noticeably lower voice, simply said, "Yes, sir."

Habersham looked at Tillerson and began to speak again, "Mr. Tillerson, is there anything to connect Mr. Crockett with Mr. Spanning? Any clear evidence that has come to light?"

"Honestly, we feel there is."

"And would your office care to share that evidence with me and my client yet? Seeing that my own team has failed to find anything about Mr. Spanning's short life to link him to Mr. Crockett. He grew up in Gwinnett

County, he had been arrested multiple times for a whole host of offenses from drug trafficking to dog fighting ... *dog fighting*, Mr. Tillerson ... and yet, somehow, Mr. Crockett shoots him in the head while Mr. Spanning is driving his car.

"Was it just his unlucky day or what?"

"Mr. Habersham, I can't tell you *why* your client killed Mr. Spanning, but the State of Georgia is prepared to prove he, in fact, did."

"I see."

Franklin could see, too. This was a play. Habersham was simply trying to bully Tillerson and get him to acquiesce on the charges – which were sketchy, to be sure – but Franklin suddenly spoke up, looking at Crockett.

It was now or never to get Crockett to talk. "What about you, Mr. Crockett? Do you have anything to say? Aren't you a little curious about how you got found?"

Jon Crockett simply sat there, staring at Franklin.

"I'll tell you how - you were a dumb kid. That's all. You got mad at something, who knows. What happened? One of your friends overdose? You got tired of your parents giving you everything on a silver spoon? Bored with what you had so you needed more? So you decided to take the law into your own hands. You and your buddies were going to clean up Graniteton, make all the crime and drugs go away, like some sort of fucked up western movie?

"You shoulda left it to the pros to handle it. The cops *were* getting these guys, you know that, and if you didn't then, you have the resources now to figure it out. Get Mr. Habersham's paralegal to look at the arrest rates and the conviction rates for drug related charges from 1987-1995. Spend some of your money to find that out. We were handling it. We didn't need punks like you trying to be Charles Bronson cleaning up the town."

Franklin, himself no stranger to acting, suddenly stopped and snapped his fingers. "Oh, that's right. You can't spend any money now, because we've frozen your accounts. Sorry, I probably shouldn't have mentioned that."

Crockett's gaze strayed from Franklin, past his face, over his shoulder to the window outside. Franklin caught it, "What? You waiting on Merrick Gose's ghost to save you? He's in Arlington, remember? Jones is dead, too, and Claiborne? We sent folks up there to talk to him and his family. He *almost* remembers you. The last time you saw him was, what? 1998? When he got married?

"Let me answer that for you. It was. You've never been to his house, never met his children, never even had a cookout.

"It sucks, doesn't it? Your best friends are dead or dead to you. Claiborne isn't talking, although we've talked to him. You know what he said? "High school was hard for a lot of us." That's it. Not, "I hope he's okay" or "Damn! What happened?

"Your boy could give a shit about you. Has he called you? Sent you an email?"

Crockett shifted in his seat and his face was slowly reddening.

"We can't get Claiborne. Or Gose. Or Jones. But we *can* get you. We have already. So tell me, just answer me one question. Why? Which one of those kids that died at River's Ford was the one that sent *you* over the edge? I bet it was a girl…" he let the sentence trail off.

31

FRANKLIN, IMMUNE TO PAIN – physical or mental - in others, reached into his jacket pocket and pulled out a small notebook, flipping quickly, he came to the names of the students who had died at River's Edge. "Let's see. If it *was* a girl, there were eight of them on that memorial – that was a nice touch, by the way – a horse with no rider. You pay for that?" Franklin shook his head, "No matter, it's lovely. Was it Annie? Or maybe Jessica?"

Crockett knew Leigh's name would be the next he called.

Crockett continued to sit, staring at Franklin. His hands clenched. Tillerson looked aghast, and Habersham had put his hand on Crockett's knee. He wasn't restraining him, he was far too small, and despite his spry appearance, Crockett was nearly sixty pounds and six inches larger than him.

Habersham stopped Franklin, "Detective, I respect your desire to get to the truth, but I hardly think this is legal and it's damned sure not polite. I wouldn't allow it in a courtroom and I'll be damned if I allow it in my own office. You'll stop this badgering or I'll conclude this meeting now and have you physically removed from here."

Franklin stared at Crockett and the man stared back. It was now or never if Crockett was going to admit it.

Crockett looked at Habersham and smiled. "Joel, may I say something?"

"Of course, Jon. Just be mindful of the company."

Franklin could *feel* it. – Crockett was about to cop to the whole thing and it was on tape … from his own damned attorney!

Crockett leaned forward and his blue eyes seemed to bore through Presley Franklin.

"Detective, I know a little about you, too. Dozens of accusations about graft and bribery, a list of censures for your conduct going back decades, and before that, you were little more than Coweta County poor white trash.

"Don't go pissing on the graves of Gose and Jones. They had more integrity in one eyelash than could be found in your whole god-damned body. You need a patsy to keep the investigators off of you, at least until you retire. Then, I'm guessing you've got enough salted away from bribes and kickbacks and other … what's that term the Feds use in RICO cases? *Ill-gotten gains?* Yeah, the old IGG, to disappear to some third world shithole and live a long healthy life because of the laws you broke."

Crockett smiled and his blue eyes glinted merrily, "I'll bet somebody finds you, though."

And with that, Joel Habersham stood up and simply said, "I guess we'll see everyone in court" and quickly separated the two men and whooshed Franklin and Tillerson out of the conference room and out to the waiting area.

Tillerson was nearly babbling as he walked out of the office and into the courtyard area. A man, obviously a groundskeeper, was struggling to start a leaf blower on a trailer laden with landscaping tools parked two spaces over from their car. As the two men got into Tillerson's Malibu, the man, deeply tanned, smiled at them and waved nonchalantly as they drove past him.

Six minutes later, Jon Crockett came out of building and walked down the sidewalk and around the corner to the Town Car. As he did, the landscaper, dark skinned from what was obviously years in the sun and walking with a pronounced limp, caught up to Crockett.

"I think you might need this, Mr. Crockett," he said with a smile, handing him two phones. Crockett knew they were the clones of Franklin's and Tillerson's. He thanked the man and walked to his car.

32

TRY AS HE MIGHT, Joel Habersham couldn't get the DA to drop the charges. The Grand Jury had met and they had voted to proceed with the case, despite the circumstantial basis of most of the evidence. He'd reached out several times to Shane Tillerson trying to cite facts, but Tillerson, perhaps scared of the case or getting pressure from Franklin and the District Attorney, would not call him back or schedule a call.

The biggest challenge, of course, was the money. Yes, he had plenty stashed where the Feds couldn't find it, plus nearly $200,000 in the safe in his home, but he didn't want to dip into that because it would cause questions to be asked. Right now, his problem was one dirty cop, but if some other smart boy buried in a computer room somewhere began to start adding things up, he might be able to figure out Crockett had other financial assets at his disposal. As it was, the accounts they had frozen were only about $132,000. Basic operating expenses anyone might expect of a real estate investor. They couldn't touch his other LLCs and it would take smarter folks than Tillerson and Franklin to understand the various trusts Crockett had created long ago for just this type of problem.

Crockett was wealthy, but like many wealthy men and women, he didn't rely on liquidity to pay his bills. The income his company generated paid the bills, but with no easy way to access those funds, it wrecked the systems he had built and kept quietly forcing him to try to generate cash legally – in ways that *could* be deemed *illegal* in real estate.

Tenants were asked to pay in cash that now had to be physically stored or used to pay bills in an economy that was quickly becoming cash free. This had to be documented on paper, lest the IRS decree he was skimming profits, no doubt inviting an audit of his other assets and the books on all his companies.

Silly as it seemed, Crockett had to pay the electric bills for three of his rentals with a money order, and so a process usually took five minutes online now took up better than three hours. For a man used to expedient systems and processes designed to free up his time, it was maddening – and extremely unprofitable.

But keeping a real estate company liquid with only the monies coming in on rents made for hard times. Crockett was staying afloat on his reputation and his long-term tenants, but it was, frankly, more than simply a pain in the ass, it was brutally hard to keep track of everything.

The real problem wasn't the murder case, it was how long it might take to get the charges dropped and get the feds to unlock the operating accounts. Barring unforeseen circumstances, the best timeframe Habersham could give him was between ninety and 180 days.

Crockett knew he could make it, but if he made one misstep, he would either be opening up a federal investigation into his business finances or possibly bankrupting his real estate company and losing nearly half a million dollars a year in profits.

In the back of his mind, of course, he also knew he had to protect *all* his interests.

Most of all, the Shady Dale Social Club.

33

FRANKLIN HAD UNKNOWINGLY put Crockett between a real rock and a real hard place.

Murder One was, in all honesty, the least of Crockett's worries.

The judge in the case, an older, no-nonsense black man named Jenkins, had allowed, based on Habersham's filings, Crockett to stay out of jail so long as he did not leave the country. He surrendered his passport and the DA's office began to slowly build their case.

Franklin, trying to put the nail in the coffin, had continued to investigate the Four Horsemen case and, while the FBI wouldn't – or couldn't – say if the medical reports and the subsequent police report had been doctored, they at least didn't say it *hadn't*.

Due to the nature of the case, it was nearly two months before Crockett was arraigned with Judge Jenkins and his courtroom with ADA Tillerson representing the prosecution, Joel Habersham, Esq. and one Jonathan Christian Crockett representing the defense, and surprisingly few people in the courtroom.

The newspapers had simply found other things to report on. This celebrity couple was having a baby, this pop star had died of a drug overdose. This war was going well and Russia was rattling their saber in some other country most people couldn't find on the map.

No one really gave a damn about a rich man who might have killed a career criminal twenty-three years before.

The DA had arrangements for Roosevelt Bidings to be flown in especially for the case to testify about the events of Dundee Bay on or about August 23rd, 1992. The APD's sole remaining Task Force member, one Presley Franklin, was to be called to testify, too. Unfortunately, that was the extent of their witness list. Franklin was looking forward to seeing Bidings when the trial actually started, but he figured he'd call him this evening to let him know how things went at the arraignment.

Unknown to Franklin, it would be over before it even began.

As the judge called the two attorneys forward, Tillerson explained the state's case. Joel Habersham, looking far younger than his seventy years, smiled at the judge and began to speak.

"Your Honor, the state has done us all an incredible disservice for the last two months. My client, who has maintained his innocence all along, has never been allowed to answer the very accusations that have been thrown at him, all the while being grievously handcuffed by having his personal and professional bank accounts seized by the Federal government, costing him thousands of dollars in lost revenues and no amount of trouble to merely operate his business. With this hamstringing, my client may be forced to shutter his company; all on this false premise of guilt foisted upon the court by the District Attorney's office. My I humbly ask Your Honor a legal question?"

Jenkins cracked the slightest smile and said, "You may, Counselor."

"With all due respect, Your Honor, in the United States, is the law of the land NOT," Habersham turned to gaze at Tillerson, "the accused is INNOCENT until PROVEN GUILTY by a court of his peers?"

In the back of the courtroom, Franklin watched, amused at the old bastard's theatrics.

Jenkins, nearly as old as Habersham and enjoying watching an artist perform, played along with the old man, "It is, Counselor"

"Well, as I have attempted to explain on numerous occasions, and at every turn been silenced, my client was nowhere near the scene of the crime that terrible day in 1991." Habersham sounded more and more like an old Baptist preacher as he began to warm up. "In point of fact, your Honor, I can provide evidence; pure," he shot a glance at Presley Franklin in the back of the courtroom, "… *unadulterated*, evidence that my client was, in fact, far removed from the scene of this heinous crime."

Presley Franklin leaned forward in his seat. What the hell was this old goat doing?

Habersham walked casually over to the table for the defense, poured a sip of water into his glass, drank it down, and proceeded to pick up a folder. Pulling a single slip of age-darkened paper from the folder, Habersham began to speak.

"Judge, I'll enter this as evidence, and Assistant District Attorney Tillerson is undoubtedly aware of this but has chosen to ignore it, relying instead on his *circumstantial* evidence, which he will undoubtedly introduce at the appropriate time."

Judge Jenkins cut him off, "Counselor, please, make your point and drop the theatrics."

"As you wish, your Honor. My point is simple, I have here, what we'll eventually call Defense Exhibit A, a newspaper clipping from September 22nd, 1991, from the Memphis Post-Herald. You'll clearly see, the date at the top and a picture of my client in the photograph on an official recruiting visit to Rhodes College.

"In Memphis, Tennessee on September 21th, 1991. The day Chad Spanning was killed."

34

TILLERSON BLANCHED and walked to the bench. Franklin stood up immediately and began walking to the front of the courtroom, where he was quickly stopped by a bailiff and made to take a seat.

Judge Jenkins looked at the newspaper clipping, one of dozens that Jon Crockett's mother had painstakingly kept as the young man, a star athlete, had been recruited and gone on visits to dozens of colleges seeking to get him to play football for them.

"Your Honor, I've taken the liberty of asking the Memphis Post-Herald to verify the dates on that clipping and send me a notarized copy from their archives. I will, if need be, enter this as "Exhibit B" if you would like me to. I feel the Atlanta Police Department owes my client an apology and the District Attorney's office owes this court one as well. I have," he paused, "*FIVE* times tried to meet with Mr. Tillerson to share this information and he has refused to return my calls."

Habersham opened the folder again, withdrawing another document. "Here are those instances, highlighted on my personal and office phone records."

Judge Jenkins looked at the three pieces of paper the old man had passed to him.

He looked at Tillerson, now standing like a recently remonstrated child.

"Counselor? Can you comment on this? Can you comment on why you have ignored the messages and calls on this document?"

"Your Honor, I ... I never got those messages."

Jenkins looked unimpressed. "Each one of these calls is at least two minutes long, indicating to me that, even if you did not answer the phone, a message was left."

He looked at Habersham, "Am I to assume you left a verbal message for the Assistant DA?"

"Yes, your Honor. I have the recordings of that as well. I would never endanger the life of one of my clients, as I'm sure no self-respecting attorney would." The old man shot a glance at Tillerson, who now looked like he was going to cry.

The judge looked at Habersham, then at Tillerson. He asked the two men to approach the bench. In a low voice, he asked Tillerson, "Son, do you realize how critical your job is? How much responsibility your office carries? To simply abandon your post – and that's what this amounts to – is damn near fraudulent. I don't know what you planned to bring into my courtroom, but sloppiness like this will never cut it when the rule of Law is the norm. Now get out of my courtroom and before you try to find a case worthy of your office's time, may I suggest you act to quickly release the holds put upon this man's financials. If this is not resolved quickly, I will be forced to find you and your office in contempt of this court. Am I clear?"

Tillerson stammered out a very quiet, "Yes sir" in little more than a whisper.

And with that, Judge Jenkins picked up his gavel, banged it loudly, and proclaimed, "Case dismissed. Mr. Crockett, on behalf of this courtroom, I apologize for what has obviously been a waste of your time and taxpayer dollars. Please keep this court apprised, via Mr. Habersham, of the District Attorney's actions in reconciling and restoring your financial accounts."

Crockett stood, smiled at the judge, and said a quiet "Thank you, your Honor."

Habersham walked over and the two men hugged. Presley Franklin, disgusted, had stormed out of the courtroom thirty seconds before. He didn't notice the well-dressed man walking out behind him was Peter Claiborne, nor did he notice when Claiborne stopped to speak to a nattily attired, deeply tanned man with a cane, sitting on a bench in the hallway.

Jon Crockett, of course, knew what had really happened the day Spanning died, and it was simple: Brandon Jones was set up for a buy on the county line and the ruse was basic – he'd be parked on the side of the road, hood up, looking like he'd had some engine trouble. Spanning would stop, offer assistance, and they would trade tool bags. Brandon was to have $24,500 in it, Spanning's was to have one kilo of pure cocaine.

Crockett had set the meet up to take place on a long stretch of the state highway that ran casually uphill nearly two miles, and when Spanning showed, Jones had said hello, made the exchange, and Gose, positioned on the other side of the county line, well into the treeline and nearly four hundred yards away, neatly shot the man in the head through his open driver side window, killing him instantly.

Jones had simply closed his hood, walked over to Spanning's car and taken the dope and the cash as well as the man's identification and pager, and then, started the car and shifted the little Mustang's transmission into neutral and let it slowly roll back down the hill. It had rolled nearly three quarters of a mile before running off the road into a creek bank and disappearing from view.

It was finally called in by a truck driver two hours later.

Crockett's pager had gone off in Memphis that afternoon, with the simple code "done." Five hundred miles away.

35

CROCKETT'S ARRAIGNMENT and subsequent release had been on Wednesday morning, and since then, Presley Franklin's life had gone steadily downhill. Swift had called him to badger him about the dismissal of Crockett, of course. The Journal-Constitution was steadily digging into Franklin's activities and those calls seemed to only come more frequently.

Crockett going free had only been the high point. Everything else was sinking around him.

Friday afternoon, he'd received a message from his union representative that IAD planned to conclude their latest investigation into Presley Franklin's potentially illicit activities as a sworn officer and their findings would be released within the next two weeks. As he was responding to that text, he got a call from – of course – his Captain, Jonathan Scott.

"Franklin, I hope you have your union dues all paid up, because your chickens are coming home to roost soon, big boy."

Trying to sound happier than he felt, Franklin smiled and spoke into the phone, "Well, Captain, I owe it all to you. Without your guidance and support, I don't know what I'd do."

The voice on the other end of the phone went from jovial to serious, "Look, Presley, for what it's worth, I don't want you to go up the river on this one. You and I both know what happens to dirty cops in the joint, and even though I don't like you professionally, personally, I don't want you to get shived from some kid trying to make a name for himself. Whatever you have, I hope there's a Plan B."

"Captain, I've said it again and again, I don't need a Plan B, I'm innocent. Justice will be served and everything will be fine. I'll talk to you later."

Franklin hung up and looked at the calendar on the kitchen wall. It was December 10th. Another five weeks and he'd have his 30 years.

Never one to simply sit on his hands, he logged on to his laptop and reviewed his personal accounts, then, changing users, he checked the other ones. There was enough money to just disappear right now. For the next two hours, Franklin pondered what to do. He hadn't exactly planned on this, but he hadn't been ignorant of it, either.

It was just, so … *worrisome.*

He decided he might as well take a vacation, so he pulled the phone out and called Roosevelt Bidings in the Bahamas.

No answer, but Franklin dutifully left a voicemail at the beep, "Roosevelt, it's Presley. I'm not sure if you'd heard, but the court decided not to indict Crockett, so the case has pretty much fallen apart. I'm thinking I might come down and see you in the next few days, maybe have a few laughs and escape this dreary Atlanta weather. Give me a call…"

He hung up and looked at the calendar again, then started to make something to eat.

Across town, the darkly tanned man from the Crockett's courtroom appearance sat in a small room in the same development where Joel Habersham's offices were located. He was wearing a Bluetooth headset and had been listening to Franklin's calls as well as through devices he had planted in the man's car and home and was furiously typing notes at nearly 100 words per minute despite the obvious challenges he should have had.

Switching between the laptop on one side of the desk and a PC on the other, he pulled up and confirmed that Roosevelt Bidings' cell phone was, in fact, pinging between three towers in Freeport.

Returning to the laptop, he sent a single SMS message out. Cryptically, it only said, "Freeport."

36

PRESLEY FRANKLIN'S CALL was returned by Bidings the next morning and the two men had commiserated. Bidings had troubles as well, an informant wearing a wire had been killed in a botched drug deal, but not before the killer had, on tape for all the world – or at least the Bahamian State Police – to hear, "And tell that crooked bastard Roos'velt Bidings he's our insurance policy."

That had created all sorts of challenges for Bidings, but he felt he was explaining them away as well as he could. At some point, he told Franklin, if he just kept doing what he'd always done, this would blow over and he'd be fine.

On the other hand, if Franklin wanted to come down, he'd be happy to see him, but his schedule was such he couldn't promise too much time to tour guide. Franklin had laughed, "I don't need a babysitter, Roosevelt, but I AM thinking about a change of scenery. Maybe you could find me an honest real estate agent to talk to?"

"You're going to move here, Presley?"

"Well, the thought had occurred to me. I'm eligible for retirement in another few weeks and since the Four Horsemen case fell apart, I figure the expatriate life might be a good one."

"Presley, that's excellent! I know some folks you can trust for housing and they'll take good care of you. I'll call you tomorrow, or no later than the day after!"

Two hours later, a process server, accompanied by a U. S. Marshall, knocked on Presley Franklin's door. Franklin, unsure what was going on, opened the door casually, "Can I help you?"

"Detective Presley Franklin?" asked the old man, obviously a retired cop.

"I am."

"I'm Deputy Silvers with the Fulton County Sheriff's Department and my companion, Special Agent DiMarco, is a member of the United States' Marshals Service. We have here," indicating an envelope, "an order for you to surrender your passport until such time as the investigation from the City of Atlanta Police Department's Office of Internal Affairs has concluded its review into allegations of illegal activities and actions in your sworn duties.

"Detective Franklin, IAD considers you a flight risk. Until the investigation is concluded, as you know, that ruling is expected in the next two weeks, you may move freely throughout the State of Georgia, but should you choose to cross state boundaries, you must inform the IAD office in writing at least 48 hours prior to taking such actions.

"Is that clear, Detective?"

"Yes sir. I guess so."

"Please retrieve your passport for us."

Franklin stepped back, closed the door, and went to his desk. He rooted around in it, found the passport, and, on a whim, made a quick photocopy of it. Returning to the door, he opened it, handed the passport to Silvers.

The man took it, opened it up, nodded to DiMarco, and then, as if on cue, DiMarco opened up the envelope he had. "Please sign here, Mr. Franklin," indicating the signature line on the bottom of the page.

"That's Detective, jackass."

DiMarco sighed, shot a glance at Silvers, and in a flat tone of voice, said, "Please sign here, *Detective.*"

Franklin read the document, signed it, and handed it back to DiMarco and the Marshall handed Franklin a copy.

"Have a nice day, Detective."

And with that, the two men turned and walked back to their car.

Franklin closed the door. *Where the fuck had this come from?* In all the investigations he'd been involved in, both personally and through the department, he'd never heard of such a thing. A flight risk?

A pragmatist at heart, Franklin had to agree, he *was* a flight risk, he'd been thinking about it for two days at least, but the reality was, he'd always figured it might come to this.

No matter, he had two other identifications he could use if it came to it. Real, government issued passports, state identifications, and plenty of money in those accounts.

He'd be fine.

He knew this all somehow went back to Crockett and the goddamned Four Horsemen case. Knew it. Like Crockett's guilt, though, he couldn't prove it, but there were other courts than the court of law.

Franklin went to his desk and pulled out a clean phone, one he'd taken off a kid in a shakedown several months before and kept in case he needed to make calls that shouldn't come from him.

He quickly dialed a number he'd long ago memorized, waited for a beep, and then hung up. In two minutes, the phone in his hand rang and the deep baritone voice of a black man simply said, "Someone called about a tile job?"

"Yeah, I got a job for you guys. Pretty good sized kitchen up in north Atlanta. The owner's name is Jon Crockett and if you'll hold on a second ..."

Franklin flipped open the file on Crockett, "...He lives at 14 Willow Oak Drive in Pickett. Nice house on the lake."

"I see. How fast do you think he needs the job done?"

"I'll bet he'd like to have it squared away before Christmas."

"Alright. It's can't be earlier than next week, but right now, eighteen-inch tile is really popular. Is that what you're thinking, sir?"

"That does look good."

"Alright, eighteen inch. I'll have a courier bring over an invoice by the first of next week. Is this the best number to reach you?"

"Yes sir. I'll look over that proposal and there shouldn't be any problems with the bid. The funds are ready when you are."

"We'll be in touch, and Merry Christmas."

The Tile Man was, Presley Franklin reflected, one of the slickest scams he'd ever run across. A killer for hire advertising in broad daylight, the signs were on light posts all over the city, they simply said, "The Tile Man" along with the phone number and if you knew what to ask for, you could either get a nice upgrade in your home or have a contract put on someone. The funny thing was, the guy really *did* do tile jobs, too, and they were damned good.

It was going to cost $18,000 to kill Jon Crockett.

37

THROUGH JOEL HABERSHAM, Crockett had requested – and received – the file the DA's office had kept on the case. In it, of course, were interesting pieces of circumstantial evidence, but, obviously, no smoking gun.

His accounts were still frozen, which was a pain in the ass, but the heat was off. He had taken out a loan from a bank, based on the transcript of the court. He'd sold the banker's daughter a house three years ago.

Habersham, not aOltogether ignorant of Jon Crockett's past (or his father's, for that matter) had advised him to see if there actually had been enough to prosecute.

"Jon, you know I loved your parents like they were my own people, and I'd never say this out of disrespect. The Crockett men have walked on the shady side of the street. Your dad did for decades and I well remember the wiretaps and the inquiries from years ago. You? You and your friends tried to do the impossible, and it destroyed parts of you and killed men who were like brothers to you. The fact this is all coming out so many years later – and the fact the DA seemed to randomly pick one murder instead of another? If I was you, I'd think long and hard about how close they got and make sure they never come this close again. You're damned lucky that a dirty cop and what might be the only airtight alibi in your life saved your ass."

So here he sat, late one night in his office, looking over the file.

Unbeknownst to all, it would seem, Crockett actually *had* been shot in 1995, while he and Peter were in Delray Beach, as part of a sort of homage to the last thing the Four Horsemen had done – the bloodbath at Dundee Bay. There had never needed to be a coverup from Crockett's gunshot wound … he'd earned it legitimately.

The real question was what the hell this cop in the Bahamas – Roosevelt Bidings – was all about.

Obviously he and Franklin were buddies and Crockett felt confident Bidings must be dirty, but, aside from being on scene in Dundee Bay eighteen hours after Crockett and the others had left the Bahamas, how did he fit in?

Another weird circumstance. Another curveball thrown, trying to open doors that had been closed for two decades. He silently hoped Bidings *was* dirty, because a real cop – the kind that ask questions and actually solve cold cases – would be taking a harder look at the house where this whole deal had, depending on your point of view, begun or ended.

Crockett stared out the window at the lake he could not see.

38

August, 1992

ABOUT THE SAME TIME that Merrick Gose was torturing 'Montay Morgan to death in a cinder block building on Pole Bridge Creek, Peter Claiborne had called his grandparent's friends in the Bahamas. He told a series of little white lies and mentioned that he had met a near-neighbor of theirs, a Mr. Allitini, who lived in Dundee and he'd like to send the man a thank-you card for the kindness he had shown him.

Patricia Attenborough, resident of Windsor Bay and member of the Reef Club, said she would be happy to figure it out, as there were only a handful of homes in Dundee *Bay*, not just "Dundee." anyhow – maybe 10 or 20 – and see if she could get Peter the man's address.

Three days later, Mrs. Attenborough called Peter back.

"Hello young man, how are you! I wanted to tell you I checked my phone directory for the Reef Club there isn't any member named Allitini. Are you sure that was the gentleman's name?"

Peter suddenly remembered Allitini had gone through Customs as Allen. Thinking quickly, Peter laughed, "I'm sorry, Miss Patricia, it was Mr. Allen. Allitini is the last name of a man in a book I was reading. Is there a gentleman in the directory named Jim or James Allen?"

Peter could her hear flipping the pages of the club directory, and then, Patricia Attenborough laughed, "Well here he is, Peter! You were right, 'Jim Allen, 15 Dundee Bay.' Did you just want his address or would you like his phone number, too?"

"Miss Patricia, if you could give me both, that'd be great. I was just going to send him a thank-you letter but having his phone number would be nice."

Mrs. Attenborough gave Peter the phone number and the address and asked him to say hello to his grandparents for her. If he ever got bored, he was more than welcome to come visit her and Roger at the condo, but she also knew school would be starting soon.

The two said their goodbyes, and as soon as Peter hung up the phone, he sent the other three men a coded page that simply said, "Got him."

39

PRESLEY FRANKLIN, now seemingly grounded by IAD, decided it was time to fly. He thought of the various places he'd traveled over the years on vacation and the pros and cons of each of them. As he sat at the kitchen table in his home, he mulled over options. The Tile Man had been paid and the young black kid that had met Franklin for lunch at a nondescript diner in Gwinnett County had assured him Crockett would be dead within ten days in what looked like a robbery gone wrong.

Now it was time to think about his options outside of the United States.

Belize had been nice, the people friendly, and living was cheap. With the money he had stashed, those assets would likely outlive him while still allowing him to live like a king. He'd liked the weather, many people spoke English, and, despite his age, the women were still attractive – and attracted – to him.

Argentina had been nice, for a lot of the same reasons. He'd gone there bird shooting five years before and knew his money wouldn't go as far, but that was like saying your boat only held forty people – you still had a big damn boat.

Mexico he'd always liked and he knew enough Spanish that he felt he could be just fine in any one of the hundreds of little villages that dotted the southern coastlines of the country. At the same time, watching the sun set in the Pacific did have a nice ring to it. He remembered a couple of tiny places like Punta Mita and Mismaloya that he could comfortably live in and the healthcare around the tourist meccas in Mexico – as an expat – was as good as he'd get in America.

And then, lastly, there was the Bahamas. With Bidings, he'd have an introduction to the illicit world of the Bahamas and that might even give him some work from time to time. The exchange rate was pretty good and American dollars were as useful as Bahamian. The internet connection would be better, too, allowing him to manage his finances as – or more – effectively.

The challenge, of course, was if he waited on IAD to rule in this latest case, they could find him guilty and *that* would be an immediate cause for him to be placed in custody. Sure, he could be bailed out, but if he decided to leave the country at that time, he'd have to deal with the possibility of bounty hunters and even the damned Marshals Service hunting him for the rest of his life.

He wasn't sure he could blend in to any other culture that well, but he also didn't want to look over his shoulder forever. Plans formed in his head and were discarded, to be replaced by still others.

He remembered a marginally famous case from Louisiana in the mid-eighties; an old sheriff, long used to playing the kind of games Franklin played, had finally been indicted on racketeering charges. Knowing the gig was up, the old man had simply eaten a bullet rather than face what he knew would be a life sentence.

Open and shut. No investigation, no outcry, not even a hard look by the police.

They were just done.

Franklin could simply disappear.

Maybe not completely, but potentially … enough? At least to give him time to get out of the country and get reestablished somewhere more congenial to retirement, even if it was under an assumed name.

But how? He'd investigated enough crimes over the decades to know what cops would look for, so how could he do it, at least with enough misdirection, to throw investigators off the scent?

He knew they'd look all over, so he had to give them some misdirection. He'd call IAD and inquire about spending Christmas with one of his sons at the boy's home in Jackson, Mississippi. This would give him a window of time before they'd notice him missing and with all the traffic at airports, he didn't think it would be easy to figure out if he'd even left the country.

The Marshals would be looking for him in the United States for months before they went overseas.

That sounded like a good plan, and since it wouldn't directly involve Atlanta cops as the primary investigators, they'd be fighting with whoever the local authorities for days or even weeks before anyone concluded anything AND the Marshals Service would be squabbling with both of the departments.

It wasn't perfect, but with his knack for detail, he knew he could pull it off. He could catch a bus out of Atlanta to Jacksonville and fly anywhere from there. He could likely jump that plane to the Bahamas, maybe bring Bidings into the loop, and use his illicit resources to help him get things moving to his final destination, too.

He decided to sleep on it and, if it still felt good in the morning, he'd put his plan in place.

40

JON CROCKETT WOKE UP at his usual 6:30 and made his way to the kitchen to start the coffee pot. By the time he'd showered, shaved, and brushed his teeth and hair, he was already on the phone with Terry, sorting out business details before many in his industry or time zone were even out of bed.

Like he did every morning, he went down the driveway to get the paper and as he removed it from the mailbox, he saw a small handwritten note was scrawled on the front page.

"Look at page 3A"

Crockett got in the house and went to the kitchen counter where he could open the paper up.

There it was, above the fold.

"Veteran Cop Under Investigation Disappears"

"Terry, can I call you back? Something's just popped up – can you give me a few minutes?"

"Of course, Mr. Crockett."

Scanning the article quickly, Crockett looked for the high points. Presley Franklin, a long-time detective with the Atlanta Police

Department, had been under an ongoing investigation from Internal Affairs and, with that ruling expected in the next week, had been granted permission by IAD to visit his son for the holiday and had failed to check in with the local authorities in Jackson, Mississippi at the required times.

Crockett smiled: Franklin was on the lam.

A Captain Jonathan Swift was quoted as saying, "Detective Franklin had an incredible career with the APD and it seems the stress of the investigation may have contributed to his decision to flee. We are currently working with state and local authorities as well as the U. S. Marshals Service to determine where the detective may have gone and if foul play may be involved."

There were other quotes, from the Jackson P.D. and even a few points referencing Franklin's legitimate career highlights. In the end, the writer conveyed, subtly, Presley Franklin was still a dirty cop whose disappearance was likely not an accident but was unlikely to end on a positive note.

Crockett smiled to himself at the situation – Franklin, chasing the Four Horsemen with such passion, only, in the end, to be forced to turn tail as his own pursuers closed in.

No matter now, Franklin was likely gone forever and the case was closed. IAD was still planning on releasing their findings in the next week, but those findings were expected to be sealed due to Franklin's suspected flight.

It was a good way to start the day.

41

JON CROCKETT COULDN'T SAY he was happy over Presley Franklin's missing status, but as the week passed with no sign of Franklin – either a body or an arrest - found, he took a dimmer and dimmer view of it. To him, a pragmatist and a doubter, it was *too* easy. He knew Franklin would have gone to ground outside the United States.

After all, Franklin understood the system and was just the son of a bitch to work it.

As the days passed and no corpse had been found, Crockett became convinced Franklin had taken his slush fund and decided to get out of the picture.

There were a million little cities he could hide in North America and if you took a broad view, a humble man with money really *could* disappear into the world at large. Especially if he had documents proving who he was.

Six days after he'd read the article in the Atlanta Journal, he called Dimitry.

The voice on the other end of the line was, as always, cool and reserved, "Yes?"

"Dimitry, I'm wondering if you could check a few things for me?"

"Of course, sir, what would those be?"

"I need to find someone that might not want to be found. A cop in Atlanta, Georgia, named Presley Franklin. He's been under an internal investigation in Atlanta and quietly disappeared. Could you do some searching and see what might be out there in the web?"

"Yes sir. You've asked me for data on him before. Would security footage be helpful? Bus stations? Train stations? Airports?"

"Actually, yes. Check Savannah's airport and Jacksonville, Florida for the last … I don't know? Ten days? Hell, check all of them in the surrounding states, too. There's a chance, since he's dirty, he had bank accounts not linked to him, but I couldn't guess what banks or even what name he might be using. I'm sure if he's got fake identities, they originated in Georgia. He's a small fish, but he could have squirreled away a lot of money in the last two decades. Maybe if you see a six- or seven-figure transaction from a private account in the Atlanta area, it could help."

"I will take care of this, sir. It will take perhaps … 48 hours? Any information I find I will share via the secure line. Should you need any additional help, I can recommend experts to assist you."

"I'll bet you can, Dimitry. I don't believe that to be the case, but I will advise you as we progress."

The two men hung up nearly simultaneously and Jon Crockett had to smile. He appreciated Dimitry's offer to assist in finding a hit man, but he wasn't quite sure if he needed to worry about that yet.

After all, Franklin had bigger things to worry about, but when Crockett caught his own reflection in the mirror of his living room, he could see his own blue eyes flashing with the fierceness of revenge. Presley Franklin was no different than the dozens of men the Four Horsemen had condemned to death so many years ago.

Jon Crockett thought of his father, dead now for years, and the rules the man had taught him to live by. They'd been in his father's Eldorado, of course; the two-tone red and white luxury monster with the stainless-steel roof and white leather interior.

"Johnny," the old man had said, "there are only two things you need to remember as a man. Number one, don't fuck with my family."

Jon Crockett, perhaps twelve years old, had nodded his head. "And number two, Daddy?"

"Don't fuck with my money. Everything else will take care of itself."

Presley Franklin had managed to do both, if only by accident.

42

THE NEXT FEW DAYS passed with bland normalcy. Atlanta was in the Christmas spirit and the malls were filled with shoppers. Crockett had flipped two properties to make some quick cash and, as usual, planned to spend the last two weeks of the year at the ranch.

Dimitry's 48-hour deadline had also come and gone, with nothing to prove or disprove Presley Franklin was alive.

With year's end in sight, Crockett boarded a plane at Hartsfield-Jackson and five hours later, he was met by his distant cousin Keith White in Salt Lake City in the old Jeep Wagoneer Crockett kept at Keith's house.

"How's the flight, Jon?"

"It's always great coming out, it's the going back that sucks, you know that. Your family good?"

"Shit, growing like weeds. Maggie wants another baby and I keep telling her 'Four is enough!' but I guess it's what I signed up for. You marry a Mormon and you better be prepared for a lot of tax write offs."

The two men laughed as they walked out of the terminal and Keith indicated the direction they were headed as they stepped out into the crisp

Utah winter. "South lot, E3. I got the Jeep all fueled up, still runs fine, but Jon, why are you driving a thirty year old vehicle that gets 12 miles per gallon? You know they invented this thing called fuel injection? Lets V8 engines get, you know, twenty miles per gallon?"

"Keith, I like the Jeep. One of these days, I'll trade it or sell it, but for the thousand miles I put on it a year, why should I get rid of it? Hell, the air conditioner still works!"

Keith smiled, "Yeah, air conditioning. Spare me. A hot day at your ranch is 80 with ten percent humidity."

In the years following the death of his parents and his divorce, Crockett had alternated spending Christmas with Keith's family or another cousin in Virginia. Despite the three-hour drive to his ranch from Keith's, he loved the west – the smells, the views, and the idea of freedom it entailed. He'd been in love with it before he ever laid eyes on it and had actually bought the ranch before he'd ever seen it in person.

Since Keith's wife was out with their kids, the two men ate a quick dinner in the city and Jon dropped Keith off at his house. Maggie had been kind enough to buy some groceries for the ranch and Keith had loaded them into the cavernous back of the Wagoneer before coming to the airport. "I reckon they'll keep in this weather," he'd laughed.

The two men shook hands and Jon confirmed he'd be there by 6 o'clock Christmas Eve to read "The Night Before Christmas" to the kids.

As the old Jeep rolled down Interstate 80 and headed east, Crockett turned the heater to "high" and rolled the windows down to enjoy the crisp air and the smell of the ever-present sage that blanketed the high desert lands of Wyoming.

It was good to be home.

It was good to *feel* like it was home.

• • •

Crockett's ranch was situated in a saddle and a valley between the towns of Afton and Hoback Junction, Wyoming. From the very beginning, he'd known it was a good sign – Afton had been the name of his maternal great-grandfather and like many athletes and competitors, Crockett was superstitious.

He'd named the ranch Afton, at least in his mind, but in a land so bereft of neighbors, no one ever had become confused by what Crockett had meant. The men and women in the area had taken kindly to Crockett and he counted several of them as close friends, even if they had no real idea what he did for a living. To them, it was about being respectful and if your views were in alignment with theirs, nobody ever gave you a second thought.

He'd hired out his neighbor's foreman as a caretaker on the ranch, mostly just to ensure the fences stayed up, the house was secure, and the wood was split. From time to time, the man's wife would buy groceries for Crockett if he was coming in on a flight for the weekend, and the couple had always offered Crockett plenty of advice on how the bottomland of his ranch's leases were doing. Down in the valley of the ranch, there was nearly four hundred acres he leased for hay and three windmills he'd had built in the saddle generated electricity he sold back to High Plains Power.

The ranch wasn't exactly profitable, but it did try to pay its own way.

Finally, the big V8 engine in the Jeep delivered Crockett to the ranch. Built originally as a bunkhouse for cowboys in 1895, he'd gutted it and rebuilt the main structure into a sleek and modern – on the inside – home with 100-mile views in two directions. Situated halfway up the side of the saddle, but on the opposite side of the windmills, Crockett could watch the sun rise from his front porch and watch it set with a walk up to the elevated patio and small outdoor kitchen he'd had built expressly for that purpose.

The house was cozy without being small and Jon Crockett knew he could effectively run his business from this office nearly as easily as if he were in Atlanta. He might not be able to flip houses as easily, but, as he'd often joked, "everyone has to live somewhere..."

Wyoming was the future ... and that future might be starting sooner than he thought.

43

ROOSEVELT BIDINGS WAS SHOCKED when the call came through from Jonathan Swift in Atlanta sharing the news of Franklin's absence.

Bidings had never met Swift, but despite what Franklin had shared about his boss, it was obvious to Bidings the man had cared about Presley and was saddened by what was either an admission of guilt on the part of Franklin's actions or a harbinger of harm having come to Franklin. So it was equally shocking when Bidings answered the phone three days later to discover Presley Franklin was on the other line.

"Roosevelt, it's Sean Jameson," said Franklin, using his alias. "I'm wondering if you and I could have a bite to eat?"

Bidings, caught completely off guard, stammered out an answer and caught himself. "Pre- ... Precisely! I'd be happy to! When did you get into town?"

"I've just gotten to the airport and thought I'd check in with you and see how you're handling things these days."

Bidings, rising to the occasion, picked up the ruse quickly. "Yes, Sean, it isn't too bad, but seeing an old friend like you right now is exactly what I need. Where are you staying in town? Do you need a ride from the airport?"

Jameson *nee* Franklin said he'd be staying at the Marriot, but if Bidings had time this evening, they could meet in the bar about seven.

Franklin got off the phone with Bidings and immediately called the Tile Man to check and see if Crockett had been killed yet. Unfortunately, the news was not good. Crockett was out of town, likely gone to his Wyoming ranch for the holidays, but the Tile Man said the job was well under control. He handled these types of jobs personally and he was positive his client would be surprised and excited as soon as the job was done.

It wasn't the answer Franklin wanted, but it was the one he was stuck with.

Three hours later, Bidings walked into the bar to meet Franklin. The two men shook hands and Bidings was obviously nervous about Franklin's presence.

"Sean," he said, using Franklin's alias, "What's happened? Is everything alright?"

Franklin smiled and nodded his head. "Absolutely! It's a shame that it seems the pressure of the job seemed to make our mutual friend take to the hills, but me? I'm doing very well. I have a nice nest egg saved up and I'm ready for retirement."

"And where will you go, Sean?"

Franklin looked uncertain, "You know, Roosevelt, I'm not sure yet. I've thought about renting a place here for the next month or so, you know, get through the holidays, and then really see what my options are.

"Do you think that makes sense, Roosevelt?"

"Absolutely! Freeport is a great place to chill and the weather this time of year is perfect. Shorts everyday, maybe a sweater in the evenings. You'd like it. Besides, there's dozens of islands you can check out, you know, take a ferry over for the day, see what you like, and…" he glanced around and nodded at the bar, slowly filling with American tourists, many of them women, "… as you can see, the scenery is very nice."

The two men smiled and the serious part of the conversation was over.

44

THE TILE MAN WASN'T SURE when Crockett would come back from his ranch out west, but he was smart enough to know that a large black man driving around rural Wyoming looking for a wealthy white man in the winter was a terrible idea.

He knew the man would come back to Atlanta and, with the practiced skill of a professional, he simply incorporated Crockett into his regular schedule. Using three different vehicles, driven by three different employees – one a young white woman – he had his team simply drive by Crockett's house several times a day to monitor it for signs of life. An older white woman came to the house every afternoon and stayed for half an hour. Checking the mail? Feeding pets? None of the lookouts knew, but it was obvious she wouldn't be important to the contract on Crockett. The Tile Man had quickly figured out Crockett lived alone, but the lack of social strings he could find on Facebook led him to believe Crockett was more reclusive than he thought.

Franklin had provided him with a decent picture and Crockett's name and address, but the Tile Man's usual methods – verify the images from what he found on social media – had failed him in this case. Nevertheless, on December 22nd, one of his lookouts verified Crockett's Town Car had pulled up into the garage and he had gone inside. The lighting wasn't great, but the man who went inside the home fit the description of Crockett – about six feet tall, light brown hair going grey, and two hundred or so pounds.

At eleven thirty that night, the last light had gone off in the house and the Tile Man went to work.

Two hours later, if Crockett's neighbors had been awake, they might have heard the two muffled gunshots and seen the muzzle flash from inside Crockett's house.

A thousand miles away, Franklin's burner phone rang and a slightly drunken Franklin heard a deep voice say, "The tile job is finished. Have a blessed holiday." Then the line went dead.

Two thousand miles away, another phone rang in western Wyoming and, when the line was answered, a single voice said, "Franklin is alive."

45

TWO DAYS AFTER CHRISTMAS, Roosevelt Bidings knocked on Presley Franklin's door at the small home he'd rented for the month and asked him if he'd like to see the scene of the actual massacre at Dundee Bay.

"Pres… Sean," he still struggled to call Franklin by the new alias, "I don't know the man who owns it, but he's a British expat. After the storm and the events of that night, as I said, the house sat empty for, I think, two or three years? In the end, the company that owned it never paid the land debts on it and it was bought for the taxes owed in … maybe 1995? 1996? I never looked it up, but it changed hands several times in the next few years and the current man who owns it has had it since he moved here in 2003 or so. As I understand it, he worked back and forth between England and here for a few years, but in the last four, he's been here almost exclusively."

Franklin, with little else to do that day, warmed quickly to the idea. With Crockett dead, his problems were pretty well mitigated, so a field trip today might be fun.

"Who's the owner now?"

"Well, officially," said Bidings with a smile, "a British company owns it, but that's not unusual here. Land ownership in the Bahamas is strange if you're a foreigner, but it can be done.

"As I understand it, he's a remittance man who left England."

Franklin looked at Bidings, "Roosevelt, I have no idea what the hell that is."

"Of course you do! What do you call them in the States? You know, a child with loads of family money that is basically just given an allowance and told to stay away? A black sheep?"

"Oh, you mean a trust fund baby?"

Bidings looked confused, but he thought the term sounded correct. "Yes. I think that's a good description of him, from what I know."

"So what's this guy's name?"

"Bradley Joyner."

The two men walked out to Bidings car and the black man put it into gear and began the three mile drive to Dundee Bay. As they turned off the main road, they met an armed guard at a stout – and closed – gate to the compound.

"Good mornin' sirs. May I ask your business here in Dundee?"

Bidings flashed his police ID and the man smiled, "It's a lovely day to be out, isn't it? To where will you be goin'? I'll just need to sign you a pass and take a photocopy of your badge."

Bidings, used to the pomp and circumstance in the affluent neighborhoods of the island, smiled and said, "15 Dundee Bay, a Mr. Joyner. Do you know if he's in?"

The guard smiled, flashing incredibly white teeth, and said, "Oh yes, Mr. Joyner is certainly at home. Do you know the way?"

Bidings flashed his own smile, "Yes sir. Have a great day."

The gate, far removed from the wreck that Roosevelt Bidings had run past that long ago day in the aftermath of the storm, swung open easily and silently and as the guard waved them through; he was picking up the phone to ring Mr. Joyner.

The two men drove down the street in silence. This was an enclave to the wealthiest of the island's residents. Here and there, they could make out what they assumed were homes through the trees and landscaping, and Franklin could see, off to his right, the suggestion of a canal while the Atlantic Ocean peeked at them from behind trees and homes on their left. The car pulled up to a massive stone wall with a simple "15" on a large wrought iron gate that swung open at their approach.

No security was evident, but Presley's trained eyes could see cameras tucked away on the wall, and here and there in the trees.

Whoever lived here liked to know what was going on.

Suddenly, they pulled through the trees and landscaping that made up the front of the property and gardens and a house, surprisingly modest, stood before them. Presley realized the size was an optical illusion.

It actually was enormous, but its true mass was so well balanced, the scale deceived you from the front. Two stories, stucco, brick, and granite, with a red tile roof. Modestly, Franklin realized it had to be four thousand square feet, and even though it was only two stories, the height of the roofline suggested high ceilings on both floors.

The men parked, got out of the vehicle, and looked around.

For Bidings, he was obviously trying to reconcile the memories of the home as he had seen it in ruin versus what he was taking in now. For Franklin, it wasn't the size of the home, it was the quality. In Atlanta, every would-be millionaire had a house at least this big, but underneath it all, you knew the stucco was fake, the frame was wooden, and the walls were probably built from the cheapest materials the contractor could buy.

Here, though the quality oozed out. Without having to look, he knew this home was steel-framed and built to last. After all, the damned thing had withstood Hurricane Andrew, the Storm That Ate Miami.

As they stood there gawking, a man, younger than they were but still in his forties and casually attired for the day, opened the huge wooden front door, walked out into the early afternoon light and, with the faintest of English accents that had obviously been bastardized by living in the Bahamas for years, said, "Hello!" and waved.

"To what do I owe this pleasure, gentlemen?"

Roosevelt and Presley both waved back and began walking up the steps that led to the front porch. "I'm Detective Roosevelt Bidings of the Bahamian State Police and this is my associate from America, retired detective Sean Jameson." The two men stuck out their hands and shook the Englishman's.

"Bradley Joyner, pleased to meet you both. What brings you out here today? How can I help?"

Bidings took the lead. "Mr. Joyner, I'm dreadfully sorry to intrude on your afternoon, but I have some questions for you and Mr. Jameson is assisting the BSP in an extremely old case. I hate to ask you this, but are you familiar with the history of your home?"

Joyner looked amused. "You mean the shootout? Why, it's nearly legend here in the neighborhood! After all these years, maybe you can actually shed some light on it. I've tried to find out more about it myself, after all, the buyer's disclosure on the deed lists things like this, but after so many years, the truth is fairly watered down. Even your own people won't tell me about it.

"Maybe you can clear things up for me, too!"

Joyner gestured towards the open door, "Please come in, and welcome to my home."

The three men walked into the house and, as Franklin expected, it was immaculate inside. Obviously, no expense had been spared, and Bradley Joyner ushered them to the sunroom overlooking the ocean.

Bidings was looking around, trying to reconcile his own memories of that long-ago day with what his eyes were taking in.

"Can I get you gentlemen something to drink? Fruit juice? Coke? Something harder? It's not often I have guests, especially from the police, so please, let me know if you need anything."

Presley thought about it for a moment and then said, "A Coke would be great, Mr. Joyner. Thank you."

"Make that two, please."

Bradley Joyner disappeared and, a moment later returned, carrying three cans of Coke. "You'll forgive me, but I've given the house staff off for the week due to the holiday and the fact that, as you can see," he looked around, "I'm here alone. So, I saw no need for them to sit here when they could make merry with their own family."

Looking to Bidings, he asked, "So what really happened here, Detective? What happened in my home all those years ago?"

For the next hour, Bidings shared his memories of the events of August 24th, 1992. The smells, the sights, the devastation. As he did, he paused here and there to ask if Joyner would allow him access to the rooms of the house to describe the scenes.

He showed where men had been executed, he described blood trails down the hall, onto the landing, and the eerie whitewashing the storm had given the first floor as the windows had been blown inward by hurricane winds and the water and storm surge had wiped away what must have been gallons of blood spilled in Bradley Joyner's living room.

Finally, the three men stood outside, on the patio of the home, as Bidings pointed out the worn chip in the brickwork of the corner where a long ago bullet might had killed a guard. He gave freely, explaining his theories of a team of killers arriving by boat in the midst of the worst storm the island had seen in decades, of the killing of the people in the home and his belief the bodies had all been taken away by those same killers as the storm began to pound the coastline.

Suddenly, Bidings stopped. He looked out to the dock, where a beautiful sportfisherman sat moored to the dock. "Excuse me, Mr. Joyner, but may I walk out on the dock?"

Joyner nodded and the three men moved out onto the dock. "Mr. Joyner, do you know if this dock sits on the same area as the original?"

Joyner shook his head, "I've no idea, but I cannot see why they'd have moved it." He pointed to the concrete and mosaic tile path that led from the dock to the back porch of the house. "That, near as I know, is where they laid it forty-odd years ago."

Roosevelt walked out to the farthest end of the dock and looked back to the house, specifically the broken brickwork from a long-ago shot to kill a guard.

It lined up perfectly. The men *had* come in by boat.

46

AS ROOSEVELT BIDINGS excitedly continued his story, Presley Franklin watched for the reactions from Joyner. He judged the man to be six feet, three inches tall, perhaps 195 pounds. His hair, receding slightly, was close cropped and his skin was the deep tan anyone living in the tropics obtains and keeps after years of exposure. He was obviously a confident man and, no matter how gruesome the story Roosevelt laid out, Joyner seemed to control his emotions. Even when Roosevelt explained the way a man had been executed in the master bedroom and the empty wall safe, Joyner took it very well.

Franklin wasn't sure if Joyner was simply that well composed or that pragmatic.

As Bidings' story finally had run its course, Franklin tried to turn the conversation back to Joyner.

"Mr. Joyner, I'll have to tell you, I've had to give a lot of people a lot of bad news over the years, and I've never seen someone take something like this so … easily. Men died here. In your home, killed by men who got away with it. Doesn't that … I don't know … make you a little squeamish?"

Bradley Joyner smiled. It wasn't a happy smile, but rather, one that expressed a degree of sadness.

"Mr. Jameson, I'm a Brit. In many ways, I guess you could say our entire country is used to the idea that others have used the places we love before us. You can't dig up a hole in London without hitting history.

"So, the idea that bad men, or at least men that someone *believed* to be bad, died here isn't foreign to me. The home I grew up in had burned down at least twice in the four hundred years it's stood, so I guess I'm used to living with ghosts, good and bad."

Franklin nodded. It made sense, in a sort of melancholy European way. "So, you're from London?"

"Oh, Hell no!" Joyner smiled. "I'd not equate myself to those hoodlums if you planned to boil me for it. I'm a Nottingham boy, born and raised, though I served with enough of the Londoners to dislike the town even more." Joyner chuckled, "Actually, I'm from a hamlet *near* Nottingham, named Strelley."

Franklin had to smile at the pride the man showed. "And you were in the military?"

"Aye! My father actually has a noble title, but in England, half the damned plumbers are technically nobility. Nevertheless, my Dad's father immigrated to England from Finland after the Winter War. He'd had enough of war and decided if England needed him to fight, he'd do it, but he'd do it when called. He actually *did* open a plumbing business and did pretty good for us.

"Granpa ended up becoming a millionaire and my father turned that money into more than you could shake a big stick at. So that's why I'm here." He held his arms out, as if the house was an answer.

"So you inherited the money your father made and just … live in luxury?"

"Not at all. I'm actually too damned thrifty. Father hated me for the decisions I made, but since I'm the eldest, he won't throw me out on me arse."

Bidings looked around the home, "So this is punishment?"

"In a way, yes. I did everything I was supposed to, got a degree from the University of Leeds, had been sent to the right schools for any young man to attend, and, a month after I graduated, I walked into the Army Careers Office in Nottingham and signed up to join. I didn't know what the hell I wanted but sitting around the spoiled brats I'd always been surrounded by my whole life had made it clear on at least one thing: being rich wasn't as much fun as poor people think it is."

Franklin and Bidings both laughed at that comment, but Joyner continued. "I guess it'd been fine if I'd gone in as an officer, but the fact I'd simply enlisted was torture to my family. Even worse? I was in Logistics, the unenviable world of bullets, beans, and Band-Aids."

The men smiled at the remark. Joyner was obviously a bottom feeder, doing only enough to piss off his family and never rise to the prominence his father and grandfather had hoped.

"Did my Phase One – what you Yanks would call Basic – at Pirbright Barracks in late 1997 and Phase Two – basically job training – at Worthy Down, in the south. I ended up at the Air Mounting Centre in South Cerney."

Since neither of the two men seemed to register the places he'd referenced, Joyner tried to explain.

"Basically, anything the British Forces have going in or coming out of the country goes through these types of centres. Think of it as security and warehousing for the armed forces – men and materiel.

"The Royal Logistical Corps is the group that does it and I did it for six years – the term of my enlistment."

Franklin was nodding his head, "I guess most of us who have never served forget how important supply is. I'm guessing it did get a little boring, though."

"Oh shit, you don' know the half of it! The good news was I knew exactly what the hell I had to do, and, by that time, I'd become somewhat of a legend for my love of mountain marathons. I did all the big ones and represented my squadron all over the country."

To Franklin, it was obvious this man was just a lazy rich kid who pissed off his family. Mountain Marathons? Guy must've been a savant, but it did explain why he was so bulky and still in shape. Joyner looked more like a rugby player – or whatever the hell they had over there - than a marathon runner.

"It was kind of the best of both worlds – I could do something tangible by serving my country and I could do something on weekends that was physically challenging, not only for the endurance aspect, but the navigation. For a boy from the country, even a rich one, it was still easy, but the competing was the real reason I did it. Plus, our executive officer at the AMC liked the fact I made life easy for him, so he cut me considerable slack for training."

The two cops were nodding their heads in unison. Joyner was grounded, even if a little strange. After a pregnant pause, Bidings asked him, "So how'd you end up here?"

The man let out a hearty chuckle, "Oh, boy, that's a story in itself. Let me give you the high spots: When I mustered out, I came here on holiday and fell in love with it. Heat, blue water, and rain that didn't last for days. I went back after a month here and told my father I was taking money from my governance and buying a small home in Freeport. He wouldn't hear of it, it would have been scandalous for the family, so he trumped up the circumstances and created a branch of the family company to buy this home.

Joyner looked around the room, then held his arms out, "I'll bet you didn't realize this is the corporate headquarters for a pipefitting company from Nottingham, did you? It took me a few years to get everything sorted out, back and forth to England and getting the house up to par, but I'm here, now. No going home."

• • •

Another hour passed as Joyner shared anecdotes about Nottingham, his time in the Royal Logistical Corps, and how he'd tried – unsuccessfully – to move into some area of the British Army that would at least let him go to foreign countries.

It had never happened, though, and, looking at the clock on the wall, Joyner suddenly caught himself and apologized to his guests.

"Dear me, we've chatted up nearly three hours. I'm dreadfully sorry, but I've an engagement tonight with a young lady at the club, so would you think me a poor host if I kicked you out?"

Neither Bidings nor Franklin had realized how long they had been there, but they both nearly jumped to their feet in their haste to not keep Joyner from his date.

As he walked the men to the door, he shook their hands and told them to call anytime they were in the area. Bidings passed his business card to Joyner and Franklin simply said, "Bradley, I appreciate your time, but I'll be leaving the country in the next few weeks. Now that I'm retired, I'm a little like you, looking for the right place to fit in."

"I understand all too well. Be safe in your travels, then, detective."

47

JOYNER STOOD ON THE PORCH until the car had disappeared around the bend in the driveway, then went back inside. As he closed the door, Bradley Joyner, whose real name was Brandon Jones, killed in a training accident in Fort Benning, Georgia and buried – at least on paper – in Wrens, Georgia, and now retired from the United States Army's PsyOps Intelligence Division, smiled.

It wasn't *all* a lie. He *had* worked in England. He and Crockett *had* bought a family-owned company in Nottingham in 2002, while Jones/ Joyner had been running logistics for the United States Army's PsyOps group operating out of South Cerney … to arm the Kurds against Saddam in the coming invasion.

He'd always had a knack for languages and accents and his nickname for the nearly fifteen years he'd spent (after his untimely death in Fort Benning) running operations in the Middle East had earned him the name Lawrence Jr. after the legendary T. E. Lawrence of Arabia.

Joyner walked over to the kitchen counter and reached into a drawer containing flatware. Reaching behind it, he removed an old Nokia flip phone and dialed a number he'd long ago memorized.

Jon Crockett answered the phone and Joyner greeted him warmly. The intelligence service had long ago purged any hint of an American accent from him, and for Jon Crockett, Bradley Joyner was simply Bradley Joyner. Brandon Jones *was* dead.

Joyner filled Crockett in with his visitors that afternoon, and in the slightly morose humor that only the British could have, Joyner explained that Sean Jameson must surely be Presley Franklin "It's simply a shame, quite frankly, Jon. People running and hiding in foreign countries is so passé. Especially when they do it poorly. At least when governments do it, they make it look good and make sure the poor bastard doesn't act the same way. You know, some linguistics here, a scar there, maybe teach you how to write with your off hand. Amateurs give this sport a bad name."

"We used to be amateurs, too, Bradley," Crockett laughed.

"I'd say not! We never did this for anything but the right reasons. Mr. Jameson, I feel, did this only for a profit-based motive. Shall I begin looking into his daily activities?"

"Yeah, I guess. And his little friend, too. Bidings. This needs to end and stay ended."

"As you wish. Perhaps you should come down to visit? Maybe a little New Years' Eve celebration? You know, I could arrange a meeting with my new friends? It's Dundee Bay, after all. The rules here have never really changed."

"Maybe so, Bradley. "Jameson" had paper out on me. Caretaker took care of that problem while I was at Afton, but I still had to put in new carpet in the living room when I got home. At least most of the mess was cleaned up."

"Ah yes. Sometimes these things do get messy. How much was the paper worth?"

"Eighteen grand."

Joyner "tsk'd" into the phone. "Amateurs! See? I told you. I'd have charged at least twenty."

"Thanks. That makes me feel better."

"Jon, remember, I delivered Saddam for twenty, also."

"Yeah, twenty *million*."

"A minor detail, merely commas and zeroes. Shall I have the staff make up your room for you? We can't continue these sorts of conversations via phone. We need to sort this out and close this last chapter."

"I guess so. See you in a few days and I'll call when I get in town."

48

NO MATTER HOW HE TRIED to play it off, Presley Franklin couldn't shake the feeling that something was odd in Freeport. The first few days, he shrugged it off to a new town and a new name, then he decided it was diet, and finally, when he confronted it, he knew it was the feeling he was being … pursued. He didn't want to risk checking in with his old sources in Atlanta, but he had the nagging feeling that the Tile Man might have fucked up. Crockett could be alive or maybe, he had flipped the script and put paper on Franklin. That would be funny, because where do you look for a man when you don't know where to look? The world was a big place.

Nevertheless, on December 30th, Franklin called Bidings to tell him he was leaving to check out some other spots and would check in with him in a month or so. Bidings, still struggling under his own poor planning when dealing with criminals and lacking Franklin's finesse or finances, wasn't surprised, but he had bigger worries. He was sad to see his friend go, but it would allow him to focus on keeping himself out of prison or an unmarked grave.

49

JON CROCKETT DIDN'T ACTUALLY LEAVE for Freeport until January 4th. The financial shitstorm he'd weathered had blown over, but he wanted to make sure anyone looking at him saw him creating money, not spending income there was no record of. He'd sold a small rental house he'd had in Cabbagetown for years and managed to do a quick flip on a duplex in Dekalb County, then booked a flight and pawned off the operations of his real estate business to his teams for the coming week.

January third had dawned cold and clear, with the promise of one of the weird weather patterns that seem to occur once or twice during winter in Atlanta. By the time Crockett had finished his coffee, the sun was gone, replaced by dark, scudding clouds and winds gusting into double digits. The temperature dropped, first into the twenties, then began to rise. By two o'clock, the rains had begun, lashing the big house in Pickett and as darkness began to fall, the sky cleared, the winds dropped, and it was warm enough for Crockett to watch the sun go down from his porch in shirtsleeves.

Jon Crockett rarely drank, at least not to excess, but that night, he sat in the big Adirondack chair on the porch with a chilled glass of Southern

Comfort. To his left sat another chair, with the table between the two. The old grey cat, Bella, sat demurely on the table beside the man. Fully a quarter of the bottle was already gone. The events of the previous months had, he realized, affected him far more than he thought possible.

Thirty years had passed, and yet, he understood all his planning, all his scheming, and all the killing had done nothing. Crime, criminals, drug use, and fucked up lives still existed.

Four Horsemen, zero. Society, one.

Was life really just about having enough sex to try to get one kid to live long enough to breed again? Amassing money enough to run away from your problems? To beg or buy some kind of joy?

He didn't know, and he reached over again for the bottle he knew didn't hold the truth, but, on days like this, seemed to offer some respite.

What the hell had they accomplished? Ruined lives? Merrick had been blown to hell in some third world shithole. Brandon was gone, replaced with a wealthy British nobleman and a stopgapped story from one of the shadiest intelligence organizations in the world. Peter, of course, had survived pretty well intact, but at what cost? Franklin had been right. What did Crockett actually have, when it was all said and done?

"The rest of us are fucked, Bella," said the man as he stroked the old cat's fur. In his mind, he saw the dead; the men they had killed and the friends they had lost. Their names – good and bad – rolled through his mind as easily as the names of streets in his neighborhood. The ones with no names stared back at him across time with the unblinking eyes that only death can endow.

"Leigh."

It all came back to her, didn't it?

("No, no, Jon, don't do this.")

To no one in particular, Jon Crockett continued, "I mean, fuck it. If I'd have had one minute's courage as a kid, then all this would never have been."

("Oh, shut up. You're drunk.")

"What if I'd have just told her what I meant?" He shook his head, the Southern Comfort had his tongue now, "Why was it so damned hard to simply tell the truth? Love is love, isn't it? I mean, is there a difference in the love we feel as teenagers versus what we are so careful to describe as adults? If I'd had half the balls of any of them, I'da told her and we coulda lived happily ever fucking after..."

("You really think that? She could have said it, too...")

"Aww, that's shit. You know it is. Girls can't say that first. No, I fucked myself and killed her, as surely as if I'd laced the shit she took that night. I've killed everything I've ever cared for, or driven it away. I've willfully destroyed every relationship I ever had. Drove my brothers from my life, shit on every woman who ever tried to love me and I tried to fix every stupid bitch I ever met as some kinda fucked up penance for all the shit from River's Ford. I couldn't say it. I couldn't even *write* it to her. Somewhere in this motherfucker," he gestured grandly at the house with open arms, "is the goddamn note I wrote her, professing my undying love for her."

Crockett's head was spinning now. "I couldn't give it to her the next day. I kept it in my jacket pocket for another five weeks. "Tomorrow I'll be brave enough." And another tomorrow. And another. And then there weren't any more tomorrows. Just dirt hitting the fuckin' top of her coffin.

"No, the devil has his hooks in me now. Funny. *We* were the Four Horsemen. Death. Conquest. Famine. War. God-damned ironic when you think about it. Spawned from Hell? Or sentenced to a life of it? We damned sure reaped what we sowed...

After a long silence, petting the now sleeping cat, Crockett began to speak again, in a harsh whisper. "You know I tried to make something work – Jen – and I managed to fuck that up, too. How can you fuck up love?

("Jon, just shut up. You're opening doors you shouldn't...")

"Is it because we're so stuck up on sex? I mean, as a teenager, you wanna screw anything you can stick it in, but when you really love someone, there's a helluva lot more to it than the squirt at the end. Is not knowing *that* where we fuck it up?

"I'll tell you where the lightning hits the goddamn merry-go-round ... you don't let the other person love *you*. You try to be a goddamn hero. Superhuman. Fuckin' Lancelittle,"

("Lancelittle? I don't think that's who you think it is.")

"Then Lancelit, goddammit! You try to be so goddamn good and what happens? They feel like they can never possibly meet your standards. Leigh was my queen and I was trying to make her see how much goddamn better I was than the bastards she was with, and in the end, she didn't think she could have me ... she'd fail to make the grade."

By now the bourbon was closing down his ability to rationalize his thoughts and as they descended into the dark chaos of his memories, he began to sob quietly and doubled over with the pain and the loss in his youth that had crippled him emotionally for many years.

A few minutes later, he seemed to recover.

"Hemingway's *The Sun Also Rises, right?* Jake Barnes is in love with Lady Brett and because of his wounds, they both know they can never consummate it. The poor bastard spends his time cleaning up after her and it isn't until the end, the *very* end, when she finally gets it. 'Oh Jake' she says, 'We could've had such a damned good time together.' And there's Jake, shot all to shit in old W-W-One and what's he got? He's got nothin'! He's in the back seat of the car with her in traffic and all he can do is hold Lady Brett and say, 'Yes, isn't it pretty to think so.'

"That's what this was. Except at least Jake got to *hold* her. I got recurring dreams of watching her die. Again and again, night after night."

("Jon, relax. We're here. We've always been here.")

In his mind, he tried to put his feelings into words. The pain had never stopped the wounds, the time passing had never healed them. He'd buried it all in his business and his schedule, but some nights, like this, when he stupidly opened the door to it, it came blowing through with all the grace of an airplane crash.

The next morning, as The Dream was playing out in his mind for the fourth, or fifth, or hundredth time that night, the alarm of the life support system signaling the crash of Leigh's vital signs in the ER coincided with Jon Crockett's alarm clock. He woke, surprised to find himself in his own bed, rather than passed out on his porch, and when he walked into the kitchen to start the coffee pot, he noted the empty bottle of bourbon in the trash and the glasses washed and placed on the mat to dry by the sink.

The cats, Bella and Cheeto, watched him from their own posts on furniture in the living room and Jon Crockett, with a surprisingly clear head, despite the amount of alcohol he'd apparently consumed, looked at them all and simply said, "It's time to hunt."

50

August 1992

IN THE EARLY NINETIES, as rock n' roll was changing from hair and heavy metal to the sounds coming from Seattle, a short-lived band named the Prodigal Sons were one-hit wonders with a song named *Unbroken*. It had all the elements that would later make bands like Alice in Chains and Soundgarden popular, but with the vocal elements more in tune with older Metallica stuff.

Crockett and Gose loved it. Lyrically, it was about at least one bad boy who wasn't about to get fucked with, but was ready to die on his little hill, defending … well … *something*.

They had worn out cassette tapes from the album, simply titled *Prodigal Sons*, and one night, while drinking beers around a bonfire, they'd drawn the conclusion that the Four Horsemen were, in the strictest sense, prodigal sons themselves.

Anyone who knew the whole story, though, would find it ironic that the young men who so loved the song would far outlive the band that spawned the discussion.

No matter. In less than three months, the lead singer and the guitarist had been killed in a car crash and whatever was left of Prodigal Sons was quietly put away. The bassist and the drummer tried to recapture their success, but without the haunting lyrics of the newly-famous and newly-dead lead vocalist, there was little they could do but return to obscurity.

Their fifteen minutes was over.

With Peter having found Allitini, he called Crockett in Graniteton and the two young men tried to figure out how to solve the challenge he presented. After Labor Day, the three of them would be leaving for school and there would little, if any, chance to catch the man.

They were about to have to be grown up and the chances of all four of them being able to be home, with actionable data and the resources to sort out Allitini, was quickly coming to a halt.

Crockett had filled in Peter on the events of Pole Bridge Creek and maintained they had a good plan – kill Allitini at the airport – but it could take weeks they didn't have to verify Allitini was adhering to his previous schedule. With Morgan gone, the man might have been forced to make changes in how he managed his time and travels in Atlanta. Peter, unable to simply drop in and visit the tower at Charlie Brown airport, had been at the Sarasota Public Library looking at the Dundee Bay development on Aero Atlases and microfilm of aerial shots from Freeport.

"Jon, if the four of us can all get here, we could take the boat out, take it right to his backdoor, kill the motherfucker and be back here in five days. No one could trace the boat and we'd all be able to get in and out in no time."

Crockett thought hard about it. Selfishly, he'd wanted all of his friends to be together one last time before the world took them away from him.

Besides, what Peter was saying *might* work. With Morgan out of the picture, Allitini might change things up, too, thinking it was the start of trouble for his organization. God knew that what Merrick had done to the man looked gang related. Allitini might be running scared and change tactics and with their only link to his travel schedule dead, they could spend a lot of time in the dirt at Charlie Brown Airport and never have a shot.

"Let me call you back, Peter. You around tonight?"

"Yeah, I'm off today."

"I'll hit you about nine."

Jon quickly paged Merrick and Brandon and the three met for dinner that night. All three of them agreed – taking Allitini at his home in Freeport would be lower risk with far higher challenges.

If they could make sure he was there.

Brandon was optimistic. "So what we'll do is simple: Hit him on a Sunday night. We know … well, we *think* we know he'll be there, right? I mean, he'd be back from Atlanta, so it just makes sense."

The others nodded in agreement. It couldn't be this weekend, due to schedules and families, but the next Wednesday, they'd drive down to Peter's, take out the Honey Chile, and go to the Bahamas.

Youth is often a lot of things, but visionary is not one of them.

On August 16th, the tropical wave that would become Hurricane Andrew began to form off the coast of Africa.

51

PETER MET THE BOYS as they got out of the Camaro Wednesday at lunchtime with a worried look. "It could get hairy. There's a storm blowing up in the eastern Atlantic, but nobody knows where it'll go. I'm not too worried, but it could slow us down the way we were coming back from the Keys. I called Grandpa and told him we were going to keep an eye on it and if it looked like it would come across Florida, we'd head the boat up or down the coast."

Gose laughed, "You mention we'd be taking it to Freeport in the meantime?"

Peter shrugged his shoulders and flashed a sheepish grin.

Crockett had briefed him on the plan and he had been stocking up on the supplies needed – fuel, food, and ice. Merrick had, mysteriously enough, asked for Peter to pick up a bag of baking potatoes from the grocery store and, when pressed for details, had merely said, "I've been playing with some ideas."

The boot of the Camaro carried a small arsenal of weapons – two Steyr AUGs, four Remington 870 pump shotguns with cut down barrels, the Model 70 Winchester Crockett and Gose had built, four 1911 Colts and nearly 1,000 rounds of assorted ammunition and magazines to feed them all.

Almost as an afterthought, Crockett carried a dry bag with $7,000 in cash and the best fake identifications they had been able to buy, along with college IDs stating they went to two schools in southern Georgia.

The four men quickly loaded their gear into the boat – Peter had wisely let the servants off today to ensure some privacy – but they'd return to work tomorrow. Claiborne planned on being in the Keys by then.

Late in the afternoon Saturday, they had refueled in north Key Largo. The weather reports had gotten worse so, from a phone booth at the docks, Brandon and Jon dutifully called home to tell both of their families that Peter's grandfather had asked him to move the Honey Chile to safer waters in case the hurricane came across Florida. It wasn't an unusual request, as the boys had done it twice in the previous years, although always with the old man at the helm.

Finally, the fuel tanks filled, Peter dug the twin 6-71 diesels into the Atlantic Ocean and pushed the boat across the Straits of Florida. The word on the weather radio and shipboard radio had gotten worse - the storm Peter had worried about had indeed gotten more powerful, but at that time Saturday, Hurricane Andrew was still considered a small hurricane - Category One and hundreds of miles from the Bahamas.

Merrick pointed out that it might be a good thing – Allitini might be caught offguard and not fly out at all. They had taken the chance and placed a ship-to-shore call from the *Honey Chile* and Allitini's servant, a man named Charles, had asked if they were on the guest list for Mr. Allitini this weekend. Brandon, ever the prankster, had said he wasn't sure, due to the storm, and Charles insisted the storm was nothing and the meetings would still be on for Sunday afternoon.

Might he pass a message to Mr. Allitini?

Brandon had merely said he and his associates would be there, weather permitting.

52

FOR THOSE WHO HAVE NEVER CROSSED the Gulf Stream in the Straits of Florida, it can be hard to imagine the looks of the water. An immense river-like tide of warm water flows from the Gulf of Mexico, picking up speed between Florida and Cuba, and begins a journey up the coast of North America that will eventually lead it to the green hills of Ireland and England.

As a result of this incredible flow, navigating from southern Florida to an island chain can be daunting to all but the most experienced captain, and in those days, with little more than a LORAN system to navigate along with printed charts, Peter choose to aim the Honey Chile south of Freeport and navigate based not only on the radio signals from the LORAN unit, but also, the depths they encountered as the boat began to come up on the Bahamas banks.

Despite the fact Freeport lay only 60 miles from the coast of North America, it could still be an incredible challenge to hit one specific spot in a veritable sea of small islands.

As the evening fell on the Saturday, August 22, the Four Horsemen set the anchor on the lee side of the ironically fitting Gun Cay.

Merrick and Jon cooked a pot of spaghetti and the four men began to go over the plans for their attack on Allitini.

Peter produced a file he'd photocopied from microfiche in the library that showed an aerial view of the entirety of Dundee Bay. Allitini's home had been circled with a red magic marker and using his grandfather's map measuring tools calibrated to the scale of the image, he had been able to produce an incredibly detailed description of the property.

"Okay," he'd said, taking out his notes, "Allitini's house is God-damned mansion. The dock, near as I can make it, is over 150 feet long, seven or so feet wide. The lot looks to be about three acres, all pretty heavily wooded, but the image I was able to find, taken from the canal that runs behind Dundee Bay, shows it to be more scrub and landscaped stuff – low lying, maybe fifteen or twenty feet tall. There's a pretty solid looking wall that forms the east and west boundaries of the property."

Merrick was looking hard at the image, which showed a large boat anchored by the dock. He pointed to it. "Is this barge going to be there?"

Peter sighed, "I don't know. The aerials were taken last year, so Allitini might have already been there. It's a damn big one, though. At least fifty-five feet. I'll bet it draws a damn bunch of water and these flats," he said, indicating the bay in front of the house, "only hold about six feet at any given time."

Brandon piped up, "How much does the Honey Chile draw?"

"About three feet and some change." He looked at the others, "If this storm starts sucking the water off that flat, which it could do if it gets strong enough, we're liable to have some trouble. We have to pay attention. Depth finder is useless in six feet of water.

"If we have to make a run for it, it could get ugly."

By now Gose and Crockett had begun checking the weapons. Crockett had a 1911 in pieces on the table and Gose was fussing over the Model 70. Both men knew the guns were in perfect condition, but the truth was, they had to do *something*. Staying busy meant staying focused.

They all realized their lives depended on this.

Brandon had pulled a Coke out of the refrigerator in the galley and set it on the table. He studied the images and Peter's notes.

"So what are we gonna do? Just knock on the door and say we're here to whack Allitini?"

Crockett looked up from where he was fiddling with the trigger spring of the 1911. "In a way, yeah. Peter, you said this is the ritzy part of town, right? Nobody really knows anyone else?"

"That's what it sure seems like."

"Then why not knock on the back door and just act lost? Act like a kid who was walking in the neighborhood and got turned around?"

The four men looked at one another, each considering what that might mean.

As an afterthought, Crockett expanded on the idea. "When they open the door, they'll be backlit from the inside of the house and Gose kills that cat from the flying bridge up top, then gives us some cover fire for the rest of us to get in the house. The shotguns'll let us get a good foothold and anyone trying to backdoor us," he looked at Gose, "will get it from the boat. With all this glass on the back of the house, he can also see what's going on upstairs, at least a little."

Gose smiled. "I like it, but I want to be inside. He killed my folks, remember?"

Crockett paused for a moment, reflected, and added, "once we get the first floor cleaned out, Gose can come in and help us sweep up. It'd be easier with an extra shooter in the house with us."

Peter raised his hand, "We gotta have somebody watching the back door and making sure we can get back to the boat."

To that, Crockett thought a moment and nodded, "Peter, it has to be you. You'll have an AUG and when Gose comes in, you'll ease out the back. We need you to be healthy to get our asses out of here once we're done."

Peter nodded. It made sense. Then, he looked at the picture of the house again, laid out on the table. "Aside from Allitini, who's gotta die tomorrow?"

No one had an answer.

The condensation from the Coke Brandon was drinking had slowly crept to the photos Peter had copied, and as the water mixed with the red ink from the notes, Brandon noticed the entire image of Allitini's house was wet with what looked like blood.

53

PETER CLAIBORNE HAD ALWAYS been an early riser. When many of his teenage friends languished in their beds until 10 or 11 in the morning on days off, Peter had always found it difficult to sleep in. Therefore, it wasn't unusual for his to wake up at five a.m., but when he did, he noticed the differences immediately.

The wind was coming hard – perhaps fifteen knots – from the East and, as he made his way up from the stateroom, he noted the Honey Chile had swung nearly 180 degrees in her anchors from the night before. Dark clouds scudded across the sky, seemingly close enough to touch. Two miles away, Gun Cay was clearly visible, but Peter knew they would face weather today.

He put a pot of coffee on and went around to wake up his friends.

Five minutes later, the four stood around the galley sink, brushing their teeth and Peter had turned on the weather radio.

The news wasn't good.

Hurricane Andrew was up to a Category 3 storm and was lining up to hit Freeport sometime before sunrise on Monday morning.

"Fuck" groaned Gose, but, with a mouthful of toothbrush, it came out more like, "*Gouck*."

The others smirked, but each realized that, as difficult as the day was going to be with sunny skies, it was now getting harder.

Crockett looked at Claiborne. "What's the play, Captain?"

"It's a couple hours to get there. We know he's got folks there this weekend. Maybe his *soldatos*, or some *capos*, but that's only a guess.

"We can run North, turn East, and get in the flats in front of the house and see what's going on from binoculars a long time before we have to kick in doors."

The other men nodded in agreement.

Their plan, as imperfect as it was, was still simple, even if the weather was closing in on them.

Two hours later, Peter was at the remote helm in the tower of the boat, looking for signs of Freeport to his immediate northeast. He'd expected it for the last five minutes and had cut the engines slightly to alleviate the choppiness they were getting from the following seas and strong winds in their faces.

With only a hint of worry, he rechecked the charts.

He knew where he *should* be, but he wasn't there. More importantly, he began to second guess where he was. Had he overrun Grand Bahama? It seemed unlikely. He rechecked his engine speeds, and the depth finder, then the LORAN numbers.

Then he realized it – he'd never factored in the winds. Not only would they have slowed the forward progress, they also would be pushing the boat *away* from Grand Bahama.

DAMN!

Quickly, he threw out the clutches on the engines, grabbed the chart he'd been using, and scurried down the ladder. Coming into the saloon of the boat, he grabbed the bigger charts his grandfather kept neatly folded in a file on the wall and spread out the Grand Bahama one on the table.

He shouted to Crockett, "Jon, what depth are we right now?"

Crockett, lounging at the lower helm, looked over at the display. "We're past the 1,000 fathom mark."

"Fuck!"

The other men quickly piled into the saloon, worried looks on their faces. "Peter, what's the problem?"

"I missed the Goddamn wind! I didn't take enough of it into account on my calculations when I plotted this course!

"Now I've got to figure out where the fuck we are."

Merrick Gose's eyebrows raised and he looked at Jon Crockett. The two said nothing, but after so many years, each could read the other's mind. "Peter…" he said, drawing it out into a question.

"Just gimme a fuckin' second!"

Gose shot a glance back a Crockett, then to the barometer mounted on the wall of the saloon.

It had dropped another half point since they had woken up.

• • •

For the next two hours, Peter, shaken, tacked steadily northeast and southeast, trying to recapture the Bahamas banks. Whether due to the storm or the sketchy power grid of the Third World, the LORAN signal, usually so crisp and clear, evaded them; here was a good signal, here a weak one. When he thought he had it locked down, it faded, adding substantially to the young man's frustration.

At the same time, he kept a worried eye on the fuel gauges. The tanks held 600 gallons, but at the rate they were burning diesel, they could be on fumes by the time they got back to the Florida coast.

…And then, he began to receive news on the weather radio that Hurricane Andrew was speeding up and strengthening.

All these things conspired against Peter Claiborne as he wrestled the Honey Chile into the gaping maw of what was quickly becoming a Category 5 hurricane.

Finally, nearing noon, Merrick Gose, sitting with Peter on the flying bridge, spotted land to their immediate south east.

Peter immediately began consulting the nautical charts he'd brought up to the flying bridge and trying to triangulate their position while Gose peered through the binoculars at the tiniest sliver of land he'd spied.

With a sigh, Peter groaned out a tired, "Shit. I think that's Saudy Cay. We're freaking miles north of Freeport and the Stream is pushing us further and further out."

He glanced at the fuel gauges again. "If we run inland, where the Gulf Stream isn't pushing as fast, we can't run fast and we run the risk of foundering. If I put this bitch back in the Gulf Stream, our fuel usage is going to go through the roof fighting the current."

Gose nodded and looked over at the depth gauge. Still nearly 200 fathoms. "How straight of a line is the bank, if we run parallel to it?"

"It won't work like that, Merrick. See, the Gulf Stream comes around Florida and hits Cuba, then the Bahamas. These outside banks act like the deep part of a cutbank on a river. All the current is here." He indicated the unseen coast of Florida, "On that side, it's fine. Here? No protection. You're either in it or you're in five feet of water."

The two men nodded. They knew their only option was to push the throttles to the stops and fight the millions of gallons of water trying to push the Honey Chile north.

By now, Crockett and Jones had come out on the deck and were expectedly looking at the men in the flying bridge.

"Well?" one of them said, to no one in particular.

"Gose found land and I found us, but we've gotten pushed a lot further North than I thought. We're going to have to push back into the deep water and fight the Gulf Stream to get around Grand Bahama and get in position."

"Well then let's get moving. You want us to bring you girls a sandwich?"

"Yeah, but you'd better hurry, this is going to get bumpy…"

It was after three p.m. when the Honey Chile laid to, south of Dundee Bay. The weather had started to close down and the radio reported small craft warnings throughout the Bahamas. The barometer in the saloon had dropped nearly to 28 inches. Hurricane Andrew had become, in the course of only a few hours, a monstrous storm, now a Category 5.

None of them had ever faced a hurricane before and, as they sat in the saloon of the boat, they discussed their options and the plan for the attack on Allitini's home.

How long before the storm would hit?

How long to navigate south of it?

Would Allitini even be there or would he have left his home for safer grounds?

Peter explained they had enough fuel for a nearly straight-line run to the Florida coast, but with the storm chasing them he wasn't sure where they even might be able to refuel. He'd already tried to raise several public docks on Grand Bahama and no one had responded. Even worse was the fact that, even on calm water, the Honey Chile, with nearly one thousand horsepower from the two big Detroit Diesels, couldn't outrun the storm, only maintain her distance.

In the sights of a killer hurricane, nobody wanted to pump any fuel, they wanted to save themselves.

The only hope of the Four Horsemen would be to get out before the storm and head south as quickly and efficiently as possible, hopefully refueling in Bimini before running the Florida Straits.

There simply wasn't a Plan B.

54

MERRICK GOSE HAD TAKEN the first watch after they anchored. Claiborne had placed the Honey Chile a little over a half mile from Dundee Bay, just inside the reefs that ringed the flats to the south of Grand Bahama. Sitting in the flying bridge, he peered intently through the twelve power binoculars Peter's grandfather kept in the bridge.

It had been no great challenge to match up Allitini's house with the images Peter had collected from the Aero Atlas and the microfiche he'd photocopied, and Gose was mildly surprised to see Allitini's boat still moored to the dock.

The house appeared abandoned and he was silently beginning to worry they'd risked all this for nothing.

Half an hour later, though, he saw movement on the corner of the house and could barely make out a man that looked as though he had some type of firearm – a rifle or a shotgun, quietly walking back and forth at the southeastern side of the house. His body language suggested he was smoking a cigarette and Gose made a note of it.

One thing was for sure, the damned back of the house *was* all glass. At night, Gose reasoned, it would be easy to see anything going on in the house through those windows, but with the diffused light of the cloud cover, the chop of the waves, and the distance, he couldn't see anything besides reflection.

He kept a steady watch on the house and the dock and at no time in the two hours he studied the home did he see any signs of life on the yacht.

At seventeen minutes after six that night, the winds had begun to pick up and gusts turned to gales. Peter decided to pull the anchor and run the risk of bringing the boat in, closer to land. Crockett agreed and then stopped.

"No, let's wait. That's our entry into the house. We'll pull anchors and come in at dusk, bump the dock and let Brandon jump off and go to the house. He'll be asking permission to see if we can lay to off their backyard.

"How long until dark?"

Peter looked at the sky, then his watch. "We'll pull the anchor and start moving at 8:15." He looked down at the deck between his feet. "I think she can take a little more before we have to go in closer. Let's get this thing figured out."

• • •

Frankie Jackson loved his job. He'd been recruited by Allitini years ago, had proven his worth in making the Atlanta market profitable, and when Allitini moved the entire operation to the Bahamas, he'd been put in charge of security. Oddly enough, the boss actually needed fewer men these days, as most of the street bosses were simply reporting to Jimmy when he flew into Atlanta. This left Jackson with a lot of free time in Freeport and he'd quietly begun to make inroads into the criminal underbelly of the city, extorting pimps, helping Allitini to levy some "street taxes" to illicit gambling operations, and getting a few crooked cops on the payroll, too.

The only time his job really sucked was if he had to spell guards around the house, which, due to Allitini's mistrust of nearly everyone, meant sooner or later, Jackson would have to "walk point" on the property.

It wasn't really a big deal, though. No one really knew who was running this outfit and even if they did, the guards at the front of the neighborhood kept most people away. The dubious reputations of the neighbors did the rest.

Tonight, though, walking the grounds in the wind and rain, he wasn't happy. As he rounded the corner of the house, into the lee of the rain, he saw a beautiful boat, the same one he'd observed anchored offshore that afternoon, making its way to the dock. It was 8:24.

• • •

At 8:27, Jimmy Allitini had been sitting in his office in one of the spacious bedrooms he'd converted on the second floor of his home, detailing his plans for new partnerships with two well-known smugglers, Jose "Carnival" Modesto from Venezuela and Cristobal "El Caro" Catalan, from northern Mexico.

Both men had been invited, along with six others who had wisely chosen not to attend due to the hurricane. Allitini had been pissed, but the truth was, if he could have, he'd have gotten the fuck out of Grand Bahama, too. This damn storm had prevented him from leaving, since he'd sent his plane on to Jacksonville for servicing and by the time the weatherman had figured out the Bahamas was going to get pounded, he didn't have an easy way out. The two men he'd used to handle the boat had disappeared two days ago, undoubtedly thinking they wouldn't be needed with the weather.

Allitini swore it was the natural reaction of every damned Bahamian – they had no loyalty and no sense of cause and effect it seemed, either. If the dumb bastards had asked, he might've let them shelter their families in the house if the storm was truly going to be bad.

If…

Fuck it. He'd been double crossed by worse, and it had never bitten him yet.

A quiet knock on the door interrupted the conversation and Akil Johnson, one of the few black men on the island he trusted, poked his head in.

"Mr. Allitini, they's a boat comin' in from tha channel. Big sportfisherman. Been layin' to off the coast for a few hours. Are you expectin' anybody?"

"Today? Hell no. Figure out what they want and get rid of them." He looked out the window, where the flamboyan trees were being tossed by the wind. "Hell of a captain, though, out in this shit."

"Yes sir. As you wish."

The trio of men continued their conversation as the winds really began to howl and the first heavy drops of rain angrily splattered the windows of the office.

• • •

Jackson watched as the young man gingerly tossed the line onto the dock and secured it, then looked around, waved to the bridge of the boat, and walked hurriedly up the dock. He looked like some college kid and walked like he was extremely nervous, and as Jackson stepped out and leveled the shotgun at him, he put his hands up.

"P-p-p-please don't shoot!

"I'm just trying to help the captain find a safe place to moor. We got cut off from trying to get back to Florida today since this storm blew up.

"W-wh-who can I talk to, Mister? Please don't shoot me!"

Jackson, realizing the kid was terrified and obviously not a threat, put the gun down. "Go knock on that door, ask for Akil. He can tell you what you can and cannot do."

"Yes sir!"

The kid didn't take his eyes off of Frankie Jackson as he backed up, around to the veranda, and knocked on the door. A man, assumedly Akil, opened it and smiled broadly.

"Can I help you, young man?" He held his right hand behind his body, where it brandished an unseen Beretta 92.

"Y-y-y-yes sir. My name is Brandon Jones, and my family and I were… are … on that boat. We were supposed to go back today but the storm has gotten so bad, so fast, and Dad couldn't get any fuel to make the crossing ahead of time. We're just trying to find a place to lay by.

"Dad says if we get in the deep water or try to run ahead of it, we're liable to get caught and founder."

"One minute, boy. Stay there, I cannot invite you in before I check with my boss."

With that, Akil Johnson slammed and locked the door, leaving Brandon to stand outside in the rain.

• • •

On the flying bridge, Merrick had used white trash bags with holes cut out for the arms and his head to act as both a raincoat and camouflage. Against his will, he'd done the same with the rifle and, as the rainfall became more intense, he was silently glad for it. Too much water could swell the wood and throw his accuracy out the window.

Obscenely, at the end of the rifle barrel, a potato was impaled on it. He'd cut a hole lengthwise in the potato with his little Gerber pocketknife, then cut another one across the narrower axis. Peering through it at Peter before unceremoniously impaling it on the rifle barrel in the saloon, he'd explained, "Oughta muffle the shot pretty well. I've been working on it the last month or so, this sorta impromptu silencer. It don't make it too quiet, but it does make it not sound like heavy artillery is outside trying to get in."

At this range, though, less than eighty yards, he didn't think it made a difference, but he hated to not put holes where he intended them to go. Today, the stakes were far higher than if he was stalking the deer and the hogs in Shady Dale.

He watched as the door opened in front of Brandon again and the black man gestured to him, then to the boat, then back to Brandon. Brandon shook hands with the black man, turned, and began walking towards the dock.

• • •

No sooner, it seemed, had his men alerted Allitini than they had interrupted again. Akil knocked softly on the door and, not crossing the threshold out of respect to his boss, spoke, "Sir, the boat is a family of Americans. They'd want to lay up beside the dock to try to weather the storm."

"What do they look like?"

"All we've seen is the kid, looks like a college student, dressed like he's on vacation. It's not a tiny boat, either, sir. Prolly 45 feet."

Allitini looked exasperated. "Fuck, Akil, why don't you just invite them to supper? Let them sleep in the fucking house? Jesus, man, what are you going to do when some real badasses come in here trying to bounce us?"

Akil, used to the verbal barbs of his boss, took the scolding well. When Allitini was done, Akil spoke up, "Yes sir. It simply seemed unlikely that any- one would be trying to do anything in the midst of a hurricane. I fear we have a lot more to go before this blows past."

"Akil, let them moor here and quit fucking interrupting my meetings with my invited guests. Unless this house in in danger of blowing away, I don't wish to hear from you again tonight. Tell Charles to get dessert ready for our guests."

"As you wish, sir."

• • •

Brandon Jones tried to act the part of terrified kid when Akil came back to the door. It was obvious Akil had been criticized for interrupting, but the man simply opened the door and spoke to Brandon, "You and your people may tie up for the storm, but do not leave the dock. My employer is not interested in you sightseeing on this property. If you take a step onto the property from the dock, my men may very well shoot you."

"Yes sir. I know my dad asked me to ask you if we can pay you for your kindness. Would $500 cover it? I can simply run back to the boat and get it? Would you like to meet my brothers? They're with me. You know, that way you'd know we're not here because we want to be here?"

Akil thought for a moment. $500? For letting them moor for the night? Chances were, the storm was going to take them anyhow, he might as well get what he could from these people.

"Yes, Mr. Jones, I'm sure my employer would happily accept a gift of $500 for his kindness this evening."

• • •

Akil watched the kid run off, jump to the dock, and scurry down to where he'd looped the line over the last cleat on the dock. As the kid ran, though, he stumbled, hit the dock, and then abruptly rolled into the water.

Nearly instantly, two young men, whom Akil assumed were the brothers Jones had talked about, jumped from the boat and onto the dock to check on him. Within seconds, Jones was back on the dock and he waved back to where Akil was watching. He saw the other boys laughing and thought of his own brothers.

Undoubtedly the boy would be getting a good-natured ribbing from his siblings.

Out on the dock, Jones looked back to Akil and mimed drying off on the boat and returning with the money. Akil, dry in the doorway, waved his agreement. The other two boys had already gone back aboard.

• • •

From the lower bridge of the *Honey Chile*, Peter Claiborne grabbed the microphone that led to the flying bridge. "Gose, we're ready to go. Remember to keep your eyes on the anchor lines on the boat ahead of you. This storm is going to pull this water clean off this flat as it builds and if we get too shallow, we won't get out of here."

Up top, Gose had maneuvered the mic handset into his impromptu rain gear and simply "clicked" the button twice. The code for "Yes."

They'd already talked about it that afternoon. Peter had gone over the charts, looking for the deepest water they could find, aware that before the storm surge of the hurricane, the hurricane would suck the flats nearly dry. He couldn't be sure of the timing, or even the amount of water they'd lose, but he knew that if they lost too much, the *Honey Chile* would stick to the marl bottom and not pull free until the storm was on top of them.

They would be dead men if that was the case.

The plan was simple, Allitini's boat drew more water and Gose would thus watch the mooring lines. If they began to slacken, the boat was sitting on the bottom. Their's would be the next.

Peter had reasoned Allitini's boat drew four or more feet to the *Honey Chile*'s thirty-nine inches, so that gave them at least an extra foot. He almost believed they could pull this off.

● ● ●

From the doorway, Akil watched for the boy to come back with his money. These damned Americans! Always clumsy! Now, the kid was making him wait and, before long, one of his men might happen along and want to get cut in on the money the boy had promised him.

Finally, after several minutes, Brandon Jones emerged from the boat. He had on a baggy sweater that came nearly to the edge of his still damp shorts, but Akil could see he had, of all things, replaced his boat shoes with some kind of work boots.

He didn't think much of it, these sunshine sailors often neglected to think they might actually get wet, so he figured the boy only had packed one set of shoes for his boat trip. Thirty seconds later, Brandon Jones stood in front of Akil, holding a damp envelope that had been hastily sealed with tape.

"Well, boy, did you enjoy your little trip?" he said smiling as he tucked the Beretta back into the waistband of his pants to open the envelope.

Jones looked embarrassed. "Not as much as the one you're going on."

• • •

Frankie Jackson had watched all this play out. The kid walking to the door, the kid falling off the dock and then waving back to Akil as two other young men — brothers? Friends? - came out to help him. He could see movement in the saloon of the boat, but the lights were very dim.

He reasoned that Allitini had allowed them to moor for the storm, but just to be safe, he decided to watch these people carefully. Besides, from his vantage point at the side of the house, he was out of the rain that was falling ever harder now.

• • •

Jones' comment didn't register with Akil immediately. In fact, if he'd actually had time to think about it, he would've known what it meant. The prospect, though, of easy money had thrown him off. Allitini paid well, but $500 was $500.

As he wrestled with the packing tape that held the envelope closed, though, the crack of thunder tore open the sky nearby. Then it hit again sounding strange and unfamiliar, and in his periphery, he sensed, more than saw, Frankie Jackson fall to the ground.

• • •

Brandon Jones winced as the crack of thunder tore open the sky and expected to see the guard on the corner of the house fall. Nothing had happened, and then, with a queer-sound, another crack, this time sounding far distant and strange, the man who had brandished the shotgun at him only minutes before crumpled to the ground.

It was time to move.

Jones had positioned his right hand in his pocket to hide the bulge of the .45 and hopefully the extra magazines he carried in nylon sleeves on his belt. The plan had been simple, Gose would kill the sentry and then kill the man at the door. As the sentry was falling, Crockett and Claiborne would hit the dock at a sprint with the extra shotgun and ammo for Jones.

No one knew what to expect but Gose. As soon as he took the trigger slack out on the man on the corner, he deftly threw the bolt on the Winchester, pivoted the rifle slightly, and fired dead center into the bullseye of darkness surrounded by light that was Akil Johnson's head.

The empty shell he'd ejected from killing the guard had not yet hit the water.

Jones winced as the bullet screamed by his head at nearly three times the speed of sound and took Akil right beside his left nostril.

Most of the man's head, from the ears back, simply ceased to exist and he crumpled backwards to the floor.

• • •

A man named Boots Swanson was in the kitchen talking to Charlie, Allitini's houseman, when he saw most of Akil's head explode. In the seconds of incomprehension following, he observed a young white man holding a large black handgun push open the door, step over the crumpled body of Akil, and lock eyes with him.

Swanson, his brain unable to piece together the things he was seeing, moved as though in slow motion as Jones leveled the .45 at him and double-tapped Swanson in the chest.

His twitching fingers tapped the butt of his Smith and Wesson, but the lack of blood flow to his brain rendered him dead in a matter of seconds. His brain simply didn't have the ability to decide to draw his gun.

Charlie, also somewhat short circuited, nevertheless had enough of a mental head start on Boots to duck and as he did, he grabbed the large utility knife he'd been using to cut a cheesecake for Allitini's guests.

Charlie Wright might be a gourmand, but he was also a thug and an expert at both killing and survival. He low crawled to the end of the island in the kitchen and maneuvered to make a low sprint to the pantry, where he could at least hole up and fight these men in closer quarters.

A man with a knife was no good against a man with a gun unless they were close enough to hug.

• • •

By this time, Crockett and Claiborne had reached the house and were inside.

They called out to Jones to signal they had his back and Jones indicated there was still an armed man in the kitchen. "One up and one down in here."

"Heard."

Crockett signaled to Peter he should help Jones and, with an AUG still slung on his back, he stepped lightly into the main common areas of the house.

A huge staircase ascended to the second floor and Crockett could hear the scuffle of feet hastily moving into position up there.

Back in the kitchen, the "BOOM" of a shotgun rang out twice in rapid succession and the heavy "thump" of the .45 signaled what was probably the end of another bad guy.

Crockett whistled, another of their codes, and got a single whistle back. Yep. The guy was dead.

From the landing above him, Crockett heard another shuffle, then the "click" of a slide being quietly worked on a handgun. Patiently, he scanned the landing.

Almost as soon as he snicked off the safety on the Remington, he saw a man rising from the corner of the landing. Like some bizarre jack-in-the-box, he popped up and with a speed that nearly belied comprehension, Crockett killed the man with two loads of #4 buckshot to the head and neck.

He could sense, rather than see, his friends easing towards him and he scanned the lower floor of the living room, trying to get a sense of who had been there. As he scanned, he reloaded the big gun while keeping it ready for another fast shot.

Two drink glasses, both nearly full, sat on the wet bar.

Two whistles.

From the living room, a wide hallway led to what he'd assumed was the front of the house and he stealthily made his way towards it. As he did, he sensed Brandon beside him. In the lowest of whispers, he said, "Crock, Peter's gone back out to the boat, Gose should be incoming."

He nodded.

The only noise was the howl of the wind outside and through the door.

• • •

In his office, Allitini had leap into action at the second shot. The first one had sounded like weird thunder, but the second, coming so soon after the first, was unmistakable.

He looked to the two men that sat in his office, "Are you two expecting company?

Both men looked surprised. At Aliitini's request, they had allowed their bodyguards to leave with their drivers, believing, as Allitini did, no one could mount an attack in a hurricane.

The two men Allitini had stationed outside the door immediately opened it to ensure their boss' safety, then been admonished to "solve this fucking problem" by Allitini.

Those two men, Americans, were both ex-military, dishonorably discharged, and, if one was to believe their arrest record, highly skilled operators with a string of crimes to their names.

In reality, they were loud-mouthed, inexperienced fools, the kind that so often brag themselves into positions far above their skills. The smaller one, named Kaiser, nodded to his partner, Gildan, and they began to slip down the hall to the back staircase, which exited into a front parlor. They would flank the intruders.

Jon Crockett had never been to any kind of military training, but he understood the discipline of the gun, as did the other Four Horseman. As he stood, quietly assessing the situation, he heard what he could only assume was a door being quietly opened in the front hallway.

Easing slightly to the side, he leveled the shotgun.

Seconds later, the plate glass window of the living room blew in and two shots, less than a second apart, rang out, undoubtedly coming from the flying bridge of the Honey Chile.

Brandon let out a soft chuckle and whispered, "Damn that sonofabitch can work a bolt gun. Sounds like a fucking belt fed weapon...."

Merrick Gose had delivered death again, if not from afar.

Kaiser and Gildan lay jerking in a pool of their own blood, dead before they had hit the ground. Two seconds later, another shot blew out one of the upper windows and the scream of a man, badly hit and bleeding out, pierced the house.

Brandon muttered under his breath only loud enough to be heard, "Goddamn, we could've just sat in the boat and let Merrick do all the work."

Crockett allowed the comment a smile, "There's a lot of house in front of us. He hasn't killed them all. They'll be wisening up now."

As if on cue, the lights downstairs went out.

• • •

From his office, Jimmy Allitini rightly surmised men had come to kill him. Right or not, he logically assumed it was because of the men who now sat in his office. With no change of tone in his voice, nor any prior indication of what he was about to do, he reached into the upper right hand drawer of his desk, pulled out a Glock 17, and calmly shot both men twice in the chest.

He stood up, walked over to the electrical panel in the closet of his office, and flipped off the breaker to the lights downstairs. Let the light draw these bastards upstairs.

• • •

On the flying bridge of the Honey Chile, Merrick Gose was frantically searching for targets. He'd lucked out with the positioning of the two idiots walking down the hallway and had silently cussed himself for a sloppy shot on the guy upstairs, but the Leupold scope's lenses were pocked with raindrops now. The last shot had been off but had still caught the man through the jugular and the carotid arteries.

He'd bleed out quickly enough.

Now it was time to move. Anyone still alive would figure – correctly – the shots were coming from the boat and if they decided to engage him and Peter, they'd have no defense.

Gose shrugged out of the plastic bags, smiled at the splattered remnants of his potato silencer, and scrambled down the ladder to the bridge and his waiting cache of weapons.

He met Peter there and the two quickly debriefed. As they did, Peter indicated the barometer, then the mooring lines of the other boat. "We've got less than half an hour before this gets complicated…"

The sun was gone now, too, the last vestiges of light were faded and the house sat, half lit. Gose snatched up the last of the Remingtons and leapt to the dock.

He was at a full sprint in two strides when he heard the next gunshot.

• • •

Jimmy Allitini calmly assessed the situation. Obviously, these two bastards had tried to set him up, and so far, it certainly seemed like they were doing a good job. He could tell from the gunfire his men had been getting hit hard, but he understood they knew the floorplan of the house.

Nonetheless, he wasn't one to shrink from a fight, so with the Glock and two extra magazines he kept for occasions like this, he moved to the door.

As he did, he looked at his watch. It was 8:39.

• • •

Merrick Gose, like some sort of pulling guard (which he had, in fact, been for a time at River's Ford) nearly took the door off its hinges as he fought to not only get into the house, but to minimize his exposure to any hoodlums looking for vengeance.

As he eased further into the dark house, he let out a soft whistle, sounding very much like, "Where are you?"

Another whistle came back to him from the living room.

He eased silently into the living room, dark now save for the dim light spilling from upstairs.

The three men huddled together to assess the situation.

"Nice shooting Gose. Not quite the plan, but still nice."

"Well, seemed better to make it seem like you weren't the shooter. Where these fuckers at?"

Crockett indicated the hallway. "There's probably at least one down there to the right. Door's closed but might open back up somewhere else – the back of the kitchen? Maybe upstairs? There were two shots in there before the lights went out. Light, like a 9 mm or something."

Brandon nodded to the kitchen. "As big as this place is, there might be a back door to the kitchen. I didn't see anything, but I was worried about that big spook with the knife we capped in there. I'ma ease in there and check it out. You guys cover me and sit tight for the next couple minutes."

As quietly as a cat, the young man began to lightly step towards the kitchen.

• • •

There actually wasn't a back door to Allitini's office, but he had added a pocket door that opened up into his bedroom. He'd had it put in on a whim when he'd bought the house, but he did like the idea of a built-in backdoor to the upstairs AND downstairs.

Just like Brandon Jones was currently doing in his kitchen, Allitini began to stealthily make his way to his bedroom, which would offer a better chance at repelling fire due to the layout of the hallways.

The only downside of the whole affair was the damned pocket door. In certain parts of the house, notably the kitchen and the pantry, you could hear the subtle opening and closing of the door. He'd bitched about it to his contractor, but the reality of living in a humid environment meant sometimes doorframes would swell and make them harder to open.

As the storm continued to batter the house, he figured the door might be a little tight.

Sure enough, he had to use more pressure than he'd have liked and the frame sent a quiet "thump" through that area of the house.

In the kitchen, Brandon Jones looked up as the sound of a door quietly being opened carried through the floor. Easing backwards to the living room, he waved the others over.

He pantomimed with his fingers someone opening and closing a door upstairs and then pointed down the hall. Then he held up two fingers, then he held up one and pointed to the darkest shadows of the living room, indicating where one of them needed to position themselves to be able to cover the main staircase and the hallway.

The three men looked at one another. In the faintest of whispers, Jones said, "Ya'll want me to cover you two?"

Gose looked at Crockett. The two men nodded. Brandon silently eased over into the corner, the short barreled Remington at the ready.

• • •

Crockett and Gose, with no discussion and operating on a level only siblings and the closest of friends could understand, simply began to move down the hallway. The two men had known each other for too long to not know what the other would do. Gose took the right, Crockett took the left. As they passed a door, they peaked inside. The windows let in enough ambient light, and in the strange style of some homes, the sparse furnishings popular among the wealthy at that time left few places or shadows from which to hide.

The first room on the right, obviously a dining room, was empty save for the table and chairs. Not even curtains hung over the windows.

Across from it, a parlor, more plushly appointed, but still stark, stood empty. The next room on the left was obviously intended as a library, but nearly devoid of books. Allitini obviously wasn't a reader.

The foyer was empty and the huge wooden doors that opened to the front were easily ten feet high.

The last door on the right was closed. Gose, using hand signals, got Crockett in position, and then gently tried the door.

It opened silently on its hinges.

As Gose eased the door open, Crockett saw a nicely decorated media room – several televisions were mounted in built-in shelves on the wall and a fireplace – of all things – sat between them. Gose indicated the spiral staircase and Crockett slipped quietly over to it, looking up expectedly.

There were lights on, but no noises escaped the room upstairs.

Step by step, he began to climb.

Finally, thirteen steps later, he peeked over the edge of the staircase.

Two men sat on the couch and Crockett took a hasty step up and leveled the shotgun on them. With less than a pound of trigger pull left before the big pumpgun barked, he realized they were dead.

This was Allitini's office and he must have been meeting with these men as the gunfight had started.

He began to back down the staircase. At the bottom, he leaned close to Merrick, "I think the cocksucker killed his own guys..."

"A meet gone wrong? I'll bet he figured we were with them."

"Well, who the fuck are they?"

"Hell do I know? I'm not the fuckin' hoodlum encyclopedia..."

"There's three doors in that office, looks like a converted bedroom or something. One's gotta be a closet and I don't know about the other two — maybe one goes to a john?"

The two men began to ease back to Brandon in the living room, letting out the faintest hint of a whistle as they went.

• • •

Back on the Honey Chile, Peter Claiborne was torn between watching how low the barometer was falling, peering expectedly through the scope of the AUG, and watching the mooring lines of the yacht in front of them.

He duly noted the name of it - "Miss Behavin'" - and its registry out of Panama City, Panama.

The thing was enormous, fifty-five in length, nearly twenty abeam, and God knew what kind of engines it had. Knowing full well how expensive it was to run Honey Chile's engines, he could imagine the fuel bill on something like this. If his grandfather's boat took 600 gallons, it seemed likely Allitini's yacht must hold even more.

Then it hit him — this was not just Allitini's yacht, it was a fuel tank, placed in front of him as surely as the Gulf dock they'd stopped at in Key Largo.

Slinging the AUG, Peter ran down to the engine bay to locate the mechanical pump he knew his grandfather kept for emergency refueling.

Three minutes later, he quietly made his way onto Miss Behavin' and walked forward towards where he knew the fuel tanks and hatches lay. In his hands were nearly sixty feet of hose, the mechanical fuel pump, and a Colt .45. He could only hope that a boat the size of Allitini's was running diesel engines.

In the faint light of his penlight, he found the hatches for the tanks and let out a silent prayer of thanks when he opened them. In the dim light, he could make out three words, "Diesel Fuel Only"

Any sounds were muffled by the wind and the waves, so Claiborne could only hope there was no one aboard. As stealthily as he could, he set up the pump, ran the hose back to the Honey Chile, and began to pump fuel.

Claiborne tried to calculate how long it might take to fill the tanks and didn't like any answers he could come up with. The little mechanical pump was great for emergencies, but for volume? It would take hours to fill his tanks with it.

Time the storm was not letting them have.

• • •

In the house, Brandon, Merrick, and Jon had pantomimed their plan. Easing slowly up the stairs, each would cover the others. At the top, they peeked around the corners. Two crumpled bodies lay on either side of them and, despite the quiet in the house, they could hear scuffling and what sounded like frantic whispering down one of the hallways.

Gose, between the other two, pulled them all together. "Okay, so there's a couple of somebody's down there" he said, indicating the right hallway, "and that way's quiet. I'm gonna ease down to the quiet end with this" he indicated the big shotgun, "and let fly a couple into the doors. If anyone's there, I'll take care of 'em.

"That'll draw 'em out," he said, nodding to the doors on the other end of the hallway, "When they do, you boys drop 'em. Then we'll go room to room."

Brandon looked perplexed, "And?"

"Kill every motherfucker that moves."

• • •

Salvatore Digiorio was an old soldier that had come to work for Allitini after he'd gotten out of prison. In his mid-fifties, he had worked for the senior Allitini, gone to prison for ten years, and then, upon his parole, had asked the father if he could put in a good word to his son. Digiorio needed to leave the U. S. and so the Bahamas offered the best of both worlds — do the work he knew how to do and do it relatively free from prosecution.

When the guns had started to pop, he'd been in the bathroom at the end of the hallway and had immediately decided to slip out of the window, onto the roof, and try to sneak back into the house. He was armed only with a handgun, but in a fight, it was better than nothing.

Dropping unobserved to the ground on the east side of the house, he quickly eased around the corner and found what was left of Frankie Jackson, minus most of his head. He could make out another boat through the rain, but the lights were dimmed.

Obviously, the action was in the house, not outside. As he watched, a man jumped from Allitini's boat and made his way to the other vessel.

Digiorio dismissed this. He couldn't shoot him from this range and he didn't know who the man was. Better safe than sorry — not a good idea to kill the wrong guy.

He continued around the back of the house and stepped into the back door. Akil's sightless eyes stared up at him.

Digiorio stepped over the pools of blood and turned into the kitchen.

He listened.

Besides the wind, there was nothing except the sounds of the wind, the water dripping from his clothes, and the sounds of the rain beating on the roof. Digiorio crept through the first floor, finding dead men and little else. He could hear voices from upstairs but couldn't make them out. It was obvious he was the last man standing, except Allitini, obviously caught – and maybe wounded – upstairs.

He decided to wait in a darkened corner of the dining room, which would give him the cover of darkness and an easy view of the door the men had come through and would likely leave by.

• • •

At the end of the hallway, Merrick turned, shotgunned the knobs on the two doors, and quickly squatted down to reload and shoot. He moved the big shotgun to his left hand and filled his right hand with the Colt.

Nothing.

While the smoke cleared, his friends, positioned at the end of the hallway, had kicked in the two doors at the end. The gun in Jon Crockett's hands barked twice, then paused, and another crashing boom echoed through the house. As he did so, the big gun in Brandon's hands spoke, too and the men both quietly called, "clear."

Crockett had scored three hits on two targets, unknown men who had brandished small pistols at him as he'd kicked open the door. Neither had been prepared for the speed of the attack and hadn't managed to get off a shot.

Despite all the noise and the intense smell of gunpowder, Merrick's ears picked up a faint groaning. Someone had been standing immediately inside one of the doors he'd hit and was now lying on the floor inside the room to his left.

Merrick pushed the door open, with the pistol down and the shotgun up, he looked into the hate-filled eyes of Jimmy Allitini. The big Colt in Merrick's hands barked twice.

• • •

Jon Crockett heard Merrick's Colt fire and he tapped Brandon and with his hands, indicated "stay here and watch."

Jones nodded and began to look over the rooms he and Crockett had just cleared. They were empty except for the plush furnishings, and a search of the closets revealed nothing of any importance.

At the other end of the house, Merrick had rudely drug the still-living Allitini to the middle of the room and placed the shotgun barrel deeply into the man's mouth. A few pellets of the buckshot he'd used to blow open the doors had caught Allitini in the groin and the two shots from the big .45 had been into the man's shoulders, rendering his arms useless. Gose had rudely kicked away Allitini's Glock.

Crockett stood in the doorway, "'Rick, oughta slow down on that a lil bit."

Allitini's eyes were wide open and he frantically nodded. Merrick removed the shotgun from the man's mouth. "You got something to say?"

"Yes! Yes! Don't kill me! I can pay you — w-w-who sent you? Look, don't kill me — how much do you want? Look — a million? I'll pay you a million to walk away right now. How much was this job worth? Couple hundred gran…"

Pain shot through the man and he stopped, groaned, and tried, unsuccessfully, to sit up. Gose knocked him back down.

"You don't have a million, cocksucker. You gonna take us to the bank? Get us a check? Fuck off."

"Look, there's cash in the safe in the closet right there." He nodded to the closet across the room. "I'm serious — there's bricks of cash in there. Take it and walk away."

Merrick looked at Jon Crockett. "What do you think, Bub?"

"That's a lot of bread." He looked down at Allitini, "How do you have it boobytrapped?"

Allitini looked surprised, "What? No way! It's just a fuckin' wall safe. I'll give you the fuckin' combination, you get the money, and then walk the fuck away."

"And why wouldn't we just take the money, double cross you, and kill you anyway?"

"What the fuck do I have to lose?"

Allitini knew his only chance would be if some of his men were still alive and would rally to help him. If he was the last one, he knew he'd be dead.

• • •

Aboard Mis Behavin', Peter listened to the steady "chug-chug" of the fuel pump while he looked around. He quietly gathered up several briefcases and two dry bags and transferred them to the Honey Chile, then set about looking over the boat.

It was beautiful. The big 8V-71 Detroits looked nearly new and he knew the boat was designed to run smoothly in all kinds of weather. He continued looking for personal items and found precious few things that would possibly link the boat to its owner. Finally, in the galley, he found what he was looking for. Behind a row of dishes and plateware, there was another briefcase. Using a butter knife from the drawer above it, Peter popped the locks and found it only held one thing - $10,000 bricks of cash. Dozens of them.

He transferred the case to the Honey Chile and checked the fuel gauges again. They were getting better, but Christ they were slow! Pumping less than ten gallons a minute, he knew their only hope was for him to transfer as much as possible before the others returned.

Whatever they got would have to be enough.

• • •

"Fuck, just open the fuckin' thing and take the money, then get me to a hospital, you fucks!"

"Really, Jimmy, your social skills are shit" replied Merrick. "We'll get there, just answer some questions. What happens when we open the safe? Signal? Burglar alarm? Talk to me or what's gone on so far will seem like child's play against what I got left for you."

"Oh, you're a tough guy? You ain't even old enough to drink. Kiss my ass, you little shit. I toldja the fuckin' combination, either open it and take the money or kill me and be done with it."

The other two had left Merrick and Allitini alone while they searched the upstairs. They'd returned with a few personal items, placed them into a garbage bag from the office, and shook their heads. The only safe was in the room Allitini and Gose were in.

"What, you guys are robbin' me? Classless little bastards. Who called in this hit? I'm tellin' you, you can't kill a guy like me without a sanction, and you three are signin' you own death warrants. You think you walk into a man's home and bring war with you and expect to live?"

"Jimmy, shut up." And with that, Merrick Gose reversed the pistol in his hands and popped Allitini in the forehead with it, knocking him unconscious.

"So, we gonna pop the safe? A million is a million. I don't think there's going to be much in the way of police action tonight."

As soon as he said that, a tremendous peal of lightning ripped through the sky and the lights — all of them — went out and returned thirty seconds later.

Allitini came to a few minutes later and realized the wall safe was open, he'd been stripped of his personal effects, and the few items in the room that indicated he lived there had been taken away.

Gose had rolled him over and roughly picked the man up by the belt — Allitini's arms were useless from the wounds to the shoulders. "On your feet, jackass. We're going for a walk, and if you fuck with me, I swear to God, you're walking days are over. If you survive the shot at all, that is."

"I can't walk, you shot me in the fuckin' crotch, you piece of shit."

"*You better figure it out, asshole, or you ain't gonna like how I get your ass down the stairs.*"

Slowly, limping and grimacing from the pain wracking his body, Allitini began to walk down the hallway. Gose looked back at the others. "I'ma take him downstairs, you guys finish up and let's get going."

• • •

In the dining room, Digiorio heard a man talking clearly, indicating he was coming downstairs. He eased further back into the shadows and made sure the safety was off on the little 32 ACP he carried.

• • •

Allitini was in intense pain. The wounds to his shoulders throbbed, the buckshot that had punctured his legs and – he hated to think about it - his groin, burned like a hot poker each time he moved.

What he really needed was a quick snort to kill this pain and get him thinking clearer. As he began to walk down the steps, he could feel Gose's hand on his neck. "No funny stuff, Jimmy. I don't want you dead, not like this."

Allitini allowed himself to hope – there might still be a way out! Like a zombie, he navigated the stairs and, to his own surprise, made it to the bottom. Gose guided him into the dining room, staying close to keep the man upright. It was easier to let him do the walking than to have to drag the body out.

Digiorio had no shot. He could see a man guiding – carrying really – his boss but didn't recognize him. In the darkness, he wanted to make sure Allitini wasn't hit and the other man was killed quickly.

It would have to be precise.

Gose, on the other hand, missed very little. Even in the dim light spilling from upstairs, he could see water on the floor and the way it had pooled in areas. Someone had come in after them. A bodyguard? Servant? Where were they? Who were they?

He leaned in close to Allitini, knowing a bodyguard would never shoot if they didn't have a clear view. As Allitini stepped over Akil's body, though, with the blood, the water, and his limited mobility due to the wounds, the man slipped and began to go down hard.

Gose, thinking quickly, reached to grab for the man and, as his body bent to the left with the man's weight, he heard the crack of a small caliber pistol and felt the burn of a bullet driving into his arm. Off balance, he, too, slipped on the blood in the doorway and went down hard on top of Akil and Allitini. Two more shots perforated the darkness but went wide.

"Boss! Boss! Are you okay!" Digiorio stepped to his immediate right to try to see where the two men had fallen and try to figure out who was who. He knew Akil's body was in there, too, so identification was even harder.

Weakly, Allitini replied, "Sal, I'm hit and this…" a meaty "thump" silenced Jimmy Aliitini. Whoever Digiorio had hit was still in business. He took a step forward and as he did, his feet crunched the broken glass that littered the floor. Too late.

Suddenly, Salvatre Digiorio gave the impression of improvised dance, as his body began to take hits from the .45 Merrick held. Eight shots, each punctuated by the flash of the gunfire, lit up the rooms and thundered through the house.

● ● ●

When the barrage of shots erupted downstairs, Jon and Brandon rushed to the staircase in time to hear the collapse of Salvatore Digiorio into a heap on the floor. Jon, the big Colt in one hand, called to Merrick, "You still there, brother?"

"Yeah, this fucker winged me, but I'll be fine." The sound of the gun's slide slamming home on a fresh magazine punctuated the young man's statement.

"Allitini?"

"Nah, he's still alive, this was some dago in the shadows."

Jon could tell that his friend was silently moving through the murk below him, waiting for another shooter, trying to draw them out, ready to dole out more death in the darkness.

"Okay, put the man in the boat and make sure he won't go anywhere, check with Peter, and then come back. We gotta load this thing up and get in the wind."

"Roger that."

Crockett could hear shuffling downstairs again, then the rough smack as Merrick tried to awaken Allitini. Finally, after several slaps to the face, the gangster began to come around from his second meeting with the butt of Gose's pistol.

"Time to wake up, jackass." Then a grunt, then mumbling, and finally, the sound of the two men moving away.

Brandon, with a now-full garbage bag of money and what paperwork he could find in the house, handed Crockett another briefcase and a duffel back he'd hastily packed with Allitini's other personal items and slung the long guns.

"Now what, Jon?"

"Let's take this shit back to the boat and get these bodies loaded up."

• • •

As he made his way up the dock with Gose's pistol pointed at his spine, Allitini's mind raced. Who were these guys? If it was a hit, they'd have just killed him and been done with it. These people were good, but they lacked the ... what? Style? Panache? Something of trained killers. Yes, they worked well together and obviously had done so for a long time, but no one had warned him of any problems in the underworld.

They weren't locals. That was for damned sure.

Beyond his boat, he came face to face with Peter and understood instantly.

"You! You're that punk from the airport!"

Peter, not one to be scared or impressed easily, simply smiled and said, "Among other things. I appreciate you letting us top off our tanks with your diesel tonight, too, Jimmy."

Allitini, his mind clouded with pain and rage, suddenly noticed these bastards were not only robbing him, they were siphoning fuel out of Miss Behavin'. "You fucks are from Atlanta! You're just common thieves. No sense of decency or honor, to come into my house, to rob me!" He turned, awkwardly, to face Gose, "What about you, cowboy? Did I piss you off, too?"

"Yeah, I guess you could say that. But I'm starting to feel a little better about it, now."

With that, Merrick Gose calmly shot Jimmy Allitini in both knees.

It was 9:03.

• • •

Jon Crockett knew Merrick Gose was going to kill Allitini as payback for the contract on his parents. His oldest friend, the closest thing to a brother he would ever have, had a dark streak in his soul, coupled with a practical one that ran beside it. Peter might not have it and Brandon's actions only hinted at it, but Crockett and Gose were cut from the same cloth. Crockett would have killed Jimmy Allitini for what his drugs had done to Leigh, but he knew the loss of one's parents far outweighed the loss of a first love.

At least, he hoped it did.

The two men quickly loaded the bags and guns onto the Honey Chile, leaving Brandon to clean Merrick's wound — a simple pass through by a non-expanding bullet. Crockett dragged the now unconscious body of Jimmy Allitini onto Miss Behavin'.

Peter looked at the now slackening mooring lines of Miss Behavin', then the rest of the Four Horsemen and simply said, "We've got less than ten minutes."

• • •

Sometime later, Jimmy Allitini woke up to the deep throb of diesel engines. The room was dark and he could sense the boat moving through a heavy chop. He vaguely remembered the events of the last … hour? Hours? He knew he'd been shot and the pain that riddled his body was testament to that. He tried looking at the watch on his wrist but it was gone. These punks! Stolen his watch? Killed his people? Jesus!

There had to be a way out of this. It was likely at least some of his men had survived. If so, he knew they'd be looking for him. Maybe even stowed away on the boat he was on, ready to rally to their boss and save his life. He found he could move, with great pain, his right arm, but his legs wobbled uselessly below their shattered kneecaps. His left leg and groin burned intensely from the buckshot wounds in them and while he could move the fingers on his left hand, nothing else worked. Gritting through the pain, he began, with sheer force of will, to move like some kind of larval insect towards a tiny sliver of light coming from under the door.

Despite his wounds, he was too filled with hatred to quit. He'd always been a fighter and if these bastards wouldn't negotiate, he would at least be heard. Let them kill him like a man, not some tortured beast in a cage.

Five inches. Then ten. A foot. What felt like hours passed by to Allitini, but inside his head, he knew they were minutes. Maybe seconds?

As he struggled across the floor, he marveled at the balls of these kids – and that was what they were – kids. Punks. Bastards. To attack his home – and the guests in it (he dismissed the fact he had killed his guests … he'd never been too big on details) – in a storm? When he had offered them respite? They were fuckin' cowards. He groaned, came perilously close to blacking out, and then, suddenly, felt the deep throbbing of the engines grow still deeper. Behind him somewhere, the RPMs of the motors got higher. 1,500. 2,000. 2,500? What was this?

"It's a fuckin' hurricane, you dumb bastards! You'll kill us all!" he screamed into his shirt sleeve as the pain wracked his body again as it rolled from the big boat getting up on plane at what must have been twenty or more knots.

• • •

On the two-way radio, Peter gave Jon instructions. "Keep the revs up, sync the engines, and watch me. We're taking the deepest water I could find on the charts, but we're doing it in the dark and I can only hope there's enough water to get out. Just do what I say and not what I do."

"Roger that."

Peter and Gose had the Miss Behavin' revved up to nearly thirty knots and every light they could find trained to the front. It was an incredibly stupid move, but one they had to do in order to get out of the path of the storm. Crockett and Jones were following at a far more sedate speed to not only preserve fuel, but to avoid any collisions if Peter's calculations were wrong.

All around them, lightning crashed and the winds were past gale force. The two boats would have to run nearly due south for almost four miles in the ever-shallower flats as they raced the storm and tried to escape into the deep water and the relative safety of a southerly heading.

After Crockett dropped off the radio, he looked over at Peter. "I'll be back in a minute, don't hit nothin' too hard before I get back."

The other man smiled and nodded. He knew what Gose was doing.

• • •

Merrick Gose made his way down to the stateroom where they'd dumped the unconscious Jimmy Allitini in the dark. The wound in his upper arm stung but hadn't bled very much. A simple wrap of gauze had nearly stopped the bleeding. Now, though, there were more important things to worry about than another scar. Opening the door and turning on the light, he was mildly surprised the gangster had moved at all, but it would all be for nothing soon.

"Looks like you'll be back on your feet in no time, Jimmy."

"Fuck you, you bastard. Why didn't you just kill me?"

"Where's the fun in that, Jimmy? If I'd have just punched your ticket, I wouldn't have the satisfaction of making sure you'd suffer like so many other folks have had to suffer because of your dumb ass. Your people, what few there were of them, didn't have it nearly as bad as some of the folks you killed."

Merrick Gose nodded behind Allitini, then, with little thought to the pain he was causing the man, reached down and rolled him over and, in the same motion, sat him up like a parent with an infant on the couch.

"Looks like everyone's here for your going away party, Jimmy!"

…And they were. All his men from the house. All dead. All piled in here, in this stateroom, in what he now realized was his fucking boat.

"So here's the deal, Jimmy: We're going to leave you in this fucking bloodbath, adrift in the middle of the Gulf Stream. Sooner or later I guess the Coast Guard will find you boys and then you can tell them who did this to you."

"Or?" Allitini said, with more hope than he wanted to.

"Or when you get to Hell you can tell the devil the Four Horsemen sent you."

• • •

As the two boats approached the reef that surrounded them, Peter cut the engines on the Miss Behavin' and marveled at her again. She was a beauty — half a million dollars, easily — and he prayed silently to a God he still tried desperately to believe in.

"Just a lil' help here, God? Okay? Maybe a dash of forgiveness, but right now? A little help and a heap of guidance. We really need it."

Merrick had come back up top and was finishing his final few tasks. He nodded to Peter. "Honey Chile is coming in astern."

"Yep. Your friends all safe and secure below?"

"Yeah, ready to ride."

Peter produced a long piece of what appeared to be shoestring. "Go ahead and get the last of our gear aboard the Honey Chile when she swings in, I need about a minute here." He began to kill all the floodlights, leaving only the green and red navigation beacons on. He had already turned off all the other electronics.

Fifty-three seconds later, Miss Behavin's engines revved nearly to red-line, she squatted into her stern, and, in the harsh floodlights of the Honey Chile, she began to race away into the darkness. As the three men watched from the deck of the Honey Chile, Peter Claiborne elegantly dove from the cabin into the sea and was just as quickly tossed a line by Brandon and hauled in.

Jon Crockett looked at Peter. "Everything set?"

"Yeah, I just hope the props don't shear on that heading. She'll get to about thirty five knots before…" he let the sentence trail off into the wind howling around them.

The two men nodded. At the helm, Crockett dropped the engines into gear and eased into the throttles.

• • •

Locked in the dark stateroom, Jimmy Allitini's mind began to slip. He heard the engines slow and then drop to idle, then perhaps three or four minutes of silence. He wanted to scream, but fear had crept in on cat's feet. Only feet away from him, he could imagine the dead bodies, turning to look at him.

To hate him for what he had caused to happen to them.

As he listened in the dark, he was sure the nearly headless Akil was planting one dead hand in front of another, crawling towards him, seeking revenge for his death at the hands of others.

"MISTAH Allitini?" He could hear the lilt in Akil's voice, gargling through the blood that had poured from his head into his vocal cords. *"Why did this happen? Why did you let this happen?"*

Salvatore spoke up next, *"Jimmy, your old man promised me a quiet gig. That punk lit me up like the fuckin' Fourth of July. How? You always were a little bitch. Even your old man thought so. You couldn't hack it Up North, so they sent you away.*

"You fucked that up, too."

Suddenly, all of the dead men in the room began to scream at Allitini, in a chorus of blood-choked and heart-rendering screams and Allitini began to scream, too.

It was nearly thirty seconds before some calmer part of Allitini's mind realized it had not been screaming, but the sound of the engines of his boat, pushing nearly to redline. He felt the big boat begin to wobble a bit from the storm and the wind, then she regained her stability. So be it. The bastards that had killed his men and stolen his boat had a death wish.

For perhaps a minute, maybe two, this continued, then, Miss Behavin', all fifty-five feet of her, needing almost five feet of water and running nearly forty knots, ripped her guts open on the coral reef that formed a ring around the flats south of Dundee Bay.

Against all odds, neither of the outdrives hit the reef, and the big boat, crippled but not knocked out, continued on nearly the same heading Peter had, with a piece of twine, tied the wheel to follow.

She began to take on water and still the big Detroits continued to push her further out into the storm, into the big water, into the Gulf Stream. Soon she was out over the thousand-fathom mark and when the water in her hull finally hydrolocked her engines, she foundered and began to sink in nearly seven thousand feet of water.

Aliitini knew none of this until he felt the engines begin to lope and then stop. He'd felt the tremendous impact of the hull when she'd hit the reef, but he was no seasoned sailor. The storm howled outside like a beast but in *the darkened stateroom, there was only the dripping of water and, in Jimmy Allitini's mind, the quiet whisperings of the corpses that surrounded him. It was nearly half an hour before the cold waters began to seep into the room where he was locked away with his dead crew.*

Miss Behavin' took another forty-five minutes to finally slip under the waves, and in that time, the dead men talked nearly nonstop to Jimmy Allitini.

• • •

Peter had climbed aboard the Honey Chile, accepted the towel Brandon held for him, and went immediately to the helm. Life and death literally hung on his actions in the next minutes. He glanced at the barometer in the saloon and grimaced at how low it was. Around the boat, the winds were gaining and the rain, moderate until now, began to pour from the sky, blown sideways by the winds..

"You boys hold on, this is going to get a little sportin' for awhile."

Gingerly, he looked at his compass, the LORAN beside the wheel, and his fingers, looking more like a concert pianist than a football player, gently caressed the throttles, bringing the boat up to the safest speed he could.

For the next hour, the four men and their boat battled the biggest storm any of them would ever see in their lives. Peter maneuvered around the reef and opened up the throttles in the big water and pushed Homey Chile up past twenty knots.

He had run the calculations over and over in his head earlier. Heading south was the only solution. Any other direction on the compass pointed to death. If they could get another fifty miles between them and the storm, based on the weather reports Jon was monitoring constantly, they might live.

Slowly, agonizingly, the storm kept strengthening. At ten p.m., after citing widespread flooding on the island and 150 mph winds tracked on the east side of the island the weather station in Grand Bahama had signed off. Brandon looked at the others and smiled. "I guess this is it."

"Yeah, I reckon so." mused Gose. Crockett nodded.

"Peter?"

Claiborne, hunched over the helm, looked back at his friends. His brothers. He checked the engines again, ensured the wheel was stable, and walked back to the saloon.

As they had done before every football game, the young men, never avid churchgoers, sat down on the plush seats of the boat and bowed their heads. Simultaneously, they began to recite the Lord's Prayer.

• • •

At NOAA headquarters for the U.S. eastern seaboard, a man named Charlie Hendrix sat in awe of what Hurricane Andrew had done. In the blink of an eye — at least in hurricane terms — Andrew had become the biggest storm in nearly half a century.

Before they'd lost Grand Bahama, the numbers had been off the modern chart. The winds were pushing 200 mph in the stratosphere and likely not much less at sea level. Instead of following the model they'd been studying, the huge storm ... the damned thing had not only tripled in size in one day, but it had also turned from the glancing blow they had predicted for the Bahamas and now the eyewall was turning nearly straight to the west.

It was going to crush Miami.

• • •

Out in the Gulf Stream, Peter wrestled with helm and tried desperately to keep his headings on track. The storm — at least this side of it — was starting to slacken and he gratefully accepted the change of clothes Brandon had brought him, along with a hastily brewed pot of coffee Merrick had wrestled out of the galley.

"I don't want to jinx it yet, but we gained nearly an inch of mercury in the glass" as he nodded to the barometer.

"Yeah. Still a long way to go. How's the fuel?"

"I've got her set between sipping and chugging, but there's no way around big motors. Her sweet spot is about twenty or twenty five knots and that's where I've got her." He gestured to the storm and the ocean that surrounded them. *"A little more drag than usual."*

"How far will we get?"

Peter looked at the charts he'd set up in the seat beside him. *"I make us to be somewhere around here,"* pointing nearly dead center between Cuba, Key Largo, and Bimini. *"If we're close, we've got to make the turn soon. I can run at this rate nearly another three hours before I get worried. We just have to find a gas station…"*

Aft, in the saloon, the others had gathered and were going over the items they had taken from house. Allitini hadn't been quite accurate, there wasn't a million in his safe. The actual tally was $374,000. Another few thousand in small bills. The real problem was the heroin.

One of the briefcases held nearly twelve pounds of it — not the black tar stuff they'd seen over and over again; shitty, low quality garbage from Mexico and South America.

This was the stuff that had killed Leigh. High end China White, proudly stamped on the foil wrapping with the symbols of the Triads that had smuggled it into America. It was deadly, and it was uncut.

Jon turned up his nose. *"Fuck me that's a lot of China. Forty five dollars a gram? Figure they'd cut it down to a twenty percent pure? What's that? Million? Million and a half? Jesus."*

"I guess he was branching out? Maybe that was the guys he whacked in his office when we got there?"

Merrick, disgusted, picked up the case and unceremoniously cut open the neatly packaged kilos and dumped them over the side of the boat in the wind and rain.

Brandon laughed, *"Well, that solved that."*

Each of the three men continued to look through the pile of materials they had seized from the house. Most was little more than receipts and *incomprehensible notes about people and places they knew nothing of. Brandon, going through the garbage bag of personal belongings he'd filled up found a keyring.*

"Hey, doesn't this look like a safe deposit box key? It's on a Trust Company Bank key ring…"

Crockett took the keyring and looked it over. "Could be. I know Mom and Dad have a box at the local branch, but, there's like 13 or 14 branches in Atlanta. Be a needle in the haystack."

Brandon shook his head, "Might be one worth finding, though…" and went back to digging through the bag of dead men's things.

Forty minutes later, Peter turned the big boat west towards Florida.

• • •

In the end, the hardest part had been finding fuel. Peter had worked the radio for nearly thirty minutes before finding a dock that was open. The storm was largely to the North of them now, but the wind and waves were still far from normal. Brandon and Merrick tied off the lines and Peter and Jon ambled into the tired looking dockside store to find a payphone. After nearly four days of being on the water with precious little time on dry – or any – land, it was a welcome respite from the Honey Chile.

One by one, each of the young men dutifully called their family to check in and assure them they had gotten the boat out of harm's way and were safe in the Keys while the storm raged through central Florida. Each of the boys had taken a moment in their own call to push the phone into Merrick's hands, trying to include him in the simple act of speaking to concerned family.

Leaving the others in the boat, Crockett and Gose walked into the little market to pay for the fuel.

Despite having plenty of supplies, the simple act of a transaction and human contact was welcome to them. The old man behind the cash register smiled and looked at the big boat, then looked the two young men from head to toe. "Where you boys running from?"

Merrick smiled, "That's about the right word, boss. We took that heap outta Boca to get out of the storm, but everything's closed down, so we been layin' to down here until we can see clear to get back north. How you been makin' out?"

The old man cackled and said, "Mmm hmmm. I believe I'd rather eat a mess of stingin' nettles than run on this storm. Ya'll's welcome to lay off here for a few hours. Weatherman says it's pounding the Okeechobee basin and fixin' to lay into Tampa and St. Pete in a few hours."

"Well, maybe we'll do that. I guess you've been kinda slow today?"

"Yeah, only folks comin' out today are the Coasties and a couple of rescue boats tryin' to save some weekend sailors who can't run this kinda weather."

At the mention of the Coast Guard, Crockett cut his eyes at Merrick. The old man caught it, too.

"You boys worried about the law? Trust me, they ain't lookin' for dopers or crooks today, they're just savin' lives. If'n any of 'em even give you a second look, tell 'em you movin' this boat for one of the folks that store 'em with me."

"Then I guess we oughta know who you are, old man," said Merrick, putting out his hand to shake, "My name's Merrick Gose and this here is Jon Crockett."

The old man shook the two men's hands like he meant it and simply said, "You can call me Bundy. Ever'body round hereabouts knows who I am, even the Coasties."

"Well, Bundy, I reckon we're indebted to you. Be okay if we lay off for a few hours? We've taken a helluva beating and it'd be nice to catch some sleep."

"You do that, boys. You do that. If'n you need anythin', just ring me up." He nodded to a radio on the shelf behind him. "Channel 19."

"We appreciate it."

Ten minutes later, back aboard the Honey Chile, Peter fired up the big engines, eased the boat out of the channel and into deeper water and dropped anchor. *They had decided to take a break and one man would stand watch while the others slept.*

Merrick volunteered to stand the watch and the other three were asleep nearly as soon as they laid down on the couches in the saloon and the stateroom.

Fifteen hours later, the Honey Chile and her crew of four docked at the nearly untouched home of Peter's grandparent's on Bird Key. The houseman greeted them warmly and immediately set out to send messages to families in Atlanta. The phone lines throughout the state had been damaged, so the old man patiently waited for operators to connect the calls, then hurriedly grabbed each of the young men to get them on the phone with their families.

The devastation the storm had wrought on the East Coast was hard to fathom — towns like Homestead had simply ceased to exist. Basic services had broken down throughout the southern third of the state and thousands were dead or missing. Hundreds of thousands of structures had been destroyed and, as the emergency entered its third day, no one seemed to be in charge.

The next day, Interstate 75 was reopened and Merrick, Jon, and Brandon prepared to load up the Camaro for the drive home. The four men sat quietly on the veranda after breakfast and discussed their next steps.

"Nothing's ever changed. We all go to ground. Normal lives — school, military, whatever. This was the last charge of the Four Horsemen," said Crockett.

The others nodded in agreement.

Brandon smiled, "What about the money?"

"Already squared away. All the money in the old accounts was liquidated and a whole bunch of cashier's checks for odd sums under $9,999 are in each of your names are in the mail to my house. As to the extra cheese from this weekend? It's split up evenly, so we just put it into our own mirror accounts in different banks to stay under the $10,000 limit so as not to attract the lepers in the IRS."

Again, a round of nodding heads. This time Merrick spoke up. "And the safe deposit box key?"

Crockett shook his head. "I don't know. That's such a long shot? I guess we could go branch to branch and see if we can con our way into the vault and check it out? Tell the truth, I don't know enough about the damn things to know what banks do and don't do."

"I'll handle it," said Peter. "I'll use Dad's financial guy and see if that helps open the door for us."

The four men sat in silence a few more minutes.

"I guess that's about it," said Brandon.

The others quietly agreed.

"Peter, you'll take care of the guns? The Winchester and the 1911s we can explain away but sawed off shotguns and Styers are a little more challenging."

"Yeah, I'm taking out in the boat this afternoon. I'll dump them in the deep water. Nobody's gonna find them."

"Then I guess it's as over as it's gonna get."

The four men stood up from the table and began to walk out to the drive-way. One by one, they all hugged.

It was the last time the four of them would ever be seen together again.

55

2014

IT WAS ACTUALLY JANUARY 6TH when Jon Crockett stepped off the plane in Freeport. The hangover from Southern Comfort hadn't bothered him, but an investor he'd bought and sold multiple properties with over the years had reached out with a couple of lucrative deals and Crockett decided Bidings just wasn't worth the lost income.

Joyner's house man and driver Stanley had picked up Crockett at the airport, explaining that his boss had been sidetracked by a few recent events and had needed a few hours to handle what he'd termed "some loose ends."

Crockett smiled and took his seat in the front beside Stanley and the two men drove through Freeport back to the house. Stopping at a grocery along the way, Crockett made a few purchases owing to the fact that Bradley had some truly weird tastes in food and, while it was always delicious, sometimes, you just needed better options. Since Joyner was a devotee of Coca-Cola, Crockett also picked up a case of Diet Pepsi.

Stanley eased the big car through the gates at Dundee Bay and pulled it into the garage and sternly lectured Crockett to simply leave his luggage and groceries for Stanley and the staff to handle.

"Mistah Crockett, you knows the drill, we'll handle the heavy lifting. Please, make yourself at home and Mistah Joyner will be back very soon. You know where everything is."

With time to kill, Crockett acquiesced, walked into the house, spoke to Valencia, Joyner's lead servant, and promptly fell asleep in the late afternoon sunshine on the veranda.

It was nice to be able to let your guard down.

• • •

Roosevelt Bidings knew his life was in danger. That morning, as usual, he had met a courier for his payments and, as criminals were sometimes prone to do, this one had thrown a wrench in the mix.

The bastard *had* paid in full, but Bidings, realizing the backpack with the payoff was far heavier than normal, had opened it in the presence of the courier — something he never did — and saw, in addition to the neatly stacked bills of cash, a box of United States quarters. $500 worth of them, all rolled neatly and placed in their orange and brown cardboard box that the banks stored and shipped them in. Bidings shook his head and remarked at the courier, "Ever'body got jokes today, huh?" The courier shrugged his shoulders and disappeared into the crowd. Two blocks later, the courier called the man who had intercepted him that morning and reported in.

"Your man has the package."

The voice on the other end merely said "Good," and then hung up.

The downside was the damn bag was *heavy*, so Bidings had simply locked it in the trunk of his car. Seemingly every time he'd try to take twenty minutes to run to one of his banks to deposit the cash, something had come up. It didn't really matter. Cash was still cash, even if it was coins.

Early that afternoon, Bradley Joyner had called and asked if the two men could meet for an early dinner and, despite the long list of things to get done, he'd decided that it was only rarely a bad thing to have a rich man as a friend.

Joyner suggested a restaurant on the other side of town and Bidings had asked if they could go to one closer to the police department. Joyner knew the place, so the two men set a time to meet and then hung up.

Roosevelt had gotten to the restaurant and the hostess had taken him to the booth in the back Joyner was already occupying. The two men talked about any number of subjects – it seemed Joyner knew many of the local politicians and more than a few hoodlums. After a light dinner, Joyner had picked up the tab and the two men walked out into the parking lot.

Bidings hadn't noticed that even though he'd gotten there *after* Joyner, the man's car was parked beside him. If he'd have thought about it, he would have remembered the spot had been open when he'd gotten to the restaurant.

That was when Joyner abruptly overpowered him, quickly knocked him unconscious and locked him in the trunk of Joyner's car after taking his phone.

56

WHEN BIDINGS AWOKE, his head was wrapped in some kind of hood, his mouth was gagged, and he could feel cable ties binding his hands and feet together. The car was still driving and Bidings tried kicking, flailing, and screaming with no success. Seemingly seconds after he'd begun rolling around in the trunk, though, the car came to a sudden stop, a door opened and shut, then the trunk opened and Bidings was hit with a sap to the side of the head and knocked back out.

Sometime later, Bidings had come to and, as his senses began to refocus, he realized his hands and feet were now tied with a sturdy rope. Lying as he had been, his arms had fallen asleep and now, pins and needles shot from his elbows to his fingers as the blood returned. He could feel gentle waves rocking what he now understood was the deck of a boat. As he took in more and more information, he realized the boat was moving slowly in one of the many canals along the residential parts of Freeport.

Suddenly, he heard the unmistakable lilt of Bradley Joyner. "Well, well, well, Detective Bidings! Welcome back!" With that, the hood covering Bidings head was carefully removed and he was propped up against the gunnel of the boat's hull. Joyner stood over him and, perhaps six feet away, at the helm of the boat, another man, his back to Bidings, steered the craft.

Joyner leaned in close, obscuring Biding's view of the other man, but, since he was busy piloting the boat, he didn't seem too threatening. "I guess you realize we're going to be asking more detailed questions about your illicit dealings in Freeport, Mr. Bidings, but just to be painfully clear, you also need to make sure you're ... how should I put it ... *incredibly* focused on each question and your answer to it.

"I won't ask them a second time."

The first faint tentacles of fear began to creep into Bidings' mind and then the small boat, perhaps only 25 feet, eased out of the canals and began to move into the deeper water of the flats to the southeast of Freeport. The sea was rougher, but Joyner appeared to have no challenge staying balanced hunkered on the deck in front of the bound man.

The man at the helm had subtly accelerated the boat and, after only a few minutes, he'd cut the engines and simply said, "Two hundred feet, Bradley."

Joyner smiled and looked at Bidings. "Nice! You know, the waters around here are funny. If we were less than a mile over there," he nodded to what Bidings thought was the south, "we could practically get out and stand on the bottom. Over there," nodding the other way, "over a thousand feet. Falls off quick. Lot of old stuff that will never see the light of day again out here on this bottom, too.

"So, let's talk." His face broke into a broad smile and he turned his head and spoke to the shadowy man at the helm, "You got the camera going?"

"Yep, all set."

"Fantastic. Well, Roosevelt. Let's start with some basics. Give your audience your full name and rank with the Bahamian State Police Force...."

"I will not."

Joyner looked hurt. "Now, Roosevelt, that's not very sociable. But, I guess you know the rules."

Bradley Joyner deftly grabbed Bidings' body with his right arm, leaned the man forward, and reached around and expertly broke the man's left pinky finger.

The winds carried away Bidings' screams.

Joyner propped the man back up and cheerfully began again. "Okay, we can edit out that little mistake you made, Roosevelt, so let's start fresh. Please state your name and rank with the BSP."

For perhaps five seconds, the man sat there. Joyner knew exactly what was going through his mind, but he also knew Bidings would answer the question. They always did.

"My name is Detective Roosevelt Bidings. Yes, I am an officer with the Bahamian State Police forces."

"And your badge number?"

"516."

"Good! That's a great job, there, Roosevelt!" Joyner's tone was the same as a teacher of young children might use with a preschooler who had just washed their hands after using the bathroom. "Now, could you please elaborate on your involvement with the El Camino street gang in Freeport."

El Camino was a particularly violent street gang that had made inroads into the Bahamian criminal scene from the Dominican Republic, but the truth was, Bidings wasn't involved with them in any way. He looked aghast, "The only thing I've ever had to do with them was to bust them! I've never taken money or payments or offered to look the other way with any of them. I swear to God!"

Joyner smiled broadly and in the same tone and excitement said, "That's awesome, Detective! See? This is going to be as easy as you want to make it!"

For another fifteen minutes, Joyner kept asking questions about dealers and individuals that Roosevelt didn't know. Bidings was beginning to relax a bit. Joyner was ... something – maybe Interpol? MI-6? But apparently, none of the illegal activities or people Bidings protected were within the scope of his investigation.

Joyner watched the man begin to relax. They always did with the right amount of misdirection in an interrogation, whether you were in Sierra Leone, Afghanistan, or Paris. He'd ask a few more questions to finish building rapport which would subtly assure Bidings his own illicit activities weren't in danger and then, he'd move in for the kill. Finally, after a few more pointless questions, Joyner sprung his trap.

"So, Roosevelt, where is Presley Franklin?"

"Who?"

Joyner made a faint "tsk'ing" noise in his throat and broke the man's ring finger less than two seconds later.

"Roosevelt, you were doing soooo good. Do we have to go over the rules again?"

Bidings vigorously shook his head.

"Good! Now, *where is former Atlanta Police Detective Presley Franklin?*"

"I swear to God I don't know! How'd you know his name? He was Sean Jameson – we were at your home! Only a few days later, he sent me a message he was leavin' an' he did not say where! You must believe me!"

Bradley Joyner smiled warmly, "Of course we believe you, Detective! You've been so honest with us so far. How or why I know Franklin was a dirty cop – or his real name – isn't important to you. What is important is this: how did you meet Detective Franklin?"

"He had come to visit Freeport last fall and we simply happened to meet. He was staying at a small place on the beach and I happened into the bar to discuss a matter with the man who worked there. He knew I was a cop and we became friends."

Joyner nodded his head. "Hmmm. Sometimes coincidence is an interesting thing, isn't it, Detective?"

"So, Franklin just happened to be in the right place at the right time and you two just started chatting about *my* home?"

"No, no, no! We'd gone out drinking some days later and had simply started talking about old cases we'd never solved. It was nothing more than that. The massacre in your home was like nothing I'd ever seen before or since. What young cop wouldn't remember that, especially with no bodies, in the midst of a hurricane?"

Bidings was trying to stay focused on the questions and the consequences of what he said. Joyner was clearly far more than a veteran of the Royal Logistics *whatever* and the fact he was bringing up Dundee Bay and Presley Franklin – not Sean Jameson – meant there was far more to it than he'd once thought.

Perhaps the man at the helm was from Atlanta, looking to find Franklin? But how the hell did he know to look here? How did he know about Bradley Joyner?

"Gentlemen, I swear by all that is holy, I don't know what Presley sought from the events in Dundee that day. He was trying to bust the Four Horsemen through Crockett," he tried to focus through the pain in his shattered fingers. Suddenly, Bidings remembered he'd been named in the case as a potential witness against Crockett. Was it possible he was the man at the helm? He looked at the man again, more of a shadow than a definite person in the faint lights of the boat's gauges.

Nodding to the man at the helm, he continued, "Jon Crockett was what he wanted, and it was only by chance we'd ever met. Franklin was the crook – that's why he disappeared. He's got money, maybe millions, squirreled away and he's simply gone; but the reason he wanted this case solved was for vanity – he wanted to go out thumbing his nose at the Internal Affairs investigation while he closed this huge cold case."

In the faint light of the helm, Bidings could see the two men smile.

"I cannot tell you why this was so important to Presley. He should have simply let the dead stay dead."

The man at the wheel turned and faced Bidings. "Well, you've done good, Detective. Real good. You've answered our questions, you cooperated fully, and now, we only have a few more things to ask of you."

Roosevelt, feeling the danger to his own life was relaxing, nodded his head, "Yes, yes. What do you need? I'll give you what you want. Mr. Crockett?" Bidings smiled up at the shadowy figure at the helm.

"You got the wrong cowboy, Bidings. I ain't Crockett."

"We need all your email accounts and passwords, the passwords to your phones – the one we've taken from your pockets tonight and the three I took from your home this afternoon, and we need to be clear on one thing: You can only help yourself and us now. Presley Franklin is going to die, and we're going to kill him.

"Are you in or out?"

Roosevelt Bidings' eyes told the man all he needed to know. Bidings was sold and 100% in for whatever the two men would ask of him. Joyner turned to the other man and simply said, "We've got what we need. Let's head back." He started the engines and began navigating back to the breakwater and the waiting dock.

"When we get to the dock, I will give you a piece of paper. On that paper, you'll write down all of those numbers and passwords. Detective, you are not my final objective, by far. Franklin is. If you attempt to contact him, we will kill you. If you don't share any contact you have from him with us, we'll kill you.

"It's really that simple. You opened up an incredibly complex can of worms when you began talking and worrying about things that don't concern you. You're honestly lucky I haven't killed you already.

"Do you get this?"

Roosevelt nodded his head.

"Good."

A few minutes later, the boat bumped the dock and while Joyner untied Bidings, the other man threw the lines and quickly moved off into the darkness with the slightest hint of a limp.

Bidings looked at Joyner bemusedly, "He's not much for conversation, is he?"

Joyner nodded, "Never has been. Maybe if you'd known him long ago? He's a good man, just one with a lot of demons he carries around."

"Did he really do the things Franklin said he did?"

Joyner, with his odd British accent, smiled, "Roosevelt, Franklin told you what he wanted you to know about *Crockett*." Joyner looked at the shadow slowly making its way into the parking lot. "Him though? You don't want to imagine the half of it. Some he did for his country and some he did for his family." The man handled him a piece of paper and a pen, "Go ahead, write it all down. Your car is parked down to the left approximately 100 meters. The keys are under the passenger side floor mat. We've been in your home but we've taken nothing other than information. Your phones have been duplicated, so the burners you had? They're still where you hid them.

"You will find nothing out of place, Roosevelt; we are extremely thorough. And not to worry, we didn't touch the money in your trunk."

The dirty cop breathed a sigh of relief and did as he was told, then Joyner patted him on the back, again, as you would a small child, and the two men parted ways.

57

ROOSEVELT COULD NOT BELIEVE he was still alive. He hurried through the parking lot, mindful of where the other man might have gone and trying to be gentle with his two broken fingers. He fully expected to still be killed, but the cop in him said if these men wanted him dead, they would surely have done so on the water and simply dumped his body.

He desperately wanted to try to call Franklin, but in his heart, he knew these men would now kill him. Joyner had proven to be a gentleman with the heart of a gangster and the other man – Crockett or whoever – was obviously not unfamiliar with violence.

No, he was safe on land. Joyner and the other man were obviously professionals, but Bidings suddenly didn't want to know anything. He also suddenly understood he'd never faced men like this before. They had money, power, and anonymity. Despite his skills at navigating the Bahamian underworld, in fifteen minutes of interrogation, Joyner had shown the man how little he really knew of life in the real world. Obviously, Joyner was far more than a rich man's lazy son.

He sat down in the car, felt under the floor mat and immediately found his keys. Moving quickly, he unlocked the trunk to check the bag. He didn't really doubt Joyner, but five grand was five grand.

Even in the dark, Bidings could tell the money – and those damned quarters – hadn't been moved or messed with. He drove away, his blood pressure slowly beginning to lower. The whole way home, he watched for a tail behind him, but none showed and he circled by his home twice to see if any other cars followed him.

Nothing.

He was safe.

He pulled into the driveway and popped the trunk to retrieve the backpack with the money and absently slung it over his shoulder and began walking up the short walkway to his home. Unbeknownst to him, that movement had acted as the final trigger to a complex series of timers and mercury switches set by Joyner's accomplice that morning and thirty-three seconds later, nearly two pounds of C-4, secured in the bottom half of the box of quarters in the backpack, had detonated against the man's body with the same effect as a Claymore mine.

From his armpits to his groin, Bidings was simply vaporized as hundreds of dollars in quarters tore through his body and the front façade of his home.

Despite the quick arrival of the police department, it was still hours before they could make a positive identification.

The investigation is still open today.

58

IT HAD TAKEN PETER – *using his father's contacts in banks and financial advisors – nearly three years to finally sort out the safe deposit key they had taken from Allitini. In those days before Google, he'd had to rely on bank officials, seemingly endless periodicals and books about locks, and plain old asking questions.*

The problem was the fact that Trust Company was a huge bank, and it had bought dozens of smaller banks over the years. When it consumed one of those smaller banks, of course, it didn't swap out the locks in the safe deposit vault, it just kept using them.

He'd been able to eliminate all of Trust Company's original branches, as well as all the various banks they had purchased in Georgia, North Carolina, and Alabama. It was like playing a chess game in the dark – frustrating. When his emotions began to get the best of him, he'd simply put down this puzzle and hit pause.

Thus, he didn't work on it every day, of course, or for that matter, even every week.

But he did *work on it.*

That damned key. He knew its shape the way an old couple knows each other's bodies. He knew the not-quite-circular shape of the head, the plain font of the "2103" stamped on it (the font, he'd learned, was called "Bookman"), the thickness of the blade, the notches, the ridges, the teeth.

Hell, he knew what each of those terms meant.

The same determination that would drive him through law school in the coming years and that had driven him on the football field forced him to not give up on this simple key.

He knew it was more than a key, it was the final step that would give them all closure.

For him, it became the key that would lock away the Four Horsemen and allow them all to get on with their lives. So, while visiting his Great Aunt Gale in Panama City in early August of 1995, he was more than a little surprised to see "his" key on her keyring.

It wasn't actually his key, but it was the exact same design. Instead of "2103," this one was proudly marked "179."

He had damned near fallen down.

He'd been helping great aunt Gale take some items to Goodwill and she had given him her housekeys, and there it was - the same style of key he'd tracked for three years — proudly riding between Aunt Gale's shed key, her front door key, and the two keys to her Lincoln Continental.

He tripped and nearly fell headlong into the flowers that lined the walkway to Aunt Gale's carport. Peter regained his composure, started his Aunt's aircraft-carrier-sized Lincoln and turned on the air conditioner, and hurriedly walked back to the house.

"Aunt Gale, this is going to sound crazy, but is that a safe deposit box key on your keyring? You know that's not safe to carry around with you! What if someone took it? Or you lost your keys?"

The old woman smiled, "Oh, Peter, it's fine. I don't have anything too exciting in it anyhow."

"I don't like it, Aunt Gale. Why, somebody could just figure out what

bank you used and rob you. If they were smart, you might not even know they took the danged thing. You need to put it in a safe place."

"Lord, Peter, you sound just like your Uncle Randy. There's nothing valuable in that box, at least not to them. It's a will, a couple of pieces of jewelry, and that's about it. Couldn't be more than two thousand dollars. I know that a lot of people would kill for less than that, but I'm too old to worry about that stuff these days."

The old woman laughed, opened her arms up, as if for an inspection, and giggled again, "Besides, look at me, I'm old. Nobody's going to hurt an old woman for a key.

"They might steal my purse, or the car, or break in and take some valuables from the house, but a common criminal? He's not looking for that key, silly. Besides, that's not from a local branch around here, anyhow."

Peter's hopes were suddenly dashed.

Damn! He finally had a lead, after all these years, and he was – at least geographically – still far removed from the damned safe deposit box after all.

"Okay, then, Aunt Gale, where is that box? What branch? You've lived here as long as I can remember. If it's so safe, respectfully, then where is the box? Or more importantly, does anyone know you have it and where to find it?"

"Of course! It's listed with the other copies of the will at my attorney's office. Don't worry, Peter, when I'm gone, someone will know about that safe deposit box in the main branch of my bank in Delray Beach."

Delray Beach. The other side of the state. Peter sighed. No getting it today. He had three weeks before school started back, so it was still possible he could get there.

Knowing when he was beat – and knowing that any more questions about the safe deposit box might make his great aunt wonder why he was so worried about it, he decided to change the subject. After dinner that night, though, he went out to his car and got the road map of Florida from his glove box.

It was at least eight hours to Delray Beach.

He also noticed Delray Beach was nearly due west from Freeport. He reached over and grabbed the car phone his father had given him for his birthday and dialed a number he had long ago memorized.

Jon Crockett's pager.

Less than a minute later, Crockett called him back from his parent's home.

"What's up Pete! Been awhile — when do you have to go back to school? We gotta get together and go fishing, or drink a beer, or something and catch up — I hadn't talked to you since Christmas."

"Jon, I'm visiting Aunt Gale down in Panama City and this is going to sound crazy, but how about we meet for a long weekend? I found a cool place in Delray Beach and we hadn't hung out in awhile."

"Yeah, I'd be down for that. When? I gotta take off work, but since I'm working for Dad doing maintenance on one of his office parks here, that's no biggie. It's only, what? Five hours? Is Delray Beach east or west of Panama City?

"Umm. No, it's near Miami."

"Dude, do you own a map? You're ON the beach where you are and you're telling me you want to drive across the state to go to another beach? Man, you been in the sun too long."

"It's a pretty chill spot, and, umm, you know, we just oughta go there. Maybe check it out on a map, I'll bet you'll like it. It's not far from some places we've been before. Let me know when you can meet me there, but we gotta be there on the weekdays.

"Besides, Gose and Jones can't be there. You talked to either of them?"

"Yeah, Brandon is losing his mind up in Missouri. Apparently, Fort Leonard Wood is not the place he wants to be all he can be. Said it's either hot all the time or cold all the time, and Merrick says that Sniper School sucked worse than boot, but he graduated top of the class. He's stateside, but last I heard, he's on the west coast. Been a couple months since I heard from either of them."

The two young men continued to catch up, neither discussing nor needing to discuss the things that had happened three years ago.

In the end, Crockett did drive down and meet Peter in Delray Beach.

One week later and nearly three years to the day of the shootout in Dundee bay, in the sixth bank they walked into, they found the safe deposit box.

Inside the small container were over three million dollars in U. S. Treasury Bearer Bonds dating from the 1970s.

The next day, Jon Crockett was shot in a liquor store holdup.

Peter Claiborne killed the shooter, and in the whirlwind of the next few days, the two men, along with their parents, had made it through the mountain of paperwork, Crockett's short stay in the hospital, and managed to get back home more or less unbroken.

Less than a week later, though, in Atlanta, Peter Claiborne, using an acquaintance of his family's financial investment banker and his own limited knowledge from prelaw classes, set up an irrevocable trust in the State of Wyoming with four members.

The Shady Dale Social Club.

59

WHEN CROCKETT AWOKE, darkness had already fallen on Joyner's compound in Dundee Bay and he noted that someone had laid a light summer blanket on him. He looked at the battered old Vostok on his wrist.

Damn! It was nearly nine o'clock!

As he stood up, Stanley greeted him warmly at the back door and smiled, "Mistah Jon, did you sleep well?"

"Stanley, you can't possibly imagine. Yes, I did, and thank you for asking."

"Mister Bradley had asked me to wake you at nine, so you could refresh yourself. We'll be serving a late dinner on the veranda at 9:30, Valencia tracked down a nice grouper at the market and she's made that up with a ginger vinaigrette. As a side, she's got some nice fruits this morning, too, so she's cut them along with a few cheeses Mistah Bradley had shipped in from England. Stilton, I believe. His favorite.

"What may I prepare for you to drink?"

"I'll just start out with a Diet Pepsi, Stanley, thank you. I'll be down in a few moments."

As he changed clothes, washed his face and brushed his teeth, Crockett saw the splash of headlights in the window. Bradley was back. It was 9:19.

The meal was spectacular and the men lingered on the veranda long after Joyner's house boy had cleared the dishes and brought out the coffee service. The talk went first to the events of that evening and the solemn report on the news that Detective Roosevelt Bidings had perished in an "accident" – possibly a gas main explosion – earlier that night. Using the information from the phones and Bidings' email accounts, Crockett transmitted an encrypted zip file via a VSP service to Dimitry to begin to try to find Franklin.

The man with the Russian name had been embarrassed by his inability to find Franklin in the weeks since the Tile Man had been killed, but a single encrypted text had confirmed his receipt of the file and his devotion to thorough customer service for all of his private clients.

Crockett placed his phone on the coffee table, "I'll get the son of a bitch sooner or later."

"No, *we'll* get him."

"To-may-to, to-mah-to. Splitting hairs."

"You know, Jon, you could simply roll it all up and go away. Franklin thinks you're dead, you've squirreled away a reliable fortune, plus what we've all invested into Shady Dale, and while I don't agree with your choice of states, Wyoming is where you've always been most happy. Just go there."

Crockett smiled, "You really think I'd let him go? After all this? Not only what he did to me, but what he knows about us?" He nodded at the house, "This place? You know that won't fly."

"Speak for yourself, remember, I'm dead. Quietly pushing up grass in Arlington."

The other man snorted. "Georgia's nice, too."

"Yeah, maybe it's time to walk away for a bit. Unless Dimitry finds something, Franklin is in the wind. One day, though, when he *does* pop up, I'll be there."

"Yeah, maybe I shoulda simply killed his ass at Joel's office that day."

"No!" He turned to the other man, "You'd have been immediately implicated, especially since your attorney *invited* him there. Besides, if their phones hadn't been cloned that day, you'd still be fighting the Spanning case in court now and they would have likely dug a lot deeper than that idiot Tillerson ever could have."

"Woulda been a helluva lot more expensive…" the man mused.

"Yeah."

60

ON THE OTHER SIDE of the continent, the dirty cop formerly known as Presley Franklin had rented a cottage in Punta Mita, Mexico, sitting on the edge of the Pacific Ocean and Banderas Bay. He'd settled into a routine now, after two months.

Get up, go to the coffee shop that looked over the edge of the bay, then on to the local markets, where he'd eventually eat a late breakfast or an early lunch and usually, buy his groceries or the makings for his dinner.

After that, he'd go back to the cottage, put everything away, and walk the beach or, since the cottage's owner also owned a small timeshare resort next door, he might go and sit by the pool, striking up some conversations with the Americans that inevitably came for the week or the month.

It was a simple life, but he was actually enjoying it. He had a driver, Auturo, who came by a few times a week to take him shopping for bigger items in Nuevo Vallarta, thirty miles east, or simply out sightseeing along the coast. An older woman, Cecilia, he'd hired to clean his cottage and wash his clothes showed up on Wednesday about 1:00 p.m. and would have the entire place looking spic and span by 3:00, when her son would pick her up in his battered old Chevy truck.

Franklin wasn't sure how long he'd stay in the cottage, but he felt obligated to find something a little more stable.

Living out of a suitcase is only appealing to those who have never done it.

Through Auturo, he'd begun to learn how this part of Mexico worked. All the cops were some version of crooked, but mostly, they just wanted a little money as a "gift" to look the other way for some real or imaginary traffic infraction. He'd realized this didn't happen very often if they knew he was an American, but Auturo had explained it was simply the cost of doing business in this part of Mexico.

In terms of bigger bribes and kickbacks, it was only a matter of scale.

Need a firearm? No problem – you paid a "street tax" to the local police and ownership was rubber-stamped. Ready to buy a home without being a citizen of Mexico? Again, pay the man and it would happen.

Thus, Presley quickly came to understand it was a sort of criminal paradise and money was the lubricant that made it all run. On the surface, though, and to those who didn't know where to look, it was simply a beautiful place for Americans and the wealthy citizens of Mexico to vacation.

It was nearly March 10 before Presley became curious as to how Roosevelt Bidings was making out, so, on a whim, he'd called one of the safe numbers the man had given him from his own burned phone.

No answer and no voice mail.

Another safe number yielded the same result.

Franklin signed, shrugged his shoulders, and simply dialed the man's regular cell phone. Again, the call went unanswered and when the voice mail system kicked on, it dutifully reported "The mailbox is full, please try again later, goodbye."

Obviously, Bidings was busy and Franklin figured the man would see the missed calls and become curious.

After he hung up the phone, Roosevelt Bidings slipped out of his mind for another week.

61

CROCKETT HAD STAYED in the Bahamas for another three days after Bidings had been killed, then returned to Atlanta and began to rethink his business model. In short order, he'd hired a property management company to handle the homes he still rented, created another LLC to pay them, and quickly flipped four houses before the end of the month. Taking stock of the commercial properties another one of his companies owned, he'd placed them on the market, intending to do a 1031 Exchange with similar properties in western Wyoming that summer.

All in all, January saw Jon Crockett taking action to move his base of operations in Atlanta to the ranch in Wyoming – post haste.

By late February, he'd had most of the furniture he wanted to keep – heirlooms from his Mother's family and other old pieces he liked – shipped to Afton and had negotiated with an auction company to take out and sell the rest of the furnishings in the house. His housekeeper, Miss Anne, had agreed to take the cats with her on the flight to Salt Lake City, where Keith would pick them all up and deliver her to Afton to get them acclimated to their new home. Crockett would be there in two days and take her back to the airport for her flight home and he had arranged a small severance program for her that would pay her salary for another year. She had, of course, bought her own home from Crockett years before.

With his home on the market as of February 25th, Crockett walked through the now-empty rooms and marveled at the shift he had allowed himself to take.

He'd planned for this moment years before, but never thought he'd actually do it.

He was leaving Atlanta. This time, for good.

What they had started so long ago was finished. Maybe not the way he'd hoped, but he had played it to the very end. There was simply nothing else to do and no clear need to do it.

He took a last walk around the grounds and smiled at what he had built. It *was* a beautiful home. Walking around to the back door, he figured this was it. He went inside, grabbed his overnight bag, and carried it out to the Lincoln. He'd leave it at the airport and Miss Anne would place it for sale and they'd split the proceeds.

The big car merged easily onto traffic moving south on Highway 400 and the man silently reflected on the last few days. Of course, he'd gone to Graniteton and placed a last bouquet of white roses on Leigh's grave. Sitting there, alone in the graveyard, he'd had the last of many conversations with the girl who had made the man…

"I'll be seeing you around, Leebo, I guess. It never really ended before, but I guess it does now. All the death, all the killing, all the fear and running and … bullshit.

"I guess we're done."

He could feel the tears, but they had never come.

"I never wanted this for us. I never wanted to twist up so many lives, to destroy so much of what I'd beheld.

"It's funny, because I never would have done it if you were alive. So much death. It never brought you back, though. It never brought back

Merrick's folks. It just…"

The sentence died off and the man smiled through watering eyes.

"And yeah, *we could've had such a damned good time together.*"

The man, seemingly smaller now, walked back to the car.

Perhaps two hundred yards away, a man sat on a bench, seeming to enjoy the bleak winter sunshine, spoke into a phone. Rising from his seat, he slowly limped back to his own car, parked several hundred yards away in an older part of the cemetery.

…

In the whirlwind of moving, Jon Crockett had spent the better part of three weeks getting Afton set up to live in full time.

He quickly learned that despite having sold much of the furniture from the house in Pickett, he still simply had too damned much of it and had finally managed to find an auction house in Jackson that would come and take some of it away to sell in their March auction. Finally, March 12th, Crockett was able to hook up his laptop in the office and begin to get things organized. It had been nearly a month of cluttered living before he began to approach something resembling the normalcy and organization he preferred.

Opening his email for what he now realized was the first time in four days, he was confronted by what many Americans fear seeing - hundreds of unopened emails, all seeming to need his instant attention.

He poured a cup of coffee began to slog through them.

Here was one from a tenant, demanding he fix a leak in the roof. He dutifully sent this to his management company and CC'd them and the tenant on his response.

Marketing and spam messages he deleted quickly, but there were dozens of other requests – the bank, verifying his new addresses, his credit card companies, asking the same.

His realtor, updating him on the latest showing of the Pickett house. *God, it never ends!*

…And there was an email from an address he didn't recognize, too. It was Dimitry, explaining and apologizing that due to unforeseen circumstances, he'd lost some of Crockett's contact data earlier in the month so he could not call.

Switching to the other email address, he quickly read Dimitry's short email.

He'd found Presley Franklin.

Crockett looked at the old grey cat, sitting in the sunshine in the window. "Well, Bella, maybe you and Cheeto will be holding down the fort for a day or two…"

He reached for his phone to place a call.

62

DIMITRY HAD FOUND Presley Franklin when the man had placed a series of calls to Roosevelt Bidings' various phones. Tracking Franklin had been slightly harder, since the number was unknown, but the hacker had soon ascertained it was, indeed, Franklin when the name on the credit card had come back as one Sean Jameson.

He was in the town of Punta Mita, on the west coast of Mexico, an hour or so from Puerta Vallarta.

As he had done in the past, Dimitry had created an extensive file based on the digital footprint Franklin left.

Debit cards, phone calls, credit cards, and, once the trap was set, it had been all too easy to triangulate where the man lived by where the phone pinged local towers.

Crockett reviewed all the materials Dimitry had prepared and then sent then in an encrypted file to Bradley Joyner. The two men had discussed, in a seemingly harmless conversation, what to do.

"So, do you think we should go visit our new friend in Mexico?"

"I think he'd be really surprised… but I worry about his overall health."

"He must be doing fairly well to live in that area, I've checked out some similar places to the one he's got and it's not a cheap place to live. I wonder where he's invested his money?"

"Come to think of it, though, I've been interested in investing south of the border for a few years now. Perhaps he's on to some interesting rental properties."

"The downside, Bradley, is that I simply don't know any real estate people I can trust down there. I'd hate to plan on doing something there only to end up losing my nest egg."

"Well, we could call Peter and see if he's got any contacts that do business there."

"That could make some sense. I'll shoot him a message and see who he might know. It very well could be he's got someone in his Rolodex that could help us navigate the local bureaucracy. I'll call you back tomorrow."

Crockett, as he had always done, reached out to Peter using an old email address of his. For years, they'd played this game to make sure Peter could never be implicated in any investigation into the Four Horseman or Jon Crockett and, as the events of last fall had proven, it wouldn't have taken a smart investigator long to put the pieces together.

So much for being so smart all those years ago…

Nonetheless, Peter did email back the next morning apologizing that he simply didn't know anyone nearby. The only clients he had that owned anything in Mexico were on the east coast or in Acapulco.

Damn…

Despite that, three days and several phone calls later, the men had a plan worked out.

63

ANYONE WHO HAS EVER FLOWN into Puerta Vallarta's airport knows the drill – the plane comes in low over the Sierras that ring the eastern side of town and then, just as it seems you will surely crash into the waiting waters of Banderas Bay, the old pockmarked runway comes up and, against all odds, the plane manages to stop and execute a U-turn. At that point, a good athlete could probably throw a football and hit the water.

The man wasn't a huge fan of air travel but had done it for years. The plane ride had been comfortable but being cooped up for hours always left him feeling cramped and sore with the old man's knees he now had. He preferred the wide open spaces and at least the option to step outside, to go for a walk, to do ... something.

He waited patiently for the tourists to scurry from the plane before he finally stood, stretched his legs, and retrieved his carry on bag from the bin above. As his legs warmed up, he easily moved through Customs and Immigration, then on to the waiting crush of timeshare resort hawkers, salespeople, and taxi drivers.

At the end of the long line of "Free Tour" kiosks and guides, he saw the old man quietly holding a placard with his name on it. Walking up, he greeted the man in Spanish.

"Como estas Guillermo?"

"Muy bien, y tu?"

"Asi-asi. Su familia?"

"Bueno, gracias."

The older man easily took the other's bag and led him out to the waiting car. As he did, they continued to converse in Spanish. Out in the sunshine, the two men both donned dark glasses and, as they settled easily into the car, the older man handed the other a sealed envelope. The little car darted easily into the traffic and headed west, to the border of the Jalisco and Nayarit states.

At the checkpoint, the *Federales* gave the driver's paperwork a cursory glance, peered at the American, and waved the car through. Forty minutes – and one stop for gas and a *bebida* later, the men pulled up to guardhouse of The Four Seasons Resort, in Punta Mita.

The guards waved the men through and the old man eased the car around the twisting entrance to the sprawling resort compound, finally pulling up to the portico. Instantly, a young bellboy moved to the car. *"Hola, senores!* Welcome to The Four Seasons. How may I assist today?"

In the rapid-fire dialect of the locals, the old man explained his friend was checking in and could the young man please get his bags from the trunk.

"Oh, si!"

The bags simply disappeared, and another young man opened the door for the American. "Please, this way, sir."

The American shook hands with Guillermo and deftly slipped him a hundred dollar bill. "I'll call you in a few days, Viejo."

"Vaya con Dios, Tiradoro..."

"Egualamente..."

There had been no one to notice the man had arrived in the country with one bag and now checked into the hotel with two. One was noticeably heavier than the other.

The next day, Presley Franklin made a new friend.

64

FRANKLIN HAD GOTTEN UP and gone about his usual daily tasks – a walk up the beach to the coffee shop for a big cup of café Americano and to read the day-old Los Angeles Times. The news never really seemed to change, he'd noticed: this star was doing this, this politician was in trouble, a fluke of a storm, the stock market went up, then it went down.

In the grand scheme of things, he was finally realizing that there wasn't anything really *new* in the news.

He finished his coffee, left a small tip, and folded the paper up as neatly as anyone can when that paper has already been read multiple times.

As he looked out over the Pacific, he decided that today was a good day to spend by the pool in the small private facility his landlord operated next door to the cottages where Franklin had taken up residence. Walking back to his place, he could feel the subtle changes in his body – the stress had left him, his breathing was not nearly as labored as it had been for the last few years when he was still a cop and worrying constantly about his illegal activities, and even his clothes were fitting better than they had – ever.

Retirement and a slower pace were all agreeing with him.

In the cottage, he quickly changed to a bathing suit and tee shirt, decided that no one would be calling him today and left his phone, and absently tucked several hundred pesos – thirty or so dollars – into his pocket.

Arriving at the pool, he greeted the two young men that worked as lifeguards and bartenders and noted the older Mexican couple who had been vacationing there for the month were already drinking, despite the early hour.

He retrieved a towel from the rack, selected a chaise lounge, and laid down on it.

When he awoke nearly two hours later, a few more people had drifted in. He had met and talked to all of them in the last two weeks except for one – a dark skinned white man with a bottle of Modelo, speaking in a rapid-fire Spanish to the bartender and obviously telling a funny – or ribald – joke.

The two men burst out laughing, then the unidentified man said, in a plain southern accent, "I'll catch up with you in a beer or so, Pee-dro." With that, he turned, and walked past Franklin to the other side of the pool. He had a limp, but it was barely noticeable.

What Franklin *had* noticed was the shirtless man, perhaps six feet, two hundred and twenty five pounds of what his daddy would have called "country strong," was covered in scars and had at least two tattoos. One upper arm announced "Death Before Dishonor" while its mate showed an incredibly detailed horned skull with a burning cross between the horns. Above the skull was some kind of Gothic lettering, and below, the word "Infidel." Most interestingly, though, was the man's left hand. It was badly scarred, and the ring and pinky fingers had been severed right at their bases.

Franklin counted at least seven scars that had to be old bullet wounds, as well as a long slashing scar on the man's upper chest, obviously from a knife wound. His right thigh, too, had been badly burned and healed a lifetime ago.

Whoever he was, he surely *looked* like a badass, and Presley Franklin got the impression that under than man's wide straw cowboy hat and wraparound sunglasses, there would be a thousand-yard stare telling about a lifetime of death in faraway places. Always for someone else, though.

The lifeguard had noticed it too, and when he and Franklin made eye contact, the young man's hands mimicked pistols firing and his face burst into a smile.

Presley decided that this was as interesting a person as he was likely to meet, so he decided to see if anyone joined the guy – he didn't look like he had a wife, or even a girlfriend for that matter, but he figured he'd simply observe for a while and see who joined the man at the pool.

Less than ten minutes later, a much younger woman, wearing what was likely the smallest bikini Franklin had ever seen, joined the man. They spoke to each other quietly in Spanish for a few minutes, laughing and smiling, and the two abruptly got up, picked up their belongings, and left.

By now, the sun was high in the sky and Franklin decided a cold beer was a great start to his afternoon. He got up, ambled over to the bar, and spoke to the bartender.

"Pedro, una cerveza, por favor?" He was learning, but he knew he'd never speak as rapidly as the native speakers. Or for that matter, the bullet-scarred man who had just left.

As the bartender handed him the beer, Presley had to switch to English, "Who's the new guy, Pedro?"

The man shrugged his shoulders. His English could best be described as "tourist grade" and so he simply smiled and said, "A bad man, I think. A *soldado*? A – how you say? Boom-boom man?" He shrugged again. Customers were customers, and customer who tipped well, like the big *soldado* who had just arrived this morning? They were special.

Franklin got it. "A gunman, Pedro. Seems like the right word."

"*Posible.*"

Just then, the young woman, this time with a sarong wrapped around her body and a small clutch in her hands, came back into the pool area. She was smiling and waving, and in broken English, she shouted in a terrible Arnold Schwarzenegger impression, "Ah'll be back, Sarge! *Una hora, mi amor!*"

Franklin had to smile. As she quickly walked out the front gate of the pool and down the path leading to the parking lot and the guard-house, the man returned, walking up to the bar and stopping beside Franklin.

"Pee-dro, how about another of them oat sodas?"

The bartender laughed and popped the top on another Modelo for the man. "Aye, Sarge. On the tab."

Presley figured this was a good of a time as any, so he turned to the man, smiled, and put out his hand. "Sean Jameson, nice to meet another gringo here."

The craggy face – with *another* short knife scar that followed the jaw-line – broke out in a smile and said, "Nice to meet you Sean! Everybody just calls me Sarge."

Sarge's handshake was powerful and Presley's own hand felt small and insecure in the man's grip.

"Where you vacationing from, Sarge?"

"Shit, myself!" The big man laughed easily, "I split time between here and my house in the States, but I think Isabella wants me to be here a little more often."

Franklin smiled, "Was that?" he nodded to where the young woman had just left and let the sentence hang.

"Yeah. Ain't she a pistol? Almost too much for what's left of me, Sean." The two men laughed and Sarge motioned to a barstool and took a seat himself.

"What brings you down here, Sean?" The man took a deep drag on his beer, "Let me guess, your wife wanted to take an exotic vacation and your travel agent convinced you this was as exotic as you needed without needin' to get immunized?"

Franklin held up his left hand to display his empty ring finger. "Not me, Sarge, somebody else can wear that ring. All she did was cost me money."

Sarge had been taking a sip of his beer and nearly spit it out. Still laughing, he held up his own nearly missing ring finger and smiled, "I just tell 'em rings don't fit anymore."

"Yeah, I'd say you got into a Hell of a fight at some point... What'd you do?"

"Oh, shit, that's a *lifetime* of stories. I was in the Corps but lost the fingers in a motorcycle accident after I had put in my twenty."

"Damn! Where'd you serve?"

"Wherever my Uncle said to go. Let me make it easy ... I've been to places you never knew there was trouble at and damned few you actually have heard of. Most of it was after 9/11, but I'd been in a few years when the towers came down. Kinda made me rethink my own plans."

The two men talked for two more beers, and Franklin could clearly see the letters on top of the horned skull tattoo spelled out "SDSC." He was about to ask what they stood for when Isabella returned and grabbed Sarge. "It's almost this old man's bedtime, so he has to go." She looked at Sarge and planted a huge wet kiss on him. "You can play with your new friend tomorrow. Right now, you have to play with your *young* friend."

Presley could see barely see Sarge wink at him from behind his sunglasses as he let the young woman lead him back towards their bungalow.

• • •

Franklin lounged around the pool for a few more hours, but Sarge had not reappeared. In the meantime, he'd eaten a couple of tacos with another beer at the bar, then walked back down the beach to his cottage.

Nearly 1,000 yards away, a man watched Franklin walk back to the cottage. A shot from this range was difficult, but not impossible with the breeze coming off the Pacific, but that wasn't his objective. Instead, the man, whom Franklin would have recognized, simply observed through a Celestron 50X spotting scope. Despite the range, he could nearly read the man's lips.

As the man watched, Franklin walked up to his little cottage, number 14, retrieved his key from under a planter beside the door, and disappeared from view.

The distant observer noticed Franklin had shown no precautions as he'd dug out the key – no furtive glances around and no subtle shifts in his body language.

He had become the ultimate soft target – a man who no longer thought he was being hunted.

The man Franklin knew as Sarge quietly packed up the spotting scope in its case, slipped that into an old backpack, and began casually walking down the beach, back towards The Four Seasons.

65

PRESLEY FRANKLIN WAS A SURVIVOR, if nothing else. He lived in a world of stimulus-response, and despite his ingenuity, his real talent was centered on his instinct for survival. He had once cared about other people, but his job, the stresses he placed upon himself when he began to work both sides of the law, and his need to protect and insulate himself at all times from anything beyond casual emotional entanglement had led him to a place of being little more than a scavenger.

There was nothing resembling altruism in his mind, his heart, or his soul.

So he truly gave little thought to dreams or any sort of premonitions – he was grounded in the facts – and when his sleep was disturbed that night with a series of nightmares, he chalked it up to something he'd eaten, perhaps indigestion, or too much sun.

The images of violence and crime scenes splattered with gore were, in his mind, more a product of undercooked seabass than a harbinger of his own undoing.

The next morning, he'd risen and followed his usual schedule, but had slept in an extra hour before going for his coffee and a sweet pastry while he read a three-day-old Wall Street Journal.

As he walked up the flight of stairs from the beach to the pool, he'd heard Sarge before he'd seen him – the rapid-fire Spanish with a hint of a drawl from somewhere in the southern United States.

He made a mental note to find out where the man had grown up, because even though the Spanish was fast, he was sure it had to have an accent, too.

"Well, I'll be damned, there he is! Sean! Come on over! Pee-dro was just opening me the best one of the day!"

The few other people around the pool were smiling. Most were tourists from elsewhere in Mexico, on vacation, and they seemed to enjoy the energy the big tattooed and scarred man oozed from every pore of his body.

Today, he still had the wraparound shades and the straw cowboy hat, but he was wearing what had to be the brightest orange swim trunks Franklin had ever seen. Pedro handed Franklin his beer and Sarge shook his hand warmly.

"How're you getting' on, Sean? I missed you last night - came back up here late in the afternoon, but Pee-dro said you'd ducked out a little while before me."

"Yes sir. I left and showered up then grabbed some dinner at the seafood place past my cottage."

"Oh, you mean *Pescadora's*? Yeah, we eat there every now and again. Good chow. You ever had those fish empanadas? I could eat my weight in those damn things."

"Nah, I had the sea bass and it gave me some fits last night."

Sarge rolled his eyes, "Man, deliver me from Montezuma's Revenge. Been a long time since I dealt with that." In his rapid fire Spanish, Sarge said something to Pedro that, it seemed to Franklin, had to be a joke about diarrhea, and the bartender laughed and nodded.

"No, no para mi!"

"So what are you up to today, Jameson? Gonna pound some beers with me? Isabella's gone to see her folks in Vallarta, so I'm pretty much going to get shitty drunk and lay in the sun." The big Marine looked around and then, in a lower voice, "Besides, not too many of us palefaces in this crowd."

Franklin laughed, "Well, what'd you expect? But that's not a bad idea, Sarge. Pedro?" Franklin held up the now empty bottle, *"Una mas, por favor?"*

In less than three hours, the men drank nearly eighteen beers. Franklin was struggling, but Sarge – for whatever reason – seemed to be immune to the alcohol. He simply kept downing them and ordering more. As he finished his seventh *Negro Modelo*, Franklin stood up on wobbly legs and made his way to the restroom. Standing at the urinal, he caught himself laughing at some of the jokes Sarge had been telling.

He was only vaguely aware that someone else had come into the restroom and was in the stall immediately beside him. He zipped up, washed his hands, and navigated carefully out into the sun and back to the bar.

He sat back down at the bar and slapped Sarge on his back, "Alright, big boy. Let's grab some lunch. I'm too old to keep this pace up on an empty stomach."

"That's a damned good idea, Sean. Pedro – *Tenemos los menus?*"

The little man behind the bar smiled and passed out two menus. Franklin started giggling again. "Sarge, where the Hell are you actually from? You've got that 'down-south' drawl, but it's like it's been watered-down."

The big man laughed. "Yeah? Well, living with a bunch of Marines for 20-odd years will do that to you. Hold on a sec..." He pulled out a phone and quickly responded to a text. "Let's go sit at a table, I gotta stretch out this leg before it locks up on me."

Sarge motioned to Pedro they would be ordering and moving to one of the tables beside the bar.

"What'll ya have, Sean — we need to get Pee-dro working on our order."

If Presley had been sober, he might have noticed how Sarge had deflected the question about where he was from, but, with the beers deadening his focus, he didn't catch it.

The two men placed their orders and Pedro dutifully rang them up. He returned from the computer to tell the men their food would be coming from the kitchen in a few minutes, and he placed two rolls of silverware and two glasses of water in front of them, and wiped down the table for them.

As Franklin looked down at his phone, Sarge loudly proclaimed, "Sumbitches'll let anyone in this dive!" and stood up, laughing.

Franklin, confused but unworried, realized his back was to the men, and as he went to stand up, a strong hand pressed him back down into his chair.

Too late, he felt the sting of the needle in the base of his neck and then the numbing warmth of drugs as they entered his system.

"No need to leave, Detective, this party's just starting."

Franklin looked up, horrified, into the smiling faces of Jon Crockett and Bradley Joyner.

66

SARGE BEAMED A BROAD SMILE at Franklin. "I reckon you know everybody here, Sean – or should I say, Presley. You fellows doing alright today?"

Bradley nodded, "Spectacular. We're sorry we couldn't get here earlier, there were some challenges with the flight. Not to worry, we've gotten that all sorted out now."

Presley Franklin's ability to think – much less move – were already weakened by the alcohol, but now, the Fentynil that had been injected into his body made him little more than a zombie.

He began to mutter, "I … I… that's not – that's not my name. I'm Sean Jameson."

Crockett leaned forward, smiling, "Oh, cut the shit, Presley. You're a dead man. You put paper on me? You tried to railroad me in court? You froze my assets? You can say you're the Pope, but where I'm gonna send you? They don't ask for I.D."

Sarge began laughing and took a sip of water. "Presley, I believe you done shit and then stepped in it. You shoulda let the dead stay dead, son.

Besides, that amateur you hired to whack poor Jon in his own house gave you up before I'd even really gotten warmed up on him. You make some truly piss-poor decisions, boy."

Suddenly, as he looked at what was left of the man's battered left hand, Presley Franklin's confused mind began to comprehend what was happening.

…And he knew he truly *hadn't* let the dead stay dead. They were alive and well and somehow, some way, the Four Horsemen were now here to judge *him*…

"You… you're Gose. You're not dead. You were *never* dead." He looked at Joyner, "and you – you're Brandon Jones. Not some lazy Englishman's son. You're alive, too."

In his faint English lilt, Bradley Joyner laughed and said, "That's great policework, Presley. Really top notch, considering how doped up you are now. Of course, between the beers and Fentanyl, you won't have any memory of this conversation or all the exciting ones we've got in store for you…"

Presley turned to Gose, still uncertain how the hell the man was alive. "You were KIA! You were given a hero's burial, Hell, you're in *Arlington*."

"Not all of me, jackass." He held up what was left of his hand, "But, yeah, there's a few bits that made it home to lie with my *other* family. Don't worry, I've been busy keeping democracy safe since I left Africa in '97, but I still consider Atlanta my home. Got a house right near where Jon used to live…"

Trying to muster some bravado, Franklin leaned back in his seat, "So, does this mean you three are going to kill me? Bury me out in the desert? Is Isabella going to slit my throat?"

Joyner smiled, "Not at all, silly. We didn't bring a shovel. We've no intention to harm you. Sarge's lady friend is, shall we say, simply some local color we … well, more correctly, he slipped in – pun definitely intended – to throw you off."

"Besides, there's a significant price on your head from the U. S. Marshals Service and their Fugitive Task Force." He looked at Gose, "What's it up to now?"

"Hundred fifty grand when I checked in yesterday afternoon. I told them I'd be there to collect it tomorrow or the day after."

Franklin stared stupidly, "You work for the Marshals?"

"Nah, I couldn't pass the physical. On the other hand, we've never turned down a bounty, have we Colonel?"

The fake Englishman laughed, "Aye."

Crockett, who had been quiet up to this point, looked at Gose, "Is that hundred and fifty dead or alive?"

Gose smiled, took another sip of water, and nodded, "They usually give you an extra fifty if the subject can still talk, especially when it comes to ill-gotten gains and possible RICO violations."

He paused, seeming to look Franklin over, "The ability to walk or be photogenic doesn't count against you."

Joyner leaned in close from his seat, "So here's the deal, Presley: You're going to eat your lunch like a good boy. After that, Crockett and I will leave. Twenty two minutes later, you and Gunnery Sergeant Gose will be leaving by the back stairs and you'll head to the parking lot where a car will pick you up. That's the last thing you'll have to do, do you understand? If you fuck around between now and then, you'll suffer a heart attack and die right here on the patio."

The adrenaline in Franklin's system was trying to counter the drugs and alcohol, and Joyner, one of the most talented interrogators in the world, could see the man's survival instincts were trying to formulate a plan.

Joyner produced a small hypodermic needle, "Presley? Fuck around, it all goes black for you before Pedro brings your goddamned snack and we'll leave your corpse laying in the sun the rest of the day. The cabana boys will all just think you passed out."

Gose leaned forward, "And if you think I'm drunk, you're wrong. Old Pee-dro is in on it and he's been feeding me beer bottles filled with soda water since the third beer *you* drank. I just told him you and I were in a drinking contest for a hundred bucks and if he helped me win, I'd give that Benjamin to him. So, don't fuck around and find out what happens if you try to get brave when we leave, cocksucker."

Jon Crockett smiled, "Well, here comes lunch, dig in boys…"

67

FOR PRESLEY FRANKLIN, everything *did* go black after lunch. He'd tried to eat – some unaffected survival gene in his body knew he needed something to try to slow down the chemicals in his system – but the taste of his oncoming death took the hunger from him.

Pedro had cleared the plates and as the man walked away, Joyner had cursed and smacked his left arm.

"Damn! That stung like a son of a bitch!"

Crockett, laughing, looked at him, "Gotta be faster down here, the damn sand bees will tear you up if you're not careful. They pack a wallop."

Just then, Crockett smacked the side of his neck and cursed. "That's what I get for talking about them." He gave out a soft chuckle.

Franklin, puzzled, couldn't see the insects, but he was sure one must be targeting him, so he looked nervously around, scanning for it.

Sarge, from across the table, saw it and stood up, "Stop wiggling, Presley…"

As Franklin froze, he felt the sting in his thigh and Joyner's strong hand blocked the swat he tried to deliver to the damned bug.

Too late, he realized Joyner had injected him with *another* needle.

The next thing Presley Franklin knew, he was waking up handcuffed to a hospital bed in Atlanta, Georgia.

• • •

It had been an old ruse, but it always worked, and as Joyner hit the plunger on the second needle, the next load of Fentanyl really went to work on Franklin.

Seemingly instantly, Joyner could see the man's eyes relax and he knew Franklin's mind was slipping even further into a nearly semi conscious state that would allow him to follow directions, answer questions, and remember none of it.

From many years of using Fentanyl in dark places to extract the truth, Joyner knew the man would remember nothing of the last hour or two. The Four Horseman would continue to be a loose end to Presley Franklin and the rest of the world, despite the man having eaten lunch with most of them.

Even better? The only answers he could give would be true ones, because the Fentanyl stripped away all the layers and only let the brain access information it had committed to memory.

It was the ultimate truth serum, and it was universally available – and virtually untraceable. He'd brought his own, of course, not trusting the quality of what he might find in Punta Mita, but he had plenty to get Franklin back to the States. Once he was in the custody of the Marshals, they could do what they wanted, but, given the state of the case, he idly thought about giving Franklin a healthy dose of it before they turned him over, just so he'd plead guilty and they could be done with him.

But Joyner also knew Crockett had other plans, and as temperamental as Crockett had become, there was no telling what might happen.

Joyner knew that keeping Franklin nearly unconscious was likely the best bet for the man's survival.

In the end, if anyone had thought to ask Pedro and the other men who worked the pool and bar area, the last time they remembered seeing Sean Jameson, he and the man they only knew as "Sarge" were singing as they drunkenly left the compound.

The song, of course, was "*Leaving On a Jet Plane.*"

68

AT 9:15 THE NEXT MORNING, a Ford ambulance pulled under the portico of The Four Seasons and a single paramedic got out, unloaded a folding wheelchair, and proceeded to one of the cottages, where three men helped another into it. While they assisted the paramedic in getting the other man loaded into the ambulance, the doorman quickly loaded the guests' bags into the back of the vehicle.

Had anyone been paying attention, they might have noticed the lights on the ambulance did not turn on until the little van was well outside the city limits of Punta Mita. In fact, those lights didn't come on until one of the men looked at his phone and simply said, "the bird's in the air."

From his seat in the front, Merrick Gose listened as Guillermo explained the situation via phone to first the airport administration and then, to Mexican Customs officials: they were carrying an American national who had suffered a heart attack at The Four Seasons and, while stable, it had been deemed necessary to fly him to St. Thomas General, in Nashville, Tennessee, for an emergency surgery that simply could not be done in the country of Mexico.

No one on the ambulance was surprised when, with two "gifts" of $1,000 apiece, the Customs man and the airport's general manager agreed to allow the man's private medical staff to load him onto the waiting plane from the tarmac and bypass the standard processes.

Guillermo assured the men that his team of three would simply help to get the man aboard, then return to the ambulance, but since time was of the essence, they would provide their identification after the patient was aboard. The stress of Customs officials asking questions and checking identification may be too much for the patient and he could suffer another cardiac arrest, potentially dying on the tarmac and creating a nasty public relations incident for an economy based on tourist's dollars.

That wouldn't be a problem, the man on the phone assured him; load the man and then they would sort everything out.

So, while it was odd to see the ambulance waved through guarded gates on the perimeter of Puerto Vallarta's airport, everything was already approved.

Shortly before 11 that morning, one text rang through on three phones in the same vehicle and the ambulance moved slowly out onto the tarmac, followed closely by a white compact car bearing the seal of the Mexican Customs and Immigration Service. In the distance, a dark blue jet was on final approach. The men on the ground watched as the Gulfstream landed and then began to taxi towards them. As the G550 slowed, then stopped on the open tarmac, the little ambulance raced up to the waiting plane.

The Customs man, Antonio Garcia, was an old veteran of the game and, at 62 years of age, he simply watched as three men in blue scrubs quickly stepped out of the ambulance and unloaded the gurney with a sedated figure on it. In the meantime, the ambulance driver had brought the patient's passport to the officer – with an envelope containing the bribe - but he had hardly given it a glance other than to note the name on the document – Presley Franklin. He wasn't a doctor, but the speed and efficiency with which the masked medics were moving – plus the oxygen mask, IV drip, and pasty white skin of the patient – convinced him the man would likely die on the flight.

There was obviously no foul play afoot here, just another wealthy *gringo* that likely wouldn't be back.

As two men steered and maneuvered the patient towards the plane, the third quickly grabbed the personal effects of the patient – three bags – and followed the others.

By now, the plane's pilot had cut the engines and the sleek aircraft had come to a complete stop. A moment later, a quiet but firm "click" emitted from the door latch and the hydraulic stairs folded silently outward towards the paramedics.

From the top of those steps, a tall figure wearing finely tailored shirt and slacks stepped forward into the bright tropical sunshine, deftly slipped on a pair of gold Serengeti sunglasses, and nodded at the men loading the patient onto the plane. He languished on the small platform, casually stretching his legs, but Garcia noted that at no time did the man make any attempt to step onto Mexican soil.

It never dawned on him the tall man was effectively blocking his view into the plane.

Garcia idly checked his watch when the three paramedics went aboard the plane and was genuinely surprised when they had all reappeared in less than 90 seconds. He walked over to them, introduced himself, and asked them for their paperwork.

All three produced the proper Mexican identification, and while it was surprising they were all from near Acapulco, nothing was out of order. He watched as they returned to the ambulance and waved to them as the vehicle drove back the way it had come.

The big private plane quickly began to turn around and taxi, and the controller in the tower, aware of the life and death situation playing out aboard the Gulfstream, had greenlighted it for takeoff on the southern runway.

The tall man had quickly closed and sealed the door, then spent a moment in the cockpit with the pilot. Nodding to the pilot as he began to taxi the jet, the man then turned and closed the door. Franklin, more heavily sedated for the trip, had been carried by the real medics he'd flown in with this morning into the stateroom at the back of the plane, where the man's private physician would look after him on the ride back to the United States.

He took a moment to look out the window and make sure the three men who had deplaned were safely in the ambulance with Guillermo, then walked quickly through the galley and back into the main cabin.

Merrick Gose, Jon Crockett, and Bradley Joyner all now sat in the civilian clothes they had worn under their scrubs when they had carried Franklin on to the plane. Unknown to Garcia as he watched on the ground, the men that had gotten back into the ambulance had only been Mexican nationals who had ridden in on the plane while Gose, Crockett, and Joyner has all arrived in the ambulance and effectively snuck out of Mexico with their prize. All of them looked up as the sharply dressed man walked into the main cabin. Peter Claiborne smiled broadly, "Gentlemen, welcome to this year's annual meeting of the Shady Dale Social Club."

69

THE GULFSTREAM ACCELERATED down the runway and took off with little effort. Climbing and banking over Banderas Bay, the plane continued to climb, first over the Sierra Madres, and then, to a cruising attitude of nearly 42,000 feet.

The four men made small talk in the cabin until the pilot confirmed they were now in level flight and would be for the next five hours. Immediately after that announcement, Claiborne's doctor, a well-built man in his forties with a shock of red hair going grey at the temples emerged from the stateroom.

Claiborne introduced the man.

"Gentlemen, this is Darren Dykes, my personal physician. Doctor, the tattooed fellow is Gunnery Sergeant Merrick Gose, USMC retired … so to speak. Next to him is Colonel Bradley Joyner, late of the U. S. Army Joint PsyOps division in the Middle East. You've read of his work, just never knew it was his. Lastly, in the blue golf shirt is Jon Crockett." Peter chuckled, "He's in real estate."

The doctor smiled at the men, shook their hands, and addressed Peter.

"He's sedated and will be for at least another seven hours. All his vitals are fine – he's actually in good shape despite the atrocious diet he's obviously had for too long. There are signs of high blood pressure, but I guess that's to be expected.

"You said he was a cop?"

Gose chuckled, "I guess so, Doc. A damned dirty one."

The doctor smiled, "Well, that would make anyone have high blood pressure." He turned to Peter, "If you gentlemen need me, I'll be back in the cabin with my patient." The doctor looked around, somewhat sheepishly, "I assume I need to have my headphones and quietly watch the in-flight movie so as to not end up sedated, too?"

Peter smiled, "We're not talking about anything too risqué, Darren, but yes, we'd appreciate you not listening to company business."

"As you wish. Gentlemen, it's my pleasure to help ya'll today. Let me know if I'm needed."

The Four Horsemen sat quietly for a few moments, until they heard the sound of the stateroom door being latched. Perhaps fifteen seconds later, Gose began to chuckle.

"You got a helluva good health insurance plan to get a doctor to leave the country on a damned house call, Pete."

"Nah, he was off today, besides, I've done him a solid or two over the years. Some research he did while he was still in medical school got picked up by one of the big pharma companies and they, shall we say, "forgot" to give him credit.

"The first check he got from them after our court date was nearly twelve million. You might say he'll now come when called."

Joyner smiled, "Ahh, the amazing lubrication qualities of money. It truly does make the world go around…"

With that, Peter reached behind his seat to pull out a legal folder and an iPad. "Gentlemen, if you will now turn your attention to the screen at the front of the cabin, we might as well go over the financials of this thing of ours…"

Each of the men dug out notebooks and pens from their bags, and two of them rooted around to find reading glasses.

"The current financial status of the Trust is at $328 million."

The three other men exhaled. Gose let out a low whistle.

"That's a pretty fair jump from last year. I guess that Bitcoin stuff is paying off?"

"And then some. Right now, all the projections I'm seeing say that market will be stable for at least another four years. If we get out in the late fall of 2018, we each walk with nearly half a billion, based only on what the Trust owns now. It'll likely be 2020 before our Uncle Sam figures out he needs to tax the stuff, too.

"Holy fuck."

For nearly another hour, Peter Claiborne went over the various investments he and Crockett had made using the monies the four men had accumulated through a variety of sources – all legal methods now - over almost twenty-five years.

Despite the fact they did this every year, Peter, ever the attorney, always tried to ensure that any of the members – his friends, to be sure – knew all the actions he had taken were in the collective best interests. He had, for the most part, quit being an attorney many years before and had become the man behind the curtain – constantly moving levers, using his contacts around the world to understand investment opportunities many people never learned about.

While he also invested his private money (and that of the others), much of his adult life had been driven by the goal of putting bad money to good use.

The trust now owned thousands of acres in Wyoming and Montana, all placed under Conservation Easements for tax purposes or, in several instances, legitimate cattle or hay operations. Bitcoin. Gold. Oil wells. Tar sands. Solar farms. Windmills.

All either producing income or creating tax breaks.

The Shady Dale Social Club – the trust he'd begun building so many years ago – was the sole client of two different accounting firms in Nevada, and another company in Reno was on retainer simply to make sure all the pieces ran smoothly and insulated the ownership from any sort of legal actions. After nearly a quarter century of legitimate operation and management, the corporate veil was nearly bulletproof, and while various entities of the Trust had been audited, nothing amiss had ever been discovered.

After nearly an hour of discussion, give and take, and good-natured joking, Peter concluded the reporting of what their money had been doing for the last year and briefly shared his thoughts for the coming year.

They each nodded in agreement, "aye'd" their support of his plan, and, as he did every year from someplace far from Nashville, Peter passed around a paper with the minutes of the financial meeting and each of them signed it, using the names documented in the trust paperwork for all registered agents acting in the stead of the owners.

"Well, moving on, Sarge, what's the plan for turning our passenger over to the Marshals?"

"Pretty simple. We'll land in Atlanta, where they'll be waiting on us. Me an' Bradley can get dressed up again in our scrubs, along with the Doc, and get Franklin deplaned. I've done enough business with them over the years that I'll just have to sign a few things. From there, we get back on the plane and fly off into the sunset."

"Which airport?"

Gose smiled, "Why, Charlie Brown, of course. Could you imagine it any other way?"

70

IN THE END, the arrest of Presley Franklin was almost melodramatic. The Gulfstream landed, Gose and Joyner deplaned with Dykes attending, and despite nearly a dozen Marshals in attendance, the unconscious Franklin was loaded into an ambulance and taken to Grady Memorial.

Gose signed off on the forms under his primary pseudonym, Rick Gesslin, shook hands with the lead on the case, and handed the man the two different passports Franklin had been using as well as a Ziploc bag with the various financial documents he'd taken from Franklin's cottage.

"The passport we used to get him out was fake, but these look pretty good, too. I suspect you'll also be able to use 'em to track down where his money is."

The Marshal looked at the passport he held in his hand and laughed nervously, "You made a fake passport with his real name? Who the Hell are you guys?" Until the bounty hunter had told him it was fake, he'd thought it was the real thing.

Merrick winked at the Marshal, "We're like the Four Horsemen in the Bible, come to judge the wicked in the dead of the night."

With that, Merrick and Bradley turned and began walking back to the plane. Dykes had already returned and the pilot had been cleared for takeoff, and in less than an hour, the big jet was back in the sky, winging to Nashville and the hanger where the owners – Peter being one of them – kept it.

As the private jet thundered down the runway, one of the Marshals, new to this kind of detail, shook his head.

"Must be nice, flying around in your own jet to bounty hunt."

The oldest of the team, a veteran named Randy Clark who was nearing his thirty years in the service, laughed, "Tell me about it. That guy is one of the most successful in the game. In the dozen or so years he's been active, he's pocketed at least five million from the U. S. alone. I heard he and his partners have knocked down a bunch for Interpol, too. If you believe the scuttlebutt, he's worked with about everybody to bust anybody. That English guy that was with him?"

"Yeah, seems more like a bum than a bounty hunter."

"Well, the word around the campfire at HQ was he brought in about a dozen or so high ranking guys from Afghanistan and Iraq. The terrorists we had on the playing cards?

"That British dude put the snatch on a whole pack of them between 2002 and 2006 and laughed all the way to the bank. When I was in the Green Zone in '08, they talked about an Englishman, a full bird Colonel, who'd been heavy into that scene with U. S. Army PsyOps. I think that's the same guy…

"They said he was the reason we got Saddam…"

The young man laughed and shook his head in amazement. "Gotta catch 'em all, I guess…"

71

JON CROCKETT WASTED NO TIME in arranging Dimitry's assistance in crucifying Franklin in the court of public opinion. Where once, those skills were used to bury stories and information about Crockett's arrest, now, the press seemed to come alive, crying for blood over the disgraced cop.

In the time it took Franklin to come out of the Fentanyl haze and be given a clean bill of health, fully thirty-two newspapers and six national magazines, along with countless television stations, had run the story and were "investigating" Franklin's decades of activities.

Try as they might, no one ever took credit for his actual arrest, only the U. S. Marshal's Service and their Fugitive Task Force.

The media simply accepted what they were told was solid investigative police work, driven by "tips" called in and "incredible investigators on our team."

But they had a field day with Franklin's life. From New York to Los Angeles, media outlets solicited – and got access to – files they should not have been able to (delivered through proxy servers, fax machines, and even the United States Postal Service). No one in the law enforcement community knew how (or at least admitted to it), but, given the nature of the case, they were only happy the information seemed to always indicate Franklin acted alone. Jonathan Swift, nervous as always, dreaded every phone call, but each one, day after day, only asked about Franklin, never indicating or implicating any other person or department in the APD.

Franklin's assets were seized, and as the narrative of a dirty cop played out over the printed page and the 24 hours news channels, "sources close to the investigation" continuously offered more damning evidence in the court of public opinion.

Of course, none of it was admissible in court, but the public had long ago forgotten the rule of law that Joel Habersham had once called into question in a courtroom in Atlanta.

Innocent until proven guilty.

The public ate it up. Ambulance-chasing attorneys began to file grievances in courts alleging Franklin's involvement in their client's case warranted a retrial or an outright dismissal.

Civil rights groups protested in Piedmont Park on a Saturday and that devolved into rioting on Saturday night. Near where Techwood Homes had once stood and where Presley Franklin's original beat had been, he was burned in effigy by a group demanding any case he had been involved with be thrown out. The Atlanta Police Department walked a thin line, trying to allow protestors to air their grievances and still allow the city to run smoothly.

In a town with such a checkered history of police corruption and the civil rights movement, the weeks leading up to Presley Franklin's arraignment were tense. In late May, his attorney, a smart young man named Robert Webb, argued and won the right to have the trial moved to a to-be-disclosed location since the Grand Jury had indeed decided to indict.

In the chambers, the two attorneys and the Judge, a man named Clemmons, discussed the case. Webb was, despite his youthful appearance, a brilliant attorney, and he knew that a change of venue was only the first step towards Franklin's only hope – a plea bargain. Turning states' evidence wasn't an option, because there simply was no indication he had ever conspired with anyone.

He'd done this to himself, bribe by bribe and kickback by kickback. It was far too early to tip their hand at a defense, because if the State thought Franklin might plea, they would really stick it to him on the charges.

Right now, he was looking at a minimum of twenty years, and if the Feds got involved, they might never let the man go. The fact he'd taken millions of dollars in bribes over the years and certainly paid no taxes on those monies meant everyone would be lining up to nail Franklin to the door. If he could simply get the man out of Atlanta, it gave them options. For the short term, getting the trial moved opened up the chance to see which agencies wanted to play ball with Franklin.

As Clemmons considered the options for a fair trial, Webb considered the far longer game Franklin's defense would require. If the man went to prison, he'd be dead before he was there a week. So any sentence was a sentence to solitary confinement, and even then, there were no guarantees he wouldn't be killed.

Right now, the best he could hope for was to get the trial moved, begin working on a plea deal with the State of Georgia and see how the Feds would handle it.

With a lot of luck, Franklin could end up doing, say, five to ten years in a minimum security facility run by the U. S. for white collar criminals.

The man *might* be able to survive that.

Right now, Webb had to get the man a fair trial somewhere else.

Finally, Clemmons turned around in his desk chair.

"Gentlemen, given the material this trial is set to discuss, the current environment in the local area, and the…" he paused, seeming to look for the right word, "overall dramatic nature of the case, I will concede the accused may indeed face a substantial challenge in finding a jury of his peers to judge him fairly.

"May I ask where the defense team would suggest this trial be moved to?"

Webb smiled warmly and began, "Your Honor, I believe any one of a number of major metropolitan areas offer my client the opportunity for a fair trial by a jury of his peers. I have taken the liberty of listing them here for your review. As you'll see, they are all relatively close to Atlanta, but do not have the history of civil rights challenges nor do any of them have the more recent problems of police corruption."

Clemmons looked at the attorney for the State of Georgia, a man named Smithson. "Counselor? Have you seen this list?"

"I have, your Honor."

"And the opinion of the state is?"

"We would prefer the trial be held in Tallahassee, Florida, Spartanburg, South Carolina, or Knoxville, Tennessee, your Honor. But, of course, that is only our preferences. You are, of course, the man who can make this decision."

"Mr. Webb? Is there any particular weight you ascribe to this list? Is the order based on preference?"

"No your Honor, all the cities on that list are equally amenable to my client and his request for a fair trial."

Judge Clemmons considered the list, then reviewed something on his computer monitor. Tapping the keys a few times, he entered some bit of data, then navigated with the mouse for nearly three minutes.

"Then I will grant the accused's request for a change of venue." He turned and faced Robert Webb, "Mr. Franklin will face the first of his preliminary court dates in Knoxville, Tennessee in three weeks. Until then, he will remain in the care of the Atlanta Police Department in their Dekalb County detention facility.

"Mr. Smithson?"

"Yes, your Honor?"

"See to it that the defendant survives these next few weeks in custody before he is transferred to Knox County's care."

"Yes, your Honor."

"You gentlemen are dismissed, thank you."

72

JON CROCKETT HAD RETURNED to Wyoming after the Four Horseman delivered Franklin to the Marshal's Service, and in the ensuing weeks, he'd quietly watched Dimitry's work pound nail after nail into the coffin of the defense. Even in the sparsely populated country of western Wyoming, he'd heard references to "that crazy shit going on in Georgia" when he'd been sitting at the little diner in Star Valley one morning, on his way to look at a small rental home he was buying.

The wait to see justice was agonizing, though. He'd stayed busy with work in the mornings and with the daily tasks of learning the nuances of his own land. Despite the change of scenery, though, he still felt the memories of the things that had impacted him for a lifetime.

Looking at the elk and deer trails along the various ridges of his land, he could hear Merrick's father teaching him and Merrick how to read the signs. Memories of hunting with Merrick and Mr. Gose in Shady Dale thirty five years earlier bubbled up constantly as he made his way through the timber and underbrush of Afton.

"See here, boys? Look at how these tracks run along here. They go over here, then over here, than double back on themselves a bit. Just like a woman, so's you can be sure, these here was made by a doe. Think of your mamas shopping at the mall.

"'Oh, what's over here, what'd I miss over there?' Get it? When men go to the store, we go in, we get what we came for, and we get on down the road. Men's got work to do."

Mr. Gose walked over perhaps fifteen feet, off of the small ridge top he and the boys had been standing on. His eyes searched the ground, and, finding what he wanted, he hunkered down and called the young men over.

"Look here, Tweedle Dumb and Tweedle Dumber." He was pointing down at the ground, to the faintest of disturbances in the leaf litter.

"See how these leaves are disturbed? Not enough to really see nothin', but if you don't look at them directly, you can see what's goin' on."

Merrick and Jon had looked and, after a few moments, the man knew the boys had seen what he was pointing at.

Merrick had seen it first, and only seconds later, Jon had seen it. A faint disturbance in the leaf cover. The older man moved a few leaves to the side, revealing a large deer track.

"This here's a big ole boy. See how he keeps off this ridge?" He pointed back to where the more obvious trail was, perhaps four feet higher in elevation. "Up there, where them does and fawns an' young bucks'll run, they'll been seen by anybody. Either side of this ridge, though, that's where your bucks are going to slip. They know they can use the wind coming up the hill to their advantage in the morning and down the hill in the evening.

"What else to you boys see here?"

Jon figured it out first this time, "These tracks run straight. He knows what he's doing and where he's going. He's not wasting time."

"Yep. That's good, boy."

Merrick was still staring at the trail, "Dad, when's he run this ridge?"

The man looked hard at the track and reflected a moment. "If I had to say, he's here an hour or two before daylight and an hour or two after sunset. You ain't gonna kill him here. He'll be holed up in the swamp," the man nodded in the directions the tracks were going, "or down in Mystery Valley," nodding back the other way, "by the time you get up in the morning.

"He ain't gettin' killed on this ridge, though."

The old man had killed that buck three weeks later, as the first slivers of daylight had exposed him slipping along the faint trail that led into a nearly impenetrable area they all called Mystery Valley.

These were the memories Crockett encountered nearly everywhere he went on his ranch. In the years since he'd bought the property, of course, he'd walked or ridden it extensively, but with the warm weather and being there full time, he'd begun to finally feel at home.

Even though the landscape was far harsher than he'd ever hunted in Georgia, he mentally began to name areas based on their similarities to those he'd found with Merrick, Peter, and Brandon all those years ago on the lease he'd learned to hunt on near Shady Dale, Georgia.

The ridge that ran immediately behind the big house had now been named the Cedar Ridge, the river bottom beyond the alfalfa field was the Swamp, although it was filled with alders and not privet, and the drop off to the south of his home, where the land began to fall away towards the Snake River Valley, had become The Bowl. The three farm roads that came together to the east of the hayfields was simply The Triangle, and the large meadow that could be seen from the big back porch of the house had become the Upper Field.

Even though they had hunted and fished it for years, the real joy the four young men had gotten from the Gose family's hunting lease in Shady Dale had simply been the feeling of safety. The problems they had there were ones that could be worked out – getting a truck out of the mudhole, dragging a deer up a hill, even using the outhouse on a freezing-cold night.

It had proven to be a respite from the life they had lived, and, while none of them had ever really discussed it, that feeling of belonging, of being a part of an ecosystem where everything had a reason, change came slowly, and the few things that could be left to chance were far easier to overcome than in the world the young men actually lived in.

Peter had said it best many years later, during one of the corporate meetings, this time in Bali, "For me, the outdoors will always be something I associate with the four of us and Shady Dale. I'd give anything to sit by that campfire again, to play Hearts or Spades at that kitchen table, to sit around after deer season and drink underage beers with those boys again."

As he stood on the windswept ridge at Afton, looking back to the Southeast where he knew, thousands of miles away, Shady Dale must surely lay, Crockett couldn't help but smile. It *had* been one of the best things in his life.

Wyoming wasn't without challenges, though. It simply didn't have the population of Atlanta, so Crockett was – not for the first time – having to rethink his business practices. Money had always been easy to come by, of course: he'd learned that from his Dad before he was old enough to ride a bike. Real estate, the way Jon Crockett played the game, was always going to offer the chance to make money.

He'd made it big as the new kid on the block in the late nineties, he'd made it as the bubble was getting bigger before 2007, and he'd managed to still generate double-digit gains after the meltdown in 2008.

Somewhere in the back of his mind, he knew he could simply coast the rest of the way through life – his various investments outside of the Shady Dale Social Club Trust all generated far more than he could spend to live comfortably, and the fact the Afton was paid off meant his actual expenses each month were far less than most families.

Despite this, the voice of his father and countless coaches from his football days sounded in his head, telling him to keep moving, keep growing, keep expanding. Sitting there on the Cedar Ridge, nearly a thousand feet above the house, looking to the northeast as two Golden Eagles rode the thermals below him, he couldn't help but be optimistic.

This was the future, already here in the present.

73

THAT NIGHT, AFTER HE'D COME DOWN from the Cedar Ridge, he'd checked his emails and the news on his laptop in the big open kitchen and was not surprised to find Presley Franklin's defense had requested and been granted a change of venue for his police corruption trial. Quickly changing email servers, he'd sent a short encrypted message to Dimitry to focus some energy on east Tennessee for social media and news reports, trying to subtly influence the local residents on the dirty cop who would be facing trial in their town.

The wild card, of course, was if the State of Georgia would allow Franklin to plea bargain on his guilt. Crockett had consulted with Joel Habersham about it earlier that week, and Habersham conceded with the current workload the DA's office had, they very well might opt for a plea in this case, then quietly bury the whole mess to avoid the public relations nightmare of yet another corrupt officer among the ranks of the APD.

The old attorney, as much as Crockett hated to admit it, was right. "What they'll do, Jon, is give him some time in some low-security setup, the kind they send insider trading guys to. He'll get ten or twenty years and be out on parole in five, maybe six years. Depending on how things turn out and who's paying attention, he might even still have a pension and his retirement benefits.

"Bastard'll probably live to be old, fat, and happy."

"What would the Feds do if he pleas at the state level?"

"Well, the IRS might try to get him for evasion, but they'd hit third in this rotation. The Feds have an even bigger caseload but would get priority. If they think he'll go away quietly, they might just sit on the case. If enough people were pissed off, you might get them to strike while the iron is hot and indict him for corruption, unlawful flight, and a laundry list of stuff he's done, but everything they've shown us – hell, even what your people found – says he'd acted alone.

"There's no master criminal at work here, just an opportunist. I doubt Justice wants to worry about it unless the state fumbles the ball in the case."

"So this guy spends his career beating the system, abusing his responsibilities, and doesn't get punished for it?"

"Sad to say, but probably not in the way you'd be happy to see, Jon. Certainly not after the trouble he caused you."

"Damn. Joel, you know that's shitty. Franklin'd be out of prison when he's sixty and just keep right on living. Pretty good retirement deal."

"Yes, and you know that's the same sort of thing that drove me from being on that side of the bar."

"I know, Joel. I know. Thanks for the insight, have a great rest of the day."

"And you, Jon. Be good."

As he sat there in the kitchen of the big log house, Crockett idly opened up Google Earth on his laptop and began looking up various spots in Knoxville, Tennessee. He'd gone to college not far from the town and knew it well from several of his father's friends who had lived and worked there. As he did, he began to formulate a plan.

A more fitting sentence for Presley Franklin.

• • •

All in all, Presley Franklin couldn't really complain about his situation. Instead of being locked down in the jail, waiting for his trial, the fact he was a cop had gotten him locked down in a safe house run by the Justice Department. Three different two man teams rotated into and out of the small apartment near midtown Atlanta every three days, and, while he could not leave the building, he was allowed to use the gym, sit on the patio, and even swim in the pool.

It was far better than what being in general population in one of the city jails would be like.

Still, he was nervous. Try as he might, he couldn't understand how he'd gotten here. He'd been on the beach, in Punta Mita, free and clear, and then, he'd simply woken up in Grady Hospital. He could vaguely remember drinking with some tourists, a old shot up soldier and his girl-friend and going back to the little cottage he'd rented, but then? His memories simply ceased until he awoke handcuffed to a hospital bed in Grady Memorial one afternoon.

Somebody had gotten him, and Webb, his attorney, had tried to get the Marshal's to share how Franklin had been returned to the U. S., but they could not – or would not – disclose the facts. The Patriot Act kept things like this safe for their people and bounty hunters.

For a man who had been so careful for so long, not knowing was the worst part of it. He was counting on Webb to get the trial moved, and to hopefully cut some kind of deal, but he also knew this was a little like playing poker – tip your hand too quickly and you'll lose. So Franklin was resigned to waiting and living under a strange version of house arrest on the taxpayers' dime.

Two weeks later, the youngest Marshal in the rotation to babysit Presley had come in and simply said, "Franklin, trial's being moved, you'll be going to Knoxville tomorrow. Your counselor is on his way to give you the scoop, but if you need anything give us a list." The young man, named Mark, glanced around the room, "I guess you know how this works."

"Yes I do. And I appreciate it, Mark. When Robert gets here, please show him in."

"Of course, Presley."

• • •

Robert Webb knew Franklin's defense was a loser, but the court system had been so diluted with petty cases and silliness that no prosecutor's office could keep up with their workload. If he and Franklin could play a long game and wear the DA down, they'd offer a plea bargain and his client would spend a few years in a low-security facility.

His request to move the trial wasn't originally part of the strategy, but the amount of fervor Atlanta had shown against the case simply added to his defense plans.

Knoxville would be fine, and since his client was receiving death threats, he certainly couldn't be held in the general population awaiting trial. Presley Franklin could live a quiet life for a few months in an apartment with the Marshals babysitting him while the wheels of justice slowly rolled on.

Webb was somewhat surprised the move to Knoxville had created some aggression on the part of the locals. There had been angry protests at the Knoxville City Hall, the mayor's office had fielded a number of calls expressing displeasure that "their" courts were being used for a dirty cop from Atlanta, and at least two effigies of Presley Franklin had been hung in the town – one on the front lawn of the courthouse and another from the Gay Street bridge nearby.

Of course, the reality was this was the work of a handful of conspirators – Dimitry's people on VOIP phone lines from around the world and his own mastery of social media had infiltrated the right groups on

Facebook and Twitter to get them stirred up. Merrick had used some of his own contacts in the Atlanta underworld – and a few thousand dollars – to send angry young men to Knoxville to add to the protests, stop traffic, and generally be a nuisance.

In many ways, it was no different than the systems he and Bradley had used for many years to push a given political agenda in faraway places, and it was ironic they did it so close to home.

Both Merrick and Bradley kept Crockett apprised of the pot-stirring they were doing, and Dimitry, as he always did, continued to monitor communications coming into and out of Robert Webb's office to find Franklin. Eight days after Franklin had been moved to Knoxville, Dimitry found the safe house.

He'd communicated the information to Jon Crockett and agreed to further monitor any and all communications for any changes.

74

FOR THOSE WHO HAVE NEVER flown into McGee-Tyson Airport outside of Knoxville, the small size can be deceiving. Despite the age, the facility is open, bright, and travelers from all points of the world can easily find themselves deplaning in the foothills of the Smokey Mountains. Four days before Franklin was scheduled for his first appearance in court, three men arrived at a home they had rented for three weeks, two having arrived on flights that afternoon and the third having driven from Atlanta that morning.

Merrick Gose had arrived first, and as he had done for many years, he'd used two different scanners to ascertain there were no listening or recording devices anywhere in the home. Working in America was a great deal easier that overseas, but he realized how unconditioned his countrymen were to the world of espionage and blackmail he'd worked in for so long.

He'd been amazed at how often he'd found "bugs" in the hotel rooms and homes he'd rented to take care of things for Jon and Bradley over the years and yet, no one seemed to ever really use any of the information they could have gathered – at least in the U. S.

It was shortly after one o'clock when Bradley arrived, carrying only an overnight bag and a backpack, and the two men caught up on the patio. Despite what the calendar said, the weather was mild with a hint of a breeze.

"Well, what do you think, 'Rick? What's our boy going to do?"

Merrick looked off in the distance, his dark eyes squinting. "Kill Franklin."

"Well, no shit. Thankee-sai for your observation of the obvious. How's he going to do it?"

Gose, ever the sniper and campaigner, leaned forward in his seat. "if *I* was going to do it, I'd kill him on the courthouse steps from across the river; rooftop shot, maybe six or seven hundred yards out. The sun'll be behind you, so the light's good. They'd likely be bringing him in the backdoor of the courthouse in bright morning sunlight, so there's plenty of contrast. At some point, he'll be walking straight towards or away from you, so there's a high probability of a mortal hit, even if the drop is wrong. Less than a second of flight time, too. If he's shooting from the north, maybe a fourth or fifth story window shot from the Hilton or the rooftop of the Convention Center? The light's gonna be tricky in either one of those because the sun is still low on the horizon. Even from a shaded area, he'd deal with some light diffraction within the lenses of the best scopes money can buy.

"And I don't like it because as soon as the shot rings out, they'll plan on trying to vector it and their first instinct'll be to look north."

Joyner's face scrunched up, "Think so? Why not south, towards the river?" The other man nodded.

"The river's always a barrier to men's minds. They forget that the bullet doesn't care what it's shooting over. Even if they hear the shot from there, it's worth at least an extra ten or fifteen minutes before anyone thinks to go look. We can add to that by closing a road or two to traffic. That'll push first response back ... I don't know ... another ten minutes?

"On the other hand, where they've got him holed up is some apartments upriver just a bit, and you could take him from this little park on the other side of the river. The problem is, we can't be sure of when they'll leave, how they'll load him in the car, and even where they'll load him. If they decide to load from the northside lot, which is the logical course, there simply isn't a shot. Besides, we can't be sure they won't change safe houses in the meantime.

"But we *do* know where the bastard is going..."

Joyner listened, mentally thinking through the plan as the sniper outlined it. The logic was sound, the timeframe seemed right, and a twenty-minute head start meant they would be far out of the area before any kind of response – tactical or otherwise – could be mounted.

The other man sighed, "Yeah, that would work, but between me and you, can Jon hit that shot? I know he could have, long ago, but ..." He let the sentence trail off.

Gose chuckled, "Easily. Two years ago, when I was visiting Afton, he and I did some long-range steel plate shooting. Sumbitch was hitting everything out to 800 yards. MOA all the way."

Joyner's eyebrows raised a bit. "Bastard shoulda worked with us."

Merrick began to laugh, "I know what you're doing, Brad, but it's not going to work."

"What?"

"This was how *I'd* do it. You know Jon isn't going to lob a 168 grainer at Franklin from a half a mile out and call it good enough. He wants Franklin to *know* who it is that's killing him."

The two men sat quietly for a few minutes, both lost in their thoughts. Finally, Bradley turned, "So how do we kill Franklin without taking out any good guys?"

"That's the real challenge, isn't it, boyo? Come on, we got another two hours before Crockett gets here, let's go for a ride. Binoculars are in my truck."

By the time Jon Crockett had landed and gotten to the rented house, the two other men, long skilled tacticians in undeclared wars around the world, had a plan Crockett would approve of.

75

FRANKLIN'S INITIAL COURT DATA had been set for June 12th, but the vagaries of judicial calendars pushed it back until June 23rd. Unbeknownst to anyone involved in his case or the protection detail assigned to him, Crockett had again shifted Dimitry's effort back to Atlanta, leaving the locals in Knoxville to find other problems to worry about. As the threats dissipated and the social media keyboard activists quieted, both Webb and Franklin became more confident in the case. Fewer eyes on the actions of the District Attorney's office meant a far better chance of a plea deal being offered, so despite Franklin's unease at being "cooped up," their plan was working.

Sitting with his client the afternoon before the first hearing was to take place, Webb went over the process.

"Tomorrow morning, the Marshals here will make sure you're up, get you some breakfast or whatever, and they'll transport you to the courthouse – it's only about five minutes from here - where you'll have the first preliminary hearing. The DA decided months ago – actually right after you fled the country – to indict, but the charges have changed a bit. That won't really change anything, but we've kinda skipped around a bit.

"Your disappearance demonstrated you are obviously a flight risk, so we're operating past what's "normal" in court. The good news is that could help with any potential appeal, but you'd be doing that from wherever they sentenced you."

"Thanks, Robert, I appreciate you thinking I'm innocent. Who's paying who here?"

"Presley, the question of your guilt or innocence makes no difference to me. I don't need to look at the evidence the state is going to bring yet, because you're basically locked into a guilty plea unless there's some technical reason for the case to be thrown out. If this goes to trial, you're likely screwed anyway. Effectively, they have all the evidence IAD collected, plus the information your captors surrendered to the Marshals.

"To add to that, if the state fumbles the ball, not to worry, the Feds could have a field day with the case, and the IRS is lined up to wring every penny they can out of you in Tax Court with evasion charges.

"Presley, saving you from incarceration or trying to salvage your tarnished reputation is the least of my actual worries. I'm trying to save your life, because if they take it to trial and they elect to send you to prison, you're a dead man, even in solitary. Somebody will want to get you, and somebody *will* get you.

"We've got to play the game, and you might not like it, but let me remind you of who took the bribes, who hid the evidence, who sold out the police department and the informants that didn't push your illicit dealings forward."

Franklin sat quietly and, for the first time, noticed he didn't lash out at the accusations Webb was speaking of. For years, be it Captain Swift, IAD investigators, even other dirty cops, he'd staunchly defend his innocence.

Not now. He realized he was caught.

Not only caught, but to tired or scared to fight.

"So then what happens?"

"They'll set a date for the arraignment, which might be a few more weeks, then we'll have some of what we call "readiness conferences" and "motion hearings" – as a cop, you know the drill. I'd expect if we actually go to court, it might be September or October."

"When do you think they'll offer a plea?"

"Usually? At the eleventh hour. Maybe a week or so before the trial is set."

Franklin seemed to think about it for a moment, stopped, opened his mouth to say something, then paused again. Webb leaned forward.

"Yes?"

"Nothin'." He looked around, "I guess I'll just get used to this place. Could you at least see if I can be allowed to take a walk every once in awhile? I mean, I can't complain about the house they've got me arrested in, but it'd be nice to be able to go for a stroll along the river. Those little walking trails are nice looking."

He looked out across the Tennessee River from the living room window, "I don't need them to let me go to the national park, just a freakin' walk."

"I'll see what I can do, Presley."

"I know you will. It's just frustrating." The man sat down heavily in the chair, "I spent a lifetime with complete freedom to do whatever I wanted. Working both sides against the middle, going and coming whenever I pleased.

"If I'm totally honest, I wouldn't give two shits about going for a walk, but now that I can't?"

Webb smiled, "You want to take a walk."

Franklin looked at the attorney, "Yeah. I do." His eyes shot back to the river and to the little park he'd seen from the porch of the safe house. Perhaps three hundred yards away, kids played on the little playground, an older couple walked along the narrow boardwalk on the riverbank, and, at one of the benches, a single man in a business suit sat, looking at his phone.

"I'll see you in the morning, counselor."

"That you will, detective."

76

AT 6:30 THE NEXT MORNING, one of the Marshals knocked on Franklin's bedroom door. "Time to rise, Detective." Upon hearing the man rustling around, the young officer withdrew, back to the kitchen, where he poured his second cup of coffee.

His partner, a man name Tristan, walked in from where he'd been on the porch. "Sleeping Beauty up?"

"Yeah, he's moving. Got him a big day today." The two men made small talk while they unpacked several sausage biscuits they had brought when they relieved the night shift team. As they sat in the kitchen, they heard the shower run, and twenty or so minutes later, Presley Franklin emerged from his bedroom in a dark gray suit and tie.

"Good morning, gentlemen." He poured a cup of coffee, then pointed to one of the biscuits, "May I?"

Tristan, caught with a mouthful, managed to say something that sounded like "Go ahead" but came out more like "Gaw'here."

"Thanks, guys. Ya'll sleep well?" The two men nodded and they continued to eat breakfast. For the next forty five minutes, the three made small talk and drank coffee as they had for several weeks. Despite the fact Franklin was a prisoner, the men on his protection detail all seemed to be nice enough. They had enough shared experiences that, on occasion, they could talk about some of the oddball things that happened as law officers.

At 8:10, the phone belonging to the younger Marshal beeped and a text message displayed on the screen. "Detective, it's time to go. The car will be downstairs in five minutes."

"You guys aren't driving me?"

"No sir. S.O.P. in cases like this is for different teams to handle different stages. This gives us an advantage in prisoner transfer – twice the men at choke points. Normally, we do this to ensure a prisoner cannot easily overpower our people and escape, but in this case, since there have been threats made against you we believe to be credible, this gives us extra eyes at each transfer point."

Tristan looked at his own phone, "White Suburban, plain Georgia plates," he said, to no one in particular.

"So you guys don't know exactly who is picking up who? Or what to look for until they text you?"

"Yep. Less chance of bad guys being able to infiltrate our plans. Using civilian tags on vehicles also gives us some anonymity in high profile cases like this."

Franklin was impressed. He remembered several times in Atlanta when high-ranking gang members had been gunned down during transfers to and from court, and even though he didn't know the particulars of those killings, he knew corrupt local officials who undoubtedly benefited from their deaths.

Hell, he'd have done it, too, if it was the smart thing to do. The Marshals obviously knew a thing or two about getting people to and from court safely.

"So, what would happen if there was a threat on the way?" he asked as they stepped into the elevator.

"Couple of different ways to play that, depending on how far they'd have to go. Obviously, evasion is the first move, but we have some people along the route for things like that. You won't see them, but they're there."

Presley decided to see if he could pick them out on his way to the courthouse.

The three stood outside for just under a minute when, as promised, a white GMC Suburban and dark tinted windows pulled in. The two men inside wore dark sunglasses and deep navy-blue suits in the bright morning light, and as the big SUV came to a stop, the driver flashed a badge.

It was obvious they had done this before. Not a word passed between the four Marshals as they opened the rear passenger door and Franklin got in. Tristan closed the door, knocked the side twice, and the big GMC was underway.

• • •

As soon as he got into the back seat of the Suburban, Franklin noted the difference in the attitude of the Marshals. These men were all business. No introductions, no greetings, nothing. Hell, the bastards never even acknowledged him. As they began to pull away, the driver, speaking with the hint of a Southern accent, finally spoke.

"Mr. Franklin, I'm unsure what the Marshals told you at the safe house, but we have intel suggesting a credible threat on your life this morning. As such, I expect you to do exactly what I say, when I say it. You've undoubtedly noticed, this is a bone-stock fleet vehicle – there is no armor, no bulletproof glass, nothing that GMC didn't put into thousands of other trucks just like this one. Anonymity is our friend here, but in order to successfully do that, we are not going the most direct way to court this morning.

"Do you understand?"

Franklin nodded.

"Fair enough."

The SUV pulled into the traffic, turning North out of the apartments where the safehouse was located. As it did, Franklin noted another white Suburban – this one a Chevrolet – making its way down the street. As he watched, the big truck made a u-turn and began to follow them.

"Uh, you boys see that?"

The driver made eye contact in the rear view mirror, "The guy busting a u-turn? Yeah. Look again, Mr. Franklin. It's some broad with a couple screaming kids in the car. She's not a threat."

Presley looked again – *damn* – the guy was right. As he watched the lady in the other Suburban, she was yelling into her rear view mirror. At the same time, a small hand waved over the back of the passenger seat.

Just as quickly as she had turned around, she turned the SUV into a small medical office on the right side of the road.

"*No threat there,*" thought Franklin, "*unless you were getting immunized.*"

As they continued further into downtown Knoxville, Franklin began to relax. Yes, it was court, yes, there was the chance he would spend the rest of his life in prison, but, he reflected, he didn't have to run anymore. Leave it to Webb now. Leave it to the courts. Leave it to a jury of his peers.

The Four Horsemen were the furthest thing from his mind.

77

THE MARSHAL RIDING SHOTGUN suddenly spoke up, "Frank…" He held up his phone, indicating a text message. "Take a left here, they think they got a guy down the street."

Frank – Presley could only assume that was the driver's name – dutifully turned left without hesitation.

From the back seat, Presley asked, "What's going on?"

The Marshal in the passenger seat simply said, "looks like someone was going to try to bounce you, Mr. Franklin. Knoxville P. D. is on it now."

Suddenly, it sank in for Franklin: *people were trying to kill him.*

Another message beeped through on the Marshal's phone.

"Grab a right here, Frank."

Two more times, messages popped up, forcing Franklin and his team further away from the courthouse. To their credit, neither of the men caring for Presley seemed worried. They were, of course, guarded, and Franklin could only assume the other Marshals that would be guarding their route that morning were now watching the wrong streets.

They had been in the car less than five minutes.

• • •

Jon Crockett stared at his phone, waiting to hear from Bradley and Merrick. He'd gotten a text a few minutes ago, indicating Franklin had been picked up, but, just like hunting, you could never be sure if the quarry would show.

So, he resigned himself to do the hardest thing in the world – wait.

Whatever would happen would happen soon, but there was no way of knowing if today was the day.

• • •

Very few things scared Presley Franklin, so it was surprising when he felt the first nibbles of fear begin at the base of his neck. He tried to reason with himself – if there was a real threat, the Marshals would be acting far differently. They would be taking evasive actions. They'd be calling in support. They would be driving faster. Instead, he could only note that Frank and the other Marshal seemed preoccupied, but otherwise, they were calm and cool.

Inexplicably, as they passed what Franklin could only assume was Neyland Stadium, Frank's phone rang. Presley was more than a little surprised, but the man continued to drive and answered it, holding it up to his ear.

"This is Rosdale."

"Yeah, he's here. No, we had some trouble, but KPD has confirmed no credible threats. We are making our way back to the secure route and expect to be at the courthouse in six minutes."

"*WHAT*? Jesus! Please repeat that…"

"Okay, patch him through and we'll pass it to him."

Rosdale – Presley could only assume that was Frank's last name – put his thumb over the mouthpiece of the phone, "Get this – this guy's law-yer" he nodded towards Franklin – "wants to be patched through to talk to his client! Where the fuck do these people get off? How the fuck do they get our numbers?"

The other man shook his head, "Shit gets crazier every day." The man shook his head, "What are you gonna do?"

"Shit! I'ma put the bastard on the phone."

Presley was more than a little surprised that Webb would have gone to all the trouble to find out how to call the Marshals who were transporting him, but he figured it must be important. Ever the cop, he noted the next stoplight - still several hundred yards down the street – had a Knoxville Public Works van parked in the turn lane past the intersection with orange cones blocking all but one lane on their side of the road. Traffic was being waved through by a dark skinned man with an orange vest and an equally bright orange flag.

Rosdale handed the phone to Franklin. "I guess you heard. Your attorney couldn't wait to talk to you, so HQ patched him through to my line."

"Make it quick, we'll be there in about four minutes."

Presley took the phone from the man and waited to hear Webb's voice. A short burst of static shot through the line, and then, assuming Webb had made the connection, he spoke tentatively into the phone, "Hello?"

• • •

From the cargo area of a nondescript van, Crockett waited patiently, then the other man's voice came over the line, "Hello?"

"Good Morning, Presley. I guess you remember who this is. I just wanted to share something with you before you have your first – and maybe last – day in court."

From the backseat of the Suburban, Franklin began to laugh, "Sorry, cocksucker, your boys missed me. The Marshals gave them the slip and I'm about to walk into the courthouse."

"Really? Because I think you're rolling up to the stoplight on Neyland and Cronan."

Presley strained to look at the street signs and realized what Crockett said was true. *How the fuck did he know?* Franklin began to look around and unconsciously moved towards the middle of the big bench seat.

"That's a good guess, just a bad one." Franklin hoped the bluff would work and he was straining to look and see who – or where – he was being observed from.

"Oh, I don't know. I didn't get this old guessing wrong. Besides, your tie is crooked."

Franklin instinctively checked his tie in the rear-view mirror. It was perfectly straight.

"Now I know you're guessing, boy. Face it, you missed me. Besides, this isn't Atlanta and it ain't the Wild West. You guys never cleaned up anything, and now? You're just pissed I know the truth. I'm another loose end you'll never tie."

There was a short pause, and Presley wondered if the call had been dropped. At that moment, Crockett's gruff voice came back to the line. The connection didn't sound as clear, but the man was there.

"Tell you what, Presley. Look to your left, about two hundred yards. See the white van parked at the service entrance?"

Franklin turned to peer out the window. Just as the man on the phone had stated, there was a white work van, with one of the back doors open. The bright morning light made it difficult to see inside, but there was enough contrast to see a man in the back, seated at some kind of workbench.

Jon Crockett spoke into the headset he was wearing as he peered through the scope of the Steyr AUG, nestled into sandbags on a shooting bench in the back of the van, "*Nemo me impune lacessit,* cocksucker…"

78

WHEN A PRISONER TRANSPORT detail for the U. S. Marshals Service loses a prisoner, either through escape or attack, the sheer volume of paperwork is simply mind numbing.

For Rosdale and his partner, Jeff Dealoach, the next few days were a blur of meetings, debriefings, and report after report. Time after time, they were forced to explain to superiors, then the Knoxville and Atlanta Police Departments, the Knoxville and Atlanta prosecutor's offices, and four separate federal law enforcement entities how their prisoner – one Presley Franklin – had been shot not once, but three times by an unknown assailants. Robert Webb, Franklin's attorney, had, in fact, not called *anyone* – he had been at the courthouse, speaking with two courthouse employees and video surveillance validated the man had not used his phone in a nearly fifteen-minute window before and after Franklin had been killed.

The coroner's report provided even less to go on – they were reasonably certain all three bullets had originated from the same place and only shards of the copper jackets had been recovered. The first had gone wide to the left, shattering the glass of the back window and destroying the phone Franklin had been holding, driving shards of the broken device into Franklin's face and punching a quarter-inch hole through the man's hand.

The other two had taken Franklin immediately below the eyes, breaking both cheekbones, breaching the cranial vault, expanding rapidly, and continuing beyond the man's broken, leaking head through the other window of the Suburban and becoming lost in the industrial complex beyond the crime scene. The best guess the coroner could produce was that Presley Franklin had been struck and killed by three thick-jacketed bullets of at least 22 caliber, traveling at least 3,000 feet per second.

Over and over again, Dealoach and Rosdale were interviewed and – for want of a better word – interrogated – for the actions they had taken and not taken. When the shots had rung out, Rosdale had reacted instantly, stomping on the gas, running the red light and evading the presumed attack. Dealoach had immediately called in a code 10-57 – Shots Fired - then jumped into the backseat and attempted to save Franklin, but seeing the mess of the man's head, he quickly understood he and Rosdale were now a code 19-39 – Prisoner Killed in Transport.

Fucked, in other words.

79

WHAT MADE THE FACTS behind the attack worse was the startling lack of them.

The Knoxville Police Department had no record of any communication or persons of interest despite the texts Dealoach had received that morning. Both men's phone records had been analyzed by numerous agencies and had proven to be digital dead ends. Even worse, the phone records for Rosdale's destroyed phone clearly showed the call that had come in, but the patched line was a VOIP that had been jumped from multiple servers inside and outside the United States before the actual call had been placed.

Through it all, their stories had never changed – the texts they had received about suspicious persons, the secondary and then tertiary routes, and finally, the strange phone call that had come through on Rosdale's phone.

Both Rosdale and Dealoach, trained observers and competent field operators, were able to describe all of the details of the ride. Unfortunately, they were men trained in a very myopic version of situational awareness, and the van Crockett had shot Franklin from was simply outside their normal threat range for a simple prisoner transport.

By the time a team of Marshals and police had arrived back at the scene of the shooting, Merrick, who had been in the orange vest and the Knoxville Public Works van directing traffic, and the van Crockett shot from – driven by Bradley – were both long gone. The vans had been returned to the motor pool where they had been stolen from in the early morning hours.

Wiped clean of fingerprints, disinfected with an aerosol that degraded DNA within minutes, and the proper license plates bolted back on.

They'd even washed them and filled up the fuel tanks.

As the days passed, there was simply no usable evidence in the murder of Presley Franklin.

The lead CSI on the case, a career man named Charlie Ottsa, worked himself into a frenzy, trying to find any physical evidence of the crime. He and his team worked in ever-increasing areas away from the crime scene, never recovering any parts of the bullet, fired cases, or any evidence suggesting where the shots could have originated.

They spoke with witnesses, each of whom gave different accounts of where they felt the shots had come from. Some claimed there had been a Knoxville Public Works van in the area, others claimed two vans.

Still others claimed to have not seen *any* vans.

It was the same with the number of shots – some swore a veritable barrage of gunfire had erupted, spraying lead all over the streets, while others said there had been only one or two.

The inability of human beings to be aware of their surroundings – the same trait the Four Horsemen had realized so long ago – had allowed them to once again kill and simply disappear into seemingly thin air.

80

JON, MERRICK, AND BRADLEY had executed Franklin, and the rest of Merrick's plan, nearly effortlessly. They stayed in the rental house for another two days, reminiscing about their pasts and enjoying each other's company. Inevitably, though, they all knew it would end, and while Merrick and Bradley would leave on the morning of the third day, Crockett's flight wasn't until much later that afternoon.

The men, brothers united by their past and a lifetime of supporting one another, hugged a long goodbye, each knowing from life it could never be a certainty if or when they would see the others again.

As he sat on the porch of the now empty rental house drinking coffee, Jon Crockett began to feel – in some dark part of his soul – that maybe this was it.

Maybe it was finally over.

He searched the hidden corners of his mind, looking for the anger, the pain, the lust for revenge. It simply wasn't there anymore. The darkness, long a part of every day, was gone.

Crockett stood, finished the last of his coffee, and began to walk inside. It was time to live. As he opened the door to the house, he smiled at the thought of a young woman he would never see again, "Isn't it pretty to think so?"

January 20, 2019 – October 21, 2021
Elk Mountain, Wyoming

Unbroken
By Prodigal Sons

I close my eyes to the death that surrounds me
I swallow my fear and harden my gaze
The enemy creeps, up all around me
But my soul is like ice while my anger's ablaze
I'm unbroken
I'm unbroken
I'm unbroken
Unbroken
I defy death and I spit on your grave
They come to sling iron and come dealin' hate
They breached these walls and sit on the throne
The angels lie silent and the Devil holds our fate
But in the end, to the end, I face these bastards alone
I'm unbroken
I'm unbroken
I'm unbroken
Unbroken
I defy death and I spit on your grave
Chicken man on the 'sixty and Red in the bush
The blood runs hot and the specters fly true
Feel the burn deep inside see the bodies as they crush
See the crucifixion in the crosshairs and the pain I imbue
I'm unbroken
I'm unbroken
I'm unbroken
Unbroken
I defy death and I spit on your grave

ACKNOWLEDGEMENTS

NO ONE SITS DOWN to write a book of any size without taking from others, and this work is no exception. Along the way, there have been many who have helped me to become the man who could tell this story. Innumerable coaches, teachers, mentors and friends all added to the person I could become, and I thank you.

I also wish to thank my parents, who have never failed to remind me that I could, in fact, do anything I set my mind to. I love you both very much, and I hope you know how wonderful you both really are.

And no one can write a book like this without those who can listen to your crazy ideas at odd times both day and night, and my brothers – Brent, Brad, and Robert – certainly helped to do that. You guys have no idea how much your help, guidance, and ideas have encouraged me as I dove ever deeper into the world of Prodigal Sons.

I'd also like to thank Sergeant Major Ron Kirby of the United States Marine Corps (Retired), for his guidance and suggestions on what it meant to be a Marine in the 1990s–and if there is a mistake in the book, I will be the first to admit that mistake was from my notes, not Ron's recollection. I truly appreciate your time and your counsel.

ABOUT THE AUTHOR

CHRIS GROOTE is a well-known ghostwriter in the business world who has finally taken the plunge into fiction with his novel Prodigal Sons. He has lived and worked in the South his whole life and professes a weakness for old guns and trucks. Chris lives in Statesboro, Georgia with his fiancé and business partner, Jamie Gilleland, two cats, and two neurotic Golden Retrievers named Griz and Ciarello, but acknowledges that he's restless to move to the wide open spaces of the American West.

www.ingramcontent.com/pod-product-compliance
Lightning Source LLC
Chambersburg PA
CBHW050611110726
47899CB00001B/64